The Captain's Daughter

Victoria Cornwall

Cornish Tales series

Where heroes are like chocolate – irresistible!

Copyright © 2018 Victoria Cornwall

Published 2018 by Choc Lit Limited
Penrose House, Crawley Drive, Camberley, Surrey GU15 2AB, UK
www.choc-lit.com

The right of Victoria Cornwall to be identified as the Author of this Work has been asserted by her in accordance with the Copyright, Designs and Patents Act 1988

All characters and events in this publication, other than those clearly in the public domain, are fictitious and any resemblance to actual persons, living or dead, is purely coincidental

All rights reserved. No part of this publication may be reproduced, stored in a retrieval system, or transmitted in any form or by any means, electronic, mechanical, photocopying, recording or otherwise, without the prior permission of the publisher or a licence permitting restricted copying. In the UK such licences are issued by the Copyright Licensing Agency, Barnards Inn, 86 Fetter Lane, London EC4A 1EN

A CIP catalogue record for this book is available from the British Library

ISBN: 978-1-78189-423-1

Printed and bound in Great Britain by Clays Ltd, Elcograf S.p.A.

The Captain's Daughter is about the true meaning of love and family. A stable family life comes in all shapes and sizes and provides a firm foundation on which to build the rest of our lives. I would like to dedicate this novel to my family. Thank you for catching me when I fall, being by my side when I stand tall and ensuring my feet remain firmly on the ground while you encourage me to reach for the stars.

Acknowledgements

I wrote *The Captain's Daughter* several years ago. I wrote it in secret and didn't tell anyone outside my immediate family for quite a long time. Since becoming a published author, there have been many people who have offered me their support, advice or expressed an interest, each giving me encouragement in their own special way. However, I would like to acknowledge my daughter, Jade, in particular, as without her *The Captain's Daughter* may never have seen the light of day and my writing career ended before it really began. One summer, over a Cornish cream tea, she patiently listened to the storyline and instantly became my most enthusiastic and helpful supporter. Thank you, Jade. Your opinion, and the interest you have shown in all my novels, are greatly appreciated.

I would also like to thank Choc Lit and the Choc Lit Tasting Panel, who believed in my novel and recommended it for publication – with special thanks to readers Katie P, Bruce E, Alma H, Sarah C, Samantha E, Alison G, Vanessa O, Barbara P, Lawan M, Prerana S, Laura A, Ros P, Betty and Sally C who passed *The Captain's Daughter* on the Panel. I wrote it in secret, afraid to tell anyone and was unsure of the next step to take as many doors seemed closed to me. You opened that door and welcomed me through, so thank you … from the bottom of my heart.

TAKEN

He took my love,
He took my trust,
He twisted my common sense.
He took my silence,
He took a knife,
And slashed my innocence.

Victoria Cornwall

Chapter One

June, 1868, Cornwall, England

The cart creaked to a halt, rocking momentarily on its old wooden wheels as the horse settled. The passenger discreetly arched her aching back to bring relief to her tense muscles and jarred spine.

'This is where we part company, Janey,' said the old man sitting beside her. Holding the reins in one hand, he lifted a calloused finger. The young woman looked to where he was pointing. 'If you follow that stone wall over the hill it will take you out to a road, turn left and the entrance to Bosvenna Manor is on the right. This short cut will take two miles off the journey.'

Janey nodded but remained seated. She felt she had troubled him enough yet was reluctant to leave.

He noticed her hesitation. 'Don't worry, maid, if you stick to the stone wall you won't get lost on the moor. The wall borders Zachariah Trebilcock's land. He's farmed here for years, married a Penhale maid from Zennor way. If you get lost he'll point you in the right direction. I lived around here when I was a young man, used to help him out now and then. He's nice enough, although he must be pushin' seventy now.'

'It's very kind of you to give me a lift, Jack.'

Jack grinned broadly, his crumpled old face not hiding the glint in his eye. 'It was my pleasure, maid. I'll make my deliveries and be here in a couple of hours to collect you. My sister, Betty, has offered us a bed for the night.'

'Are you sure your sister won't mind me staying?'

'No, she won't mind you. The journey back to Truro is too far to make today. Best we rest up first.' The old man at her side winked at her. 'Not sure she will be so keen to have me though.'

'Why not?' asked Janey.

'Last time I was here I took her husband drinking. John didn't return home and she was frantic with worry. Two days passed before he turned up.' Jack chuckled. 'Says he woke up in a pigsty three miles away and didn't know where he was. If you ask me, I think he knew exactly which direction was home, but decided to stay put. A tongue lashing from my sister is nothing to rush home for.'

Janey smiled and climbed down from the cart. She stretched her legs, tentatively bending her knees to encourage the circulation back. The journey had been long and arduous, on an unforgiving wooden seat and over uneven roads. They had been travelling for three hours and she felt exhausted, but she remained determined. A vacancy for a lady's maid at Bosvenna Manor had arisen and she was resolute in her plan to secure it.

Moments later Janey watched Jack drive away. She shook out her blue dress, patted her hair into place and turned to follow the Cornish stone wall. Looking around she realised she stood on the very edge of Bodmin Moor, with its vast expanse of granite strewn moorland stretching as far as the eye could see. The gorse bushes were in full bloom, their bright yellow flowers a stark contrast to the brown crunchy grass that swathed the undulations and stony tors of the moor. She had never seen anything so beautiful and wild. It seemed to beckon her with open arms, inviting her to explore its natural beauty and meander around the ruins of the Bronze Age settlements.

But Janey had no time to fritter away. She followed the track that ran alongside the stone wall, made by moorland cattle as they followed their daily route to graze the moor. Cattle, sheep and ponies, owned by the local farmers, were allowed to graze on the moor during the summer months. This practice resulted in the animals grazing at will, enjoying a natural existence unlike any other farm animal. Janey felt as if she had stepped into another world.

As she walked and enjoyed the sun on her face, she gave thought to the interview she was attending. She had never held a position of a lady's maid before and it was important she gave the right impression. At only twenty years old she knew she was much younger than the usual age of thirty years expected, but Janey had ambition and a good education, which she felt would be an advantage above any contenders for the position. She took the advertisement out of her reticule and read it for the hundredth time to reassure herself that, unusually, age had not been stipulated.

> *'In a Gentleman's family, near the village of Trehale, wanted one lady's maid. She must be neat in appearance, literate, honest, trustworthy and proficient in needlework and the dressing of hair. For name and address apply to the office of this paper.'*

Janey folded it neatly and replaced it inside her bag. While doing so she noticed for the first time the sound of granite stone on stone carrying towards her on the mild breeze. She looked for the origin and in the distance saw a figure of a man methodically repairing the stone wall. He chose a stone from the pile at his feet and skilfully slotted it into place, continuing the pattern of the original builder. At first she thought it must be Mr Trebilcock, the owner of the farm, but as she approached him she realised his body was more agile, athletic and younger than a man 'pushin' seventy'.

A loud bleat from a lamb caught her attention as a herd of sheep trotted past her and settled nearby. Janey had not seen young lambs feeding naturally before. She couldn't help but gasp in wonderment at the vision and, with an unusual lack of decorum for her, she spread her arms out behind her, tilted her face to the sky and sighed in delight. *I love it here*, she thought, feeling the warmth of the sun on her face and the gentle breeze kiss her skin. The rhythmical stone on stone sound ceased.

Janey turned back to him. The man had stopped mid lift, a forgotten stone held in his hand, and he was watching her. Embarrassment flooded her cheeks that he had seen her impulsive behaviour. Head down she marched on with purpose, focusing hard on her shiny boots that peeped out from under her dress at each hasty stride. She was aware, from her peripheral vision, that he had dropped the stone and slowly straightened – and that his eyes never left her. She knew that the track would soon pass by him and the thought of being so close to him unnerved her, however, she concluded sensibly, if she diverted to give him a wide berth it would look ill-mannered.

Yet this dark stranger, with his tanned skin and dark brown hair, heightened her senses as she could almost feel his eyes follow the curves of her body. She felt like an animal being watched by a predator. The feeling both discomfited and annoyed her. She decided she would look up and meet his stare as she drew closer. If he smiled a greeting she would too and all would be forgotten. If he did not she would glare back at his rudeness and discourteous behaviour. She took a deep breath and looked up.

He was no more than six feet away and she was soon past him, yet that moment in time would be forever etched in her mind. His eyes were the darkest brown, with dark lashes and brows. They penetrated to the core of her soul making her heart lurch in her chest. It was as if a lightning bolt sizzled and crackled between them, for they were connected in time and space and nothing around them existed at all. He looked to be in his mid-twenties, serious and bold in manner. He did not smile or bid her 'good day' but continued to stare at her unabashed. She dropped her gaze in shock at his poor manners and instantly admonished herself for doing so. She walked on but she could still feel him watching her until at last she followed the stone wall around a corner. She took a deep, shaky breath.

Why was her heart thudding in her chest and her cheeks so flushed? Nothing had occurred out of the ordinary to cause such an extreme reaction within her. He had not threatened her or attacked her, yet somewhere deep inside she knew he was a bigger threat to her mind, soul and body than anyone she had ever met before.

Miss Petherbridge gave the finishing touches to the accounts for the day and sat back in her chair to study them. Master James was due to return from Bath at the end of August, following a stay with his friends, and Lady Brockenshaw wanted to give a party to celebrate his return. She would have to find another source to provide the extra milk, pork and duck required. She was not impressed by the standard of produce recently delivered by her usual supplier. It would do them good to know they had competition.

She looked around the room with satisfaction. No other member of the domestic staff had their own office, not even the butler, yet she had two. There was the housekeeper's room, known as *her* parlour, where the upper servants would gather to take tea, and this room, her very own office. She ran her hand along the wooden desk where she undertook all her administration tasks. Her pride in her position of housekeeper was palpable as she liked to walk the corridors of the manor like a strutting peacock; her uniform and keys her feathers. She had worked her way up from the position of scullery maid. Now she was housekeeper to one of the richest families in Cornwall. She had declined marriage and children in order to achieve her ambition and, although she was immensely proud and satisfied with the way her life was, she knew her appearance did not convey this as her tall skinny frame, serious bitter face and tight lips gave the impression of resenting her life and everyone in it.

There was a knock on the door. It opened and Mary, one of the chambermaids, popped her head around it.

'Miss, the girl applying for lady's maid is here. Shall I take her up to the mistress?'

Miss Petherbridge sat up and rested her forearms on the table. She was well aware that the lady's maid position was the only servant to report to and be hired by the mistress herself; however she felt, under the circumstances, she should meet the woman before taking her up to Lady Brockenshaw. She picked up the letter the applicant had written, scanned the beautiful script and, looking over the top of it, asked Mary to send her in to her.

There were several striking things that Miss Petherbridge noticed when the girl entered the room. She was a girl, not a woman and therefore too youthful for such a position. She was very pretty with arresting green eyes. She was neatly presented, with a sense of fashion, but, most importantly, she represented everything she herself was not, causing her to take an instant dislike to the girl. She did not ask her to sit down.

'Miss Janey Carhart, I presume,' she said.

The girl nodded. 'Yes, miss.'

'We received your letter. Your writing is beautiful but you appear too young for the position. I would not want you to get your hopes up.'

'I had hoped that what I lacked in years would be made up for by my education,' the girl replied.

Miss Petherbridge looked at the writing and admitted she was curious about this girl.

'Where did you learn to write so well?' she asked, slowly waving her letter requesting an interview as evidence.

'My father was a captain, miss.' This did nothing to diminish the housekeeper's curiosity and her expression must have showed this as the girl continued to explain further. 'He believed education was important for everyone and taught me to a boy's standard.'

'Yet,' Miss Petherbridge queried, 'you entered domestic service at thirteen years old.'

'I was orphaned at thirteen.'

Miss Petherbridge lifted an eyebrow. 'Did you have no other family to care for you?'

The girl looked down at her feet momentarily, then lifted her chin to meet her steady gaze.

'None that would own me, miss.'

Reluctantly the housekeeper admired her candour. 'It cannot be easy for you to admit to that, but I admire your honesty. A quality that is important in a lady's maid.' She got up. 'Follow me. I will take you up to Lady Brockenshaw.'

Miss Petherbridge led Janey along a passage towards the back stairs. They passed the servants' hall, where the servant who had met her on her arrival had hung her bonnet and shawl on the coat stand.

They climbed the narrow servants' staircase, which led to the main entrance hall on the first floor where the family and their guests entered the building. Once in the main hall, and probably as a matter of habit, the housekeeper ran a finger along the ornate hall table. She nodded in satisfaction, but was less impressed with the flowers in the vase. Janey got the impression, from her expression, that someone would feel the sharp edge of her tongue later that day. Their footsteps, and the jangle of the housekeeper's keys, echoed through the hall as they proceeded to the drawing room.

'I hope you realise that a lady's maid is a very different position to what you have held before now,' said Miss Petherbridge. 'It can be a lonely existence. Due to the position's unique intimacy with the lady of the house, the lady's maid is trusted by no one. The domestic staff will be concerned you will title-tattle to the mistress and she in turn will be wary you will title-tattle to the domestic staff. Are you prepared for that?'

Janey opened her mouth to reply but Miss Petherbridge was not really interested in her thoughts. 'I have been in service since I was twelve,' she continued. 'When I was twenty-nine I became a lady's maid for ten years. I then took up a position as housekeeper, as no lady likes a lady's maid that is too old. Having said that,' she said, looking pointedly at Janey, 'no lady likes to have a maid too young either.' She hesitated and looked like she was about to say something but changed her mind, adding abruptly, 'Wait here.'

She disappeared inside the room and left Janey outside. She could hear the soft murmur of voices inside and it wasn't long before the door opened again.

'Lady Brockenshaw will see you now,' Miss Petherbridge said, formally, before leading Janey inside. She introduced her to her mistress and immediately left her alone with her prospective employer.

A small dog ran to greet her, before returning to settle down before a welcoming fire, which crackled softly in the grate. However, to Janey's surprise, the room was inadequately lit resulting in much of it being in shadow. Lady Brockenshaw, dressed in a high-necked dress of the darkest blue, sat stiffly in a chair by the window, appearing to gaze out. Her silver hair reflected her mature years, while its severely parted style and low, tight chignon showed a distinct disinterest in bending to the will of fashion. A portrait of a young woman, with vibrant auburn hair, smiled down on them. Janey recognised the tilt in her chin as being the same as the older woman who had yet to look at her. White lace trimmed her collar and cuffs and helped soften her stiff countenance, as did the frail, fragile hand tapping the seconds of time away on the arm of the chair. The tapping stopped.

'Miss Petherbridge has filled me in briefly regarding your work history,' said Lady Brockenshaw, without turning round. 'I also understand your present employer has written a very good letter of recommendation. You work for the Reskelly family as a housemaid?'

Janey nodded, but as Lady Brockenshaw was not looking at her she cleared her voice with a small cough and answered, 'Yes, ma'am.'

'Good, that's about thirty miles away. We don't encourage followers. I assume you are not walking out with anyone from this area.'

'No, ma'am, I just arrived today.'

Lady Brockenshaw nodded in satisfaction. 'Good. Miss Petherbridge feels you are too young and inexperienced but I want qualities in a maid that are, perhaps, a little different. I also understand your father was a captain. A captain of what?'

'A merchant ship called the *Emprise*,' Janey replied. 'He transported coal, ore and china clay and brought back timber, citrus fruits and wine from France, Spain and Italy.'

Janey was beginning to find it a little disconcerting being interviewed by someone who had yet to look at her and was even more confused by what Lady Brockenshaw asked next.

'There are some roses on the table,' she said, abruptly. 'Describe them to me.'

Janey looked at the red roses and hesitated at the strange request.

As if sensing her confusion Lady Brockenshaw turned to her. 'I see Miss Petherbridge has not warned you. I am almost blind, Carhart. My sight has been deteriorating for many years. I see very little now.' She turned opaque eyes to Janey. 'The ability to see is so much taken for granted. One does not appreciate the gift until it is lost. I miss the emotion that accompanies seeing something beautiful. In my heart I am eighteen, my last clear image of myself was when I was forty-two, now ...' Her voice trailed off as she indulged in a memory.

Janey studied the five roses arranged in the glass vase, aware that whatever she answered would determine her success at gaining the position. She thought about how best to answer. Snippets of poetry came to mind but none seemed appropriate, yet a literal description seemed inadequate.

'Their colour is a deep blood-red of crimson joy,' she said, softly, 'and their petals are dark folds of scented velvet. A symbol of love, longing and desire ... yet elegant and regal.'

The fire crackled in the grate as Janey's words hung in the air between them. She waited anxiously; perhaps she had overdone the description in her haste to give a good impression. Lady Brockenshaw finally let out a sigh.

'Beautiful,' she said, with a smile. 'I think we will get along very well.'

She got up and made her way to the call bell, her fingers grazing the furniture and walls to guide herself to her goal.

She pulled at the bell. 'Miss Petherbridge will show you around and discuss your duties. She is an excellent housekeeper, but her manner can be a little stiff. I fear her nose may be put a little out of joint by my employing you. She may feel the position has come too easily for someone with no experience, but I am tired of my visual isolation and you will connect me to the world I miss so much through your words. However, Miss Petherbridge has earned her status through the years and exhibited excellent dedication. It would serve you well to stay on her good side.'

There was a knock and the door opened. The housekeeper entered and was informed by Lady Brockenshaw that Janey would commence her employment the following week. Miss Petherbridge visibly bristled at the news. Janey smiled to offer her friendship. It was not returned.

Moments later Janey was being marched around the manor by the housekeeper as she briskly relayed the duties of a lady's maid.

'Do not speak to your betters unless asked a question and reply in as few words as necessary. Do not speak to other staff in their presence unless absolutely necessary and if this is the case do so as quietly as possible.' They passed into the dining room and out again to the master's study. 'A sign of a good servant is one that is not noticed by the members of the household. Staff shall not receive any friend or relative to the manor unless I or Mr Tallock, the butler, has given permission.'

Janey was shown into the well-stocked library and following that, the music room with its grand piano. 'The cost of breakages will be deducted from your wage which is twenty-four shillings a year. You are expected to be punctual to start work and attending meal times. Meals are served in the servants' hall,' she turned to Janey, 'which I believe Mary has already shown you. It is your bonnet and shawl on the coat stand, is it not?'

Janey realised Miss Petherbridge did not miss a thing. Before ascending to the attic to see her room, she was led into the main kitchen where she was introduced to some members of the staff.

Mrs Friggens, the cook, was a round and rosy-cheeked woman with a cheery disposition and a tendency to be bossy. Janey could understand this as she had a lot of responsibility and instantly liked the woman. Then there was Mary and Lizzy, who undertook chambermaid and kitchen maid duties. Mary was a plain girl with a forthright manner, whereas Lizzy was blonde and quiet. Next was Charlotte, the scullery maid, who was timid, but appeared hardworking. Charlotte was the only one to greet her with a smile, but it was cut short by Miss Petherbridge stepping between them.

'I do not have the time to introduce you to every member of staff on the estate, Carhart. There are too many and I have the impression that you will have no qualms about making your own introductions.' Her nostrils flared slightly as she looked down the bridge of her nose at Janey and waited for her to reply. Janey bowed her head in acceptance, which seemed to please her. 'I will show you to your room now,' she said, leading the way out. Janey obediently followed.

She was led to the servants' quarters in the attic. The corridor was dimly lit and a faint odour of damp reached Janey's nostrils. As they walked its wooden floor, Miss Petherbridge began to list her own personal duties.

'You will be responsible for maintaining the mistress's wardrobe: mending, laundering the delicates, starching and ironing the collars ... all the usual care of her dresses.' She smiled insincerely at her before continuing, 'Other duties include laying out her clothes, helping her dress and dressing her hair, etc.'

They now stood outside a door of one of the rooms. 'As you may be aware, she cannot see so you will have extra duties which is why your writing made you stand out amongst the other applicants. You will be expected to write the mistress's letters as she dictates them and read her personal correspondence to her. You will also be expected to read books and poetry to her and, finally, walk her dog.

You are permitted to change into your day dress to carry out this task. The mistress retires for a nap for two hours in the afternoon; it is during this time you are expected to take her dog out. You are not afraid of dogs, are you?'

'No, I am not,' replied Janey, recalling the small, quiet dog by the fire.

Miss Petherbridge opened the door into a small single bedroom with a bed, a chest of drawers, a washstand with a matching pitcher and bowl, and a chamber pot placed under the bed.

'This is your room. As a lady's maid you have certain privileges, one of which is having a room to yourself. You are expected to keep the room tidy and you are not permitted to have too many items crowding the room.'

Janey entered and looked around. It was the first time since entering service that she had a room to herself. At last she could have some private space, be it only ten foot by ten foot. On the bed lay her uniform, a black dress with a starched white apron and frilly cap. She lightly touched the fabric, feeling its stiffness between her fingers.

'How long have you wanted this?' asked the housekeeper, who remained in the doorway.

'Since entering service,' replied Janey, surprised at the emotion welling up inside her. Miss Petherbridge observed her shrewdly.

'So you are ambitious,' said the woman. Janey felt cornered in the room as the housekeeper's body now blocked the door. 'With your education and parentage,' she continued, 'you, no doubt, feel that life as a domestic servant is beneath you. Now, as a lady's maid, you are a little above *them*.'

Janey shook her head in denial, but underneath wasn't quite so sure if there was an element of truth to what Miss Petherbridge had said.

'Perhaps you plan to be a housekeeper one day. Don't think you will be filling my shoes, Carhart. I don't plan on going anywhere. It is well to remember that.'

Janey took a deep breath of fresh air and smiled. She had been accepted for the post. It was quite an achievement at her age. Her parents would have been proud if they had lived, but then if her family had lived she would not be in the position she was in now. Life would have been very different – if her actions had not caused their deaths. Her uncle blamed her and Janey grew up believing the same. She had been trying to make up for it ever since by being the best she could be and worthy of still living. It was a daunting task.

The sun was still shining and Janey walked back the way she had come. She remembered the dark stranger on the moor and her heart quickened. How sour she must have looked; perhaps this time when they met she would smile and bid him a good afternoon, after all they would be practically neighbours.

As she approached her step slowed. He was gone, the repaired stone wall the only evidence he had existed at all. It was solid and beautiful, ready to protect the animals within against whatever the wild moor threw at it. Janey felt a sense of disappointment. She told herself it was because the sheep and their lambs had moved away to graze elsewhere, or perhaps it was the chill in the air turning the sunny day colder. It may also be, she had to admit, that she didn't like the thought that the man had been left with a bad impression of her – although why she should care she did not know.

She saw Jack waving in the distance, patiently waiting in his cart at the crossroads. Returning his wave she picked up her skirts and ran towards him.

Chapter Two

Out of courtesy, Janey informed her uncle of her new position. He did not reply. He never did. His continual rejection hurt her every time, so she did what she had always done since entering service – immersed herself in her work.

She soon fell into a routine that formed a structure to her day. Rising early, she brought Lady Brockenshaw her tea in bed, discussed and prepared her clothes for the day, and helped her to dress. Whilst her mistress breakfasted with her husband, Janey tidied her room and sorted out potential washing and mending. After breakfast she escorted her ladyship to her boudoir, where Janey remained with her for the rest of the morning. During this time she read her correspondence to her mistress and replied on her behalf; other times she read books and poetry, chosen from the manor's extensive library. On warm days, Janey escorted Lady Brockenshaw around the gardens or on a carriage ride. Throughout the day, especially during these excursions, she would describe in detail what she could see so that her mistress was able to enjoy as much of the experience as possible.

However it was when Lady Brockenshaw retired for a nap that Janey enjoyed her duties the most. After changing into her day dress, she would fetch her mistress's little King Charles spaniel, called Charlie, and head for the open space of the moor. During these walks she was free from her other duties and away from the remaining staff.

Only a few of the domestic staff had welcomed her. Mrs Friggens and Mr Tallock accepted her as a new member of staff and, although they did not fully agree that a girl of only twenty should have such a position, were not threatened by her. She was not a cook and would never be considered for a butler post. These facts allowed them to be generous and treat her in the manner her position warranted. The remaining indoor servants, led by Mary, treated her with suspicion, just as Miss Petherbridge had warned and the housekeeper did little to discourage it.

On her first day of work Miss Petherbridge made it abundantly clear she did not agree with her mistress's choice. She showed her resentment by rarely addressing Janey and did not invite her to take tea in her parlour to discuss the running of the house, an invitation that was preserved for the higher members of staff, of which she was one. This blatant snub by the housekeeper, which surprisingly was not contradicted by the butler who appeared to take a submissive role to his peer, gave momentum to Mary's treatment of her and where Mary led, Charlotte and Lizzy followed. The remaining indoor staff watched silently from the sidelines, mindful of who wielded the power over them. It was not Janey they had to curry favour with, it was Miss Petherbridge's displeasure and Mary's sharp tongue they had to avoid.

Mary and Janey had only one thing in common – they were both twenty years of age. There the similarity ended. Where Janey had risen through the ranks, Mary had not and took no joy in domestic servitude. She hated working within a big house and resented the class divide and the submissive role she had to take. Where Janey was educated and well spoken, Mary had disliked school and where Janey had no close family to confide in, Mary's family was large and lived in Trehale.

Envious of Janey's position of superiority, Mary took pleasure in pointing out to Lizzy and Charlotte what she believed to be the detrimental changes Janey's presence was making in the household. They noticed that Janey's opinion was valued by Lady Brockenshaw and her influence showed in the change of their mistress's dress and hairstyle. Suddenly the cage and crinoline dresses she had worn in the past were no longer desired and a dressmaker was commissioned to make dresses incorporating a fashionable bustle. Once satisfied with a centre parting and low chignon, their ladyship began to wear her hair high with decorative combs and slides.

The servants could not understand why a blind woman should be so concerned with fashion. Janey, however, did and her ladyship valued Janey's unique empathy for her position. Their relationship quickly became close and within days her mistress had stopped using her surname to address her. This unusual privilege was noticed by Mary and the housekeeper and resentment for Janey grew. If she could change how her ladyship dressed, they asked themselves, what other changes could she make? It was their alienation and missing her friends from her previous job that led Janey to take comfort in a most unlikely source.

Lady Brockenshaw doted on her only son, James, often talking about him with such pride and indulgence that Janey grew to admire the portrait she painted of him with her words. While Janey dressed her hair, Lady Brockenshaw would retreat to her memories of his childhood, taking joy in relating these stories to her captive audience as she combed and pinned her hair from behind. Then, of course, there were his letters.

James Brockenshaw was an avid writer, if not a regular visitor. Letters regularly arrived, written in his familiar neat hand and it was Janey who opened and read them to her mistress. His letters gave his mother great joy, providing an escapism as he described his adventures, his plans to visit, but overall they reflected a considerate son who adored his mother and enjoyed her love in return. When Janey held his letters in her hand and read the elegantly written words that he had not long before written, she began to experience an intimacy and a strange closeness with the man she had never met. If she had not felt so isolated and alone in those initial weeks she may have seen the letters for what they were, but in her loneliness any kind word held value and she appreciated it all the more. Soon she found herself looking forward to reading his letters as much as his mother did hearing them and she replied to his correspondence in the neatest handwriting she could produce.

He had spent much of the summer with his friends in Bath but was planning to return next month and his latest letter told his mother about the friends he hoped to bring with him. Suddenly the topic in his letter changed and she found that she was reading praise from him to the writer of his mother's letters. Janey's voice trailed off as she read the last sentence, her face blushing at his praise. Her mistress's voice broke into her thoughts.

'My son never misses the opportunity to bestow a compliment,' Lady Brockenshaw announced, smiling. 'I shall enjoy James being home again. Life can be rather dull without him.' Janey reread the last sentence to herself again, taking pleasure in his words. Her hand shook slightly with excitement; a connection had been made between them, as fragile as a spider's web but a connection none the less. During a time when the majority of her peers resented her presence he had reached out and touched her with his praise – and she savoured it and thought more of him for it.

As James's arrival date neared, the tension and excitement rose in the servants' quarters as extra work was created for all. The guest bedrooms were thoroughly cleaned, extra wine delivered and extra food deliveries were arranged. Miss Petherbridge directed the operations like a major in charge of an army, thriving on the responsibility and position as supervisor and, while she took stock of her orders in her office, the latest delivery arrived. Lizzy heard the cartwheels trundle into the yard before the other staff and she looked out of the window, as she wiped her red chapped hands on her apron.

'Who is that?' asked Lizzy, craning her neck to get a better view. The girls, including Mrs Friggens, joined her to look; even Janey left her sewing to see what had taken their interest. She instantly recognised the man unloading a churn of milk from the cart in the back courtyard. It was the man who had been building the stone wall.

'That's Daniel Kellow,' replied Mary, nudging her way to the front to get the best view. 'He owns the farm next door. He is a friend of my brother,' she added, proudly.

'He's lovely!' Charlotte, the scullery maid, sighed. Mrs Friggens rolled her eyes and went back to her cooking, whilst the four girls watched in silence, each one admiring the strength in his body as he unloaded another churn of milk and half a slaughtered pig. His shirtsleeves were rolled to his elbows, showing muscular forearms tanned by the sun. With ease he lifted the heavy items onto his shoulder and carried them to the dairy and cold room. He did not appear to notice the girls watching and they followed his movements, mesmerised by his animal grace.

Finally he finished, climbed up into the cart and picked up the reins. He casually turned to look at them, his smouldering eyes homing in on Janey – and he winked, before flicking the reins and driving his cart away. Janey sank back into the shadows, mortified he had caught her watching him and had singled her out. What an arrogant man. Did he think she would be flattered by a twitch of his eye? His crass behaviour could not have come at a worst time. Lizzy and Charlotte's attitude towards her had only just begun to thaw. She did not need this stranger to come between them.

'He winked at you!' exclaimed Charlotte, turning to Janey.

'No, he didn't,' denied Janey, resuming her seat at the table and taking an interest in her sewing. She stabbed at her needlework as the girls circled her and began to question her further. Mrs Friggens saw her discomfort and ordered the girls to return to their chores.

'If you girls have any sense you'll keep away from Daniel Kellow,' she said, looking at Lizzy. 'He'd take you in and spit you out in a blink of an eye. He doesn't suffer fools gladly.' The implied insult did not register with Lizzy.

'How does he own a farm? Most are tenant farmers around here, aren't they?' Lizzy asked.

Mrs Friggens returned to the bread she was making.

'When he was a lad he was caught thieving in the village by Zachariah Trebilcock, the farmer who owned the neighbouring farm. Well, Zachariah, in his wisdom, gave the boy a home as he had no family.' She looked about her to see if there were any eavesdroppers. 'He's illegitimate and his mother had died.'

Janey felt a surge of sympathy for the boy of all those years ago, if not the man he was today. She pretended not to listen but her ears strained to hear.

'Mind you,' Mrs Friggens continued, 'I bet there were times Zachariah wished he hadn't. There were many an occasion he had to bring Daniel home after some fight or other and, of course, when he was a young man of sixteen ... well,' she rolled her eyes, 'there were quite a few fathers knocking on their door and warning him off their daughters, I can tell you. Not that the daughters minded.'

Mrs Friggens rolled the dough into shape to place in the range. 'Give him his due, though, when Zachariah was took bad with arthritis and could hardly move his hands, Daniel seemed to settle down and started running the farm. Zachariah would have had to sell the farm if it weren't for him. Eventually he changed his will so everything was left to Daniel, as Amy, Zachariah's wife, had died three years before. Six months after Zachariah changed his will he was found dead, his head bashed in.'

Janey pricked her finger and looked up. She stemmed the bleeding by popping it into her mouth.

'Rumour has it Daniel did it to get the farm,' added Mary.

Mrs Friggens made a face but didn't say anything to disagree with the comment.

'He's a murderer?' asked Charlotte, with horror.

'He was never charged, but where there's smoke, there's fire. Daniel and Zachariah were the only ones on the farm that day. There were no witnesses and who benefitted from his death? Daniel did,' replied the cook, placing the dough on a baking tray. She picked up the tray and spun around towards the range. 'I'm not saying anything, or accusing anyone. All I'm saying is steer clear of Daniel Kellow, like everyone else does. He's trouble.'

Janey threaded her needle, images of Daniel Kellow building the stone wall on the day of her interview invading her concentration. She had been alone with him; what if he had attacked her or killed her? No one would have known what had happened to her. She shivered at the thought. Yet, she concluded as she continued to sew, there was nothing threatening about his wink, just arrogance that she would be charmed by him. There was certainly something about Daniel Kellow that drew you in by an invisible force, whilst his dark eyes had the power to hold you there. A man whose presence could change from being one of a threat, to one of boyish charm, in a wink of an eye. There was no doubt about it, the man was trouble and she would do well to stay clear of him.

'I think he's handsome,' said Mary, returning to the window to watch him in the distance. 'Besides, nothing was proved. The villagers keep away unless they want his help.'

Janey had an urge to join her at the window, but instead returned to her sewing with a little more vigour than she had before.

*

The day had finally arrived when James Brockenshaw returned from his summer stay in Bath. He arrived late in the morning, striding into the hall, filled with confidence in his welcome and his position within the household. His friends were to arrive later in the day, a guest list that had extended to six more than the original number. Mrs Friggens was informed of this shortly after his arrival, following his casually imparting of the news to the butler. On being told of the changes the cook had almost fainted in shock for the number had doubled in size. She soon set to work but her usual relaxed manner vanished and did not reappear until the guests left three days later.

Janey had been returning to her mistress's bedroom and found herself at the top of the stairs to the hall at the moment of his arrival home. She had just settled Lady Brockenshaw in the drawing room with her husband, Lord Brockenshaw, who was a short, round, gouty man with a bald head and large sideburns. He had never acknowledged her, as his philosophy was servants were there to serve and not to have conversations with and his wife's lady's maid was no exception.

Janey heard James's voice first. It was friendly and cheerful and drew her to the bannister to look down on the hall. He was politely asking after the butler's family and his health, whilst handing him his top hat and coat. He was just how she had imagined him to be, aristocratically handsome, tall and slender with fair straight hair and noble features. He was charming and, in turn, one was charmed by him. Janey Carhart drank in the vision of him and was captivated.

His father must have heard his arrival as he came into the hall to greet his son. They shook hands. Soon jovial laughter wafted up to Janey who sat down on the top step to watch through the bannister rails. Shyly she observed James exchanging some pleasantries on nothing of importance and then he followed his father into the drawing room. Janey imagined a happy embrace between mother and son. She sat for a moment. The hall below now seemed empty without him. Already Janey wanted to see him again, to be able to watch him move and hear him talk. Was this love at first sight, she wondered? Her heart was pounding and her mouth had turned dry. A mixture of desperation at wanting to see him again yet terror she would make a fool of herself in his presence caused her stomach to ache inside her. These feelings would never come to anything, he was the son of a lord, she a lady's maid, yet she felt in her heart that any man she would meet in the future would be compared to James Brockenshaw and found wanting.

'Lady Brockenshaw wants her blue shawl. She said you would know which one,' said Mr Tallock, entering the servants' hall where Janey had retired to starch some collars.

Janey hesitated, then went upstairs to fetch it and made her way to the drawing room. She had wanted this to happen all afternoon, yet dreaded it too. She entered the ornately furnished room, made cosy by dark red fabrics and numerous leafy green plants, and took the shawl to her mistress. She shyly looked about her to find Lord Brockenshaw and his son reading the papers and drinking whisky by the fire. James's long legs were stretched out before him, crossed at the ankles. The men did not acknowledge her entrance. While she was attending to her mistress, Charlie jumped over his legs to greet her and she was aware James sat forward to follow the dog's movements. He saw her outstretched hand gently fondle the dog's ear in greeting. His gaze ran up her arm to meet hers, and rested there for a second longer than was necessary. Then the connection was over and he sat back in his leather chair and returned to his paper.

Janey left the room, heart thudding. She returned to her duties but his eyes stayed in her mind. The memory banished all thoughts of Daniel Kellow's dark smouldering eyes, because now James Brockenshaw had entered her world and he was everything she had imagined him to be.

Janey stepped back to admire her work. 'Finished, ma'am.'

Lady Brockenshaw carefully felt her hair, the decorative comb and the tendrils by her ears and at the nape of the neck. Her hair was plaited and lifted high at the back of her head to mirror the shape of her new dress, which incorporated a fashionable bustle. She stood and felt the line of her dress and the beading on her bodice.

Instinctively knowing what her mistress needed, Janey described the dress to her.

'Your dress is silk taffeta. The colour is a deep blue, like the sea on a sunny day. The folds and fabric reflect the light as it falls and drapes to the ground. The glass beads resemble drops of dew held by an invisible cobweb. The comb in your hair is blue to match your dress. You look lovely, ma'am.'

Lady Brockenshaw smiled.

'I feel lovely, thank you, Janey. You are a dear.'

Lord Brockenshaw knocked on the door and entered to take his wife downstairs. Janey was left to tidy the room, but upon hearing carriages drawing up at the entrance she paused at the window to watch the guests arrive. The evening celebrations were about to begin for the landed gentry, while the domestic staff worked frantically in the depths of the house to ensure all ran smoothly and the evening was a success. Janey felt an outsider looking out on to a world she had no part in. Not for the first time she felt she belonged to neither one group nor the other.

Chapter Three

At the end of the three days the guests took their leave and waved goodbye from their carriage windows. Calmness descended on Bosvenna Manor once more and Mrs Friggens, the cook, finally reclaimed her sense of humour again.

Where once the day had been filled with picnics, the playing of cards or lawn croquet, the manor was now empty, quiet and, to James's mind, boring. James's time in Bath had been filled with attending balls, going to the theatre and visiting his club. He knew the return to Bosvenna would require a transition and to prepare himself for the change James had invited his friends to Cornwall. Now they had returned to Bath and James was left in the company of his aging parents. To top it all, only this morning, James had discovered that his favourite horse had become lame.

'It's good of you to drop by, Daniel,' James said, greeting his neighbour with a handshake. 'I hear you have a way with animals and thought you could advise me.'

Daniel hadn't wanted to come to Bosvenna Manor. He had just finished stacking the hay into his barn ready for winter, when a breathless lad had come running over the hill saying he was needed by the master to look at a horse. He was just about to send a message back saying he was too busy, when the possibility of catching a glimpse of a certain girl who happened to work there entered his mind and changed it.

Daniel acknowledged the greeting with a nod and a word. 'James.'

'How are things at that farm of yours?' asked James, with a friendly smile, ignoring the fact that Daniel had used his Christian name rather than 'sir' or 'mister', which was due his station. Daniel did not believe he was subordinate to any man, least of all James. However, James had the good sense not to take offence as Daniel knew about horses and it was his knowledge he needed.

'Summer has been busy, but autumn is almost here and things should settle down soon.'

'I see the reapers are at Pendrift Farm today.'

Daniel nodded in agreement. 'They moved there after helping me. They are making the most of the dry spell. What seems to be the problem?'

Customary country greeting undertaken, both men looked at the fine horse tied to the ring in the wall.

'Honestly, I don't really know. She's had all summer getting fat and lazy in the field and my first attempt at a good ride to bring her into fitness before the hunting season starts and she's just not right.'

Daniel looked the animal over. The mare was a fine specimen and, despite James's description, was not carrying too much weight.

'All her shoes are sound, she's not had an injury, yet she acts up and is not fluid in her movements. Frankly, I'm at a loss.'

Daniel looked in the horse's mouth. 'A horse can injure themselves in a field just galloping around when playing.' He gave the horse a gentle rub on the nose as a thank you and went on to feel its back. 'What's she like to canter on, to the left and right?'

James recalled his last ride for a moment. 'I do believe she feels stiff when turning left, not so bad turning right.'

Daniel nodded thoughtfully. He proceeded to run his hand down each leg in turn, taking notice of the muscle conformation, the tenderness and the wasting.

A dog's joyful barking could be heard in the rose garden, beyond the courtyard wall, but neither man took any notice.

'I think her problem is more long-standing than you may think. Take a look at her front hoof, it is wider and forward growing, unlike the others.'

James stood in front of the horse to get a better look.

'Are you saying she has been shoed poorly?'

'No, if it was the fault of the farrier it would be more than likely all the hooves would be misshapen. It is unlikely a farrier would do a bad job on just one hoof alone.' Daniel stroked the horse along its shoulder. 'See here ... and here. There is muscle wasting and tenderness. It has resulted in your horse walking stiffly, which in turn causes the hoof to grow wrong. This has been going on for probably more than a year.'

James did not answer. Daniel looked up at him to discover what had taken his attention.

'Well, well, if that isn't a sight for sore eyes.' James smiled as he looked across the courtyard. Daniel followed his gaze to find the cause of his loss of interest. It was the girl he had hoped to see and she was walking gracefully into the courtyard, carrying a bunch of pink roses in her arms, with a small dog trotting beside her.

'Be back in a minute,' James said, and strode off to greet her.

Daniel straightened. His jaw tightened. He did not like being dismissed as if he was a servant. It irked him even more to see James confidently approach the girl. Something he would have liked to do himself, if he had the skill. He watched, with irritation, as James easily struck up a conversation with her, making the girl smile and eventually laugh.

No doubt he was complimenting her on how the rose of her cheeks matched the colour of the roses she held. James Brockenshaw had the gift of the gab and the girl seemed to lap it up. It was to be expected. What girl would not be flattered to have the attentions of a wealthy and, some would say, handsome man? Daniel felt uneasy. James reminded him of a fox stalking his prey, his smile, his manners, his charm belying the deadliness of his intentions. Voices coming nearer brought Daniel suddenly to his senses and he realised that James was bringing the girl over.

'This is Lady Jane Grey, Lady for short,' said James, patting the horse on the neck.

Daniel stood to the side. James thought the horse warranted an introduction, unlike him. The girl avoided looking at him, which allowed him to look at her. She was clean and tidy, with a fresh bloom to her cheeks, and she wore a pale yellow dress with small green flower buds that matched her eyes. For the first time he wished he had changed his shirt before coming to Bosvenna Manor.

'I've been trying to find out what is the matter with her. She's a gentle horse. Come, stroke her.'

The girl looked a little alarmed as James took her hand and guided it under his to stroke the horse's neck. Daniel averted his gaze and focused on the dog. He was glad when the girl slipped her hand away and hid it underneath her roses.

Daniel returned to examining the horse, perhaps a little more zealously than before, while James continued to focus his attention on the girl.

'I warrant roses are your favourite flowers.'

'These flowers are for Lady Brockenshaw, sir. She asked me to pick them while I walked Charlie this afternoon.'

'Then tell me, what do you consider the most beautiful flower? I would dearly love to know.'

'I love wild flowers. They are more beautiful than anything cultured by man.'

'That cannot be,' said James, in all seriousness. 'Man has crossbred plants to produce the clearest of colours and strongest of perfumes. Surely nothing can compare to what science can produce ... the best of all worlds.'

The girl shook her head. 'I disagree. Nothing is more beautiful than nature intended. Nature, in its own way, has cultivated the wild flower over hundreds of years and it has resulted in flowers that are more varied, more pure and vibrant than any flower grown in a hot house. They can grow in the most inhospitable of places with a wider range of fragrances than any gardener or scientist can produce. But perhaps what I like best about wild flowers are that they have been allowed to be themselves, grow in a way that nature intended, without constraint. They are the more beautiful for it.'

The two men had fallen silent, the horse now forgotten. Her use of language had intrigued them both. One had been made the more curious by it, the other felt a great chasm open up between them. Her speech was articulate, educated, and was quite unlike any other domestic servant within the house. It had been the first time Daniel had heard her speak.

'You sound as if man stifles growth and beauty,' said James, softly.

'I did not say that, sir,' the girl replied, dropping her gaze, then lifting it again to meet his. 'A man has the power to do so if he chooses ... just as he has the choice not to.'

With encouragement from Daniel, the horse's rump nudged James to the left, breaking the spell between them. James laughed, unaware of Daniel's part in it.

'I think our gender has been firmly put in our place,' James said to him. He looked at Janey with renewed admiration. 'Daniel, let me introduce my mother's new maid. Janey Carhart.'

Daniel stiffly nodded and Janey acknowledged his greeting with a slight, stiff nod of her own.

So now he knew her name, but it was not how he

envisaged learning it. In his mind he would have introduced himself and asked her, and she would have gladly told him herself. Instead he had learnt her name from James Brockenshaw's lips – a man she appeared to find attractive. Daniel could not hope to match any comparison made between them. Particularly today when he was dressed in his work clothes and James dressed for riding. When James had the ease of conversation and banter, and Daniel felt, if called upon, he would have difficulty stringing a coherent sentence together. What a fool he had been to wink at her when he saw her through the window.

'Daniel here thinks my horse has been lame for more than a year and I have not noticed.' So he had been listening, thought Daniel, irritably. 'I fear Daniel must think I do not look after my horse well.'

'I did not say that,' retorted Daniel. 'Horses are prey animals, they put up with a lot of pain before they show it. Showing vulnerability in nature is the fastest way of being singled out and hunted.' He could not help but glance at the girl as he made this point.

'Here speaks a man who has no vulnerability to show,' James said, with a loud laugh, oblivious to the discomfort he was causing.

Janey could not meet Daniel's gaze, which irritated him all the more. It was time he was going.

'Your horse has chronic pain, from arthritis or injury, the cause does not matter. Her riding days are over.' He picked up his jacket that he had taken off on his arrival, in preparation of taking his leave.

James's smile left his face. 'Are you suggesting I have her shot?'

'You have the gift of putting words into people's mouths. I recommend she retires to become a pasture buddy for the younger horses on your estate. They can learn from her and she will provide them with a constant security within the herd. She could also be put into foal. Her condition will withstand the weight of a foal inside her and her bloodline will then continue. However, she must never be ridden again. It would be cruel and painful for her and dangerous for you.'

James watched Daniel stride away.

'I fear Daniel lacks a sense of humour, Miss Carhart,' said James. He smiled down at her as she watched Daniel's receding figure. 'May I escort you back to the servants' hall before your roses wilt in this heat? Your face is too pretty to wear such a frown.'

He beckoned the stable boy over with a flick of his fingers. 'Stable Lady in a thick bed of straw. I will visit her later.' The boy touched his cap and led the horse away.

Later, James thought, he would give instructions for her to be shot.

Miss Petherbridge looked down from a second floor window. Her lips thinned in annoyance as she watched Master Brockenshaw displaying an interest in the Carhart girl, who was smiling and radiant in her pretty day dress – like a yellow flower ripe for the picking. No good would come of it. It never did, thought the housekeeper. The Carhart girl was not the first servant girl to be on the receiving end of a gentleman's flattery. She had seen it all before and it usually ended with the servant's dismissal. No genteel family wants to be reminded of their son's youthful dalliance, least of all the son himself.

Miss Petherbridge smiled as she checked the line of the curtain. Perhaps she would not have to put up with the Carhart girl for very long after all, she thought. Satisfied with the neat folds of the curtain, she continued her walk along the length of the corridor, her keys jingling at her belt, and the swish of her black dress echoing about her.

James Brockenshaw. Janey's ink slid across the paper, sweeping elaborately the letters of his name. Somehow the action of writing his name brought him closer to her, forming an intimacy that did not yet exist. She wrote her own name, interlinking the Js like a sign of betrothal. She knew what they were – just silly girlish scribbles by the light of the candle, but as she lay in her bed ready for sleep it helped to calm her and make sense of the growing attentions he had shown her in recent days.

It had started that sunny afternoon when she had accidently interrupted the examination of his injured horse. He had not minded and even greeted her as an equal. At first she was lost for words, until his cajoling had made her laugh and any tension was broken. On escorting her back to the servants' hall he had even kissed her hand. Thank goodness no one had seen. She had watched him walk away, touching the back of her hand to her lips, still feeling her skin tingle at his touch. She hugged the encounter to her breast like a precious secret and would always treasure the moment he had first truely noticed her. It was a far cry from Daniel Kellow's rude behaviour which either involved staring, winking or veiled warnings. What was he trying to imply by saying, 'Showing vulnerability in nature is the fastest way of being singled out and hunted.'? James Brockenshaw was much more polite and easy-going.

The following day she had seen James again. While reading to Lady Brockenshaw he had entered the room looking for a broadsheet. When he saw her he had smiled at her – a smile just for her. A tender smile, a caring smile and she, Lord help her, had smiled back. How forward of her to smile at Lord and Lady Brockenshaw's son. She should have stood and curtseyed or nodded submissively, but she hadn't. She had smiled back at him like an equal and his smile had widened.

Now each time someone entered the room she held her breath in anticipation it would be James. Janey shook her head in disbelief as she realised she thought of him by his Christian name. She must be careful for he had no real interest in a servant such as her. Yet, she mused, when he looked at her he made her feel special, beautiful and desirable, as though the class difference between them meant nothing at all.

Yesterday he had visited his mother in the library and found Janey reading to her. Much to Janey's horror he had decided to stay and listen. Lady Brockenshaw teased him about his new-found interest in the *Sonnets of the Heart*, but was happy that her son chose to spend his afternoon with her. She had settled back in her chair to listen to Janey's initial faltering words.

Janey had cleared her throat and began to read. Her soft voice had filled the air. It felt as if the printed words transformed on her lips, coming alive as the author had intended them to do. Her audience had listened intently and did not speak until she had finished, for to do so would have vandalised the beauty of the moment.

Janey smiled to herself as she remembered looking up to see James staring at her. Lady Brockenshaw was talking but neither was listening as they gazed at one another. He had mouthed the word *beautiful* and she had silently replied *thank you*. He had left shortly afterwards and, although Janey watched for him, he appeared to have left the estate and was not seen again until the following morning.

Today he had joined her on her afternoon walk with Charlie. He had accidentally come across her as she walked along the moor and had fallen into step beside her. She had asked after his horse, and he had told her of his hopes of buying a new one. He had teased her, flattered her and at one point took her hand to help her over a stile. He was polite and gallant and left her to walk the last part alone so as not to cause gossip that may harm her reputation. Janey felt safe with him, protected and charmed. It felt natural.

Janey wrote his name, the ink once again sliding across the paper, sweeping elaborately over the letters. The action of writing his name brought him closer to her, forming an intimacy that was in fact growing as prolific as poison ivy.

James watched the amber coloured brandy move around the edges of his glass as he gently swirled the contents. He found a perverse pleasure in testing how close he could make the spirit touch the edge without it sloshing over. The pleasure was made the greater knowing his father would hate to see good brandy go to waste should it spill. This was borne out when his father finally snapped.

'Stop doing that, James, you know it irritates me.'

James breathed in the aroma from his glass, filling his nostrils with vanilla that transformed to a mixture of wood, fruit and spices. He took a mouthful and let it linger on his tongue before swallowing. If only all irritants could be blocked out with a glass of brandy, he mused. But they couldn't and wouldn't. His father was the latest irritant and he had heard this particular lecture before.

'Come, Father, I thought we were going to enjoy an after dinner brandy together. You should have warned me you would spend the entire time pacing up and down and preaching a sermon.'

'A sermon that has been long overdue,' Lord Brockenshaw shot back. 'Today William Menhennit called on me. He told me you owed him a large sum of money from a gambling debt. It was humiliating. Of course I paid him and apologised on your behalf.' He wiped his forehead with a handkerchief. 'How many more people are going to knock on my door wanting payment for some misdemeanour you are responsible for?'

'He is no better. He's a gambler too.'

'He's a magistrate! He also has the money to throw away if he wants. You, on the other hand, do not. I do not. Your mother and I are to blame. We spoilt you.' He placed his walking stick against the desk and eased himself down into a chair. 'We chose not to have more children after her sight deteriorated but it meant you were our only child and was duly spoilt. I cannot keep paying your debts, James. It has got to stop.'

James poured himself another glass. 'I really think, Father, you are taking this all too seriously. It is not unusual for a gentleman to owe money to someone, just take from one pot to pay the other.'

'You mean I take from my pot to pay for yours.'

James raised his glass in mock salute. 'Yes, after all, what's yours is mine.'

Lord Brockenshaw looked uncomfortable. 'Not yet it isn't. Anyway, what's mine may not be as much as you think it is.'

For the first time his father had James's full attention. 'What do you mean?'

'I mean, James, that it takes money to run an estate such as this. When I inherited Bosvenna Manor it had thirty indoor staff, a thousand acres made up of numerous farms and moorland, plus money in the bank. Over the years the staff have dwindled. We can only afford to keep ten indoor and six outdoor staff now. I've had to sell off a number of farms and,' he said, looking pointedly at James, 'I have a son who likes to gamble and waste money. You take it for granted that I will pay you a large allowance, fund your lavish lifestyle and pay your debts.'

'Well, pardon me for breathing,' mocked James.

His father thumped the desk with his fist. 'Damn you! Do you take life seriously at all?'

'No, as you do it for me,' said James, getting up to look out of the window. 'Does Mother know that you have sold so much land?'

'Our financial situation is not helped by your gambling debts and lavish spending habit,' said his father. James waited for an answer. 'No, she does not and I do not plan to tell her. She thinks the world of us and I couldn't taint that view. Her last vision of you is of a cheeky, loving boy, not the rake you are now. I don't want to be the one that spoils it for her.'

James nodded.

'The thing is, Father …' He spread his arms out wide. '… life is for living now. I really can't see the point in working like a dog to keep an estate going that loses money like water through a sieve. I'm all for selling the place and buying a townhouse in the city. The country bores me, the people bore me.'

Lord Brockenshaw was incensed. 'Bosvenna Manor and the estate has been in our family for six generations! Have you no sense of loyalty, family pride, responsibility? How are you going to explain to your son you sold his inheritance because you preferred to gamble and speculate in risky ventures?'

'I seem to recall that you lost a good deal of money to that fellow, Phillips.' James poured himself a third glass. 'Did you not realise that investing large sums of money in a venture that did not exist is always a risky business?'

'I was hoodwinked. He led me to believe I was buying shares in a ship called *Adonis*. He was to run the enterprise and I would receive half the profit. He showed me the ship's documents.'

'Indeed he did and you did buy half of a ship. Only the ship was lying at the bottom of the sea at the time and no use to anyone. Next we hear this new "salt of the earth" business partner has left the country for America with the money and not the manners to say goodbye.'

'Don't you think you've had enough?' snapped his father.

James swallowed the brandy and, as a man succumbing to the fog of inebriation has a tendency to do, placed his glass on the table with excessive care.

'You're quite right, Father, I have had enough. Enough of listening to your lectures. I'm off to bed and, by the way, I need to purchase a new horse to replace Lady. I'll head into Falmouth tomorrow and stay with Edward. He can help me choose one.'

'Edward?'

'Edward Hamilton, the nephew of Sir George Richmond. I met him at boarding school. I'm sure he will appreciate my presence more than it is here at the moment. Please inform Mother that I will be gone in the morning. I fear that if I say goodbye I may be tempted to tell her all that has transpired here this evening.' He smiled at his father. 'We wouldn't want her to learn that her husband is no better at handling money than her son is, would we?'

He left the room and swept through the hall, leaving his father alone to contemplate the price of the horse and how he would explain to his wife why their son had left at such short notice.

Lady Brockenshaw received the news of James's sudden departure with surprise but hid her hurt well that he had not told her himself. She hid it so well that on relaying the news to others it was with a matter of fact air, as if it was inconsequential. So it was something of a shock to Janey to learn from Lady Brockenshaw the following morning that

James had left and she did not know when he would be returning.

Janey had been putting away some gowns when there was a knock on Lady Brockenshaw's door and the housekeeper entered.

'Today's menu, ma'am. May I read it to you?' said Miss Petherbridge as she approached her mistress. Lady Brockenshaw waved her hand to stop her.

'My son has left. Inform cook we shall not need the quantity as originally thought and perhaps something a little lighter.'

Janey hesitated over what she was doing but quickly regained her composure. She was able to hide her surprise from her mistress, but Miss Petherbridge had noticed and took a perverse pleasure at seeing her pain.

'May I be so bold as to ask when he will be returning, so his quarters can be prepared accordingly?' Miss Petherbridge asked, as she noted Janey's hands shaking and her ineffectual attempt at hanging a dress.

'A week ... or two. I will inform you when I know the exact day, Miss Petherbridge. Now on a lighter note ... the church roof is in need of repair and Reverend Smith is raising funds by having a dance in the village hall a day after the harvest festival service. The more people who attend, the more money they will raise. My husband and I have therefore decided to grant all the staff who wish to attend an evening off. That includes you, Miss Petherbridge.'

Miss Petherbridge visibly bristled. 'I don't think a dance is my cup of tea, ma'am, but I thank you for the generous offer.'

Lady Brockenshaw held out her hand to Janey.

'Janey, I insist you go, and all the other staff who wish to. We can manage for one evening with a skeleton staff.' Janey opened her mouth to speak but her mistress cut her off. 'I insist, as I want you to tell me all about it the following day. So it is settled. Now if you will leave, Miss Petherbridge, I can continue to get ready.'

Miss Petherbridge left the room, annoyance etched on her pinched face. She would inform the staff of Lady Brockenshaw's offer after the main meal this evening. She had no doubt the younger members of staff would be thrilled, but she would not be attending the dance herself. She found the whole shenanigans unpalatable and saw no good in allowing staff time off to attend dances, no matter the cause. Such frivolity bred insolence and laziness and standards would drop. She would have to keep an eye on things.

Chapter Four

It was the evening of the dance to raise funds for the church roof. A buzz of excitement simmered amongst the servants as they gathered in the servants' hall waiting for Miss Petherbridge to dismiss them for the evening. Eventually, she arrived, with Mr Tallock beside her.

'Here are the officers ready to inspect their troops,' whispered Mary, under her breath.

Miss Petherbridge surveyed her staff with an air of distaste. It was plain from the expression on her face that she did not agree with the arrangement.

'It is very considerate of Lord and Lady Brockenshaw to allow this unprecedented favour and allow you time ... additional time,' she emphasised, 'to attend the dance. It is my duty to remind you all,' she looked pointedly at Mary, 'that you are representing the Bosvenna Estate and I therefore expect you to act accordingly. There must be no drunkenness, no gossiping and no followers. The doors will be locked at eleven thirty.' A groan could be heard from somewhere near the back. 'If you wish to stay out later you must make alternative arrangements. There will be no excuse if those of you who are working tomorrow are not at your posts prompt, sober, clean and tidy. Do I make myself clear?'

The group responded that she had.

'Then there is no more to be said. You may go.'

The September evening was warm and a thousand stars, sparkling like precious diamonds, littered the clear black sky. Only in the depths of the countryside was the night sky so beautiful and vast, displaying infinite galaxies like fine jewellery. The wooden patten shoes the girls wore on their soles to protect their best boots made a rhythmical beat on the road surface and echoed around them as they walked en masse to the neighbouring village.

Janey followed quietly behind. Since James's sudden departure she had felt quite down. The days now seemed long and dull without the hope she may catch a glimpse of him, or he may spring out of nowhere and speak to her. It may have meant nothing to him but to Janey their encounters made her float with excitement. She knew it was silly but her feelings seemed to take on a life of their own where he was concerned, and she had trouble controlling them. It affected her appetite, the beat of her heart, her ability to breathe and the swings of her mood. Unfortunately where his presence affected them to the positive, his absence did the exact opposite and she was left wishing her days away until he returned.

Tonight's event had given Janey something else to focus on, but it meant being in the company of the other girls. Lizzy and Charlotte glanced at her several times over their shoulders, and, after some nudging and whispering from them, so did Mary. Eventually they fell back to walk with her. Janey grew wary.

Mary appointed herself as spokesperson and glared at her.

'Are you going to tittle-tattle to her ladyship?'

'I don't know what you mean.'

Mary rolled her eyes. 'Tell her how the evening went. Tell on us.'

'She will want to know how the evening went,' said Janey, quietly.

'I told you she would!' said Mary, triumphantly.

'But I have no intention of tittle-tattling. It is one thing to relay back the music that is played and the dances I may dance, it is quite another to relay back who got drunk, who kissed who and what gripes the staff have about work.'

Mary's eyes narrowed. 'How can we believe you?'

Janey opened her arms. 'Because I want to have a good time. I want everyone to have a good time. I have no intention of spoiling anyone's fun or getting anyone in trouble. Please be reassured that anything I relay back to Lady Brockenshaw about this evening will not be derogatory.'

Confused faces looked back at her.

'What does derogatory mean?' asked Mary, suspiciously.

'Spoil anyone's reputation,' explained Janey.

A short silence followed as everyone took in what she had said. Eventually Mary smiled and, much to Janey's relief, so did the rest of the staff.

'Well, that's all right then,' said Charlotte, linking Janey's arm whilst Lizzy linked the other. 'Let's have some fun.'

They trudged on towards the village.

'Miss Petherbridge told us you were going to keep an eye on us. I didn't really believe her,' confided Charlotte.

'I'm glad she isn't coming. I can't imagine her dancing,' added Lizzy, with a giggle.

Charlotte turned her attention to Mary. 'Are you going to dance with Alfred?'

'I've gone off Alfred,' Mary replied, her gaze lingering on the gardener ahead of them. 'I've got my eye on someone else tonight, and no, I'm not telling!'

Despite Charlotte and Lizzy's best efforts to persuade her, Mary refused to elaborate. Eventually their voices trailed off as the sound of music and laughter reached them, long before the cosy lights from the village hall windows could be seen in the distance.

Like moths attracted to a flame, the villagers and inhabitants of the surrounding farms made their way to the lighted hall. The girls' excitement grew as they approached it. At the entrance they hastily removed their patten shoes and lined them up neatly outside before entering the joviality and warmth created by the dancing villagers within.

Janey had never attended a dance like the one that greeted her within the walls of the hall. Before starting life in domestic service she was a child of a well-to-do family and dances like this were not part of their social scene. Since entering domestic service opportunities like this were rare and did not correspond with her one afternoon off a month. Servants forming relationships were not encouraged and this side of life seemed to have passed Janey by. So it was something of a shock for her to see men and women dancing together. These people all appeared to know one another, linked by either friendship or blood.

Janey soon realised that many of the Bosvenna staff came from the village and surrounding areas. The lively music was provided by the Willis brothers, middle-aged identical twins who, as Janey later discovered, were well known in the area. Their fiddle playing was mesmerising for they played with such skill and speed that to watch them was entertainment enough. They began sober and in harmony but as the night grew older their competitiveness intensified – resulting in them becoming even more entertaining to watch. Distraction and sabotage soon replaced their attempts to outplay one another. Hats and music sheets were displaced with a furtive twitch of a bow as they jostled for position and stamped on each other's toes. Yet throughout their brotherly capers, the gay vibrant music continued flawlessly and each tune was enthusiastically celebrated with a drink from their own private supply of alcohol. Janey learnt that the alcohol would eventually dampen their competitiveness and replace it with laughter and a drunken sway until, without warning, they would collapse in a stupor and need to be carried home. The evening usually ended, Charlotte explained to Janey, with each man clutching their precious fiddle to their chest and being transported on a tide of men out the door into a waiting wagon.

Janey had never seen two grown men look so alike before, with their red hair, beards and bandy legs. She would have been happy to watch them all night, which was just as well, as no one had asked her to dance.

Mary, Charlotte and Lizzy soon left her and it was not long before they were dancing and laughing with the others. Abandoned, Janey was left to wander the room and try not to be too inconspicuous. She bought herself a glass of fruit drink and used it to hide behind as she watched the others dance. She longed to join in and was aware that several men were looking in her direction, but no one asked her. She was a stranger and no man was brave enough to be the first to ask.

'I don't believe we have met before,' said a cheerful voice from behind her. Janey turned to see a silver-haired man with a friendly smile and a clerical collar. 'Allow me to introduce myself. I'm Reverend William Smith, the vicar here and the organiser of this little festive celebration to raise funds for the church roof.'

Janey shook his hand. 'I'm pleased to meet you, sir. I'm Janey Carhart. There seems to be a good turn out.'

'Indeed there is. There are even some from the Methodist chapel. Their preacher will not like that. Are you from the manor?'

Janey nodded, wondering if there was a rivalry between the church vicar and the Methodist preacher in the village.

'It was very kind of Lord and Lady Brockenshaw to allow us time to attend.'

To her surprise the vicar snorted. 'All is not what it seems, however I should not look a gift horse in the mouth.'

The vicar smiled at her. 'I asked Lord Brockenshaw for a donation, instead he has made this offer. He's a wise man. To all it looks like he has been generous and supportive; in reality any funds raised from allowing his staff to attend comes out of your pocket, not his. He has the public acknowledgment that he has been supportive but it has cost him nothing. At one time he was a generous donator to good causes; not any longer, I fear. Do you think I sound ungrateful?'

Janey looked at him. He had a kind face. 'I think you sound disappointed in Lord Brockenshaw, reverend,' she replied.

'Indeed I am, but perhaps we all have expectations of people that are hard to live up to. Take me for example, people have very high expectations of their vicar, don't you think?'

'I suppose they do,' said Janey, not really sure where the conversation was leading.

The vicar tapped his glass. 'This looks like fruit juice, does it not?'

'Isn't it?' asked Janey.

The vicar opened his jacket to show a silver flask within. Janey's eyes widened. He tapped the side of his nose.

'I may be a vicar but I like a tipple. As you can see I do not live up to high expectations either. Very few people in the world do and perhaps it is unfair to expect them to.' Abruptly he changed the subject. 'Why isn't a pretty thing like you dancing?' he asked, quite affronted.

'No one has asked me, sir.'

The vicar immediately put down his glass and held out his hand in a dramatic gesture. 'Well, we can't have that.' He smiled. 'You and I share my dark secret,' he said, tapping his hidden flask. 'From now on, should you require my counsel, you can depend on me to help. To mark this momentous bond we must seal it with a dance.'

Janey laughed as he swirled her onto the dance floor.

They danced the next two dances, which in turn encouraged others to ask her. This resulted in Janey being rarely left without a partner for the next half hour. She started to enjoy herself immensely, picking up the steps of each Celtic dance with ease and a little help from each partner. Suddenly, she realised in horror that at some point in the evening Daniel Kellow had entered the room and he was now watching her.

From gliding around the room and not making a mistake she started to stumble and miss her cues. When the dance came to an end it was with a sense of relief that she left the dance floor to hide amongst the crowd and away from his gaze. Hateful man. Why did he have to spoil everything? Janey bought herself another glass of fruit drink. She took a sip but the taste had changed and she eyed the old lady standing next to the bowl. Mary came to her side.

'Edith has been adding her home brew again, I see. Mark my words, by the end of the night half the people will be drunk and the other half trying their best to be. It's potent stuff that,' she said, nodding to Janey's drink.

Janey noticed Daniel Kellow through the crowd still watching her. Needing courage, she downed the glass in one. Mary immediately grabbed her hand.

'Come meet my brother.'

'Which one is your brother?' asked Janey as they jostled through the crowd.

'This one.' Mary swung Janey in front of her and into the path of her brother. Janey found herself facing a thin, pox-marked lad of eighteen who was introduced to her as Matt.

Matt looked a little surprised to have his sister fling a woman in his path, although not at all disappointed. She looked at the man beside him and realised it was Daniel Kellow.

'Janey wants to dance with you, Matt,' announced Mary.

Janey looked at her in surprise.

'That looks like news to her,' replied Daniel.

Mary made a face and, ignoring Daniel, spoke to her brother.

'Will you dance with her, Matt?'

From the look of horror on his face, Janey suspected he had never danced with a girl before. She felt a little sorry for him, especially as Daniel appeared to find the idea amusing.

'Daniel will dance with you,' said Matt, looking sick with fear.

It was Janey's turn to be horrified. 'I don't want to dance with him,' she blurted out.

'I don't remember asking you,' replied Daniel.

'You can dance with me,' said Mary, coyly, looking up at her brother's friend.

Janey shot her a glance, understanding, for the first time, why Mary had engineered this meeting. Daniel was the man she 'had her eye on'.

After a short painful silence, Daniel reached for Mary's hand. Smiling, Mary followed him onto the dance floor.

Matt and Janey silently watched them. A new tune filled the air and Janey grabbed Matt's hand. 'Smile, Matt,' she said, leading him onto the dance floor. 'We'll show them how to dance!'

Unfortunately, the dance was a nightmare. She soon realised that Matt really hadn't danced before and lacked all coordination. They bumped and slipped their way through the steps like a pair of newborn foals. Much to Janey's annoyance, Daniel and Mary knew all the steps and although Daniel did not dance the steps but walked them, he did it with such predatory grace that if she hadn't decided she hated him, she would have found him a pleasure to watch.

She tried not to look but found herself stealing glances in their direction. Her spine stiffened when she saw Daniel smile down at the delighted Mary. The brief hestitation was enough for Matt's head to collide with hers in a sickening thud. The injury should have brought them to tears, but instead they both burst out laughing in relief as it had brought their dance to a much-needed premature end. They returned to the edge of the floor still giggling when Daniel and Mary joined them.

Janey thanked Matt for the dance by planting a quick kiss on his cheek before leaving. Mary tried to do the same to a scowling Daniel, but he turned his back to get another drink before she reached her target.

The vicar left and as he went out the front door, ale, brought into the hall by the landlord of the public house down the road, was carried in through the side door. The villagers grew even noisier as the potent alcohol started to infiltrate the celebrations, loosening tongues and dissolving inhibitions. Mary and Janey watched from a safe distance.

'I don't think Daniel is going to ask me to dance again,' Mary said, eventually, as she watched Daniel talking to her brother and drinking a tankard of ale. 'He must like someone else.'

Janey stole a glance at him and at that moment he happened to look up. Quickly she looked away.

'Men like him know they are good looking and they expect every woman to drop at their feet. I have no wish to dance with him.'

'Really?' challenged Mary.

'Really,' confirmed Janey.

A smile lit up Mary's face and she reached for Janey's hand. 'Listen. It's the "Wedding March Dance". You don't need a partner for this one. Come on.'

Janey wasn't sure she liked the sound of this dance but

Mary assured her it would be fun. Mary jostled her into the line of women and began to explain the dance, which culminated with a random couple coming together and walking down the aisle of dancers who clapped in time to the music.

As Mary explained the steps more people joined the line, women on one side, men on the other side facing them. Head bowed, Janey tried to concentrate on Mary's instructions, until she noticed a pair of familiar legs join the male line. With dread she lifted her gaze to see Daniel Kellow standing patiently. Fortunately, he was not looking at her. He seemed to have someone or something else on his mind. He looked up and down the line, as if he was calculating something. Just before the music started he took a sidestep, swapped places with the man to his left and slipped into the line again without anyone noticing – except Janey. She was about to ask Mary if she had seen it when the music started up and the dancing began.

Janey found herself swinging around with a rosy-cheeked, middle-aged man who was grinning from ear to ear. She was about to strike up a conversation when the next part of the dance started and she was encouraged to dance a figure of eight linking arms with women she did not know but were all laughing and calling to others in the line. Their happiness was infectious but they came to a standstill when the new couple formed and skipped behind their line to the top. The crowd cheered as the young man offered his arm to the young lady and they walked down the clapping aisle ready to begin the dance again.

This time Janey was swung around by Matt. She had not noticed him joining the dance and cried out in delight at seeing his familiar face. Once again she was off and a new couple was formed. To the crowds' amusement they made an odd couple as the man was very short and the woman very tall. Disgruntled and embarrassed, the woman grabbed the man's hand and hastily dragged him down the aisle of clapping dancers.

Again Janey was swung, this time by an elderly man, so she slowed her steps in order not to knock him over before leaving her partner to dance the figure of eight. As she approached the bottom of the line she realised she would be one of the new couple formed and she looked across to the male line trying to work out who it would be. Realisation slowly dawned on her as Daniel's deliberate, measured steps walked behind the male line to meet her at the top. Her steps faltered and slowed, but she could not avoid the inevitable. They arrived and faced each other as the other dancers, apart from Mary, clapped out a beat and formed an aisle for them to walk down. Janey's feet were fixed to the spot. She could not move or take his arm if it was offered. To touch him would be—

To the delight of everyone in the room, Daniel reached down and scooped her up in his arms as if she weighed no more than a child, and carried her down the man-made aisle.

'What are you doing?' Janey whispered, embarrassed.

'Carrying my "wife" down the aisle,' he said, quietly.

'I'm not your wife!'

'Don't I know it!'

'But I didn't want to dance with you.'

'Well, you can't have everything you want in this life,' he replied as he continued on.

'Everyone is watching.'

'They are meant to.'

'It's humiliating.'

'It's dancing.'

She reluctantly put her arm around his neck to give herself support.

'Mr Kellow, put me down.'

'I will not,' he said, nodding his head in greeting to someone in the crowd.

'You are not taking me seriously! You planned this!' she accused. 'I saw you standing there, working something out. You planned to humiliate me like this because I wouldn't dance with you earlier.'

'You flatter yourself, Miss Carhart,' he replied, emphasising her title.

He stood back in the male line, with her still in his arms. The other dancers tried their best to dance around them.

'You are trying to show me up in front of everyone!' she ground out under her breath.

'I think you are doing a good enough job of that on your own,' he retorted back, holding her even more firmly.

She gave his shoulder a shake. 'Why couldn't you just offer your arm? Why did you have to pick me up?'

'Would you have taken my arm if I'd offered it?'

She hesitated to answer.

'Thought not,' he added.

Someone bumped into Daniel and he threw them an irritated glance and moved further down the line to stand apart from the dancers. People in the crowd began to nudge one another and a few dancers slowed and eventually stopped. The dance began to disintegrate but the couple did not notice and the music continued.

'You've obviously not danced this dance before,' Daniel retorted. 'A couple can walk down the aisle any way. Look.' He nodded to a man carrying a woman on his back, both raucous with drink and laughter.

Janey strained her neck to see.

'Perhaps, if you relaxed a little, you might actually enjoy it.'

Janey gasped. 'I was relaxed and enjoying myself until you manhandled me!' she argued back. 'You are no gentleman!'

'Gentlemen by name don't always behave like gentlemen.' He was becoming more than a little annoyed now.

'I don't know what you mean.'

'I've seen you simpering after James Brockenshaw. I bet if he picked you up you wouldn't be getting so mazed.'

'The reason I'm mad at *you* is because I don't know you. How dare you pick me up as if we were on more intimate terms?'

For the first time he looked down at her and she was taken aback by the look in his eyes. She wished she hadn't spoken the word *intimate* as it immediately conjured up images of them together. She realised he was thinking the same. The music stopped and they were brought back to the reality of the village hall and the realisation they were encircled by a watching crowd. Embarrassed, she fought back in the only way she knew – with words.

'Put me down this minute, you heathen!' she shouted at him.

The crowd around them gasped and hurt flashed across his face, quickly followed by a mask of anger. With one sharp movement he dumped her onto the floor. She grabbed at his shirt as she fell, pulling off a button and tearing it in the process. As she stumbled to regain her balance he walked past her and off the dance floor.

Janey stood in the centre alone. Mortified, she looked about her at the sea of faces turned her way. Some people were shocked, others were smiling, whilst Mary appeared furious. Janey walked off the floor, her legs shaking with rage. To her relief the music struck up again. Charlotte and Lizzy came over and offered words of comfort, but Mary was nowhere to be seen.

Eventually, Charlotte said, 'Lizzy and I are leaving soon. Are you walking back with Mary?'

'We can't leave her to walk home by herself,' said Lizzy.

'No, we can't.' Janey needed to make it up to Mary. She could see she was upset. 'I will find her and walk home with her,' she replied. So the arrangement was agreed and they said their goodbyes. She turned to see Daniel was leaving too with his arm around a woman. He did not look over to her and to Janey's surprise she felt disappointed. She concluded that to be an object of desire one minute and ignored the next was bound to confuse one's emotions, even if she was the one that had done the rejecting.

She found Mary standing next to the hall clock.

'Charlotte and Lizzy have gone home. Shall we?'

Mary shook her head. 'We have plenty of time, so why don't we stay another half hour. Did you see Daniel leave? I know what he will be doing tonight.'

'Mr Kellow is of no importance to me,' replied Janey.

Mary looked at her. 'I think he likes you.'

'You don't humiliate someone if you like them,' Janey replied, looking at the clock. Time really was beginning to drag.

Mary considered her words. 'Do you like him?'

Janey shook her head. 'Absolutely not,' she replied. So why did her voice not ring true even to her own ears?

Daniel and Sally entered her home as they had done many times before. Since Daniel was a teenager he had visited the widow. She was uncomplicated, made no demands and enjoyed her single status. Married for ten years to an impotent man she made no secret that she did not plan to marry again and tie herself to one man alone. This suited Daniel as he had the comfort of a woman without the responsibility and they both knew where they stood.

Tonight he was high on frustration and it showed as he reached for her before they even reached the bedroom. He caged her against the wall and kissed her hard trying to block out the image of a pretty face with green eyes and full pink lips. Sally matched his urgency, as she clawed at his back and fought kiss with kiss. The green eyes taunted him in his head, inviting him to thread his fingers through the smooth, shiny, chestnut hair in his mind. Sally's curly, black locks caught in his fingers and tore him from his thoughts. He tried again and ran his hands over her body, his mind flashing up Janey's hourglass figure and small waist. Yet where Janey's curves went in at the right places, Sally's came out and no matter how Daniel tried to trick his body into believing it was Janey in his arms, his body would not be fooled. He slowed his onslaught and Sally sensed the withdrawal. Reaching for his belt she began to undo it. She enjoyed Daniel's visits the most and didn't want him to stop.

He reached for her again but this time he pulled away her hands and held her against him, closing his eyes and feeling the full length of her body against his. He nestled into her neck and imagined Janey once more. Sally didn't look like Janey and after tonight, knowing what he knew now, she didn't feel like Janey. It was no good. This woman in his arms wasn't the damn woman that plagued his dreams at night and his mind in the day. This wasn't like him. This wasn't the Daniel Kellow he knew. She'd messed up his mind and what he thought he wanted in life, and yet he hardly knew her. Damn the woman. Daniel moved away from Sally.

'What's wrong, Daniel?' she asked as she looked at him resting his forehead on his forearm against the wall.

He didn't answer at first, then turned and reached out to touch a black ringlet of her hair. He felt its softness between his fingers, twirling and shaping it.

'You're a fine woman, Sally. I'm just not up to it tonight.'

He didn't want to hurt her feelings by telling her why. At thirty-seven she still turned heads, but she was no longer what he wanted. Unknowingly she helped him make his excuses.

'You don't look well, Daniel. Are you sickening for something?'

He nodded. He was … just not from an illness.

'I'd better be going,' he said, giving her a kiss on the cheek.

She looked worried and he didn't want her to worry.

'I'll be fine. Don't worry about me.'

'Are you walking home or did you bring your horse?'

'I brought my horse. She's stabled in Nick's shed by the hall.' He paused at the door as he made to leave and without turning asked her, 'Sally, are you happy with the life you lead?'

She smiled. 'Of course. Strange, you of all people should ask me that.'

'Don't you wish you were married again, with a child or two?'

Sally's smile faded a little. 'Well, maybe once, but marriage didn't suit me. I didn't marry the right man and I don't want to make that mistake again.'

'If you did find the right man for you, would you marry again and have children?'

'Who'd have me?' she replied with a laugh. 'I know what people say about me.'

He touched her cheek with his palm. 'You are a good woman, Sally, don't let anyone tell you any different.' Daniel kissed her cheek again and made to leave but Sally caught his arm.

'If the right man came along, Daniel, and he asked me, I would marry him that day, but it ain't going to happen 'cos the right one don't come by very often.'

He made to leave but she stopped him again. Looking at him closely, she gave his arm a squeeze. 'Now take some of your own advice. You are a good man, Daniel, and don't let anyone tell *you* any different. Is it that girl you're sickening for?'

'You are a fine woman but not a wise one,' he teased.

She playfully slapped his arm at his insult.

'Get out, Daniel Kellow,' she said, laughing and pretending to push him out the door.

After he had gone, she sighed. He was a good man, she thought, no matter the rumours about him killing a man. He had rejected her tonight yet somehow manoeuvred the situation so *she* was the one telling *him* to leave. She smiled again and shook her head in wonderment. There were not many men like Daniel Kellow. A worm of unease moved inside her. Daniel's mind had been elsewhere tonight and he was talking of marriage, which was so unlike him. Perhaps she had been closer to the truth than she realised. Perhaps Daniel did have feelings for the girl who had humiliated him. What if he did not visit her again? Sally no longer found Daniel's rejection so easy to accept, especially if a pretty girl was the cause.

Chapter Five

Daniel saw the lights going out in the village hall as he approached Nick's shed. Matt stood outside amongst a small group of villagers, one of them being Mary. Daniel decided to look no closer as where Mary was, Janey must be too. He wanted to avoid the woman and just go home and to bed.

Matt called his name but he ignored him and went into the shed. As he fitted his horse's bridle, an out of breath Matt entered.

'So glad you came back, Daniel. I was afraid you'd gone home.'

'Just leaving now,' replied Daniel, reaching for the saddle and placing it gently onto the horse's back.

'It's that girl we danced with. I'm worried for her.'

Daniel didn't want to ask but he did, hating himself for wanting to know. 'Why, what is wrong?'

'Bosvenna Manor's doors are being locked at eleven thirty and I don't think she's going to get there in time.'

Daniel began tightening the girth with a bit too much vigour, making the horse sidestep. He took a deep breath to slow himself down and redid the girth more gently.

'Then she should have left earlier,' he answered.

'She was waiting to walk back with Mary, but Mary had arranged to stay with Mam tonight.'

Daniel slid his hand between the girth and the horse's stomach to ensure the skin had not wrinkled. 'So?'

'So, she's had to walk the three miles back by herself and there's no way she will reach the manor in time before it is locked.'

'As I said, she should have left earlier and not waited for

Mary. This mess is of her own making. Anyway,' he added, 'I don't think she'd accept my help if I offered it.'

Matt stood watching Daniel, a worried frown on his brow. 'I'm worried for her, Daniel, and I don't have a horse to catch up with her. You see, Mary turned the hall clock back by half an hour and Janey didn't know until she saw the church clock.'

Daniel led his horse outside and mounted, but Matt stood in his way.

'I know you can help her get in and I know you won't leave a woman alone in the dark. Anything could happen to her.'

Daniel manoeuvred his horse around him but Matt grabbed the reins and held out Janey's patten shoes. 'She left these behind, she was that much in a hurry. You can give them to her when you find her.'

Daniel looked down at the wooden shoes in Matt's outstretched hand. If he had been here he wouldn't have left Janey to walk to the manor alone in the dark and, as much as it irked him, he knew Matt knew it too. He took the shoes from him, muttering, 'Damn woman,' under his breath as he turned his horse around. Placing them in his waistband, he urged his horse into a brisk trot in the direction of Bosvenna Manor. It was not long before his silhouette was swallowed up in the shadows of the trees that lined the narrow road.

Janey had been walking as quickly as she could for half a mile and time was running out. Luckily for her the moon shone down brightly on the road making the track appear like a silvery grey ribbon stretching out before her and leading her home. The night remained still and surprisingly mild, whilst in places the shadows of the trees cast black lacy patterns on the road to mark her journey. The lights and noise of the village hall grew more muted as she went further into the isolation and silence of the countryside.

How had she found herself in this impossible situation? One minute she was waiting patiently for Mary to accompany her home, the next a sickening panic assailed her as she realised the church clock was much later than the village hall clock and unless her feet grew wings she would not reach Bosvenna Manor before the doors were locked.

To top it all Mary had told her that she was spending the night at her mam's. She claimed that she had told her of her plans at the beginning of the evening and that she would not be walking home with her.

Had she told her? Surely she would have remembered. Lizzy and Charlotte didn't seem to have known. Whatever the cause for the breakdown in communication, Janey was now walking alone in the dark and feeling increasingly vulnerable. What if someone came along and attacked her? No one would hear her screams or come to her aid. No one would even know she was missing until morning.

Janey's heart began to race as she lengthened her stride. Stubbornness and the late hour stopped her from turning around. She didn't feel she knew Betty, Jack's sister, well enough to wake her at this late hour and beg for a bed for the night. Mary had made it quite plain there was no room at her house and she was beginning to realise that once she reached the manor the door would be locked. However there were stables in the back courtyard and there was also the gig shed. She could bed down there and enter the house as soon as the doors were unlocked in the morning, hoping she would not be seen.

An animal screeched in the wood beyond the hedge and startled Janey. She began to shake, her heart thumping in her chest so loudly she could hear it pulsing in her ears. Her mouth was dry and a flush of heat ran through her to fade away when her brain rationalised it was an animal and there was no need to run. *Calm down*, Janey whispered to herself, *you're getting yourself all worked up. Just keep going another two miles and you will be safe.*

She was about to start her journey again when another sound caught her attention. A rhythmical clicking noise that was familiar yet alien in this lonely environment. She held her breath to listen and recognised the sound of the smooth trot of a horse in the distance. Elation that perhaps she could ask for help was quickly transformed to fear of the unknown rider heading her way. All her worries of being attacked came flooding back and, as much as she would have liked to think she was brave and not one to panic, she also understood that the wisest thing to do was keep herself out of harm's way and hide. She needed to reach Bosvenna Manor unharmed, it didn't matter that she was late, she had already reconciled herself to the fact it would be a straw bed for her tonight.

The silhouette of a rider, appearing and disappearing in the shadows of the trees, emerged as Janey slipped from the road into a gateway and behind a hedge. Crouching down she waited in the dark for the rider to pass, ignoring the brambles that caught in her hair and dress. She dared not move and strained to listen as the hooves came nearer. The horse seemed to be slowing down. If the rider had decided to walk his horse from now on it would mean she would have to hide for longer than she had thought. She frowned in concentration, hoping and praying that the rider would pass by as she listened to the horse's hooves scrape on the stony road. All hope faded when Janey realised that the rider had eased his horse to a stop opposite her hiding place. She froze.

Some minutes passed and the rider remained there. Only the occasional scrape of the horse's hooves on the road told Janey they were still there. Had he stopped to light a pipe? Was he waiting for someone?

Janey remained hidden, praying he did not know she

was there. After all, what choice did she have? She could hardly come out and start walking. What had begun with her hiding from an unknown danger was beginning to feel as if she was in fact now trapped there. Another minute passed, another scrape of hooves on the road surface closely followed by a cold breeze enveloping her and making her shiver. Then a man's voice broke the silence.

'We can stay here all night, Miss Carhart, but I have better things to do. One of them is sleep.'

Janey groaned. She recognised the voice and, quite frankly, he was the last person she wanted to see right now. And to be caught hiding, the shame of it. She remained where she was and asked the most stupid question she could have asked in the circumstances. She instantly regretted it.

'Who are you?'

'The heathen,' the voice replied.

'Lord have mercy,' Janey thought, unaware she had spoken the words out loud.

'It's a little late for praying,' Daniel replied, without humour.

Janey picked her way out of her hiding place, disentangling a bramble from her hair and dress on her way to stand before him in the moonlight. Her best dress was muddy at the hem and her hair had partially fallen down. She knew that she looked small and a little dishevelled, but she still tried to muster some dignity. After making a big show of brushing off her dress, she tilted her chin up and met his gaze head on. He looked furious.

'Good evening, Mr Kellow,' she said as if there was nothing out of the ordinary. 'Now, if you will excuse me.' She turned and headed towards Bosvenna Manor.

To her annoyance he walked his horse beside her, his dark looming shadow at her side. At first she tried to ignore him, but how can you ignore someone like Daniel Kellow?

'You really don't have to accompany me,' she said.

'I know,' was his clipped reply.

'I am quite safe.'

'You are now.'

'I was before.'

'Is that why I found you hiding in the mud behind a hedge?' he asked, angrily.

She threw him a scornful look. Despite the anger on his face his body was relaxed as he rode beside her, as if he made a habit of riding the roads late at night.

'You don't have to do this for me.'

'I'm not,' he replied.

She looked up at him, but he remained focused on the road ahead.

'I'm doing it for Matt, he was worried about you.'

An awkward silence fell between them.

Janey sighed. 'Mr Kellow, I will be fine. Thank Matt for me but I am really quite all right.'

'Matt says the doors are locked at eleven thirty which means you have nowhere to sleep tonight.' It was a statement not a question. 'Matt thought I could help.'

Janey turned on him in horror.

'I will not stay at your place,' she said, indignantly.

Images of her sleeping under his roof entered both their minds. Daniel gritted his teeth.

'I don't remember offering a bed.'

His retort made her blush at her assumption and she looked away; it was her turn to focus on the road.

'Matt knows that I can get into Bosvenna Manor when it is locked.'

Janey stopped and turned, her hands on her hips. She frowned up at him.

'You know how to break in?'

He pulled the horse to a stop too and nodded.

'Why does that not surprise me?'

'Because you have a poor opinion of me, Miss Carhart, although I don't understand why.'

'Did you steal from there?'

'I did not.'

'But you have stolen before?'

'As a half-starved child I stole food to survive.'

Janey removed her hands from her hips. 'Why would you break in, uninvited, to the manor?' she couldn't help asking. Breaking into property was just not something she could understand or had come across before.

'Who said I was uninvited?'

Silence descended between them. She could no longer see anger in his features. Even in the moonlight she could see his dark eyes had softened. He looked away and eased his horse into a gentle walk. She fell into step beside him.

'When I was a teenager I knew one of the scullery maids. She's long gone now, married with two children, I believe. If I remember rightly her bedroom was the third along the corridor in the servants' quarters.'

Janey gasped. She put her hand out to ward off any more information.

'Mr Kellow, I don't want to know about another woman you have chosen to spend your nights with, thank you very much.'

She had already seen him leave with one woman tonight. She did not need to hear about his past escapades too.

'It means, Miss Carhart, you can be sleeping in your own bed tonight … unless you would rather be sleeping in mine?' He was taunting her and from the sound of his tone it seemed he took a perverse pleasure in annoying her. She gave him a withering look to show him she would quite gladly slap him – if she could only reach him.

'How on earth did I get myself in this situation?' Janey muttered to herself, her footsteps echoing on the road.

'It is not your fault.' His tone had softened as if he felt a little sorry for her.

Janey marched on with determination in her step. She did not want his sympathy even though the evening had gone horribly wrong for her.

'Mary turned the village hall clock back so you would leave late.'

Her steps slowed and she became wary.

'Why would she do that? I thought we were becoming friends.' She turned on him. 'It's all because of you. She likes you but you singled me out.'

'I danced with you. I also danced with her,' he said, logically.

'She *really* likes you.' Janey shook her head in disbelief that Mary could be so vengeful.

'I've known Mary for years. Believe me, Mary likes no one but herself.'

Again silence fell between them. Janey's steps were slowing. She was tired. She had walked the three miles to the village, danced many times and had another two miles to go; all this after a full day's work. Another cool breeze travelled along the road and whipped her skirts around. Janey shivered. She felt defeated.

Daniel dismounted, startling her.

'You are tired and you are ruining your boots.'

'I left my pattens at the hall,' she mumbled.

'They are ridiculous things anyway. Can't understand why you women still wear them. Get up and have a ride back to the manor.' It was an order, not a request.

'I can't ride,' she protested, but he ignored her and moved her by the shoulders to stand by the horse.

'No time like the present to learn,' he said. Bending down, he took hold of her leg and lifted her upwards.

She had no choice but to grab the horse's mane and twist her body so she could sit side-saddle. She found herself looking down at him with a surprised look on her face and the warm body of a horse beneath her. She wasn't sure what surprised her the most: to suddenly be on the back of a horse or to have Daniel Kellow's hands beneath her skirt and touching her leg. It did not seem to have bothered him at all for he was getting ready to mount.

'What are you doing?' she demanded.

He raised an eyebrow at her as if he couldn't quite believe she was asking him that.

'If you think I'm walking you are quite wrong, Miss Carhart. Scoot over, I'm coming up.'

She did not move but scowled back.

'You either scoot over or I'm sitting on you,' he snapped and, with ease born from experience, he mounted and sat snugly behind her, her buttocks between his thighs, his right thigh touching the back of hers. She sat speechless as he wrapped his left arm around her waist, while his right held the reins. He eased his horse forward with a click of his tongue and a squeeze of his thighs.

As the horse walked she felt his warm chest against her back. She leaned forward to break the contact, hoping he would not notice, but he did. He firmly but gently pulled her back against him.

'Don't sit forward or she'll think you want to gallop,' he said, gruffly.

She did not sit forward again but sat stiffly keeping her eyes on the road.

'You really haven't ridden a horse before, have you?'

She shook her head.

'Are you scared of horses … or is it me you're scared of?'

Janey didn't see the point of lying. 'I think, at this very moment, I'm a little scared of both.'

'Well, I might be able to help with one if not the other,' he whispered into her ear.

She shivered involuntarily at the caress of his breath. To her relief he took it as a sign she was cold and wrapped his coat around her.

'Just relax your body and let it move with the motion of the horse. It will be more comfortable for her to carry you if you are more fluid in your movements.' Her body remained stiff. 'Close your eyes and feel the movement,' he said, softly.

Janey closed her eyes.

At first she was only aware of his body behind her, his strong warm arm about her waist and his hand on her right hip. She kept her eyes closed and soon she felt the gentle sway of the horse beneath and how his body also swayed as one with the animal. She started to sway too and she felt herself relax, her shoulders lowered and the tension she did not know she held flowed away from her. She was so tired and his warmth wrapped around her helped her to sink into the comfort and protection that surrounded her.

'That's much better,' came his voice through the night, but Janey was lost in the swaying of their bodies as if they were in a ritual dance. She had never been so close to a man before, images of his thigh touching hers teased her mind and she could smell him, ale and soap with the fragrance of—

She felt Daniel gently remove something from her hair. She opened her eyes to find a fragile green leaf held gently between his fingers. She looked at it, but it was the soft caress of his breath on her cheek that held her attention. She realised how far she had relaxed against him and how close they both were. She sat up straight and this time he let her. It seemed Daniel also felt it was better that there was a little distance between them after all.

Silence descended and left them with their thoughts. Thoughts Janey would rather not dwell upon, so when Daniel's husky voice attempted to strike up a conversation, she was glad of it. She suspected he was not a man for polite conversation so appreciated the effort it must have taken him.

'Do you enjoy working at Bosvenna Manor?'

'Yes and no,' she replied, sadly. 'I am a lady's maid and I enjoy working for Lady Brockenshaw but the staff do not like me. I don't know why. I try to be friendly but it is as if they don't trust me.'

'Why should they trust you? A lady's maid position is higher than the likes of Mary. Why would they believe you want to be their friend when you are their superior?'

'I'm not their superior,' Janey argued.

'You are by rank, by education, by how you speak. The likes of Mary want to know where they are with people. When someone steps outside their given role it must be for a reason. They become suspicious as they would not do it themselves.'

'So I should give up trying to be their friend?'

'You should just be yourself and fulfil the role you have.'

'You seem to know a lot about domestic service hierarchy,' she grumbled. 'Did you learn it from your scullery maid?'

'Yes, among other things.'

Janey could only imagine what the *other things* were. She decided not to ask.

'Why are you so different?' Daniel asked. He sounded genuinely interested.

'I'm not.'

'Your speech, the way you carry yourself. You are not like the others.'

All her feelings of rejection came bubbling to the surface. She had the need to confide, unburden or purge herself of the full story she rarely told.

'I come from Falmouth and until the age of thirteen I attended St Christopher's School for Girls and had private tuition from my father when he was home. My father was the captain of a merchant ship. He was well respected and made a good living from it. We had a large house and I had a happy childhood, with strong family morals to anchor me.' She waited for Daniel to say something. She would say no more unless he wished to hear it.

'Go on,' he coaxed from behind her.

'One winter a scarlet fever epidemic hit the town. I heard my friend was ill and went to visit her. I wanted to give her my doll for comfort. My mother forbade me but I visited her anyway. It was a foolish thing to do. I didn't understand what the consequences of my actions might be.'

'What happened?'

Janey took a deep breath. 'I brought the fever home with me. I fell ill and survived it. My mother and sisters did not.'

'They all died?'

She nodded as she felt him wrap the coat a little tighter around her.

'My sisters caught it from me and died first. Mother's grief was all-consuming and weakened her. She fell ill with the fever too. It was not long before she also succumbed.'

'And your father?'

'He was away at sea at the time. Word reached him that his wife and daughters had died. He took the news badly. The last sighting of him was at the bow of his ship before he stepped over the side. I will never know if he took his own life because he thought he had lost all of his children or if I was not worth returning for.'

She blinked away the tears that always threatened to rise up when she thought of her family.

'My uncle blamed me and was reluctant to take me in, so instead he secured me a post as a laundry maid with a family in Truro.' She gave a soft hollow laugh. 'At thirteen there is little for a girl to do but go into service, particularly if there is no one to offer them a roof over their heads. Since then I have felt that I just don't fit in, wherever I am. I'm too educated for one class, too poor for the other. It's not a nice feeling, not fitting in. It's lonely.'

She bit her lip; she had said too much. She hardly knew him yet she had just spilled her life story to him as if she'd known him all her life. She shouldn't have said so much. She abruptly changed the topic. 'I'm sorry for insulting you at the hall tonight.'

'I've been called worse, although you are the first to insult me to my face.'

She could well believe it. Only a fool would risk insulting Daniel Kellow to his face. She couldn't help smiling.

'That's better,' he said. She glanced around to find him looking down at her. The moonlight had cast its magic, softening his dark eyes even more as he held her gaze. She looked away.

'I don't usually go around insulting people. I'm just not used to being manhandled.'

'I'm not sure I like my dancing being described as being manhandled,' he teased.

'It was too forward. I didn't know you. It was ...' She struggled to find the right words. '... too intimate.' She wriggled uncomfortably. He steadied her with a protective hand.

'A woman likes to become acquainted first before such closeness.' Janey was aware she was sounding a little pompous, but she was only telling the truth as she saw it.

'I've had no complaints before,' countered Daniel.

She could well believe it.

'Then I must be different.'

The sound of his laughter surprised her.

'You certainly are,' he replied.

She tried again to explain. 'A gentleman wouldn't behave

that way.' She felt him tense behind her and the air became charged.

'Gentlemen are not always what they seem.'

'I'm not explaining myself very well. Mr Brockenshaw, for example, he wouldn't just lift a woman up in public.'

'It takes more than a title to make a man a gentleman.' Daniel's voice had once more become curt and she knew he had taken offence.

She tried to explain again. 'It's about etiquette, manners.'

'I'd rather a man was true to himself than hide behind etiquette and manners.'

'But we can't all behave that way. Say what we want, behave how we want.'

'Perhaps not, but perhaps we would be happier if we tried.'

Janey heard his challenge. He was accusing her of being someone she was not. Of trying to be the person she hoped the other staff or her uncle would love, instead of just being herself.

Her eyes began to smart. Daniel's barb had hit home. He had spoken the truth although he knew it would hurt her. He had not liked being compared to James Brockenshaw and had retaliated. She was only trying to explain her reaction at the dance but somehow her meaning had got muddled and he took it as an insult. She had offended him. She wished she had not spoken.

The gatehouse at the entrance of the road to the manor came into view but Daniel steered his horse off the road and into the woods.

'We'll cut through here and enter the gardens at the back of the house. I can tie the horse up under the trees while we make our way across the grounds. It will be dark inside so listen to my instructions so you can find your way around the house without a candle.'

Without waiting for a reply he explained how he had made his way through the house at night as a seventeen-year-old boy.

She listened quietly until they came to the edge of the wood. Then he helped her down from the horse. His manner was businesslike and although he was not rough, any gentleness he had shown earlier had gone. She felt that the sooner he got rid of her, the sooner he could be off to his bed for the night.

He firmly grabbed her hand and led her to the dairy window. She watched as he pushed each corner of the metal frame in turn until he heard the latch inside work loose. It dropped off its peg at the base and the window opened. For the first time Janey noticed that the window's middle catch halfway up the frame had long since been broken.

Janey slipped Daniel's coat from around her shoulders and handed it back to him. 'Thank you,' she whispered as he quickly put it back on.

Then he waved her closer and once again he reached down under her skirts and lifted her up to enter the window.

Here Daniel had made a mistake. He had assumed Janey would know how to climb through a window and expected her to have put one leg through when he lifted her. What he had failed to realise was that there was not much call for a captain's daughter to climb through windows. She lay stranded on the granite sill, her top half through the window and her bottom at the level of his face. As much as she appreciated his help, a view of her bottom was not part of the deal.

In her haste to move forward, Janey kicked with her legs and felt one foot connect with Daniel's face with a sickening thud. She twisted to look behind her to find him holding his jaw. He glared back at her and did not appear to appreciate her whispered apology. He grabbed both her legs to stop them moving.

'I'm going to lift you through,' he ground out and the next thing she knew her hips were lifted clear of the sill and thrust forward. She slowly slid over the worktop and onto the cold slate floor like a seal pup sliding off a rock.

Daniel looked through the window and appeared relieved when she stood up, unharmed. She was in.

'Remember to shut the window when I go,' he whispered. He reached into the back of his trouser waistband and held out her patten shoes.

'You had them all the time?' she whispered, confused.

'Would you have got on the horse if I had given them to you?' he asked.

They looked at each other with a measured stare. Feelings of distrust and hurt pride emanating from both sides.

She looked in her reticule. 'I have something for you,' she said, changing the subject, and taking something out she reached towards him with a closed hand.

'I don't want your money, Miss Carhart. You may not consider me gentlemanly enough for you, but I'm not so low as to expect payment for helping you.'

Before she could respond he closed the window in her face and marched angrily away, rubbing his jaw. Janey, frustrated that he did not give her an opportunity to explain, lifted herself on tiptoe to watch him striding across the yard into the gardens beyond, his body eventually swallowed up by the shadows of the trees. She looked down and slowly opened her hand. There, sitting in her palm, lay Daniel's button.

The atmosphere in the room was cold as the ill-fitting windows allowed cool air to circulate, which was advantageous for a dairy. As instructed by Daniel, Janey unlaced her boots and carried them in her left hand whilst under her arm she carried her pattens. Her right hand she used to guide her way. She remembered his instructions as clearly as if he spoke them at her side as she walked. 'Use the smells emanating from the pantries to guide you through the kitchen wing,' he had said. 'Avoid the creaking floorboards on the left of the stairs.' 'Be careful when opening the door near the servants' stairs, it jams.' 'Count the window recesses to guide you in the dark.' Finally she arrived at the servants' quarters.

Her trailing fingers counted the doors until she came to her own, reached down, turned the handle and slipped inside. She found her candle and lit it, breathing a sigh of relief to see her familiar things about her. She was safe at last and undetected.

She lifted her candle and took it to the mirror that hung from a nail on the wall. The candlelight cast shadows that danced around the room but her image remained clear. She had never seen herself so untidy before. Always neat in appearance, the woman who stared back at her looked dishevelled and rosy-cheeked. Yet there was something else different about her reflection that unnerved her. Her eyes sparkled with a fervour of excitement that she had not seen before. Janey did not know this woman and it frightened her. She blew out the candle and her reflection disappeared in the darkness.

Snuggling down into her bed, Janey thought she would be too tired to relive the night's events. Yet, as she waited for sleep her mind replayed images in her head, which would later tease her subconscious and meddle with her dreams. She smiled as she remembered the feel of Daniel's body against her own. The warmth of him, the smell of him was firmly etched in her mind. She touched her lips with her fingertips as she finally recognised the fragrance of the soap he used. She smiled. 'Sandalwood,' she whispered to herself as sleep finally arrived to claim her. 'Daniel smelt of sandalwood and he smelt so good.'

Daniel waited in the shadows of the grounds beneath her attic room window, which still glowed from the soft light of a single candle. He pulled his coat tighter about him feeling the chill of the night for the first time. Only moments ago he had Janey wrapped within its folds and now he felt the loss of the woman he barely knew.

Women were always difficult to understand, thought Daniel, but Janey Carhart was a strange mix. Tonight, she had shown vulnerability, yet at times had been stubborn. She was prim, but there were moments he'd glimpsed her sensuality. She had been wary of him, yet shared her innermost fears. A beguiling package all wrapped up in a comely figure of natural beauty that he knew he would find hard to banish from his thoughts when he finally reached home. Yet he believed that she would quickly forget him. She had made it plain what she wanted in a man and she did not find those charms in him.

The light from her candle was finally extinguished, plunging her attic room into darkness. Daniel knew she was now safe in her bed. It was time for him to go home.

Chapter Six

Next morning Janey lit her bedside candle and watched it twist and turn in the dark as it cast a soft amber glow around her room. Dawn was still an hour away and Janey had woken early, resulting in this unexpected time of solitude and peace. She lay watching the flame struggling to survive in the draughty room. Time and time again, just as it appeared to have been extinguished, it would strengthen and grow taller once more.

Daniel's dark chocolate brown eyes and words would not leave her mind and reluctantly she had to admit he had spoken some truth. She could not influence friendships with the other staff due to their natural distrust of her position. She could only earn their respect by carrying out her duties to the best of her ability and be true to herself. In time, perhaps, they would trust and accept her, however she had no desire to be made a fool of by Mary again, or be intimidated by Miss Petherbridge any longer. She had a right to be here and the sooner Mary and Miss Petherbridge understood that the better.

The melted wax, which had pooled around the base of the flame, spilled down the side of the candle. It cooled quickly in the chilled atmosphere to form a cascade of smooth pearl droplets. As the candle struggled to stay alight, it was transforming into a new kind of beauty that was not lost to Janey.

The sky began to lighten and Janey slipped from her bed and dressed. She stood in front of her pitted mirror, pinned her cap on her head and smoothed the skirt of her uniform down. With some relief she recognised the neat, tidy woman looking back at her. This reflection was safe. Yet, she began to realise, in truth she was a woman desperate for approval and love. A woman who had climbed the servants' hierarchy to prove to herself, if not her uncle, that she was worthy of existing. She despised that desperation. Daniel Kellow appeared to have no such failing or weakness, despite his background. Daniel, a dark, brooding man of few words, who, despite his abrupt behaviour and lack of manners, had been the only one to come to her aid last night. She must be more self-assured like Daniel. She braced her shoulders. Today, from this day forward, she would fulfil her role completely and earn the other servants' respect, if not their friendship. The woman looking back at her no longer looked quite so desperate; from the thrust of her jaw, she looked positively determined.

Mary arrived late for work and looked as if she had not slept. Her face momentarily brightened when she saw Janey. 'I was worried all night what had become of—'

Janey did not want to hear. She grabbed her arm and took her aside, making Mary wince with pain.

'You lied and betrayed me,' accused Janey. 'If you do anything like that again I will report you to Lady Brockenshaw and you *will* be dismissed.' She let go of Mary's arm with a shake. 'Now get on with your duties, Mary, before I report you for being late.'

Janey had no intention of reporting her, but she allowed the warning to linger in the air that she might. Mary needed to learn a lesson, as things were about to change.

Miss Petherbridge stood in the doorway of the main kitchen surveying the scene. She had expected at least one member of staff to be missing and the kitchens to be in chaos, yet everyone appeared to be at their posts fulfilling their duties to her satisfaction. However, although she could not put her finger on it, her sharp eyes and years of experience had sensed a change.

As she turned away to go to her office the Carhart girl's voice caught her attention. She tilted her head to listen.

'Mary, when you make up her ladyship's bed, I want you to change the bottom sheet. The present sheet has a tear in it.'

'She's blind, she won't notice,' grumbled Mary.

'Thank you for stating the obvious, Mary, but in this house we have standards. Replace the sheet and ask Miss Petherbridge if she wishes it to be mended or used for rags.'

Miss Petherbridge waited for a retort from Mary, but surprisingly none was forthcoming. She returned to her office, sat down at her desk and opened the ledger to study the housekeeping accounts. She pursed her lips as she stared at the numbers, but in reality her mind was elsewhere. She had been right to sense a change. The Carhart girl had a new-found confidence and now delegated without apology or hesitation. Something must have happened to make this change, but what?

Miss Petherbridge felt uneasy. She did not like not knowing what was going on within the household. In fact, she prided herself on how much control she wielded as although Mr Tallock was head of the domestic staff and an excellent butler, he hated confrontation and was prone to nerves, so often deferred to her. Despite this, she had the uneasy feeling that her position was under threat from the Carhart girl. She should view her as an ally, but she didn't. Youth was no longer on her side and as much as she detested this knowledge she loathed seeing her potential replacement even more.

It was not long before Miss Petherbridge saw further evidence of the change in Janey. The evening meal had come to an end. As usual Miss Petherbridge stood, picked up her teacup and offered her usual invitation to the senior staff to discuss the issues of the day with her in her office. For months Janey had not intruded on the ritual evening meeting, despite her position warranting an invitation. No invitation had ever been issued from the housekeeper so she had politely remained seated. Today was different. Janey had risen from her chair and made it clear she would not be excluded any more. Sensing danger Mr Tallock interceded.

'What a good idea that you attend also, Janey. It was quite amiss of me not to have invited you before. A direct link to her ladyship's views will be most valuable.'

The housekeeper's eyes narrowed; her chance to dismiss her had gone. If she refused her now it would be going directly against Mr Tallock, and unity between the two senior members of staff was of utmost importance. Silently she led the way to her office where they all took a seat. Janey sat quietly listening to them discuss various issues, from the menu choices for tomorrow, the quality of the food bought, to the ordering of polish for the master's riding boots. As the discussions finally died down Mr Tallock turned to Janey and asked if there was anything she wished to add.

Janey put down her teacup. 'I've noticed this past week that Lady Brockenshaw has not been drinking all of her tea.'

The housekeeper sniffed. 'I hardly think that is a major issue.'

'But worth mentioning, I think.' Janey smiled at her. 'She usually enjoys her tea but she dislikes the taste and I was wondering if the tea is different or the teapot has been cleaned using a different scourer.'

Mr Tallock and Mrs Friggens looked to Miss Petherbridge.

'This past week you say?'

Janey nodded.

Silence descended while Miss Petherbridge thought for a moment. 'I have changed the supplier. I usually buy the tea from Tridinnick Stores but I've changed to Mrs Tully's shop.'

'I have a suspicion Mrs Tully may be up to her old tricks again, mixing cheaper brands with the stock of quality tea to make it go further. She learnt those tricks from the baker,' said Mrs Friggens, looking at Janey. 'He mixes rice with his dough to make more loaves which is better than before. It used to be sawdust.'

'I think perhaps we should change it back, Miss Petherbridge,' said the butler. 'Thank you for highlighting it, Janey. Is there anything else?'

Miss Petherbridge made a note, her nose wrinkled as if she had smelt a bad odour in the room.

'Lady Brockenshaw also loves your shortbread biscuits, Mrs Friggens.'

Mrs Friggens visibly preened. She rarely heard the compliments expressed in the dining room. Miss Petherbridge often failed to give adequate feedback from her menu consultations with her ladyship, an issue that never failed to frustrate the cook.

'She mused that she would love to eat them every afternoon. I suggested it may become boring but then we went on to discuss all the extra ingredients that would maintain the interest such as nuts one day, apple pieces on another day, chocolate and so on. We decided, however, that you would be the expert and would have many more ideas on the added ingredient.'

Miss Petherbridge's eyes darted to the cook who was basking in the unexpected praise.

'I do indeed. I could add spices, blueberries or strawberries. I will start tomorrow.'

'That's a wonderful idea. As you can understand her

ladyship relies on her other senses all the more due to her lack of sight. She will appreciate your skill more than most.'

She was good, thought Miss Petherbridge. Her observations were acute and without causing offence she had brought up two problems and identified solutions. Janey Carhart had made her mark in the informal meeting and her regular attendance was therefore assured. I will have to watch her closely, the housekeeper decided, and be prepared to destroy any further rise in her status by whatever means necessary.

The week that followed was a happier time for Janey. Looking back she did not know how she had the courage to stand up to Mary on that first morning. From that day on they were cordial to each other and their position in the hierarchy was fixed and adhered to. Knowing where each other stood seemed to settle the other servants too and Janey found it a relief to not worry about trying to fit in. It was as if an invisible heavy burden had been lifted from her shoulders. She found that with this release she became more relaxed and started to smile more frequently. Conversation came easier to her and the staff, in turn, responded. Soon, she realised, Mr Tallock began to refer to her on certain matters and Mrs Friggens often asked her what the family thought of the meals. She relished this inclusion, and the atmosphere in the kitchen became friendlier, yet remained as efficient as ever. Miss Petherbridge was the only one who did not take well to the change. She remained aloof from her staff and from Janey in particular, but Janey realised, with relief, she did not mind.

'Janey!' Charlotte was furiously beckoning to her at the end of the servants' hall. 'There's someone at the back door for you! Quick, Miss Petherbridge is upstairs so she won't see.'

Janey quickly followed Charlotte to the back door. A boy, a cap in one hand and a bunch of wild flowers in the other, was waiting for her.

'Are you Miss Carhart?' the child asked, nervously. He was clean, about fourteen years old and although he was neatly dressed his clothing showed he was from the working classes. He glanced over his shoulder nervously, then back at her.

Janey nodded to confirm that she was.

'Been told to give you these.' He held the flowers out to her with an outstretched arm. His cheeks reddened. 'They're not from me,' he added, hastily.

Bewildered, Janey took them from him. 'Thank you all the same.' She sniffed them, their aroma filling her nostrils on this cold, sunny early October day. 'Who are they from?' she asked, touching their blooms.

'I promised not to tell,' said the boy.

Janey glanced up. She had a sneaking suspicion he would have liked to tell her very much.

'That is very loyal of you. However, would it be breaking your promise if you told me what he looked like? Is it a *he*?'

The boy nodded, his lips pressed firmly together.

She watched the boy over the top of the bouquet. She adored wild flowers. Someone had gone to a lot of trouble to pick these and she wanted to know who. Her intensive stare made the boy fidget as she held her precious gift against her heart.

'I respect him too much to tell you, miss. He wouldn't want me to say,' blurted the boy before escaping around the corner. Janey followed and watched him run along the gravelled carriageway that led from the main entrance of the house to the estate gate. The sound of his footsteps grinding into the gravel slowly receded as the distance between them grew.

Lost in thought, Janey did not at first see the rider on a black horse approaching. He drew level with the boy, who immediately stopped and respectfully touched his cap in greeting. They exchanged a few words before each going their own way. Janey's breath caught in her throat. James Brockenshaw had returned.

She could not move. His appearance had brought a rush of the girlish feelings she had not experienced since his departure two weeks and six days ago. Her senses churned in the pit of her stomach as he approached, and dismounted from the lathered horse. A stable boy, unnoticed by Janey, was waiting for him and after a few quick words from his master led the prancing horse, nervous of its new surroundings, into the nearby stable. James turned to face her, smiled, and to her surprise, came striding over to her with an aristocratic confidence and took off his top hat.

'Good morning, Miss Carhart. Are you keeping well?'

'Quite well, sir. We were not aware you were returning today.'

'It was a spur of the moment decision. I had a desire to see the natural beauty Bosvenna holds,' he said, his eyes never leaving her face. Janey felt heat rush to her cheeks. 'I intended to write to my mother to inform her of my arrival, but thought better of it. I realised I would arrive before the letter, so I did not bother.' He opened his arms. 'So here I am, at your service.' He did a mock bow and Janey couldn't help but break into a smile.

'You tease me, sir.'

'And you me,' he countered. Confusion knotted her brow. She was about to protest, but he had already turned his attention to the flowers in her hands. 'Those are beautiful. Beautiful flowers for a beautiful lady.' He stroked them with the back of one finger as if caressing her cheek. 'An unknown admirer, perhaps?'

'I don't know who gave them to me,' she confessed, 'but I am not so persuaded I have an admirer.'

'You are too modest, but modesty becomes you.' His finger momentary touched her fingers leaving a burning imprint upon them. 'Indeed you must have an admirer, but perhaps not unknown?'

Her mouth went dry. Was he hinting that he had given them to her?

'If I recall correctly, wild flowers are your favourite?' He replaced his hat and touched its brim with his whip handle in salute. Smiling she dipped a curtsy in return.

James turned on his heels and left her with a memory of his boyish grin in her mind and her body reeling with emotion. James Brockenshaw, son of Lord Brockenshaw, who had always been charming, was now flirting with her and hinting of admiration! She hurriedly returned inside, with her precious gift clutched in her arms, and headed for the servants' quarters. In the sanctuary of her room, she breathlessly selected her best ribbon, wound it around the stems and hung it upside down from a protruding nail in the wall. She stood back and looked at the flowers, their modest scent slowly filling the room. She couldn't contain the smile on her lips or calm her beating heart. She hoped they would dry well and last forever, preserving the memory of his gift for years to come. She did not expect the encounter to be repeated or their relationship to grow. He was the son of her employer and from a different class, but at least now she would always have the flowers to look upon and cherish.

The mild temperatures and the torrential showers, which blighted the first few weeks of October, resulted in an abundance of brown fungi breaking through the sodden soil. It infiltrated the lawns of the estate, the grass verges by the roadside and the golden, orange grassland of the moors.

Convoluted, foaming trails of gushing water also brought the moorland to life, snaking their way through the patches of gorse and white moss that laced the sodden moor. The ground was treacherous to walk upon and best avoided as dress hems and shoes were soon soaked and the ground slippery under foot.

James tipped the whisky back into his throat. He had spent the morning visiting the tenant farmers with his father, more out of duty than any real interest. He acted the role to keep his father off his back and bring peace to the house, but he had not enjoyed it. Grubby farmers, spawning dirty brats and smelly animals. He had no interest in their lives, their gossip or what they planned to sow next year. How he hated this house and estate. He refilled his glass and crossed to the window to watch the heavy rainfall. This place choked him so much that at times he felt he could not breathe. He wanted to travel and see the world, to make Bath or even London his permanent residence, to attend balls, gentlemen's clubs, gamble the night away. However, despite his desires, his birthright and his parents' wish was for him to remain here. Here, in the middle of nowhere, where the most exciting thing to happen was the weather. This was where his destiny lay and it made him feel sick.

His one comfort was his horse. The black beast had turned into a fine purchase. Not content to wait for the formal hunting season to start in November, he had attended his first cubbing hunt, held the previous week. It had proved a good opportunity for the horse to gain some experience in the field. It had been an exhilarating and successful ride, with four fox cubs killed. His fellow hunters had complimented him on his steed and James had wallowed in their praise. He was now eager for the fox hunting season to begin. His father was not so enthusiastic about his purchase, particularly when he discovered how much it had cost him. James had wanted to show the horse off again and had sent word to the only man whose praise was worth having when it came to horses. The only man James acknowledged knew more about horses than he did. Only Daniel Kellow had refused to come. Today, the memory still irked him.

The rain had eased considerably and James watched his mother's dog run out into the garden, followed by her maid. He smiled to himself as he watched her gracefully pass through the iron archway, which formed the entrance to the rose garden. He finished his drink with a quick tilt of his head, put the glass down and left the room.

Janey picked her way along the wet path through the dormant rose garden, careful not to slip on the slimy slate. Skirting along the wall of the kitchen garden, she followed the path down to the shrubbery and away from the manor. Charlie was delighted to escape the house where the bad weather had imprisoned him these past few days. Janey had also missed their walks and the freedom she felt leaving the estate. The air was damp and the overcast sky threatened rain at any moment, but Janey didn't care. She could not help smiling as she watched Charlie's tail wag vigorously with each new scent he discovered, each new object he investigated. Charlie barked suddenly and James stepped out into her path.

'I have been discovered,' he said, laughing, holding up his hands in mock surrender. 'Did I scare you?'

'You did, sir. I was not expecting you to be here.' She looked around nervously and was relieved no windows of the house could look down upon them.

'I fancied a stroll after a busy morning. Would you do me the pleasure of accompanying me?'

Although Janey was concerned that they may be seen

walking together, she felt she had little choice in the matter and silently fell into step beside him. A silence descended as Janey absorbed the reality of their situation. Her nervousness that they might be observed by his parents showed her how silly her romantic dreams about him had been.

James looked down at her. His eyes studied hers for a fleeting moment as if he had the urge to impress her and was weighing up just how to do it. His next words proved her right and she couldn't help but find his intention endearing.

'I have spent the morning visiting my tenants. It is important for me to see how they are faring, offer advice if necessary and see if all is running smoothly.' He looked away and tapped a bush with his cane. 'My father looks after things when business calls me away, but when I am back I like to oversee things.'

'It must be a great responsibility, sir. I'm sure they appreciate your interest.'

He was pleased with her reply. 'They seem appreciative.'

'It must also be a burden,' she replied, intuitively. Her response caught him off guard. He came to a halt and stared at the shrubs planted in the valley below.

'You see that bush there and that one there?' He pointed his cane at various specimens. 'My great uncle planted them. He loved to travel; he would return from his trips with a variety of plants as souvenirs. He had the freedom to travel whilst his brother was tied to the estate. I am tied to the estate, but I think I have inherited my great uncle's interest in the world.' He looked at her keenly. 'Have you travelled?'

'No, sir. My father visited many countries, but I have not had the opportunity to travel outside of Cornwall.'

James laughed. Suddenly she felt inadequate and unworldly, but James did not notice.

'I plan to visit every country in the Empire and I will one day.'

'I believe you can do anything you put your mind to, sir.'

'I believe I can.' He smiled triumphantly.

The heavens opened, forcing them to bow their heads against the pelting raindrops. James grabbed her hand.

'It's raining. Follow me. I know the perfect place to shelter.'

James led her through the driving rain, down some steps and pulled her into a stone grotto. Charlie followed them inside, shook himself dry and sat down to watch the rain outside. Janey looked about her.

'This place is lovely,' she whispered. 'I didn't know it was here.'

'The walls are decorated with crystals and minerals collected from the abandoned mines in the county.' James pointed to one. 'That one is clear quartz.' There were others too: black, silver and green rocks glinted and shone back at them. 'I used to call it the fairy grotto when I was a boy.' He leaned against the wall, watching her. 'I used to hide here to avoid my Latin lessons. How I hated them. It's a very lonely existence being an only child. Do you have siblings?'

She always found it painful to talk of her sisters and her sadness showed in her voice.

'I had two younger sisters but they died.'

Unusually, he did not voice his sympathy for her loss. A feeling of unease churned in her stomach. It was as if she had not spoken at all.

'I hated being an only child. All my parents' attention was, and still is, focused on me. Sometimes I feel I cannot breathe.'

His eyes showed genuine hurt and Janey instinctively took a step closer to comfort him. She stopped herself just in time but he took her hand anyway and held it in his own.

'Do you realise that these past few weeks have only been bearable because of you? I swear I would not visit my mother so often if it wasn't for the hope of seeing her maid.'

'You must not say such things, sir.' Gently she tried to withdraw her hand from his but he would not let her.

'I can say what I like, when I like and to whom I like,' he said, smiling at her.

'If Miss Petherbridge or Mr Tallock knew, they would see that I was dismissed.'

'The she-devil and her sidekick can go to hell for all I am concerned.'

Janey smiled at his nickname for them. How could she not?

He lifted her hand and kissed it. 'Say my name, Janey.'

'I couldn't, sir. I mustn't. Please don't ask me.'

She felt the path she had been treading these past months had suddenly shown itself to be dangerous and treacherous and she was unsure what to do. She was attracted to this man, but her dreams had been built from a position of distance and safety. Today, their relationship had changed again. He was demanding more and it would put her in danger. Her position, her home, her reputation was at risk for she knew he would never acknowledge her as anything more than a servant in public. Yet, if she denied him she still risked a dismissal and a loss of a home.

'Say my name. I need to hear it from your lips.' He seemed so vulnerable and earnest in his request.

'James,' she whispered as he kissed her palm.

The sensation of his kiss travelled down her arm. It was not unpleasant, but she was afraid to encourage him further. Not here, so close to Lady Brockenshaw's home. She was attempting to gently ease her hand away when he lurched forward to kiss her. She quickly sidestepped and made a show of calling the dog. She dared not look at him.

'I must go. Her ladyship is expecting me.' She grabbed Charlie's collar. For some reason that she could not explain, it was important she was no longer alone with him.

'You do realise I like to hunt?' He did not sound amused and the turn in conversation both unnerved and confused her.

'I do.'

'It is not the kill I enjoy, although there is a degree of satisfaction seeing the fox killed by the hounds. No, what I enjoy most is the chase.' He let his gaze wander over her body. 'I have a reputation of being a good huntsman and the prospect of an exciting chase makes me all the keener.'

He suddenly offered a charming smile, which left her wondering if she had imagined his sharper tone. He took her hand and began to kiss each fingertip in turn. 'You are extraordinarily beautiful, my dear. Do you fear me?'

'You ... overwhelm me, sir,' she replied, truthfully.

'Overwhelm? I like the sound of that,' he mused.

He opened his lips and took her ring finger in his warm, moist mouth. His provocative gesture embarrassed her. Appearing pleased at her reaction, he slowly withdrew, gently sucking and caressing her finger with his tongue as he did so. 'But what I like most of all is making you blush, which I will look forward to doing, time and time again.' He bowed his head in farewell before stepping out into the rain and leaving her alone.

Janey began to tremble. She was unsure if it was the cold atmosphere within the stone grotto chilling her bones, excitement at his promise or fear of his threat that made her shake so.

Miss Petherbridge's shoes tapped along the windowless passage of the servants' quarters, her keys jingling in tune to the sway of her walk. She had a mind to inspect the Chippendale window seat which was now stored in the lumber room in the female quarters. The upholstery was damaged and required an overdue repair.

She unlocked the door of the little room and peered in. The room, largely neglected for lack of habitual use, was cold, dark and cheerless. An abandoned wicker baby carriage lay on its side. Next to it sat a cylindrical commode made of ash and decorated with tulipwood banding, the beauty of the wood hiding its primitive function. Chairs, stools and tables were recklessly stacked, long forgotten and gathering dust. Fortunately, the Chippendale was near the door and after a quick inspection her work there was done.

She was about to leave when she heard someone leaving one of the servants' rooms. She looked out and saw Janey shutting her door and walking down the corridor to the stairs at the far end. When she had gone, the housekeeper left the lumber room, quietly shut the door and made her way to Janey's room.

Miss Petherbridge made regular checks on the servants' rooms but she always gave them notice. Today, however, she did not feel so generous. The Carhart girl had raised her curiosity and she had time on her hands, a bad combination in certain circumstances but not in this one. She wanted to know more about the girl. It bothered her that she could not fault her as her confidence grew each day. She turned the handle and entered her room.

The room was tidy and the bed immaculately made. Dried flowers hung from the wall and books lined the windowsill. One pair of best shoes, highly polished, sat neatly below the window and on the far wall hung a single framed embroidery, lovingly sewn with miniature cross stitch depicting in great detail a beautiful woman in a Grecian dress. Miss Petherbridge peered at it, snorted and continued looking around the room.

She was about to leave when a plain journal on the bedside table caught her eye. Using a single finger, she lifted the cover and flicked it open. The private musings of a young romantic girl lay out on display before her. She turned the page, then another. And another. One page in particular caught the housekeeper's eye. She instantly recognised the name, lovingly written and decorated with hearts, flowers and intertwined with ivy and ribbons. Again and again the name had been drawn, the care, tenderness and imagination evident for all to see. James Brockenshaw.

The housekeeper shut the book with a thump and stared at the closed cover. A sense of unease set in. What if, by some strange turn of events, the attraction became mutual? What if Janey Carhart should become the next Lady Brockenshaw? The idea that she would become her mistress was abhorrent. The housekeeper, her mind racing, withdrew from the book as if it exuded an offensive odour.

She did not have the authority to dismiss the lady's maid, only Lady Brockenshaw could do that. She could not express her concern to the mistress, there was no proof that anything was going on between the two of them and to accuse Janey was also to accuse the young master. Lord and Lady Brockenshaw would consider it insulting to have suspicion placed on their only son. He was heir to the estate and would never dally with a servant or, even worse, fall in love with one.

Suddenly Miss Petherbridge had a desperate desire to leave the room. She would have to think about the situation. She needed to plan. Whatever happened she wanted Janey Carhart gone and off the estate before she rose above her station, or dragged them all down with her.

Chapter Seven

Reverend William Smith looked down from the ornately carved pulpit to the empty seats below. The service had been well attended this morning and his sermon on temptation appeared to have gone well. At least the congregation had listened, whether they put it into practice when they returned home was quite another matter. He doubted very much if old George would stop drinking to excess every Saturday night or Richard Nankivell's greed for profit would stop him selling poached pheasant in his little shop. He had learnt over the years that if a vicar was to be accepted and trusted within the Cornish community he must remain non-judgmental. After all, how can a shepherd tend his flock if he howls like a wolf and fills them with fear?

He gathered his notes together and paused to listen. The congregation still lingered in the churchyard and he could hear their voices through the open doorway. He smiled at the gentle hum of gossip interspersed with the occasional laughter, for it signified that although this village was small, its community was strong and full of life.

For the first time he noticed one of his flock still remained in the doorway. He descended the pulpit stairs and waited for the person to make themselves known. The girl entered and the vicar instantly recognised her as Lady Brockenshaw's maid.

'Hello, Janey. Can I help you?' he enquired.

She hesitantly approached, trailing her fingers along the end of each pew as she walked down the aisle.

'I enjoyed your sermon, reverend.'

'I'm glad to hear it.' He watched her with a steady gaze.

She smiled nervously at him, as she drew near. There was a short silence. 'Does Lady Brockenshaw wish to speak to me?'

She shook her head. 'It was on Lady Brockenshaw's insistence I came to see you. She is quite well and sitting in her carriage with Lord Brockenshaw.' She traced the wooden carvings of the pulpit with her fingers. 'It's a beautiful pulpit. Was it carved locally?'

'As much as I like the pulpit, I don't think Lady Brockenshaw believes you need to talk to me about carpentry skills,' he said, smiling kindly to soften his words.

'Lady Brockenshaw senses I am not quite myself. She is very sensitive to other people's emotions.'

'I have often thought that myself.' He sat down in a pew and patted the seat beside him. 'She feels that if you cannot tell her what is bothering you then you might wish to speak to me?'

Janey nodded and took a pew.

The vicar waited as the young girl twisted a white handkerchief in her lap. 'Something is troubling you. Perhaps I can help?'

Janey lifted her gaze to search his face. He knew she was wondering if she could trust him. He had seen that look many times from his parishioners and he had learnt over the years to wait patiently, for they usually came to the conclusion they could and would open their hearts to him. It wasn't long before Janey did just that.

'Sometimes I feel like I'm walking in the clouds and at other times I feel I'm in so much trouble that I'm drowning.'

'Go on,' he encouraged, gently.

'I can't tell you the details but I'm in this situation and I don't know which path to follow. At times this path,' she said, waving her right hand, 'seems so exciting, everything I've ever wanted. The answer to all my dreams, yet I feel this knot of anxiety right here.' She made a fist and placed it on her stomach. 'I feel uneasy, frightened, a feeling that it's wrong. That if I take this path there is an air of impending doom waiting for me.' She shook her head. 'I'm not explaining myself very well.'

He patted her hand. 'On the contrary, I think you are explaining yourself excellently. You feel you have to make a choice and you don't know which choice to make.'

She nodded, a smile curving her lips.

He reached out and gently held her left wrist. 'And what of this path?'

She looked at her left hand, the wrist encased in the reverend's warm, soft hand, as if she hadn't seen it before.

'This is nothing.'

'You see nothing at the moment, but that doesn't mean there's nothing down this path at some point in the future.'

'I don't understand.'

'I mean if it doesn't feel right, perhaps it is because it isn't right at this moment in time. Have you asked God for guidance?'

She nodded. 'Every night, but He hasn't told me what to do.'

'It sounds like he is telling you, but you are not listening.' At her confusion he explained. 'If a child runs into the road and is about to be crushed under the wheels of a carriage, do you hesitate to run out and save the child from certain death? No, of course not, because you know it is the right thing to do. You know it is right, there is no doubting your actions.' He made a fist and laid it on his heart. 'You know it is right in here. It seems to me that if this situation is causing you such worry then perhaps it is not right for you to tread this path and it's God's way of telling you this.'

He reached for a Bible and read an extract from Proverbs. 'Trust in the Lord, my dear, seek his will and he will show you which path you should take.'

He looked up from the pages and saw tears threatening to spill from Janey's eyes. 'Have I upset you, child?'

She shook her head. 'No, reverend. At times I have felt as if I am going mad. I usually pride myself on having sound judgment but lately I have begun to doubt myself. I have felt like the moral anchor of my life is being slowly cut away from me and I fear once it's gone I shall be at the mercy of the rough sea.' Her smile was brittle. 'Thank you for your guidance. I am sure all will be well.' She stood up. 'I must go. Lady Brockenshaw is waiting for me and I don't want her to think I am taking advantage of her good will.'

'I am always willing to listen.'

'I know. Goodbye, reverend, and thank you.'

He watched her leave. Despite her smile being a little brighter than when she had arrived, Reverend Smith did not feel satisfied. She had spoken of a threat to her moral anchor. If a situation or, as he suspected, a person was trying to manipulate her feelings and beliefs to the extent of causing her to doubt herself, then that person was dangerous. That person, be it man or woman, would not stop merely because Janey had chosen not to follow them down that path. One can follow a path by choice or by force. He hoped to God it would not be the latter.

Janey breathed in the fresh air of the countryside. She relished the freedom her dog walking duties gave her and usually skirted the moors, but today she had changed her course and headed for the nearby wood. She tried to convince herself that the choice of walk was as a result of wanting to explore further, but in truth her behaviour was slowly changing.

Since speaking to the reverend, all those weeks ago, she had grown even more cautious of entering into a relationship with James. Such a relationship could only lead to her destruction. Her reputation, her job and her home would all be at risk. It was wrong for James to pressure her so. How do you rebuff a man that was the son of her employer? He was from a class so far above her own that she was at a disadvantage in all respects as he had so much more experience and power than her and her way of life depended on him.

Yet, she continued to feel emotionally torn. It would be so easy to succumb to his charms, devour the scraps of affection he promised her and ignore the voice in her head that told her he would soon tire of her. To avoid the dilemma, she had tried to distance herself from him.

If she heard him in a room that she was about to enter, she would leave and return later. If he came into a room whilst she was in it, she would make an excuse to withdraw. If she saw him watching her, she averted her eyes, and today she avoided the moor as she had seen him ride out on his horse and knew he may wait for her as he had done before. She had to admit, his coercive behaviour was verging on predatory and caused the feeling of unease inside her to grow a little each day. Unfortunately her avoidance of him only seemed to make James more determined to pursue her.

So today, for this hour, on this unusually mild day, Janey felt free. Free of the manor, free of her duties and – for a brief time – free of James. A carpet of crisp, golden leaves lay thick on the ground of the ancient wood, hiding the tangle of roots that spread out beneath the gnarled trees. How much they must have seen, mused Janey as she strolled along, feeling at the same time humbled by nature's beauty and grace.

The woodland sloped down to a river that meandered through the valley. Its flow gurgled over stony falls, became still in deep waters or surged with purpose forming fast flowing currents. The beauty of the river belied its strength as it insidiously cut at its boundaries, eroded the bank and hid treacherously unsafe edges. How precarious the undercut earthy banks were, Janey soon discovered when, to her horror, Charlie disappeared off the edge of one and fell in the water below. She screamed.

There was no time to waste. Janey ran to the river's edge and stretched out for Charlie's collar, but the current was too strong and swept the little dog further away from her. She ran along the riverbank, shouting for help. Charlie paddled furiously with his white front paws as the water carried him to a deep pool, edged by a crumbling bank. Janey knelt down and stretched out to reach him again, but the earth crumbled away beneath her and she was forced to clutch at the tufts of grass to regain her balance. She stood up and stepped back to safety.

'You can make it, Charlie, come on, swim to me.' She could see the little dog was beginning to tire.

In answer to her cries, a man emerged from the shadows of the trees and came half jogging, half sliding, down the steep embankment on the other side of the river. He slid to a halt near the bottom, as a mild avalanche of earth settled around his feet. His face, which had been obscured by his cap, was now clearly visible. It was Daniel Kellow.

Daniel hadn't seen Janey Carhart since the dance. He had spent the last few months trying to forget about her by working hard and avoiding any visits that might take him to the manor. Yet here she was, on the verge of hysteria and waving her arms about like a mad woman. It wasn't quite how he had imagined their next meeting to be, which to his annoyance had been often, despite his best efforts.

'It's Charlie!' Janey screamed at him. 'He's in the river!'

'Where?' Daniel looked for a child, but could see none.

'There! Her ladyship's dog is in the water!' Janey dropped

to her knees and reached out a hand to the little dog. 'Here boy, here boy. You can make it, swim to me.'

Daniel noticed the wet, sleek head of a dog paddling furiously towards her. The deep water had a gentle current that resulted in Charlie paddling with all his might just to remain still. He was tiring and would soon give up.

'Stop calling him,' Daniel ordered. 'You are encouraging him to stay in the deep water, just let the river take him and the current will bring him here to the shallow side.'

Janey was furious. 'Are you mad? The river will take him further downstream!'

'He will save himself if you stop interfering!'

Janey would have none of it. 'No, he won't. He doesn't have any sense.' He could see her mounting anger. He would have found her amusing, even endearing, if a dog was not suffering between them. 'Help him! Now!' she shouted at him.

No one dared tell Daniel Kellow what to do. Only Zachariah and Amy had had that privilege. Yet here was a chit of a girl ordering him to save a dog that was quite capable of saving himself if she would just shut her mouth for a few moments. He glared back at her, swearing under his breath. Janey did not flinch.

Furious, Daniel took off his cap and spun it to the ground with a flick of his wrist. His boots and coat soon followed. He waded into the river, the water soaking him to mid thigh. Janey smiled and clasped her hands as if offering up a prayer. Although Daniel would normally have taken pleasure in being the cause of such happiness, today pleasure wasn't what he was feeling. Grudgingly, he picked up the dog, which resembled a wet otter rather than a canine, turned abruptly and carried him back to his side of the river. Janey's smile fell from her face as his rescuer turned around with his hands on his hips, a frown on his brow and a smug smile in his heart.

'Why have you taken him to the wrong side of the river?' she asked, bewildered. 'I'm here.'

Daniel shrugged. 'You should have said. It's too late now.'

'No, it's not. Bring him back.'

Daniel looked over at the dog with a mock look of sympathy. 'I couldn't do that. He is resting.' He was right. Charlie had settled himself down on a slab of stone to dry off in the afternoon sun.

'But ... but I'm here. What am I to do?'

Daniel made a show of beating the leaves out of his coat. 'There's a bridge further down. I'm off.'

'No!' Janey screamed. 'Don't go! Charlie may wander off. What if he gets lost?'

'Not my problem.' Daniel was beginning to enjoy himself.

'Please, Mr Kellow!'

A little respect at last. He looked up and waited.

'Mr Kellow, I shall be in awful trouble if anything happens to him.'

Daniel rubbed his chin, pretending to think. 'Have you a lead?'

She nodded enthusiastically.

'Give me the lead and I will tie him up.'

Without waiting for an answer he waded back into the water and was soon looking up at her. She leaned down from the bank to pass him Charlie's lead but he grabbed her wrist instead. She instinctively braced herself.

'What are you doing?' she asked, warily. His hand enveloped her wrist with ease and although he did not hurt her, his grip was as strong as any shackle. He ignored her question and raised an eyebrow.

'You look worried, Miss Carhart. Do you not trust me?'

She tilted her chin. 'I have no reason to trust you. You took my dog to the wrong side of the river.'

'And you *ordered* me to rescue it. No one, Miss Carhart, tells me what to do.'

'If, Mr Kellow,' she replied, haughtily, 'you had saved my dog straight away, I wouldn't have had to tell you to save him.'

She looked down at him from her advantage of height on the riverbank, her chin set in defiance. He wanted to wipe the haughtiness off her face, yet he saw fear in her eyes and his more basic instinct was to wrap her in his arms. In the next instance he had done both as his body reacted and he yanked her into the river.

One minute Janey was on dry land, the next minute she was submerged in the river's bitter depths. Daniel quickly reached for her and Janey came spluttering to the surface in his arms, found her feet and stood up in the hip deep cold water. She glared at him, shook him off and attempted to wade to the other side of the river. Daniel followed, trying to hide his smile.

The crossing was not easy for Janey as her dress was sodden and heavy. She drunkenly made her way to the edge, but time and time again her skirts pulled her over with their weight and clinginess. Daniel offered to help her, barely concealing his laughter, but each time she angrily smacked his help away. She eventually made it to dry ground and swung around to face him. He stood on the riverbank a few yards away, dripping wet and still laughing.

'I'm soaked through!' she grumbled, tugging at the buttons of her sodden jacket. She dragged the heavy garment off and dropped it to the ground. 'Look at me,' she said, spreading her arms out wide so he could see her spoilt clothes.

Daniel turned to face her. The smile on his lips faded away.

'How on earth am I going to dry my dress in this

weather? How am I going to get home? Look what you've done to me.'

Daniel was looking. He had often wondered what she would look like undressed. Some nights the image came between him and his sleep. Yet here she was, standing before him in the sunlight and he could see all that he had imagined. Her wet clothes formed a second skin on her body: shapely legs silhouetted against the wet fabric; the pink skin of her breasts was visible through the transparent wet fabric of her bodice; and her nipples strained against her undergarments. Daniel inwardly groaned.

'Look at me!' the woman cried.

His gaze meandered downwards again, drinking in every curve to lock away in his mind. 'I am,' he whispered, hoarsely.

Janey looked down at herself and saw what Daniel could see. With a shout of disgust she picked up a clod of earth and threw it at him. The clod of earth easily missed its target and, annoyingly for Janey, Daniel burst out laughing again. She would have found his laugh endearing and contagious if she were not so angry with him. In her rage, she picked up another. It was only as it left her fingers did she realise that the weight gave a hint of the stone concealed within. This suspicion was soon confirmed as it found its target. The muddy stone hit Daniel in the middle of his forehead, his laughter abruptly stopped and he toppled like a felled tree backwards. His arms and legs lay spread out, like a starfish, from his apparently lifeless body.

'Oh Lord, have mercy!' Janey gasped, watching from a safe distance for any signs of life.

Daniel did not move.

'Daniel?' No answer came. Charlie, ears pricked, sat up expectantly. 'Daniel?'

Worried, Janey picked up her sodden skirts and walked towards him. Her patience ran out the last few yards and she ran to him. She fell to her knees by his side and roughly prodded him. 'Daniel? Say something!'

Nothing. She prodded again. With a sickening lurch of her heart she put one ear to his chest to listen. To her relief she heard a heartbeat, but it was short lived. In a flash Daniel had grabbed her wrists, flicked her over onto her back and pinned her hips with a thigh as he held her wrists at the level of her head.

'You could have killed me!'

He did not scare Janey, she was too angry at him for pretending to be dead.

'Well, I didn't, did I? More's the pity,' she shouted back.

'Are you usually such a haughty shrew?'

'You bring the worst out in me.' She shook her head to try and dislodge the wet strand of hair covering her eye, but annoyingly it would not budge. 'You pulled me into the water on purpose.'

'I also saved your dog's life!'

She shook her head again trying to dislodge the strand of wet hair that stuck to her face like a limpet. 'I am wet through because of you!'

'You deserved a drenching! Will you keep still!' he blasted.

She gave up and lay still, exhausted from her effort of getting out of the river.

As they listened to their panting settle, they looked everywhere but at each other. After a moment Daniel grudgingly apologised.

'I didn't mean to pull you in. You provoked me and I reacted before I knew what I was doing.'

'Is that an apology?'

Their eyes met and his face softened.

'It's all you are going to get,' he said, gently. He released one wrist and with the crook of his little finger lifted the strand of hair from her face and carefully laid it by her head. 'You are soaked,' he murmured, half to her, half to himself. He touched her cheek with the back of his fingers and with a slow downward movement stroked her soft, smooth skin. 'Are you cold?'

Janey shook her head, touched by his sudden gentleness. She had not seen this side of Daniel Kellow before. His fingers touched the corner of her mouth and ran across her soft lips. Mesmerised, she followed his eyes as he gazed at each feature, seeing in their deep brown a softness that made her feel the most precious thing in the world. She felt as if she had a million butterflies inside her, tumbling and fluttering, threatening to spill up through her chest into the fresh air. Her anger towards him was forgotten.

His fingers left her lips and slid through her hair behind her head as his thumb lined her jawline. He was going to kiss her. She held her breath. He lowered his head until he was less than a breath away, but came no closer. His face lingered above her, sharing the same air, waiting and giving her time to react to his advances.

The butterflies melted to a molten pool inside her. The desire to be kissed by him was threatening to overwhelm her. She waited, wanting him, needing him to kiss her, but he did not move. Janey could not wait any more. She tilted her head and kissed him first.

Whatever Daniel was expecting it was not this and his initial shock delayed his response, but not for long. Like a starved man needing nourishment, he drank in her kiss, taking over the lead with his experience and desire.

His kisses, at first gentle and teasing, became hungry and sensual and she gladly matched their fervour. It was now she who was drowning, drowning in sensations that blocked out the world. For that moment in time nothing else mattered and she wanted it to go on forever. But nothing lasts forever. Janey was brought abruptly down to earth with a thud when Daniel suddenly pulled away from her.

'Someone's coming,' he whispered, urgently.

Janey's eyes grew wide as she heard a man shouting in the distance.

'Has he seen us?' Her question was answered by the man himself.

'What's going on down there?'

Daniel's warmth left her body as he sprang to his feet and pulled her to hers.

'It's Billy Bray,' he said, positioning her by her shoulders so she faced him yet stood between him and the man descending down the steep embankment. 'He's the village gossip. There's nothing that goes on that Little Billy doesn't know about.'

Janey was horrified. Miss Petherbridge would be furious if a member of her staff was found cavorting in the woods with a man. Daniel slipped his coat on her and fastened the buttons. The large, dry coat not only warmed her, but covered her transparent bodice. He retrieved her wet jacket and pressed it into her hands.

'He's a weird looking fella,' he told her, quietly. 'You can never tell which way he's looking, but he means no harm. He's got his cart up in the road. He can give you a lift home.'

'You are going to leave me?' asked Janey as Daniel fastened the lead on Charlie and passed it to her.

One minute they were kissing like passionate lovers, the next he was putting her on a cart with a complete stranger.

Daniel pulled on his boots. 'You'll catch pneumonia if you walk home.' He offered his arm. 'Come on,' he said as he helped her up the steep embankment.

As soon as she saw Billy Bray she realised why he was nicknamed *Little* Billy. No more than four foot high, with wide bowed legs and a limp that reminded Janey of a small boat being tossed on a rough sea, the little man slowed down his descent and waited for the couple to approach.

'Billy. How are you?' Daniel said a little too loudly and with a big smile on his face.

Billy Bray was immediately suspicious; Daniel didn't often smile.

'What's going on 'ere then?' asked the little man as he appeared to look at both of them at the same time.

'Bit of a mishap with the river, nothing serious.'

The man, who was in his mid-forties and had hands the size of shovels, wasn't convinced.

'He thinks I've been mistreating you,' Daniel said under his breath as they approached. He gave her a reassuring wink. 'Don't worry, I don't have much of a reputation to lose but I'll have a word in his ear to make sure he doesn't ruin yours.'

'You all right, miss?' asked Little Billy as they approached.

Janey knew what he was alluding to and although Daniel had pulled her into the river she didn't want this man to know.

'Yes, thank you,' she replied.

'Can you give Miss Carhart a lift back to Bosvenna Manor?' interrupted Daniel.

Little Billy's crooked eyes noticed Janey's wet clothes. 'I can. If that is what you wish, miss.' Janey told him that it was and thanked him for his help. With a curt nod, Little Billy turned and led the way back up the embankment. They followed and in no time at all, they arrived at the road where an old horse and cart waited patiently.

Where had the passion of a few moments ago gone? wondered Janey. It felt as if any closeness between them was well and truly in the past as Daniel lifted her onto the duckboard of the cart as if she was a piece of lumber.

'You should keep your dog on a lead next time you choose to walk by a river,' warned Daniel as he tucked Charlie down by her feet. Janey's gaze searched his face, but he refused to meet hers, preferring to glance at Little Billy and ramble on in a voice that was unnecessarily loud.

Why was he behaving as if nothing had happened? Did the kiss mean nothing to him? She had not planned it. There had been no forethought, just an explosive passion that had risen up inside her and would not be quenched. Did he not realise that he had lit that fire inside her? He had not nurtured it, or tried to force it as James Brockenshaw had done, but he was the cause for it. She did not normally behave in that way. It was her first passionate kiss and she was glad it had been with him. Shaken, she realised the kiss had meant a great deal to her, if not for him.

'I don't feel I've done anything wrong,' replied Janey, in a measured tone. 'How was I to know he would fall in?'

Daniel pulled himself up on the cart step and leaned forward until his nose almost touched hers.

'Are you telling me you don't regret your actions this afternoon?' he asked.

She should refuse to answer. He was baiting her about her forward behaviour. Her heart vibrated within her chest, but she refused to drop her gaze. She needed no reminding. The memory of their kiss had seared itself into her brain. Dark, black pools darkened Daniel's eyes as he looked at her. He was waiting for an answer.

'No, Mr Kellow, I do not,' she replied, calmly.

Daniel smiled. 'Good.' He jumped down from the duckboard. 'I was hoping you would say that.'

He joined Little Billy, who was stroking the horse's head, and exchanged a few quiet words with him out of earshot.

Janey's curiosity piqued, she craned her neck to see what they were saying, but the conversation was over before it really began and soon Little Billy was climbing up beside her to sit in the cart. With a flick of the reins, they were off.

Warmed by Daniel's coat, Janey finally began to relax a little. She stared straight ahead, refusing to say goodbye to Daniel, but as they approached the first corner she thought better of it and turned at the last moment to wave goodbye. To her disappointment he had already gone.

Charlie settled down by Janey's feet as the cart rumbled over the rough track. She lifted her wet skirts off her legs and rearranged them more comfortably as Little Billy quietly chewed on something foul smelling in his mouth. She studied the horizon in an attempt to enjoy the ride; however, the encounter with Daniel still played on her mind. She realised she could no longer deny that she was drawn to the man, despite knowing that he had probably killed someone. Eventually Janey broke the silence. She needed to know more about Daniel Kellow.

'Do you know Mr Kellow well, Mr Bray?'

'Since 'e was a nipper,' came the short reply.

'How do you find him?'

'Bit of a troublemaker when 'e was young but an 'ard worker now.'

'I have heard rumours, Mr Bray.'

'That don't surprise me,' was his non-committal reply.

Janey tried another tactic to get the information she wanted so desperately to know.

'Perhaps I would learn if there is any substance to the rumours from someone who knows.'

'I know all there is to know about this parish. Born and raised 'ere, everyone knows me and I know everyone,' boasted Little Billy, puffing up his chest like a cockerel fluffing his feathers.

'Is there any truth behind the rumours, Mr Bray?'

'Well depends what rumours you're talking about,' he replied, raising an eyebrow.

Little Billy was not living up to his reputation of being a gossip much to Janey's frustration. She parried his question with one of her own.

'There is more than one?'

Little Billy shook the reins to gee up his horse. 'Well, 'e's a regular visitor to widow Sally, until a few months ago, that is. She won't say why but my guess is 'e's tired of 'er. She's getting on a bit, you know and Daniel's good looking enough to want something a bit more young and tender to grab hold of. Begging your pardon, ma'am.'

Janey blushed. She wondered if she was considered young and tender. She wasn't sure she liked women being described like joints of meat.

''E owns a farm left to 'im by an old man called Zachariah Trebilcock, who took 'im in as a boy. As a lad 'e always came out on top of any fight ... of which there were many, so no one dares cross 'im now. 'E doesn't take kindly to fools, you see. Keeps 'imself to 'imself up on 'is farm with 'is brood of waifs and strays. And, of course, there's the matter of 'ow Zachariah died.'

Janey was relieved he had brought up the death of the old farmer.

'Do you think he killed him?' she asked.

Little Billy scratched his head. 'Only Daniel, Zachariah and the Lord know that. I think there were a lot of sour grapes that Daniel got the farm, but why would Zachariah, with 'is 'ands swollen with rheumatism, be up a ladder? 'E could barely move 'is 'ands, let alone climb fifteen feet 'igh!'

Janey moved uneasily in her seat. She didn't like what she was hearing. She mulled over what he had said then eventually asked, 'May I enquire, Mr Bray, what did Mr Kellow say to you while I was waiting in the cart?'

Little Billy spat out what he had been chewing. ''E said if I was to breathe a word to anyone about what I saw ... and,' he said, casting a glance at her, 'I saw it all ...' Janey blushed again. '... 'e would ensure I would not be able to 'ave any more children. 'E said treat you like the lady you are and take you back to Bosvenna as soon as I could. If I did as 'e asked 'e would lend me 'is prize boar to service my sows next year, free of charge.'

Janey raised her eyebrows; she wasn't sure she liked being part of a deal that involved pig reproduction either.

'And will you tell anyone, Mr Bray?'

'What, and ruin a pretty maid's reputation and risk Daniel coming after me? One thing I know for sure, when Daniel says 'e'll do something, 'e keeps 'is word. I can assure you, miss, my lips are sealed.'

Janey smiled in relief which disappeared just as quickly when he added, 'Anyway, I don't want my 'ead bashed in one night by a stranger.'

The cart rattled on.

'How many children do you have, Mr Bray?' she asked after a while.

The strange little man spat again. 'Twelve children, with one on the way.' He started to chuckle. 'Perhaps I should spread a bit of gossip, miss. Daniel would be doing me a favour stopping me 'aving any more children, don't you think?'

Janey joined in his laughter. This weird little man, with an odd sense of humour, had a soft heart and she had a feeling that she had made a new friend.

Chapter Eight

'The flooding must have distressed the Queen,' said Lord Brockenshaw as he lifted a spyglass to examine the news-sheet more closely.

His wife was resting on a cosy seat by the fire but turned her head to her husband.

'My dear?'

'The flooding at Windsor, my love, must have caused great distress to the Queen. Let me read the piece to you from *The Illustrated London News* regarding the heavy rain they have endured there:

'*The extraordinary quantity of rain that has fallen in most parts of England during the last three weeks has caused the overflow of many rivers and the flooding of extensive tracts of land ... The waters also rose considerably at Windsor and Eton where the scene was indeed remarkable as viewed from the north and east terraces of Windsor Castle. For several miles the natural course of the river and its windings were lost in a succession of inland lakes. Between Maidenhead and Staines thousands of acres of meadow and pastureland were inundated, the ditches, watercourses and rivulets being filled to overflowing. At Eton College portions of the playing fields were under water ...*'

'The illustration is quite remarkable,' he added, looking at the picture with his spyglass.

'Perhaps she has drowned.' James was in no mood to be sympathetic with the monarch. 'No one would know if she had, she hasn't been seen for years. For all we know she may have died when Prince Albert did.'

'James!' Lady Brockenshaw was a staunch royalist.

'I'm sorry, Mother, but what is the use of a monarch when they do nothing but hide away in Scotland?'

'He has a point, my dear,' conceded his father.

The evening was drawing to a close and James had had another restless day. The Yuletide festivities had livened up the last few weeks at Bosvenna Manor but now it was January and only the dark days of winter spread out before him. He had hoped his mother's maid would provide a diversion from the boredom of the country but she was remaining elusive. With a house full of servants it was near impossible to get her alone and he suspected she was doing her best to avoid such a situation. He was aware that what had started as a bit of entertainment with a pretty wench was fast becoming an obsession. It would do him good to get away for a while. He made up his mind, at that very moment, to do just that.

'I'm going to visit Edward in London at the end of the week.'

Both his parents turned to him in surprise at his sudden announcement.

'I was hoping you would start to take over the running of the estate, learn the ropes so to speak, begin to take the burden from off my shoulders,' said Lord Brockenshaw.

'I have visited the tenants.'

'Once, at the start of winter. There is much more to learn if only you showed the interest.'

'This is your home, James,' said his mother, visibly upset. 'Yet all you want to do is escape from it. I feel you have only just arrived!'

James came and sat beside her, patting her hand as if he would a child.

'Mother, dearest, I have been here since the autumn. If I am to bag myself a rich filly I need to be where the debutantes are.'

'Will you stay with Edward in his London residence?'

'Yes, Father. You need not worry about the cost of my accommodation.'

'You will still manage to incur costs, I am sure.'

'Oh, I do hope so.'

'My dears, please do not argue,' interrupted Lady Brockenshaw. 'You know how I hate it.'

A short uncomfortable silence followed. Lady Brockenshaw felt the need to fill it.

'What will you do to occupy yourself in London?' she asked.

'Edward has an American friend staying. I expect Edward will want to show him the sights, give him a taste of England.'

'And you plan to accompany them. Does Edward know?' asked his father.

'Not yet, but he has asked me several times to visit during his friend's stay, so he will be delighted I am available.'

'Why is he so keen for you to meet him?'

'His friend is a businessman who dabbles in stocks and shares. Edward seems very enthusiastic and is considering investing.'

'And involving you too.' Lord Brockenshaw shook his head. 'Just as well you have no money to invest. An investor has to be prepared to stomach the losses as well as the gains. Gambling is no way to do business.'

'You have no adventure, Father.' James let go of his mother's hand and poured himself another drink.

'It's easy to be adventurous with other people's money.'

James slammed his glass down and his mother jumped.

'Don't start another argument, please,' she wailed, touching her temple. 'I feel a headache coming on.'

'I'm sorry, my dear,' her husband replied. Pushing himself up to standing, desperate to distance himself from his son, he added, 'I need to finish off some paperwork in my study. You will not be long for bed, my dear?'

James moved away as his father kissed his mother's head.

'No, in fact I think I will retire now. James, are you still there? Would you be a dear and ring for Janey to take me up?'

'It will be a pleasure, Mother.'

James rang the cord and sat down on a suitable chair that gave him a good view of the room. He crossed his ankles, bid his father goodnight, sat back and waited for his mother's maid to arrive. The tension that had filled the air so suddenly had already started to dissipate and James, feeling more relaxed, raised a glass of whisky in mock salute at his father's exit.

'You will write to me, James?' asked his mother as she waited quietly by the fire for her maid to arrive.

'Of course, Mother.'

'I will miss you.'

'And I you, Mother.'

'He loves you too, James. He is just anxious for you and your future.'

'He has no need to be.'

His mother fell silent and, believing he had satisfactorily reassured her, he turned his attention back to the closed door and waited for Janey to arrive.

He watched Janey silently enter the room and touch his mother's arm. He knew she was aware of him but her avoidance at making eye contact, which had initially irked him, now gave him the freedom to observe her intimately without constraint. With enjoyment he allowed his gaze to wander over the curve of her hips and bottom as she removed her mistress's footstool. He took delight at the shape of her breasts as she moved about, the narrowness of her waist as she straightened her body, and, much to his own surprise, the smoothness of her neck that was brushed by a tendril of her hair. She moved as gracefully as a dancer, had the poise of a lady and the pureness of a nun and James wanted her like no other woman before. The more unattainable she appeared, the more he wanted to have her.

His mother was speaking to him.

'I'm sorry, Mother, what did you say?'

'I said goodnight, James.' His mother was standing at the door, Janey at her side with eyes cast down looking at the floor.

'Goodnight,' James replied, absently, as he noticed his mother's book lying on a nearby table. It was the book she liked to have read to her before she went to sleep. 'I'm off to the library to catch up on my correspondence.' He stood and made a show of gathering up his news-sheets. 'I will see you in the morning.'

His mother nodded and the two women left but James did not follow them. Instead he took a chair and placed it behind the door where it would be hidden from immediate view when the door was opened. He sat down and as before crossed his legs at the ankles to wait. James enjoyed hunting, but he also knew that sometimes the hunter waits for the prey rather than always chasing it. He sat looking at the book knowing it would not be long before Janey returned to collect it. James may not be a patient man, but he knew how to wait.

He had started to nod off when the door slowly opened. At first he could not see her but he knew it was Janey. She stood, hidden from view, surveying the room and unaware that James sat behind the door waiting. Satisfied the room was empty, she spied the book on the table and entered. James quietly shut the door behind her. The well-oiled lock clicked into place, making Janey spin around in surprise.

'I thought you were in the library.' She was instantly wary, her eyes darting to the shut door behind him.

'I am not.' He raised an eyebrow. 'You look worried. Did I frighten you?'

Janey shook her head. 'No, just surprised.' She picked up the book and held it against her chest as if for comfort or even protection. 'Your mother wanted her book, sir.'

James walked to the mantelpiece and, for want of something to do, picked up a small ornament of a crying woman and turned it in his hands. It was a sorrowful, ugly thing that he had always hated but it had been a gift to the family decades before and had been part of the house and his life for years. James had always despised what it stood for; who wanted to witness someone else's tragedy? He placed it back on the mantelpiece but this time facing the wall.

'I feel you have been avoiding me, Janey.'

'No, sir.' The denial was too ready in coming to be the truth.

'Don't lie. You are better than that.' He looked at her and she had the good grace to look away. 'So you have been. I thought you cared for me.'

'I'm in a difficult situation, sir. Please understand.'

'What is there to understand?' He feigned being hurt. 'I just want a friendship, nothing more,' he said, circling her.

'I'm sorry, sir. I didn't mean to appear ungrateful.'

'I only single you out as you are educated. I have no one in this house to have a sensible conversation with. My parents are old, my friends live miles away. I thought you understood.' She watched him move around her. 'I am leaving at the end of the week as I have business in London.'

'You are?' She seemed surprised, even relieved. James's jaw tightened. He had the urge to hurt her back.

'You must think a lot of yourself to think I would want a relationship with a servant.'

In a few chosen words he had succeeded in casting doubt in Janey's eyes. Doubt about herself.

'I'm sorry, sir.'

He regally nodded acceptance of her apology and approached her. He eased the book from her hands and casually looked through the pages, aware that she could no longer leave the room without having to explain to his mother why she had returned empty-handed. James walked away and back to the mantelpiece. Anxious to retrieve the book, Janey followed as if she was on his lead.

'The book, sir, your mother will be wondering where I am.'

'There is always someone wanting your time. Someone more important than me.'

'Not at all, sir.' She reached for it but he lifted it away.

'Is there someone special in your life? A man, perhaps?'

Janey shook her head, but her hesitation told him something she was unwilling to share.

'No, sir. Please, the book.' Again she reached for it. With ease and precision he lifted it just out of her reach.

'It's a simple question, one between friends.' He suddenly stepped forward in a clumsy attempt to kiss her. Janey hastily stepped back. James paused with his head bowed. Anger rose up inside him and threatened to spill forth. He took a deep breath and straightened. The fear in her eyes soothed the rising tide inside him somewhat. The sound of his father outside the door ensured he pushed the book into her hands.

'Mother will be waiting,' he said in a clipped tone. 'You had better go.'

His father entered as his wife's maid left.

'I am sorry about earlier, James. I should trust your judgment. You are a man now.'

'Is that an attempt at a compliment, Father? If I had

known you would bestow one on me I would have told you about the investment opportunity earlier.'

'I wasn't aware a compliment from me was so important to you,' replied his father as he picked up his spectacles.

James examined his drink. 'Nor I, Father. Nor I.'

James's continual advances made Janey feel as if her world was spinning out of control. In the beginning it was the difference in their stations that shone a light on the madness of any relationship between them. Over time, his persistence and manipulation of her slowly poisoned any feelings she thought she held for him. However, it was Daniel's kiss and his gentle touch, by the river in the valley, which turned her romantic thoughts of James to the ashes they were now. James was leaving at the end of the week and the day could not arrive quickly enough for her. All Janey had to do was avoid him and soon he would be gone.

So when Janey saw James riding over the hill towards her, during her afternoon walk, she had no hesitation in darting into a disused building to hide. She stood quietly, with Charlie at her heels, listening for the beat of his horse's hooves as they approached. She had no interest in the disused granite building with its fallen in roof, piles of sacking adorning the earth floor and the strangulating ivy that was making claim to the walls. A few more years of such neglect and nature would repossess the land it stood on as its own once more, but to Janey, for this moment in time, it was a place to hide.

The hoofbeats stopped outside and James dismounted. He had seen her and Janey felt sick with anxiety.

'Why are you hiding from me?' asked James as he swept into the roofless building.

What could Janey say in reply? Once again she felt stupid for hiding and doubting him.

He plucked at the fingers of his gloves and cast them aside one by one onto the sacking.

'You drive me to distraction, Janey. Can't you see that I find you incredibly attractive? Yet you treat me so badly. I must be in love to keep coming back for more.'

He came closer and lifted her chin so she was forced to meet his gaze.

'I don't know the reason, but it is not necessarily love.' Janey looked towards the entrance.

'You doubt me?' She did not answer so he tilted her chin to face him. 'Do you doubt this?' He pressed her against the cold stone wall and kissed her roughly on the lips. James moved back to study her reaction, but she refused to give him the pleasure. Stony-faced, she focused on the wall behind him.

'I see you need a real kiss.'

'Please, sir. I need to leave.'

'You leave when I say you can leave. You are under the misapprehension that you have a choice in the matter. A real kiss I want and a real kiss you shall give me.'

She tried to move away but it only excited him more as his tongue protruded deeper into her mouth, heightening her indignation and the feeling of violation. She tried to move her head but he grabbed it ruthlessly and continued his onslaught. Managing to turn her head at last, she gasped for air.

'Please, James. James!'

Ignoring her he reclaimed her mouth and grabbed her bottom, kneading it as if she was a whore. She struggled to free herself but he was too strong.

'What the hell is going on here?' an angry voice demanded from behind James.

Janey felt a surge of relief that someone had interrupted him, then instantly shrank with shame as she recognised the voice. Sunlight shone brightly on her as James moved aside.

His movement unveiled her downfall to the newcomer, whose shadow came to loom over them in the confines of the old stone walls. She saw Daniel's stricken expression when he recognised the woman in James's arms.

'What the hell are you doing here?' demanded Daniel. It was not clear who he was talking to but James's arrogance assumed it must be him.

'Daniel. How are you?'

'Get out!'

James almost laughed at the order. There was nothing wrong with being caught with a woman. He was a man after all and, no doubt, Daniel had had his fair share of a roll in the hay.

'What are you talking about?'

'You are on my land. Get out.' Daniel's voice was controlled, but deadly as he stood his ground.

'How dare you talk to your betters in this way?'

'Get out. Now!' Daniel shouted. 'Or the foxes will be having a fine supper tonight.'

'Are you threatening me? You murdering oaf!'

'As they say, the first kill is the hardest, after that it's easy.'

James visibly paled.

'This is my land and you are trespassing. Get the hell out before I throw you out!'

James picked up his gloves. 'You have not heard the last of this, Kellow,' he said, marching out. Swearing with indignation, he mounted his horse and in a flurry of flying mud, galloped away, forgetting the woman still trapped inside.

'I'm glad you arrived,' said Janey. Her words sounded false as she wished it had not been Daniel who had found her. Still shaking from the onslaught, she wanted to be alone. She prepared to leave, but Daniel barred her way with his arm.

'Not yet,' he ground out, angrily.

Janey focused on the muscled forearm in front of her.

'You shouldn't have spoken to him like that,' she said, quietly. 'He may cause you trouble.'

'Your lover does not need your protection.'

She looked up at him. 'He is not my lover.'

'Not your only lover, you mean.'

'He was forcing himself upon me!'

'Why did you meet with him here if you are not lovers?'

'It is not what it appears,' she argued, pushing his arm away.

Daniel followed her to the door. 'He was kissing you! He had his hands all over you!'

'Whatever it looked like it was not so!'

Daniel halted her with the crook of her arm. 'I heard you crying his name! God Almighty, woman, if I'd known you were that easy I would have had you myself by the river!'

Janey slapped him.

Daniel grabbed her shoulders and pressed her up against the wall. 'Why here, Janey? Why my land? Perhaps you like the thrill of being discovered? Did you want me to find you?' He touched her forehead with his, the fight leaving his shaking body. 'Give you a sick pleasure, does it? Seeing two lovers at the same time?'

'You are not my lover!' she said, hating his insults yet also hating to see his hurt.

'Do you not think I know that?'

'*He* is not my lover,' she whispered.

Daniel closed his eyes, their foreheads still touching. Slowly he released her shoulders, taking in what she had said.

'I'm sorry. I should not have touched you.' He stepped back. 'He will never marry you, Janey.'

'I know,' she replied.

'The best you can get is to be set up in a separate house, leading a life as his mistress, bearing a brood of bastards without a name.'

'I know.'

'He is no gentleman,' he continued. 'A gentleman does not leave a woman alone with a murderer.'

It was the first time the rumours about him were laid out between them. She knew he was waiting for her response and that it was important to him.

'I see no murderer,' she replied, gently.

'What you see is not always what it seems.'

They stood facing each other, the fragile bond between them now in tatters.

His view of her had changed and this injustice gave her strength. She gathered up her shawl.

'Perhaps you should remember that, Daniel. James and I are not lovers, never have been, nor ever will be.'

She pushed past him and left. She could not bear to look at him any longer, or her heart would start to break.

Daniel raked his hair with a trembling hand. He did not believe her. Why would a lady's maid call Lord Brockenshaw's son by his Christian name? He knew she was attracted to James. Why else would she be alone with him in an isolated building on the edge of the moor if there was not something going on between them? What chance did a farmer have against a powerful man of the gentry with land and money to provide her with comforts, if not a wedding ring?

Daniel picked up a piece of granite and threw it angrily at the one remaining window. Its glass shattered into a hundred shards, just as his heart had done when he first entered the place just a few moments ago.

Chapter Nine

Janey looked at Daniel's coat, which still hung from a hook on her bedroom door. It was the first thing she saw in the morning and the last thing at night, its dark form like a guard stationed by her side. She lifted its sleeve and held it to her cheek. She could still smell the sandalwood soap he used, despite the time that had passed. The realisation brought tears to her eyes. He was near, yet so far away.

She should feel happy. James had left the same day as Daniel had found them together. She had felt a great weight lift from her shoulders that James was no longer around, yet a deep sadness had replaced it. A sadness that was linked to this man. The cause ranged from the humiliation that he had caught her with James's hand up her skirt, to anger that he had not believed her explanation. She had only met Daniel on a few occasions and, in truth, barely knew him, yet she still had a burning need that he should think well of her and – at the moment – he did not. She carefully let his sleeve fall and ran her hand along the rough cloth. She wanted to see him again, to explain – and to say goodbye, as she could not stay here. One day, James would return home and she did not want to be around when he did. So she had started to apply for other positions and it was a matter of waiting to get a response.

Miss Petherbridge simmered with jealousy as she watched Janey from across the table. The staff had just finished their evening meal and Janey was entertaining Lizzy and Charlotte with some trivial anecdote that had captured their attention. Janey looked at ease amongst them, her easy rapport feeding the housekeeper's resentment of her.

'Have you heard about it, Miss Petherbridge?' The sound of her name brought her back to the servants' hall where she realised all of the staff were looking at her and waiting a reply.

She refused to be rattled. 'About what, Mr Tallock?' she replied, carefully placing her fork on her plate.

'Scarlet fever is rampant in Bodmin at the moment.'

'No, I had not, Mr Tallock.' She smiled without humour. 'Unfortunately there is always some fever doing the rounds.'

'Fever always gives a cause for concern,' said Mr Tallock, pushing his plate away. 'Lovely meal, Mrs Friggens.'

The cook thanked him.

'Trehale's an isolated village,' he continued. 'Fortunately it often escapes such fevers but when it is as prevalent as it seems to be at the moment in Bodmin, we must do all we can to prevent it reaching us here. If the village succumbs there will be many cases.'

'The working classes are more at risk, Mr Tallock,' the housekeeper replied.

Mary raised an eyebrow as all of them sitting at the table were working class.

Finishing her meal, Janey disagreed. 'Not always. I lost my mother and sisters to scarlet fever. At the time we were living in Cromwell Street in Falmouth, a very middle class area.'

'It is a wonder you did not follow them.' It was a spiteful thing to say but the housekeeper could not stop herself. It was Janey's turn not to be rattled.

'A wonder indeed,' she replied, in a measured tone. 'I bring this up because it is best to remember that the fever does not care what class you are from or age. We should all take precautions.'

Miss Petherbridge waved a hand at Charlotte to indicate she should clear the table.

'You place yourself in an authoritative position, Carhart. Perhaps you should enlighten us with your expertise.'

Janey did not reply immediately but Mr Tallock encouraged her to continue.

'Scarlet fever can present in mild forms as to be of no consequence, but it can also be a very serious disease indeed and fatal.'

'You tell us nothing we do not already know.'

Janey ignored the housekeeper. 'Onset is often sudden, beginning with a sore throat, shivering and a headache. It develops on the second day into a rash behind the ears, which spreads to the arms and legs. Those suffering fever should be kept in bed, even in mild cases. Particularly if the weather is cold and for a considerable time after the eruption has disappeared.'

'Are you suggesting that any member of staff who has a headache should be put to bed?' Miss Petherbridge scoffed.

'I'm suggesting more than that.' Janey turned to Mr Tallock in the hope of a more sympathetic ear. 'I suggest anyone who has even the mildest symptoms should be isolated from the remaining staff. The staff member who is taking on the nursing duties should not mix with the rest of the staff before changing her clothing and washing. The linen and bedclothes used should be well boiled. Anything that cannot be washed with a solution of chloride of lime or boiled should be burned. A container of the solution ought to be kept in the room for such purposes.'

Janey turned to Mary who was listening intently. 'I've also read that another measure which tends to prevent the spread of the disease is to oil the patient's skin daily, while it is peeling.'

Miss Petherbridge scraped back her chair as she stood abruptly making everyone turn to look at her.

'Thank you, Miss Nightingale.' She surveyed her staff.

'But for now scarlet fever is in Bodmin which is twelve miles away. I don't think it is helpful to spread fear and panic. There is work to be done. Mrs Friggens, we will leave dessert for today, I think everyone has had their fill, thanks to Janey's storytelling.'

'I saw my mother and sisters die, Miss Petherbridge,' replied Janey, in an icy tone. 'I would have given anything to have known how to nurse them. It may have made a difference.'

Miss Petherbridge gave her a withering look.

'I have heard that guilt can be a motivator to become the expert. I see now that it is true. We will hear no more about it.' She looked at the others. 'Mr Tallock, I wish to discuss the accounts with you, if you are available. The rest of you ... get back to your chores.'

She turned and left the room with the butler following obediently behind. For the first time in days the servants' hall fell silent, as quiet as the newly dug graves at Bodmin cemetery twelve miles away.

Mrs Friggens broke the silence. 'Take no notice of her, Janey. She doesn't know what she's talking about sometimes.'

Janey started to clear the plates and Mary came to help her.

'I was six when I caught the fever. I didn't have it bad but my friend died,' Mary said.

'Well, let's hope it doesn't come here.' Mrs Friggens covered the pie she'd baked. 'The village children had whooping cough last winter. Little Ben up at Treluggen had it real bad, don't think he'll ever be strong in the chest again.'

'Can you catch scarlet fever twice?' asked Mary, with concern.

Janey grew pensive. 'I'm not sure.'

Mrs Friggens started to wipe the table clean. 'It seems all the reading you did concerned new patients and not yourself.'

'At the time I didn't care about me.'

'We must all care about ourselves, Janey Carhart,' exclaimed Mary. 'If we don't care about ourselves why should we expect anyone else to?'

The enticing sweet smell of hot pasties drew the vicar from his study, along the modest hall of the vicarage and down three stone steps to the warm, welcoming aromas of the kitchen. His housekeeper had just placed three golden pasties, fresh from her oven, on the table and had begun to wrap one in a cloth. She looked up and smiled at the vicar who had been led by his nose to her baking.

'Should have known it wouldn't take you long to arrive. There's only one thing that will make a Cornish man down his tools and that's a pasty.'

The vicar chuckled. 'Is that one Daniel's?'

The housekeeper nodded.

'Give it to me, I'll take it out to him.'

A minute later the vicar was picking his way through the adjacent graveyard with a pasty in one hand and a tankard of water in the other. In the distance he could see Daniel Kellow's bent form, building the wall that bordered the grounds. Two weeks ago a storm had felled an old oak tree, its trunk and branches destroying the brick wall as it crashed to the ground.

Despite the carnage being on view to all that passed by on the nearby road and causing quite a stir so that several people came up to the church with the sole purpose of seeing the destruction, only one of his parishioners had offered to help. That one was Daniel Kellow.

The vicar was embarrassed to admit that at first he was

quite taken aback. He had known Daniel since he was a troubled boy, but as an adult he had kept very much to himself. Yet it was this quiet man who had offered his help, not one of his God-fearing flock. A man he would never find sitting in his congregation and who made it no secret he was an atheist.

True to his word, Daniel had returned the next day and spent the week cutting up the wood and stacking it by the vicarage, giving clear instructions to let the wood rest for a year before using it in the fire. Yesterday he had started on the wall and it wouldn't be long before that too was finished to a very high standard. When the vicar had offered to pay, Daniel had just scoffed that perhaps for payment the vicar should have a quiet word with God to let Daniel into heaven when the time was right. The vicar wasn't sure if he was serious but said he would pray for him, as he does for all his flock. Daniel had just grunted and returned to his work.

Just as the aroma of a freshly cooked pasty had drawn the vicar from his work, it did the same for Daniel. He straightened his back and, following his nose, turned his head to see the vicar approaching with a smile on his lips. The warm crusty parcel was handed over to grateful hands.

'You are doing a fine job, Daniel. I really appreciate you taking time away from your farm to help out.'

'Now is a quiet time. In a couple of weeks I will have more work to do to keep me on the land.' Daniel bit into the pasty.

'How are things up there? Edna still got her feet firmly under your kitchen table?'

Daniel smiled fondly at the sound of her name.

'I wouldn't want it any other way,' he answered.

'I always think a woman makes a house a home with the little things she does that you don't even notice at the time. A tablecloth for special occasions, flowers in a vase, the smell of wax polish or the warming pan in your bed at night.'

'Edna is a bit like Amy in that respect. She cooks, cleans and mends but she's not into the fussy side of keeping house.'

Both men thought for a moment before the vicar spoke again.

'My wife, bless her soul, enjoyed the ... what you call ... fussy side of housekeeping. I didn't think about it until she died and it was that, as well as her company, I missed the most. To walk into the house and see fresh flowers in the vase brightened my day. It meant my wife had been there and left her presence in the room. Silly really, but after she died my home became a house once more ... that is until I found Olive, my housekeeper.' The vicar looked appreciatively at the brick wall. 'Edna rules the roost, I suppose.'

Daniel was enjoying his pasty. 'She thinks she does,' he said, between mouthfuls. Both men laughed.

The wooden wheels of a trap drew their attention away from the wall to the nearby road. They watched silently as the trap came into view, its red painted wheels turning on the stony road. Wrapped up warmly against the chilling breeze sat Lady Brockenshaw, enjoying a rare trip out with her maid by her side.

The vicar lifted a hand in greeting and they watched Janey's lips move, informing her mistress of the vicar's presence. She in turn raised her hand to acknowledge it, her eyes staring unseeing into space. The vicar voiced his greeting but his attention was on Janey who had not taken her eyes off Daniel Kellow for the entire time. She gave a tentative smile to him in greeting and the vicar looked at Daniel, eager to see his response, thinking there must be some form of friendship between them. He couldn't mask his surprise when Daniel ignored her acknowledgement and turned his back on her.

Janey's smile instantly faded and the trap rattled away down the road bringing the brief encounter to an end. The vicar frowned. He knew Daniel would not mince his words where men were concerned but he had never seen him be rude to a woman.

'What was that all about?'

Daniel defiantly bit into his pasty, but inexplicably it turned to sawdust in his mouth and he found it difficult to swallow.

'You aren't still mad at her are you?'

Daniel looked away and said nothing. He made to take another bite but he could no longer stomach the food and tossed the remainder of the pasty to the birds.

In absence of any explanation the vicar continued. 'I heard the village gossip about what happened at the dance. Surely you are not holding a grudge against her for what she called you that night? It was months ago.'

Daniel took in a deep breath. 'No. We have had words since,' he said. 'It is of no concern of yours, reverend.'

The vicar watched Daniel return to his work but saw that Janey's appearance had troubled him as several bricks were picked up and discarded as unsuitable in quick succession. He had lost his building rhythm.

'It appears to concern you though.'

'I appreciate your interest. I know it's kindly meant, reverend, but there is nothing between me and Miss Carhart to mend or otherwise.'

The vicar would not be put off. Perhaps if Janey had not come to him all those weeks ago, in such distress and confusion, he would have let things go, but he suddenly felt protective of the little creature. He hoped that Daniel wasn't the person who had been upsetting her. He concluded he probably wasn't. Daniel may be many things, but you knew where you stood with him. He was not a manipulator and no one was left confused by what he thought of them.

'She appeared hurt by the rebuff.'

'Appearances can be deceiving.'

'Life is too short to fall out with one's acquaintances.'

'Is that a quote from your Bible?'

'It is a quote from me.'

Daniel stood up, giving up for a moment on the task in hand.

'Falling out with people does not upset me. I can live quite happily without anyone pretending to be my friend. I know what people around here think of me and I do not care. The fact that I no longer wish to be on friendly terms with Miss Carhart does not upset me, so don't let it upset you.'

'You shouldn't be too harsh on her.'

Daniel handed him the cloth the pasty had been wrapped in, hoping he would take it for a sign to leave him but the vicar remained.

'We all need friends.'

Daniel grunted. 'Some more than others,' he replied and returned his attention to the wall he was building.

Using his best theatrical sermon voice the vicar spoke behind him causing Daniel to halt.

'Two are better than one; because they have a good reward for their labour. For if they fall, the one will lift up his fellow: but woe to him who is alone when he falleth; for he hath not another to help him.'

Daniel looked up frowning at the vicar's speech.

'And yes, Daniel,' the vicar said, nodding defiantly, 'that was from the Bible. Life without a friend is like death without a witness.' Satisfied with his sermon the vicar turned and walked away, halting momentarily to see Daniel staring after him before continuing on his way back to the house.

Daniel watched the vicar until he was out of view. It wasn't often someone challenged him or offered their advice. Daniel's eyes were drawn back to the road. The trap and its occupants were long gone and the road stretched like a silver ribbon into the distance. He hated how Janey continued to stalk his mind despite his best efforts to forget her. He turned his attention back to his work, picking up a brick and assessing its size and where it would best fit, but the words of the vicar continued to play on his mind, together with the face of Janey Carhart.

Spring had arrived in Trehale. What should have been a time of renewed vigour, growth and optimism for the coming year was marred by the arrival of scarlet fever in the village. It had spent the winter visiting households up and down the county, creeping unseen into people's homes, schools and workplaces, to invade their bodies and, for some, take their lives. No one knew how it came to Trehale, for the onset was so sudden that no one could pinpoint the first victim.

The staff at Bosvenna Manor, isolated from the village by work hours and distance, heard about the illness's arrival through the gardener. The joy of village life was eerily absent, he said. Even the Sunday service congregation had dwindled to four stoutly elders who did not fear death.

Life in the servants' quarters continued as normal but each day more news of another victim succumbing to the fever was brought to them. Fear breeds fear and Mr Tallock, in his quiet authoritative way, tried to contain the panic. He addressed his staff informing them that he suspected some of the news was embellished and that every illness was being put down to the fever. This may have been true but even he grew concerned when Miss Petherbridge took herself off to her office and remained there, in isolation, on the pretext of sorting out the accounts.

Mr Tallock was the one who discovered that she was in fact ill. He found her, sitting at her desk, her account book untouched and her pale forehead resting on her forearms. She looked up with bloodshot eyes and insisted she would be all right but Mr Tallock would have none of it. He informed Janey, who arranged for her to be put to bed. Despite her illness, which blanched her complexion and etched dark shadows beneath her eyes, Miss Petherbridge was still able to voice a hate filled warning to Janey as she was helped away.

'Don't think you are going to step into my shoes while I'm gone, Carhart. I will have to die first before you take my postition!'

Mr Tallock came to Janey's side. 'Pay no heed to Miss Petherbridge,' he said, producing a handkerchief and wiping his brow. 'She is unwell.'

Janey grew concerned. 'Mr Tallock, are you ill? You don't look well.' She sat him down and made him a cup of tea. He took the cup in shaking hands and took a sip.

'Rest assured I am not ill.' He gnawed at his bottom lip. 'I fear she will not make a good patient.'

'Then what is the matter? Please tell me,' she coaxed.

Mr Tallock's smile faded a little.

'I fear it is only a matter of time before others fall ill. Despite Miss Petherbridge's fears, I may lean on you for your knowledge and direction in this time of crisis.'

Mr Tallock wiped the palms of his hands on his trousers. She saw that they were trembling.

'I have been the butler here for ten years and I trust that Lord and Lady Brockenshaw have not found me wanting. Miss Petherbridge and I complement each other with our different methods of leadership.' He took a deep breath as if to summon up the courage to go on. 'I know this job inside out and relish it. Minor crises are of no consequence: the cancellation of guests, the news-sheet's late arrival, the wrong wine delivered. Once in a while a bigger crisis occurs. Staff stealing, for example, or a water pipe bursting and, as in this case, the threat of fever. There is no sense in how these things affect me.' He placed his hand on his stomach. 'But sometimes I feel a sickness come upon me, my heart races as if it would burst from my chest, my hands ...' He held them out in front of him and looked at his trembling fingers. 'See how they shake. Miss Petherbridge has made it easy by always stepping in and taking charge whether it was at my bidding or not. I must confess I have allowed her to and been grateful for it.' He took another breath as if once again, just by thinking about it, he was having trouble breathing. 'Now she is sick and not here and I dread what will occur now I am on my own.'

Janey took both his hands in hers and gave them a little shake. 'But, Mr Tallock, you are quite wrong for you are not alone. You have me.'

Mr Tallock managed a smile. 'It is good to hear you are up to the challenge, Janey. For I have a dreadful feeling it is knocking on our door.'

Lord Brockenshaw fell ill during the night. His valet, John, was the first to notice his sheets drenched in sweat and his cheeks flushed with fever. Janey sent for the doctor and it was not long before a howling gale and driving rain blew Doctor Barker into the manor. He removed his hat and shook the raindrops from its brim, while at the same time a servant helped him out of his coat. He was immediately shown to Lord Brockenshaw's room where he remained for some time, before seeing Miss Petherbridge and Charlotte the scullery maid, who had also fallen ill.

An hour later Doctor Barker was shown into Lady Brockenshaw's breakfast room by Mr Tallock. She sat stiffly in her seat, her face ashen and drawn with worry. The windowpanes rattled against the storm outside but the room within remained silent and tense. Doctor Barker opened his mouth to speak but it was Lady Brockenshaw that broke the silence.

'Good morning, Richard. How is my husband? My maid has informed me he has been taken unwell in the night. I do not wish my husband ill but I would not like to think you have wasted your morning being called here.' She nervously smiled at her own attempt at a joke but her eyes still showed her concern.

'I am sorry to tell you, Elizabeth, that my morning has not been wasted,' he replied, softly.

Lady Brockenshaw reached for Janey's hand, as she stood quietly at her side.

'We have known each other most of our lives, Richard. Speak plainly as I will be relying on my staff at this time and it is therefore important they understand what you have to say.'

The doctor sat down opposite her and took her other hand.

'George is very ill. We cannot be certain until the rash appears, however I believe it is scarlet fever.'

Lady Brockenshaw gave a little gasp, her grip tightening on Janey's hand.

'I can also confirm that your housekeeper and scullery maid also show similar symptoms.'

Janey interjected at her mistress's enquiring look. 'We have put Miss Petherbridge and Charlotte to bed, ma'am.'

'Is it serious?'

The doctor released her hand and sat back. 'Your staff are younger and have a fighting chance. I'm afraid George's age and heart is against him.'

'But he will live?' It was a desperate question but the doctor's sombre mood had already paved the way for the inevitable answer.

'I have never lied to you, Elizabeth, and I will not now. I believe it will be a miracle if George survives this. I will prescribe medicine to help fight the fever and make him more comfortable but he is not strong.'

'Then we must pray for a miracle, Richard. For I don't know how I will live without him.'

The doctor did not stay long, the fever had given him little rest over the preceding weeks and he already had a string of further visits to make before the day was out.

In the servants' hall a few minutes later, Mr Tallock told the assembled staff of the doctor's findings and the mood was sombre. Janey looked around at the faces now turned to her, waiting to hear what she had to say. Who was she, she silently questioned herself, to dictate how things should be done? She observed the faces looking at her, some older than herself, most with more experience in service and all nervous of the situation that had developed that morning. Someone had to take charge and it had to be done quickly. Janey took a deep breath and began to speak.

'Mr Tallock has told you what the doctor has said. It is a grave situation but I think ... I know,' she corrected herself, 'that if we are willing to be flexible with our duties and supportive of others in theirs, we will be able to contain the fever.' She nervously licked her lips before continuing. 'I am going to nurse Lord Brockenshaw, Miss Petherbridge and Charlotte but I cannot do this on my own. I will need one volunteer. This will mean that we will have four staff members unable to work their usual duties: Miss Petherbridge, Charlotte, myself and one other. To run the house in the normal way would be impossible. I therefore recommend that we close the north and west wing. This means no blacking the grates, cleaning, lighting of fires, changing of flowers, nothing in these areas. This will reduce the workload.'

A few staff nodded in agreement at this novel idea.

'I and my helper will sleep in the Nanny's room next to the nursery, where we have made up beds for Miss Petherbridge and Charlotte. Lord Brockenshaw's room is just along the corridor, so this means we can nurse the sick and sleep without leaving the second-floor east wing. All food and change of linen can be left in the corridor and we will collect it from there. No other staff member is to enter this area. I believe this will help to contain the fever and prevent infection of others.'

There was a murmur of agreement from the staff, relief, no doubt, at not having to be in contact with the patients.

'John, your duties of valet are not required at the moment. I spoke of flexibility in our duties. I am not a nurse but I am willing to nurse. John, we need someone to keep the copper hot so linen and towels can be boiled. There will be other duties such as carrying coal for the fire. I know you will be willing to help out and support the other staff in this time of need.'

'Leave it to me, Janey,' the valet replied.

She turned then to speak to Lizzy and Mary. 'Lady Brockenshaw is aware of my recommendations and agrees. She wishes to remain in her bedroom and parlour and will not require her frequent changes of dress during this time. However, she will require one of you to take on my duties as well as your own and the one that volunteers to help me. Do not be afraid to ask for help from the others. We must all help each other.'

Lastly she looked at Mrs Friggens who stood at the back of the room. 'I would be grateful of your expert knowledge in providing nutritious foods for the sick. I was thinking along the lines of thick, smooth soups to provide fluid and sustenance when the throat is sore and appetite poor. Do you agree?'

Mrs Friggens nodded. 'And perhaps a nice rice pudding that can be eaten cold or hot?'

Janey smiled, if Mrs Friggens was on her side others would follow.

'That would be wonderful.' She smiled. 'Now, let's not delay. There is work to be done.'

The staff dissolved into their various roles, a renewed purpose emanated in the air.

Mr Tallock smiled at Janey as she made her way up the stairs to the second floor; his praise was genuine. 'That was very good.'

'Thank you, but as I have learnt over these past months, words are nothing; it's the action that counts.'

It wasn't until Janey reached the second floor that she heard the footsteps rushing up behind her. Turning, she saw Mary appearing from around the corner to stand and watch her. She waited, expecting Mary, known for her forthright, questioning personality to voice her opposition to all her recent suggestions, but to her surprise Mary said nothing.

'What do you want?' Janey finally asked her, becoming unnerved by Mary's watchfulness as she continued to stand on the stair. To her surprise Mary gave her a big smile.

'I've volunteered to help you,' she said as she pushed past Janey. 'I'm not surprised you're shocked,' she continued, cheerfully. 'I shocked myself!'

Quite bemused, Janey followed her onto the second floor, for Mary was the last person she thought would volunteer.

Chapter Ten

To everyone's surprise, including the two women themselves, it soon transpired that Janey and Mary worked well together. The women found themselves as equals with the hierarchy of servant position no longer present to cause friction or resentment. As a result, a new Mary emerged. Gone was the sour-faced and sharp-tongued girl. In her place was a gentle and softly spoken carer whose hands-on skill and observation of her patients' needs matched the tenderness of any trained nurse. Unknown to all, and most of all Mary herself, she had a natural affinity to care for others, and on the second-floor east wing of Bosvenna Manor she had accidently stumbled upon her calling in life.

During her years in service, Janey had often snatched moments in her employer's library, to scour the family's medical books for information on how to treat the illness that had killed her family. Isolated from the outside world, Janey put that knowledge into action and Mary, enthralled by her knowledge, absorbed every new piece of information eagerly.

By the second day the distinctive red rash appeared on Lord Brockenshaw and Miss Petherbridge, confirming the diagnosis, and the news was relayed to her ladyship by Mr Tallock. Doctor Barker visited daily but despite their best efforts Lord Brockenshaw remained gravely ill.

'How is Charlotte?' came Lizzy's worried voice through the closed door, which formed the demarcation line between staff. On one side was the corridor that connected the wing to the rest of the house, on the other was Lord Brockenshaw's dressing room, where Janey stood leaning her cheek against the cool wooden panels. Despite working in four-hour shifts with Mary throughout the night, which allowed them both to snatch periods of sleep, she was beginning to feel exhausted.

'Charlotte still has a high temperature but Doctor Barker is pleased with her progress.'

'And Miss Petherbridge?'

Janey considered how best to answer her. In truth, despite being unwell, Miss Petherbridge took every opportunity to be difficult. She resented having to depend on Janey for all her needs and her hostility oozed from every pore of her skin. 'Frustrated that she is unwell.'

'Mr Tallock has written to Master Brockenshaw on the mistress's behalf, but there seems to be some confusion where he is lodging at the moment. He's worried the young master won't arrive in time.' Lizzy hesitated. 'You know ... before the good Lord takes his lordship.' Janey listened to Lizzy shuffling on the other side of the door. 'I almost forgot. This came for you.' An envelope appeared under the door.

Janey looked at the unfamiliar writing. It was the third she had received; she had a feeling this one would contain the same as the others.

'I'd better be going. Mr Tallock will wonder why I am so long.'

Janey listened to Lizzy's footsteps receding down the corridor before opening the letter. It was as she feared, another rejection to a job application. She was considered too young and inexperienced for a lady's maid post and too experienced for a kitchen maid's post. She would have to consider another position but few came with lodgings. Time, however, had not been on her side. James would be returning early and her self-imposed isolation meant she could not apply elsewhere. She felt like a cornered animal while a predator approached.

She returned the letter to the envelope and shoved it deep inside her pocket. She wondered what Daniel was doing right now and if he ever thought of her. Probably not, she concluded. The last time she had seen him he was helping the vicar. She had hoped he would offer her a smile in greeting or wave. She did not realise how raised her hopes were, until he turned his back on her and they came crashing down.

'One drachm of chlorate of potash, simple syrup and four ounces of water. Mix one table-spoonful every four hours in as much water.' Mary placed the bottle she had been reading on the table beside her and sat down opposite Janey. 'What's a drachm?'

'It's a measurement of weight,' replied Janey. 'Doctor Barker recommended filling the mixture to the line on the glass. You are very good at reading, Mary.'

Mary smiled back, pleased with the compliment. 'Charlotte's rash is drying. Her skin is covered in scales.'

'We must start to rub oil onto her skin. I have already started Miss Petherbridge's treatment.'

'Does she mind?'

'The treatment she does not mind. As for me being the one doing it, that is something else.' Janey studied Mary over the rim of her cup. 'Mary, do you have plans when things return to normal?'

'Plans? What do you mean?' asked Mary.

Janey placed her cup back on the tray. 'I hope you don't think I'm about to speak out of turn but I just think your skills are wasted as a servant. You would make an excellent nurse. Have you ever thought of training to be one?'

Mary laughed but her laughter soon died when she realised Janey was quite serious.

'Are you making fun of me?' she asked, her eyes narrowing.

Janey shook her head.

Mary snorted. 'People like me don't become nurses.'

'Why not?'

'Because …' Mary shrugged. 'I don't know. I don't know anyone who is a nurse. I don't know if I could.'

'Would you like to be a nurse?'

'I would love to be a nurse … but me? I wouldn't know how to go about it.'

'The Royal Cornwall Infirmary in Truro undertakes nurse training.'

'Move away from Trehale?'

'I used to live in Truro. There is a nurses' home on the hospital grounds. I often saw the nurses walking to their morning shifts wearing their starched aprons and hats. It is not something I aspire to but I see you have a natural gift for it.'

A light shone in Mary's eyes. 'Would you help me write a letter, Janey?'

'Of course,' said Janey, smiling.

They sat in companionable silence once more and finished their tea.

Eventually Mary said, 'I'm sorry for what I did at the dance. I've never apologised properly and I should have.'

'It is forgotten.'

'It was wrong of me. I was jealous of Daniel singling you out.' The sound of his name brought a lump to Janey's throat and for a moment she could not speak. 'I've always had a liking for Daniel but he has always looked at me as his friend's younger sister. When I saw him watching you I knew he had a fancy for you.'

'It is in the past, think no more of it.' Janey didn't want to talk about him. His rejection by the church still felt raw.

'I've never seen Daniel look at a woman like he looked at you. Matt told me that Daniel helped you get into the manor that night.'

Janey gave a weak smile and made a show of gathering the cups.

'Are you walking out together?' asked Mary.

'No. Daniel has lost interest in me, if he had any to begin with.'

Mary looked genuinely saddened. 'Oh, I'm sorry. It's not like Daniel to change his mind so easily. When he sets his mind on something he usually means it.'

'Well, he has realised his folly and I gave him no encouragement. Let's not dwell on what will never be.'

'I'm sorry if I ruined things, Janey. You would make a handsome couple.'

'You did not ruin anything, Mary. There was nothing to ruin.'

Mary touched her arm, compassion on her face. 'Yes there was Janey.' She smiled encouragingly. 'I saw it, even if you didn't.'

Miss Petherbridge looked at the bottle of cod liver oil by her bed. The Carhart girl would be arriving soon to massage the lubricant into her peeling skin. Another daily humiliation she had to endure, along with the girl's attentions to her hygiene and toilet. Carhart also brought her written daily updates from Mr Tallock, all of which praised the girl's efforts. The housekeeper could tell that the girl was unaware of the contents of the notes, which were nothing more than the butler's crude attempt to reassure the housekeeper that all was running well in her absence. He did not want her to worry, he had written. Worry? She had done nothing but worry since the Carhart girl had taken over her role.

At least now her strength was returning, as this morning she was able to feed herself with a spoon. Perhaps she could muster enough strength to administer the oil too? She stretched her frail hand and clumsily grasped the bottle, easing it closer, bit by bit, until she was able to hold it more firmly in her hand. It felt far heavier than she had expected. She dragged it off the bedside table and onto her lap, where she attempted to twist the lid free. Her fingers lacked the strength required and the lid did not move. Exhausted, she let the bottle rest on her lap and realised that the simple task was still beyond her. She grunted in frustration and pushed the oil aside with a swipe of her arm. It rolled off the bed and smashed onto the wooden floor, spilling its reddish brown liquid, mixed with shards of glass, outwards onto the adjacent rug.

The Carhart girl would arrive soon to see what the noise was about. She would be understanding and efficient, thought Miss Petherbridge bitterly, despite the responsibility and workload in recent times. The housekeeper looked down at her own thin, scaled body, which had let her down. The humiliation she had to endure at Carhart's hands was at times too much to bear. She looked across at Charlotte, who lay sleeping in the nursery bed next to her. Damn Janey Carhart, she seethed. The girl hadn't even given her a room of her own.

Miss Petherbridge and Charlotte made full recoveries. Lord Brockenshaw did not. Two weeks later his body, swollen from fluid that his failed heart could no longer pump away, was prepared for the photographer. Despite her blindness, Lady Brockenshaw insisted on arranging for a memento mori, a post mortem photograph that had gained popularity in recent years. She wanted a keepsake of her husband that could be passed down through the generations and she therefore insisted he was dressed in his best suit for the photograph. She did, however, stop short of having his body propped up in a chair and his eyes painted open as preferred by some. She wanted an image of him in his natural state as Doctor Barker had informed her he looked at peace.

The household adopted deep mourning. Black armbands were worn by the male servants, black ribbons by the female staff which matched the sombre mood which descended upon the house. Miss Petherbridge marked her return by ordering that all the curtains be drawn and all the clocks be stopped in respect for their dead master. Each mirror was covered by a single black drape to prevent his spirit becoming trapped on earth and John, Lord Brockenshaw's valet, sat by his body to watch over him until burial.

Janey, now out of isolation, was once more by her grief-stricken mistress's side and felt more tied to her post than ever before. There was no laughter in the house during those initial weeks, only sadness for the loss of a respected master, compassion for the widow left behind and uncertainty at the changes ahead. Bosvenna Manor and estate now had a new master, a master who had yet to learn of the death of his father or return home to claim his inheritance.

Daniel had not ventured into the village for the past month. Spring was always busy on the farm and the grip of scarlet fever did not encourage such a visit if there was no need. Thankfully, the fever had finally slipped away, worn out by its own ferocity and leaving a Lord, three adults and five children buried in the churchyard nearby.

Daniel emerged from Digory's alehouse feeling relaxed and at peace. He had spent the afternoon supping ale with Matt, who, much against Daniel's better judgment, had dragged him to the village for a drink to celebrate finishing the ploughing early.

They had spent the afternoon putting the world to rights until Matt had turned the conversation to the events at Bosvenna Manor. Daniel sat quietly, his expression impassive, while he listened to his friend's idle chatter. Occasionally, he would throw in a casual question. If only his friend realised that below the bored façade, Daniel drank in every word he spoke, like a thirsty man in a desert drinking the spilled water drops from another man's cup. It wasn't the manor he was interested in, or Mary come to that. It was the news of Janey. She had not been taken ill, as he had at first feared, but in fact had taken charge. She had even managed to impress Mary, who now had a new respect for her, as well as a growing friendship.

The two men parted ways just as Daniel heard a woman's voice call out to him. He recognised it immediately and turned to see Sally approaching, a smile on her lips and a swing in her hips. He sat on the granite stone wall, stretched his long legs out in front of him, crossed them casually at the ankle and waited for her to reach him. He gave her a lazy smile.

'Long time no see,' she said, smiling, whilst parting his legs and stepping between them with all the familiarity as if they had shared a bed the night before. 'Where have you been hiding yourself?'

He ignored her question. 'How are you, Sally?'

She pouted her lips like a petulant child. 'Missing you. Not seen you since the autumn. Thought you were hankering after the married life.'

'It was just a passing phase.' He looked her over. She still remained very pleasing to the eye. Her black curls bounced in the sunlight as she moved provocatively between his thighs. 'You are a tease, Sally,' he said.

'No more than you. When are you going to visit me again?'

'I'm not a man to plan ahead.'

'Drop in tonight. That's not too far ahead.' She took his hand and placed it behind her waist. 'You know I miss you. Other men don't hold a candle to you.' She slid his hand downward until it cupped her buttock. 'I'll make you something nice to eat.'

'Like what?'

'You name it and I'll do it.'

Daniel knew what she was suggesting and it had nothing to do with food. She was inviting him to a feast and not for the first time in recent weeks he realised how starved he was. He was tempted. Unfortunately his attraction to Janey resulted in every morsel ripe for the picking being found wanting. He wondered, as he openly admired Sally's curves, if it was all in his head. If Janey was standing here right now and he could directly compare the two, would Janey really be so much more attractive to him? A movement caught his eye and he glanced over Sally's shoulder. As if by some twist of fate, Janey was standing by the apothecary door watching him.

'I must be off. I have things to do,' whispered Sally seductively in his ear. 'Promise me you will visit.'

Daniel nodded absently as she kissed him on the cheek and left. He did not say goodbye. He had more important things on his mind as Janey was approaching. He braced himself.

He had questioned if his attraction to her was all in his head. Seeing her again he knew it was not. It was much deeper and pulled at his gut like an invisible rope. Her brown hair shone in the afternoon sun and reminded him of the deep sheen of freshly husked conkers. A stray strand of hair bounced against her cheek at her rapid approach and her skin glowed with the natural freshness of youth. He wondered, not for the first time, how she would smell if he was to bury his face in the crease of her neck.

He had turned his back on her the last time they met. It was bad manners. He felt his body tighten in readiness to defend himself against a verbal onslaught that only a woman could give.

'Good afternoon, Mr Kellow. Lovely weather we are

having.' Her voice, overly bright and a little shaky, made him wary. What was she up to? He dropped his gaze to the basket she was twisting nervously in her hands.

'Of course, it could rain tomorrow,' she added, less brightly. 'Spring weather can be very changeable.'

A rose hue blossomed on each of her cheeks when he failed to reply again. She looked for an escape from his silence. He suddenly realised she might leave and although he was confused, angry and hurt by this woman, he knew that he did not want her to go.

'I see you are in mourning,' he replied, gruffly, nodding to her black cloak. The blush in her cheeks reddened further as she pulled at the collar of her cape.

'Not my favourite colour, but Lady Brockenshaw wishes me to wear it.'

'Lord Brockenshaw's funeral was the first funeral in the village where half the immediate family were missing.'

'They have used the telegraph and left messages at a number of Master Brockenshaw's friends but they have not tracked him down.'

They both fell into an awkward silence at James's name. Janey eventually spoke to tackle the subject.

'That day ... in the barn. It was not how it appeared.'

'I know what I saw. One day you are kissing me, the next you are kissing him.'

'He was kissing me.'

'His hands were all over you, lifting your skirt.'

'I tried to stop him.'

'Not hard enough it seems!'

'It's difficult. He is my employer.'

Daniel shook his head as if to shake away her protests.

'Say no! It is not hard to do. If he is such a gentleman he would stop. You were alone in a secluded building ... *my* building, for God's sake!'

'You have no idea what it's like as a woman, as a servant, whose home and income depends on her job. You are a man, beholden to no one. You own your own house and farm. He is a man of wealth, of position. I am a servant. My work, my home, all that I have, depends on the Brockenshaw family.'

Daniel didn't want to hear her case. In truth he knew it was difficult for her but he couldn't bear the thought that she had allowed Brockenshaw to grope her.

'You seemed capable enough to take charge of all the servants when the fever took hold, so I don't buy your story of not being able to tell a lecherous dandy to keep his grubby hands off you.' Beneath his stony composure, anger and frustration was boiling up inside him. Images of Janey and Brockenshaw together played in his mind as clearly as if he was seeing them before him now. Her calm voice broke his thoughts.

'You seem to know a lot about me?' she said, watching him coolly. Daniel felt like a child caught stealing sweets.

'Matt prattles on sometimes whether I want to hear it or not.'

'You also seem overly concerned with my virtue.' Daniel humphed as if her virtue was the last thing he was bothered with. 'Yet other women's virtues ... or lack of them,' she added pointedly, nodding towards the road Sally had walked down, 'do not seem to bother you at all.'

'She's a good woman.'

'I hear she's very good at what she does ... she's just not too fussy with whom.'

'You disappoint me. I didn't think you would listen to gossip.'

Janey sighed. 'I'm sorry. It was a wicked thing to have said. I don't know what came over me.' He could see that she felt terrible about what she had said, yet she had said it and he believed it was jealousy that had driven her to utter the words. The thought made his heart leap.

'Do you judge everyone based on gossip?' he asked, quietly. 'Do you judge me?' Her answer was important to him, but she refused to give it.

'I came to build bridges but instead I have turned into a spiteful shrew. I'd better go.'

Again, Daniel didn't want her to leave. He realised he would rather be here arguing with her than not with her at all. She was already walking away from him and he had to stop her. Say something, he told himself, say anything to stop her walking away.

'Matt told me,' he blurted out. She turned to look at him, waiting for him to speak. 'Matt told me that you are helping Mary to apply for nurse training.'

'She will make an excellent nurse,' Janey replied. 'It is a shame I am not more successful for myself.'

For the first time today Daniel wanted to be generous to her.

'You saw something in Mary that no one else did.' It was a compliment and they both knew it. She smiled shyly in return which tugged something deep inside him. He wanted to see a lot more of her smile. Suddenly he recalled her earlier words.

'You said it was a shame you were not more successful. What did you mean?' he asked. Her smile faded.

'It doesn't matter. As you said, if I can take charge of the staff at Bosvenna Manor, then I am more than capable of clarifying my own position.'

So, he thought sadly, she was going to ask Brockenshaw to set her up in a house and become his mistress. She eased the neck of her cape and Daniel saw for the first time the stiff material had rubbed her neck raw in one area.

'You should be in colour, not widow's weeds. Tell her ladyship it doesn't fit.'

'I couldn't. It would disappoint her.'

He watched her walk away, the perfect lady's maid, perfectly turned out, carrying out her duties perfectly. Suddenly something dawned on him.

'It's not your fault, Janey,' he called after her. Janey turned to look at him, her head tilted quizzically to one side. 'It's not your fault your family died. Life is cruel and we are beholden to what it throws at us. You don't have to be perfect all the time. Just be you. You are good enough. Believe me you are good enough.'

She blinked and faltered as his words hit home.

In what he hoped was a more comforting tone, he added, 'Tell her the cape hurts, she will understand.'

He watched her walk away. The words were out and he couldn't take them back, but at that moment in time he had seen deep inside her mind and her eagerness to please. Her prim little steps echoed on the road surface, and her basket, which had been a prop to fidget with, was now held firmly in the crook of her arm.

Daniel watched her until she disappeared from sight. *Just be you*, he had said, and he had meant it, for he was sure he had seen the real Janey Carhart. She was the girl that had sighed with delight at the beauty of the moors when he had first seen her. She was the girl that in a furious temper had thrown stones at him. She was the girl that blushed so easily when embarrassed. She was the woman that he wanted and no other would do.

He would not be visiting Sally tonight or any other night for, he had to admit, Janey still had a hold on him.

Lady Brockenshaw's hand, laced with blue veins under translucent skin, felt along the collar of the cape where its material and stitching had become stiff with age. She lifted it off her lap and handed it out to Janey.

'I quite understand. You should have told me sooner,

Janey.' Janey took the offending article. 'Throw it away. I appreciate your honesty. Any other maid would have taken advantage of my blindness and just not have worn it.'

Charlie padded across the room and snuggled himself upon his mistress's feet like a pair of living slippers. Lady Brockenshaw sat patiently while her maid started to unpin her hair and prepare her for bed.

'James should be here with me now, looking after the estate, been by my side at his father's funeral.' Janey said nothing. 'If my daughter had lived she would be with me and I would not be alone in the house.'

Janey tried to comfort her. 'You are not alone.'

'True loneliness can be felt in a crowded room. I might be in a house full of staff but my son is not here and he should be.' Janey proceeded to lay out her nightgown. 'After months of searching, my brother has traced him.'

Janey looked up and saw the reflection of her mistress in the mirror. The old lady's eyes were filled with tears.

'He has been in America.' She laughed with no joy. 'No wonder he stopped writing. Chasing another dream, no doubt. As a little boy he would become obsessed about something or other, a new toy, a horse, something he would scream and scream for, yet once he got it he would lose interest.'

Responding to Janey's guidance, Lady Brockenshaw stood and lifted out her arms while she was undressed. She continued her monologue. 'We spoilt him as a child. We felt guilty, you see, that he had no siblings. His older sister had passed away shortly before he was born. But James has grown into a spoilt man who gives no thought to anyone. He should have let his parents know he was leaving the country. He should have told us.' She stepped out of her gown and her nightdress was placed over her head. 'His ship docks in Bristol next week. My brother is going to meet him and break the news of his father's death and demand he returns home. I just hope to God that he will finally show an interest in the estate and be responsible.'

'I'm sure he will,' Janey said, softly, as she led her to her bed.

'You are such a dear, Janey. You cared for my husband so well at the end and you have become more a companion to me than a maid. I know Miss Petherbridge hates that I call you by your Christian name rather than Carhart. I know it is not the norm, but you are quite simply the best maid I have had. I know I can rely on you.' She took her hand and patted it softly. 'Remember you can rely on me. If my daughter had grown up to be as nice and caring as you I would have been very proud.'

Janey entered her room at the end of the day feeling energised and empowered. It had been an eventful day. Mary had received an offer of an interview for nurse training and Lady Brockenshaw's words of support had touched her heart. Even Mr Tallock had openly condemned Miss Petherbridge for directing a scathing remark at her during dinner. The housekeeper had not liked the reprimand, which felt all the more sharp coming from the man who rarely made them.

Feeling more supported, Janey came to a decision that she should have made a long time ago. If James tried to make advances toward her, she would tell him firmly that she was not interested. Perhaps, in the past, she had sent him mixed messages. Not any more.

Janey looked around her tidy room. Usually, she carefully hung her uniform in the wardrobe but tonight she tossed it over the back of a chair in rebellion. She quickly removed her remaining undergarments and stepped into her white cotton nightgown. Thankfully the warmer evenings meant that she no longer had to dive into bed to avoid the freezing floor and chilly atmosphere. Tonight she took advantage of this and stood in front of her mirror, slowly unpinning her hair to let large soft waves fall about her shoulders in the candlelight. For the first time, Janey noticed the excitement in her eyes. She had seen it before on the night she had returned from the dance. The excitement of being with Daniel had put it there and, she suspected, he was the reason it was there now. He had said she was good enough. Good enough for who? For him?

His coat still hung on her door. She slipped it from the hook and put it on, wrapping it around herself to soak in its warmth. Daniel had been right. She had spent most of her life trying to be perfect. She had been so busy trying to please others, she had forgotten herself. Instead she had become a chameleon, changing to fit in with her surroundings in the hope of being forgiven for surviving the epidemic that had directly and indirectly killed her family. Somewhere on this journey she had lost herself and Daniel had seen it. More to the point, Daniel had voiced it in a way that was so clear and blunt that it had shocked her to the core. He had said she was good enough, but who did he see? Who was she? If she could do anything what would she want to do?

Not to be a servant or anyone's mistress, that much she knew. She thought for a moment. She knew she loved being outside with the wind in her hair and the sun on her skin. She would love to walk through the countryside with her hair loose and a purpose in her life. She loved animals, she would love to have her own garden and grow her own vegetables. She smiled to herself at the thought of having her own home. Warming to her imagination she realised she wanted to experience love and passion with a man she loved, and who loved her. Daniel Kellow came to mind.

In the semi-darkness of the room she wondered what it

would be like for Daniel to touch her. He was experienced. How would he find her in comparison? She pulled his coat aside and looked at herself. The soft glow of the candle cast dancing shadows across the curves of her body. She thought of Daniel's animalistic attraction and saw her eyes darken with desire. The woman in the mirror yearned for his touch. A woman she hadn't known existed until now.

She retreated from the mirror, took off his coat and slipped under the safety of her bedcovers. The memory of Daniel's kiss beckoned her into sleep. In her dreams he was waiting for her. He was gentle, demanding and passionate and she did not want it to end.

Chapter Eleven

James held the photograph of his father in his hand. He appeared to be peacefully sleeping with an open book placed on his chest as if he had fallen into slumber whilst reading. The whole scene was staged, of course, the clarity of his figure a telltale sign that it was his corpse he was looking at. The long exposure of a photograph gave those in life a blurring as they tried to remain still, not like the dead where the clarity was so great they could be there with you now. Strange, thought James, that one looked more alive in a photograph when dead, than alive and blurred like a ghost.

He sent the photograph spinning across the polished oak table top with a flick of his fingers. He could not stomach looking at it any longer. The truth of the matter was he felt guilty for not being here, guilty for all the disagreements he had had with his father over the years and guilty for not feeling bereft. He should be distraught for losing his father, he should feel a pain that felt like his heart had been wrenched from him – yet he felt nothing but a growing nausea of guilt for not feeling sadder. He expected his father to walk into the room at any moment. He could almost hear his familiar voice that sounded both despairing and disapproving at the same time at his son's lack of motivation. Perhaps the numbness he felt was due to his inability to accept he was dead. How could you mourn someone when his death did not seem real?

He had learned of his death three days ago, yet his father was already half rotted away in the family crypt. He had missed his illness, his death and his funeral. There was no closure on what should be one of the biggest events of his life. Trust his father to not be present to hear his news of prosperity. The news of his death was like having a rug pulled from under him. He had imagined telling his father of his gift for making money on the stock market, boasting to him that for the summer he had lived well on money he had earned himself, travelled to America, made plans to travel further and to make even more money. He had looked forward to his father's shocked face, then congratulatory slaps on the back that at last his son had found direction and wealth, and that he always knew he would amount to something someday. Yet his father had not waited for him to return. On the day that should be his triumph, his father had already upstaged him by dying.

'What were you doing in America?' His mother's voice broke into James's thoughts and he reached for his glass of whisky.

'Researching, Mother.' He took a long drink and savoured the burning in his throat from the fluid. 'London is one of the main cities for business ... only matched by New York.'

'And what sort of business have you been researching?'

'Stocks and shares, Mother. You wouldn't understand.'

Lady Brockenshaw pursed her lips in annoyance. He had still not apologised for his lack of consideration regarding not letting her know where he was.

'Enlighten me,' she ground out.

'I have gone into business with Coogan Davenport, an American associate.'

'The American you mentioned in your letter?'

He nodded.

'He introduced me to the world of stocks and shares. In layman's terms, you buy shares when they are low, wait until they rise and then sell them at a profit.'

'And you do the buying and selling?'

'God no, I have an agent do it for me. I just watch the markets and decide what to buy and when to sell.'

'What happens if they fall?'

'One loses money if one has to sell, or one waits it out until they rise again and sell at the right time.'

'And you were successful?'

He got up to pour himself another drink but there was less than a glassful left. He rang the bell for more.

'Indeed I was. I am. At least I earned enough to travel and live which also, I'm pleased to say, required very little work.'

'I'm very pleased for you.' She did not sound pleased, thought James. 'Now that you have got that out of your system you can concentrate on the affairs of the Bosvenna Estate.'

'I don't think so.'

'James?'

'Cornwall is not where things are happening, Mother.'

'That's where you are wrong. Cornwall is exactly where it is happening! You have inherited Bosvenna and you alone must be here to run it.'

'Let's not talk about this now.' James was beginning to lose patience.

'Now is exactly when we should talk about it, too much time has passed already. I didn't know where you had gone. You should have left word!'

'I said let's not talk about it now, Mother!' He stood up again and irritably rang the bell.

The butler entered and quickly left to carry out James's curt order for more whisky.

'The bank says there is not much money left. I need you to turn the estate around,' Lady Brockenshaw informed her son.

James rubbed his throbbing head. 'I never asked to be the only child and inherit this albatross.'

'Yet you would not turn away the money it has brought in over the past or disown the title that goes with it.'

'I will see you are all right but as you quite rightly say, Bosvenna is mine and I can do with it what I like. If I choose to live here, I will. If I choose to employ a manager and spend my life in London, or travel, I will, and if I choose to sell it, I will. This is my life and neither Father nor you can do anything to stop me.' He ceased his tirade abruptly, realising too late that he had spoken as if his father was still alive.

'An estate with an absent owner decays. It needs a family inside it to keep it alive. You are now Lord Brockenshaw. You need to be here, to oversee the tenants, to be part of the community!'

'No, Mother. I do not but you are right ... I am Lord Brockenshaw, and I need no woman to tell me what I can and cannot do.'

The bank manager shuffled through the papers and looked over his glasses to observe the new Lord Brockenshaw. He was young, fashionably dressed and sat tapping his walnut cane on his shoe in measured irritation. The bank manager coughed.

'Well, as I have mentioned to your mother, there is not much cash in the bank, but plenty in assets. You could try raising the rents but as they are quite high already and not due for a couple of months that does not help you in the short term or may not be a viable option. If they are too high people won't pay because they can't and this will just result in tenants falling behind with their rent. Then there will be eviction costs, looking for new tenants and, of course, if the rent is too high new tenants will be difficult to find.'

He watched the tapping cane and wondered if his client was even listening. 'You could look through the accounts and see what savings can be made, it will take time and work but many estates have been saved by streamlining their costs. Your father did leave money in the bank, it's enough to continue to run the estate for a few months, but not enough to provide the lifestyle you are hoping for.'

The bank manager coughed nervously. The man sitting opposite him did not look as if he would be willing to curtail his expenses. 'Do you have anything you wish to sell?'

'Bosvenna Estate itself.'

The bank manager smiled. 'We both know that is not an option. Your father has made a clause in his will that the estate is not to be sold for ten years after his death.'

'I need no reminding,' was the curt reply. Even in death his father was taunting and controlling him.

'You could turn the estate into a business. I understand it has large function rooms. You could rent them out for dances, meetings, weddings. It's a new idea but I've heard it can be successful. It will take organisation and a business mind but the results would be well worth it. It would become a profitable estate that you can improve upon and leave to your descendants, while still remaining your home.'

The tapping stopped.

'I want a loan.'

'You do?'

'I do.'

'How much?'

'Half the worth of the estate.'

'That's a very big sum!'

'But possible?'

'It would have to be a loan against the property. You understand this means that the estate is collateral?'

'I do.'

'And if you fall behind in payments the estate will be at risk.'

'But a loan is possible?'

'It depends what it is for. I need to be reassured that your venture is viable.'

James was prepared for this. He slid across an illustration of a street lined with rundown houses. He had never visited the street or had any interest in the houses but the paperwork served his purpose.

'I plan to buy these houses and renovate them,' he lied. 'I can then sell them at a profit, however I need money to buy them. I plan to have them completed within ten months. I will be able to repay the loan in full and the profit can be used for the estate.'

The banker lifted the papers and looked through the pictures. He asked a few questions on price and costs and James answered them to his satisfaction.

'Well, I wasn't expecting this. I wasn't aware you enjoyed this sort of venture.'

'There is a lot you do not know about me. Do I have the loan?'

'I see no objection.'

'Then let's sort the paperwork out, I have no time to waste.' He dragged the illustration from the table and watched the banker find the appropriate paperwork. 'I need not tell you that this is confidential. I do not wish my mother to know.'

'Everything between a banker and his client is confidential, Lord Brockenshaw. You can rely on that.'

'I'm glad to hear it,' said James, leaning back in his chair. The tapping began again as he waited for the banker to prepare the appropriate paperwork and set the loan in motion.

He silently congratulated himself as he watched the older man across the desk. The morning had been a successful one and he would soon have the money to put his true venture into motion, a venture that did not include a street of pitiful houses. No, it was the stock market that beckoned and a thrill of anticipation started to grow inside him as he waited to sign on the dotted line.

James returned home energised. The money would be in his account within a few days. If he chose wisely in which shares to invest, he could double his profit, sell and move on to another venture. The possibility of amassing huge wealth was fast becoming a drug to him.

He marched along the corridor of Bosvenna Manor, his long strides echoing on the wooden floor. He was heading for his study, when he spied Janey coming out of his mother's room. It was the first time they had seen each other since his return and she looked shocked at his sudden appearance.

'My God, it's Janey Carhart! What a sight for sore eyes.' He caught her arm and pulled her to him. To his surprise she pulled it away and began to walk in the opposite direction. 'Hey,' he called, grabbing her skirt, drunk on his successful visit to the bank, if not on the alcohol he had already consumed that morning. 'Where are you going?'

'I'm working, sir.'

'Is that all you have to say? I return and all you say is, *I'm working*.'

She pulled her skirt away from his hand. 'Sir, please don't,' she said, coolly. She turned to go again, but he grabbed her wrist, anger bubbling up inside him.

'And I say stay!' For a moment his angry tone appeared to unnerve her but her courage returned and she slowly turned to face him.

'Mr Brockenshaw, Lord Brockenshaw,' she corrected herself. 'I feel anything between us is inappropriate. I do not wish your attentions or encourage them. I want them to stop. I am your mother's maid. I do not wish my position to be jeopardised and your special treatment of me makes me uncomfortable.'

'You don't mean it.'

'I do, sir.'

He wanted to laugh at her, but found he couldn't. 'Don't be stupid,' he said, reaching for her again.

She shook him off, roughly. 'I said don't! I'm not interested. Now leave me to get on with my work.'

'A man can get tired of the hunt, Carhart.'

'Good, then stop hunting!' She began to stride away, but he followed her.

'You upstart! You bitch! Don't think you will be working here for much longer.'

She turned and pinned him with a stare.

'Do your worst, Lord Brockenshaw. I will not change my mind and if you dismiss me your mother will want to know why. Will you tell her, or will I?'

James watched her walk away, speechless. He had never had a woman say no to him. His good looks and family pedigree, if not his money, ensured that. To have a servant turn *him* down was hard to take in, but his feelings of shock quickly changed back to fury. He spun around and stamped away in the opposite direction, slamming the door of his study behind him.

Lady Brockenshaw and Miss Petherbridge had heard it all. They had been discussing the menu for the following day when James's raised voice was heard in the corridor outside, followed by Janey's quiet but firm replies. They listened in painful silence, neither speaking yet both pretending not to have heard. Finally, the argument outside was over and they could hear the sound of their footsteps receding in opposite directions.

Lady Brockenshaw took a shaky breath. 'As a loyal employee, Miss Petherbridge, I can trust you to remain discreet.'

The housekeeper folded the menu away. 'Of course, ma'am.'

'Then let the conversation we have heard never be mentioned again ... to anyone.'

The housekeeper smiled. 'As you wish, ma'am,' she replied. 'As you wish.'

Bodmin was a thriving market town, linked to the neighbouring town of Wadebridge by a steam railway. It was one of the busiest towns in Cornwall, with a growing population and a grand County Court building taking centre stage in its spacious town square. Yet, despite the busy streets, shops and alehouses, Daniel hated it. To the north of the town towered the gaol, with its small barred windows and indomitable boundary wall. It looked down on the town with a sombre air and despairing lost souls locked in its belly.

To the south of the town, and equally as imposing, was the Lunatic Asylum. Its wards spread outwards like the spokes of a wheel from a central tower. Each one had small evenly spaced barred windows looking down on the hospital grounds, which were enclosed by yet another tall boundary wall. The steep vertical structure kept the inmates in and society out, segregating itself from the outside to form a self-sufficient world inside. Behind the grey stone walls were the outcasts of society, the mentally ill, the physically and mentally disabled, and the unfortunates, whose behaviour just wasn't understood by society.

On the same grounds loomed the workhouse, which housed the paupers, unmarried mothers and the homeless. Daniel knew that at the root of his dislike for the town was the certain knowledge that, but for the good fortune of meeting an old farming couple called Zachariah and Amy, who had seen good in him, he too would have eventually found himself an inmate of any one of those large foreboding stone buildings.

He had spent the morning at the crowded livestock market amongst the throng of men looking for the right purchase to add to their herd. Today he had gone to observe, to watch the state of the market and the price animals reached at auction. Daniel knew farming would soon change. Industry was growing and the old farming ways would soon be forgotten. He knew that, in the not too distant future, the expanding rail links would connect more towns and villages in Cornwall and beyond. Daniel understood that if he was ready and willing to change he could take advantage of this.

His farm was self-sufficient but he wanted to expand. He hoped to increase his herd of cattle, and with the extra milk they produced, sell it to the local villagers. He had already made contacts with local farmers and together they hoped to organise a collection of milk from different farms to sell to the villages of St Tude and St Mabe. They also knew that when more railway links were developed, milk could also be transported at speed to the towns and villages further afield.

Daniel wanted to be a part of that but it would mean expanding the size of his herd, which took time and money. Time he had and, in the past, he had used it to sell some of his produce to the Bosvenna Estate to earn extra money. That source of income was no longer an option as he could not stomach the thought of providing produce to the Brockenshaw family. His hatred of James had seen to that. However, Daniel was a patient man and a driven one. He had already begun to rent out his boar and bull for breeding, which was proving lucrative. His ultimate goal was to build a solid future for the family he hoped to have one day, as he wanted his own children to never experience the childhood he had suffered.

Before collecting his horse to ride home he took sanctuary from the noisy crowds in the Cat and Fiddle alehouse. The meat pie he had eaten wasn't as good as some but it sufficed. Nursing a jug of warm ale he contemplated his next move.

The alehouse had been quiet as the midday rush had dispersed out into the streets, but all that changed as a crowd of young smartly dressed men stumbled through the doors. Already high on spirits drunk elsewhere and laughing and talking much too loudly, their presence immediately affected the peaceful atmosphere of the building. They took over several tables and chairs, banging the table in unison until a barmaid took their orders. Amongst lewd remarks and raucous laughter she escaped to the bar, where the landlord took over the order and sent her upstairs out of harm's way.

Daniel did not turn around but kept himself to himself. He had no interest in the young men, at least not until he heard a familiar voice that made his hackles rise.

'So gold it is!'

'Indeed. I have it on good authority that if we buy now, while it is low, we will reap excellent rewards in the very near future.'

Daniel had not heard the second man's accent before. He suspected it was American.

'It cannot possibly go wrong as gold will never lose its value. How do you know it will rise so quickly?'

'I have friends with plans to corner the market. They tell me it's a good time to buy but we need to be quick.'

James shook Davenport's hand across the table, ignoring their raucous friends who had no interest in stocks and shares.

'Then it is settled. Gold it is, and with such inside information I can invest heavily.'

'Indeed! To the markets!'

Their tankards smashed into each other in salute and they settled back into their chairs, returning their attention back to their companions.

James's mind, foggy now with alcohol, began to wander and his attention was caught by a lone figure sitting at the bar. The last time he had seen the man he had been in a derelict building where he was rudely interrupted and ordered away by the upstart. The humiliation and anger he had felt then flooded back and in a voice raised to be heard he turned to his fellow companions.

'Have any of you straddled a servant?'

Their laughter quietened.

'No one we would confess to,' came a nervous response.

'Come, come, we know it goes on. I have a wench, a comely pretty thing, who is only too grateful for a master's touch.' Daniel froze. 'She pines and whimpers for my company. I can only but oblige.'

Their laughter brought Daniel to his feet. He needed to get away.

'She sighs and begs for more and it's good entertainment, I must confess. Don't you think, Daniel Kellow?'

James's walnut cane arced in the air and came down in front of Daniel, like a barrier, blocking his exit from the alehouse. Daniel stared at its shiny gold tip glinting in the firelight. 'I think you may know her, Kellow,' James goaded. 'Her name is Janey.'

Daniel did not reply. He dared not trust himself to speak or move, not because he was scared, but because there were too many witnesses to the action he would like to take. Oblivious to his mounting anger, James turned to his friends.

'You see, this man here would rather have had his hands up her skirt but instead, mine were.'

Daniel startled everyone as he snatched the cane. He made a show of looking at it as everyone held their breath. He tapped the cane against his hand to examine its sturdiness and then raised it as if about to strike, but he did not. Instead he slowly lowered it down.

'Carrying a cane means to abide by certain rules or risk loss of that privilege,' said Daniel, offering its handle to the American.

Davenport cautiously reached out and took it and in doing so condoned Daniel's action. With measured strides, Daniel left and disappeared amongst the crowds in the street. James was livid and made to follow but Davenport stopped him.

'Leave him, James, we have business to discuss. Don't risk another confrontation. He did not rise to the bait. You may not be so lucky next time.'

Later, after relieving himself against a dimly lit wall behind the alehouse, James found himself lurching along the narrow alleyway that ran alongside it. Inside he could hear his friends laughing loudly and the sound beckoned him to return to their newly formed gambling table. He staggered on, noticing for the first time the silhouette of a man at the end of the alleyway, leaning casually against the wall of the Cat and Fiddle and barring his way to the street bathed in sunlight.

The stranger stood and turned towards him to wait for his approach. The man's feet were set squarely with his shoulders, bracing himself, filling the small space and blocking out the light. James staggered on, comfortable in his position in life that the man would stand aside once he reached him. He did not and it wasn't until James came face to face with him that the man finally lifted his chin, to show his eyes that had been obscured by his cap. James, with sickening realisation, recognised Daniel just as he was slammed up against the wall by him. His feet barely reached the ground as he hung in mid-air supported only by Daniel's fists buried in his coat collar.

'If I ever, *ever*, hear you speak her name in public or talk about her in such a degrading way again, I'll kill you!'

James struggled to break free but failed. Gasping for breath his reply was no more than a hoarse choked whisper. 'Take your hands off me, Kellow.'

Daniel slammed him up against the wall again.

'You try my patience, Brockenshaw. You ain't fit to clean her shoes.'

James's eyes widened. 'My God, man. I believe you're jealous!'

Daniel slammed him against the wall again. James winced as his head banged against it. He was not a match for Daniel Kellow's strength, but he knew how to hurt him.

'I've had her, Kellow.' He savoured the look of shock on Daniel's face before adding with relish, 'Right up to the hilt!'

Daniel's fist flew through the air and made contact with his jaw. James slid to the floor like a wooden puppet with severed strings. Daniel stood back breathing heavily.

'You'll pay for that, you murdering oaf!' threatened James, rubbing his jaw. Daniel was unmoved.

'The advantage of having a reputation such as mine, Brockenshaw, is that it attracts scum. Right now I have two paid witnesses who will swear in court that at this moment I am at the Red Lion drinking with them. Now, hear me well. If I hear you saying anything to harm her reputation, I'll hunt you down and finish the job!'

Daniel left as quietly as he had arrived, disappearing into the busy street at the end of the alleyway. James propped himself up against the damp stone wall to nurse his bruised jaw and bleeding lip. He could still hear his friends' laughter from within the alehouse, but his own good spirits no longer matched it and he had a mind to leave early. He would not forget that Daniel had ruined his night.

'I think their behaviour was atrocious!' Mrs Friggens dropped the bread dough onto her floured board and began to knead it with vigour. 'This house is meant to be in mourning yet the young Lord Brockenshaw and his friends have been drinking and laughing as if they are at one long party.'

'Indeed,' Mr Tallock agreed. He inspected his reflection in the back of a silver spoon, found it not up to standard and resumed his polishing. 'Thank the Lord his friends have now left. Perhaps we can get back to some semblance of normality.'

'Poor Lady Brockenshaw, that's all I can say. She's grieving for the loss of her husband and her son seems to be celebrating it.'

Miss Petherbridge paused in her writing. She was making a list of provisions required for the house. Unusually she had chosen to be sociable and sit at the same table where Mr Tallock and Mrs Friggens worked, each at opposite sides of the table.

'Janey has been a great support to her since her husband died,' said Mr Tallock, picking up another spoon to start the process of cleaning again. 'I've heard Lady Brockenshaw say she has become more of a companion than a lady's maid.'

'I thought as much. I've hardly seen her, except at meal times.' Knowing it would rile the housekeeper, the cook added, slyly, 'She'll be wanting to have the wage of a lady's companion to go with it.'

'I don't think that is appropriate, Mrs Friggens,' replied Miss Petherbridge, tapping her pen in annoyance.

'Nevertheless, I think Janey is better than just being a lady's maid and I for one wish her well in all she does. We must all strive to better ourselves.'

'Well said, Mr Tallock,' agreed Mrs Friggens, but Miss Petherbridge ignored them both.

'Do we need more brandy and whisky?' she asked, returning to her list.

The butler coughed in embarrassment. 'Indeed we do,' he said, 'only the establishment we usually order our spirits from are reluctant to fulfil another order at present.'

Both women looked at him in surprise.

'Why?' asked Mrs Friggens.

'It seems they are unwilling to supply any more until they have had their account settled.'

'Lord Brockenshaw usually deals with them,' said Miss Petherbridge.

'Well, it appears he has not and I have the unfortunate task of bringing the subject up.' He proceeded to sort the polished silver into separate piles, before adding, 'It's just a matter of choosing the right moment.'

There was a knock at the back door and the butler disappeared to see to it. Conversation halted until he returned.

'It's a telegram for Lord Brockenshaw,' said the butler, placing it neatly on a silver tray.

Miss Petherbridge voiced what they were all thinking. 'Telegrams are seldom good news, Mr Tallock. I suggest you leave the matter of the spirit account for another day.'

'I am inclined to agree. I think one lot of bad news in a day is enough for any man.'

Chapter Twelve

James looked at the telegram in his hand and tried to muster the courage to read it. The last few days had not been good to him. His friends had left three days ago and time had dragged ever since. He was feeling restless and irritated by everything around him. His mother was melancholy and his capacity to be patient with her had all but vanished. It was just as well that she appeared to prefer the company of her maid these days. The same maid who had rebuffed his advances and made him feel like a schoolboy being reprimanded by his headmaster. To top it all, he had also been warned off by Kellow and the more James was told he could not have something the more he wanted it.

The telegram continued to taunt him, but he still resisted. He had taken out a substantial mortgage and used it all to buy shares in gold. The shares had increased steadily. If he had sold them last week he would have made a substantial profit, but the more they had increased in value the more he had been tempted to hang on for just one more day. His first repayment would be due at the end of the month. He had nothing in the bank to pay it but he planned to sell the shares before the due date. It was a waiting game but the arrival of the telegram could only mean one thing – Davenport had urgent news for him. He drained his glass in one gulp and tore it open.

GOVERNMENT FLOODED MARKET. PRICE OF GOLD PLUMMETED. PANIC BY INVESTORS. RIOTS IN NEW YORK. ALL IS LOST.

James's face paled as the words began to dance before his eyes. He had lost everything. Later the papers reported that two American speculators had attempted to corner the New York gold market, which had caused the shares to rise. On discovering this, the American government had flooded the market resulting in investors scrambling to sell before the shares plummeted further. Within minutes the gold market had collapsed as angry crowds besieged the banks to withdraw their life savings. In a frenzy of desperation and panic, angry crowds attacked bankers and rioted. The government were forced to send in troops to quell the riots that broke out but it was too late for many speculators and investors who had taken out loans. Within hours many were wiped out financially and ruined.

The consequences of the collapse on September 29th, 1869, or Black Friday as it was later referred to, would have a knock-on effect for other shares and investors and last well into the following year. For James its devastating consequences were instantaneous. He had in his possession worthless shares that he could not sell without making a substantial loss. His bank loan repayment was due within days and he did not have the money to pay it nor would he in the foreseeable future. Without a very large injection of money, the bank would claim and sell the Bosvenna Estate for payment. He had been Lord Brockenshaw for just a few months and he was about to lose everything.

Miss Petherbridge placed the footstool into the already crowded lumber room. It had been a favourite of the late master but now it had become an object of annoyance as Lady Brockenshaw repeatedly tripped over it. In an unusual fit of despair she had ordered the housekeeper to *remove it at once*. In the absence of Mary, who had been accepted for nurse training and had left the previous week, and the Carhart girl, who was taking her ladyship's dog out for his daily walk in the grounds, Miss Petherbridge had removed it. Casting a last look at the furniture stacked about her, she turned to leave. She saw Janey entering her room and stepped back into the shadow of the lumber room before she was seen.

Janey Carhart. The sole cause of her pent-up jealousies and resentment. A chit of a girl who had secured a position she was not qualified for, endeared herself to the majority of the staff and become a firm favourite of her ladyship, to such an extent that she was even granted liberties that she, as Lady Brockenshaw's loyal housekeeper, had never been given. She was nothing more than a scheming girl wanting advancement and who had taken advantage of the bereaved Lady Brockenshaw to make herself indispensable to the old, blind woman. Miss Petherbridge waited until Janey was in her room before she stepped out of the shadows where she had been hiding. She despised her own behaviour, but since her illness she found it difficult to face the girl. During her fever she had been forced to depend on Carhart. The girl had tended to her most personal needs, had seen her aging body disrobed and had fed her like a baby. The humiliation she felt, and still felt whenever she recalled the experience, swamped any gratitude she should have felt. She had been knocked off her perch and she now had the burning desire to do the same to her.

Miss Petherbridge made her way down the corridor and the stone spiral steps to the servants' quarters below. James Brockenshaw appeared before her, smelling of alcohol, a little unsteady on his feet and blocking her way. He appeared as surprised to see her as she was him.

James could not meet her gaze and was sweating profusely. They both knew he had no right or acceptable excuse to be climbing the female servants' staircase, which led to their rooms. Her sudden appearance had knocked him off his stride and as he struggled for an excuse, he reminded her of a child caught misbehaving.

Miss Petherbridge looked down on him from the higher step. She had known James since he was a spoilt child and recognised the feverish glint of danger in his eyes. He was on his way to see Janey and Miss Petherbridge felt that no good would come from the encounter. As housekeeper, she was responsible for the welfare of her staff and should refuse him entry to the female quarters.

'Sir, may I help you?' She watched James struggle to find the right words. 'Perhaps you are on your way to the lumber room for a particular piece of furniture?'

James's eyes lit up at the lifeline of an excuse she had offered. He nodded enthusiastically.

'Yes, Petherbridge, I am!' The whisky on his breath wafted across her face.

'Then perhaps I can take the liberty to remind you, as you so rarely enter this area, that the lumber room is the last door on the right.' James frowned. The housekeeper realised that the alcohol had slowed his mind and he would require a little help. 'I only tell you this as your mother's maid is up there alone and her door is the last but one on the left. I should not like to think you would mistakenly enter her room, sir.'

James's eyes met hers for the first time. He smiled. 'Of course, Miss Petherbridge, thank you for your consideration.'

Miss Petherbridge studied him silently. It was not just danger she saw in his eyes, but lust too. Euphoria coursed through her veins as she continued to block his ascent. She had the power to refuse him entry and save Janey from a horrible fate or move aside and allow Brockenshaw to carry out his shameful intentions.

Miss Petherbidge smiled, inhaled deeply, savoured the moment, then stepped aside.

Janey removed her day dress and hung it on the rail. The house had been in mourning for six months and although

Lady Brockenshaw would remain in black for the next two years she had decided that Janey could change into her day dress to walk her dog, rather than dress in mourning clothes and risk spoiling them.

Janey heard footsteps outside but thought no more of it until the door burst open and James stumbled into the room. With a flourish, he slammed the door shut behind him. The aroma of whisky accompanied him and Janey grew wary.

'You shouldn't be here,' she said, calmly, whilst shaking inside.

His glazed gaze raked her body as he swayed in front of her.

'I think you should leave, Lord Brockenshaw,' said Janey, carefully reaching for her uniform. 'You should not be here.'

'This is my house!' said James, tearing the uniform from her hands. 'I can go anywhere I choose!'

Janey realised, with mounting horror, that it was no mistake he was in her room.

'James,' she said, softly, using his name as he had once asked her to do, 'you don't look well. Perhaps I can get you something. Let me dress and I will get you a cup of tea.'

He laughed harshly. 'James. *Now* you call me James! Only a few days ago I was not *good enough* for you!'

'Please, sir, let me go downstairs and get you something to drink.'

'I know your little plan,' he said, wagging his finger at her then tapping his nose. 'You want to escape. I scare you.'

Janey's mouth felt dry. She did not know how to best answer him.

'You think I don't know about you and Kellow. You made eyes at me when you were bedding him.'

Janey shook her head in denial, but she knew it would do no good.

'You are a whore, Janey Carhart, and whores should be treated as whores!'

Janey backed away. 'Please, sir, I don't know what you are talking about. Please leave.' He grabbed her arm and she pulled it away. 'Please leave me alone. Don't touch me,' she begged again. For the first time, she saw the lust in his eyes – and it terrified her.

'Did you know that Kellow attacked me for merely mentioning your name?' asked James as he swayed toward her. 'I wonder what he would do if he knew I was here now.' He clutched the neckline of her bodice. 'He has a temper. It will lead him to the hangman's noose one day.'

With a wrench, James tore Janey's bodice away exposing her to his eyes. She retreated until she felt the metal frame of her bed form a barrier at the back of her legs. Politeness would not save her. She would have to fight or be lost. She ran for the door but he grabbed her around the waist, holding her tight as he tried to kiss her. His stale breath filled her nostrils and invaded her throat.

She hit him, slapping, then thumping with tightly balled fists. Some hit his body, others went wide of their mark before he grabbed her arms and pinned them to her sides. She tried to kick, but her stockinged feet made no impact. She tried to avoid his mouth, arching and twisting in his grasp, but he pulled her hair and dragged her head back to a painful degree. Suddenly her arm became free and she reached up blindly to attack his eyes but his thundering smack caused her head to whip to the side, dazing her and making her head spin. She turned in disbelief, not quite believing he had hit her. Another followed and blood flowed into her mouth. Her vision blurred and she felt herself roughly pushed onto the bed to be covered by his heavy body.

As she lay stunned, he ripped at her clothes, kneeled on her limbs and violated her body with his hands. In a last attempt to escape she tried to push him away but he was too heavy, too strong, too drunk on power and control. His rough groping hands tore at her tender flesh and exposed her to his eyes. Humiliation at her degradation overwhelmed her. With each grope of her body, her spirit withered a little more. She no longer had any strength or will and she withdrew from reality in order to survive. She became detached from her body and searched for something to focus on as he attacked her person. Her safe little room, all that she owned in the world about her, was her only witness to the attack. Her notebook lay discarded on the floor beside the bed. Its contents lay open, displaying her girlish writing, evidence of her fledgling love for him – silly, naive love for a man that now took joy in degrading her.

Something rolled across the floor and came to a halt within her view. It was Daniel's button from the dance that she had been unable to throw away. In her mind, numb with shock, it appeared to invite her to focus on it for strength. She stared at the little object. It was a symbol of the outside world, something to keep her mind off her humiliation. Suddenly James entered her with a rasping violence, causing pain and tearing, stripping her of her virginity, her naivety and her joy of life.

As he rutted her body she was no longer there. Her spirit had withered, her soul had died. Time no longer existed as the ordeal seemed never-ending. Finally the deed was done and he withdrew to stand and look down on her, leaving her exposed, her limbs twisted like a broken rag doll.

He spoke as if all was normal but she did not listen, she did not care. She felt used and discarded as if she was no more than sacking tossed aside to rot away. She was vaguely aware of his departure but she remained still as if dead, an empty carcass with nothing left inside.

After some time she tried to move her bruised limbs, the action bringing her back to the reality of her room and the evidence of the violence about her. Slowly and tentatively she drew her knees up and rolled on her side; hugging them tight to her, she started to rock rhythmically for comfort. Her lips crusted with dried blood, her aching body tender and sore, she finally let go of the emotions she had held back in order to survive. Tears spilled from her eyes as she silently sobbed like she had never sobbed before.

Despite the warm autumn sun shining down on her skin through the sitting room window, Lady Brockenshaw felt troubled. Something was wrong. Her sense of foreboding had grown and despite wanting to know the cause of it she also dreaded finding out. The feeling had started yesterday when Janey had not returned to her duties following Charlie's walk. Miss Petherbridge reassured her she just had a headache and that she had insisted Janey went to bed. Her duties were filled by Lizzy for the remainder of the day. Was it the fact that Janey had succumbed so quickly to a mere headache or Miss Petherbridge's unusual leniency that lit the flame of her concern? She did not know but if she was unsure of the legitimacy of her feelings her uncertainty disappeared this morning.

Janey had hardly spoken while she attended her mistress's needs. She appeared distracted and forgetful and for the first time Lady Brockenshaw had to direct her. When the door to her rooms opened and other staff entered to attend the fire or remove trays, she felt and heard Janey jump at her side. Usually a proficient hair stylist, this morning she had found the task impossible and Lady Brockenshaw, unable to bear witness to her distress, told her to stop and undertook the chore herself.

When asked to reveal the cause for her change in behaviour Janey would not say. When pressed further she begged not to be asked and on the edge of tears swore she would never tell *anyone, ever*. Lady Brockenshaw was at a loss and felt Janey's distress as if it was her own, but her distress multiplied when James entered the room and Janey fled.

Lady Brockenshaw sat tapping the arm of her wooden chair with the tips of her fingers, waiting for her son to sit down. It was only eleven o'clock and he was already at the decanter. She waited patiently while James grumbled that it was almost empty and rang for the butler to refill it. She waited while Tallock entered and nervously told James there was none in the cellar.

'Why the hell not?'

'The vendor will not supply any more until the account is settled, sir,' replied the butler, nervously. 'I'm sorry, ma'am,' he added to Lady Brockenshaw, 'for speaking of such vulgar matters in your presence.'

'Why hasn't it been paid?' she asked, for a moment sidetracked from her thoughts and the inevitable confrontation to come. 'James?'

James did not answer.

'I presented the bill to you last month, sir,' Mr Tallock reminded him.

'I know, I know.' James waved him away. 'Get something else, wine, brandy.'

'We have no brandy, sir.'

'Then wine, damn you! Get out!'

His mother was shocked at his outburst. 'James.'

'I'm sorry, Mother. He annoys me.'

'Tallock is an excellent butler. Why have the bills not been paid?'

Defeated, James suddenly collapsed in a chair, covering his face with his hands.

'Oh God, Mother. I've made a mess of things.'

Hearing her son's despair, Janey was temporarily forgotten.

'James, dearest, what is wrong? Tell me.'

He rubbed his face, wincing as he caught the scratch on his cheek, which he had passed off to his valet as having been caused by a bramble whilst riding.

'Oh, Mother, I've done a terrible thing. You will be so angry with me.'

Her feeling of dread grew inside her and she waited to hear his confession. James took a deep breath.

'I bought shares in gold in the American market but the shares have dropped in value.'

'So you have to wait until they rise again?'

'They will not rise to the price they were when I bought them.'

'You will make a loss, but you have time on your side to wait until they rise, to lessen the deficit?'

'I do not have the luxury of time, Mother.'

'I don't understand.'

'I borrowed the money. The first repayment is due in a few days.'

Realisation began to dawn on her.

'And you cannot make the repayments?'

He shook his head. 'No.'

'Who did you borrow it from? You could speak to your lender. I'm sure they will understand.'

'It was the bank.'

'Bank? Was it a big loan?'

'It was.'

'How much?'

'Too much.'

'A bank would not loan money for a customer to play the stock market.'

'They did not know.'

'You have been fraudulent? What did you borrow against?'

'Bosvenna.'

Lady Brockenshaw rubbed her breastbone as a pain started to build up inside her, along with her anxiety.

'How much did you borrow?'

'Half its worth.'

'Oh God, James, how could you? What does this mean?'

'It means, Mother, the bank will want its money back and we have none to give it. So they will claim the estate and sell it to get its money.'

The crushing pain grew and she struggled to catch her breath.

'What about the servants? What about the tenants?'

'What about me, Mother! What about me!'

Suddenly her fury broke forth.

'It's always about you, James! You have ruined us! How could you? You ruin everything you touch!' Suddenly she remembered her maid and demanded to know the truth. 'Have you ruined my maid as well?'

James looked up, surprised at her sudden change in topic.

'Your maid?' he asked, in all innocence.

'Have you ruined her too?'

'I swear before God, Mother, I have no interest in her!' Indignantly he scoffed, 'If she is out of sorts it is nothing to do with me.'

'Do you swear, James, that you have not touched her? Swear on your life that you have not hurt her.'

'I swear on my life I did not touch her. May God strike me down, Mother, if what I say is an untruth.'

Lady Brockenshaw listened to his claim of innocence. The same tone he had used numerous times when accused of a minor misdemeanour as a child. Back then, she chose to believe him as her judgment was clouded with inexperience and the doting love of a mother. Today she was more experienced and this was no minor misdemeanour. Yet she could not bring herself to believe that he was lying. The pain in her chest was becoming unbearable.

'Then I must believe you, although God may not. I love you, James, but you have disappointed me to an unbearable degree. I want you to leave this house and do not come back while I am still alive.'

James's shock quickly turned to fury. As he stomped from the room, he almost collided with Mr Tallock as he entered the room with a bottle of wine. Bewildered, the butler addressed his mistress.

'Ma'am, is there anything I can do?'

Lady Brockenshaw inhaled slowly before she spoke again. 'Yes, Tallock, there is,' she said, politely, as if all about her was calm. 'Fetch me the doctor. I have a pain in my chest.' She rubbed her breastbone, wincing as a tear trickled down her cheek. 'I do believe my heart is breaking.'

The weeks that followed saw a marked deterioration in Lady Brockenshaw's health. Doctor Barker paid frequent visits, as did her brother, Phillip Fitzwilliam. The staff became aware that an awful rift had formed between their mistress and her son and that he had been banished from the estate. Furthermore they became aware that the reason had something to do with her brother's more frequent visits, his interest in the estate's accounts, and meetings hurriedly arranged with the solicitor and banker in town.

The staff, desperate for more information, soon realised that their only route of finding out what was going on was closed to them. Janey Carhart, who was constantly by her side and privy to Lady Brockenshaw's concerns, had changed. She no longer ate with them or lingered to chat. Her self-imposed isolation was so complete that it was as if she was no longer there.

Although Janey would always remember the details of

the attack, she would not be able to recall the weeks that followed it. It was as if her mind tried to protect her by closing down and shutting out that painful period in her life. She became emotionally numb, unable to believe the events of that sunny autumn afternoon. While birds sang outside, her world had been torn apart in the room that had been her own private safe place. How could this thing happen to her? Had she been responsible, as he had accused her?

Again and again, she replayed the events that had led to the rape. She had to tell herself that she must not let his accusations twist her common sense. She was not responsible for his violence. She did not deserve such degradation, which had left her feeling tainted, worthless and bearing an overwhelming sense of shame. A shame that was so consuming that it affected the way she dressed, the way she carried herself and how she even viewed her own body. She felt the shame so keenly that she was sure anyone she met would see it too and know what had happened to her.

So she isolated herself from the other staff, and ate her meals alone. Mr Tallock grew worried and watched with a fatherly concern over the maid that had become a shadow of her former self. Lady Brockenshaw did not notice Janey's quietness for she too was melancholy. She spent long periods in bed, her swollen ankles a stark sign of her failing heart, each day growing more dependent upon her maid who would rather be anywhere but on the Bosvenna Estate.

The nights were the worst for Janey. She moved her mattress across the floor to block the door so that if anyone should enter her room at night she would be woken. However, she still found it difficult to sleep and, when she did, vivid nightmares threaded in and out of her dreams, causing her to wake in terror. She took to hiding a kitchen knife under her pillow and carrying it in her apron during the day. Whether she could ever bring herself to use it she did not know, but she felt safer with it on her person. When anyone spoke to her she pasted on a smile and tried to act normally, but everyone was aware that something was not right. Her smile was brittle and she looked so very tired.

Only Miss Petherbridge took the change in Janey's behaviour in her stride, accepting her absences at mealtimes and meetings with no more than a smile or a raise of her brow. Mr Tallock wondered if the maid had shared something with the housekeeper that would explain the change in her, yet when questioned Miss Petherbridge told him he was worrying about nothing – as usual.

Eventually, Mr Tallock could take it no longer and invited Janey to the office. He sat down opposite her, spoke to her gently and expressed his concern for her welfare.

Janey watched him through dry eyes and wondered if he could see who she really was now. She was ruined, her future was uncertain and she was damaged for any husband she might have had as no man would want her now. Mr Tallock looked nervous and was sweating and Janey found herself feeling sorry for him. He found this sort of thing so difficult and she didn't want him to suffer. What good would come from telling him the truth? What help could he offer? No one would take her side against a gentleman. So she had reassured him she was well, and with relief, he accepted her answer.

So the weeks that followed saw two women grieving at Bosvenna Manor. They were bonded by their sadness, which, although caused by very different reasons, was connected by a common thread. Lady Brockenshaw grieved for the loss of her husband and son and Janey grieved for the person she once was.

Chapter Thirteen

Torrential rain and gusting winds marked the beginning of November. The heavy showers sent people scurrying through the village streets to seek shelter, dodging the constant streams of water that overflowed from the gullies by the roads. Mary had not been replaced since her departure two months before. This led Mr Tallock and Miss Petherbridge to realise that financial problems may be at the root of the rift between their employers. This did not bode well for the security of their jobs.

Janey continued to isolate herself and had no interest in their gossip as a new realisation had started to dawn on her that she could no longer ignore. It reared its head in the form of nausea that left her violently retching into her chamber pot each morning. She knew she was with child as she was suffering the same symptoms her mother had years before.

Lady Brockenshaw did not suspect. Besides, there were other changes afoot to occupy her mind. She was dying, she confided to Janey, and James had financially ruined them. Her brother was frantically trying to find a way out of the financial mess they were in, however she knew it would prove useless. Janey was not to feel obliged to stay on her account. She gave her a reference that she had privately dictated to Doctor Barker. 'Use it to your advantage,' she had told her, 'and find another position elsewhere.'

Janey took the reference but knew there would be no position for a woman with child. That night she wrote to the only family member she had left, her uncle, to tell him she was with child. She would stop short of telling him it was as a result of rape. The shame at such an admission was still too great.

Hel Tor stood alone on Bodmin Moor. It was majestic, mystical and dominated the surrounding barren landscape, with its long-forgotten Stone Age settlements decaying at its base. It was formed following the Ice Age, which had exposed its granite to wind, ice and water, leaving in its wake smooth-edged granite blocks precariously balanced on top of one another. Yet it had stood for thousands of years and would remain standing for a thousand more. Their strange shapes, as if piled high by some gigantic hand, had a special significance and stood as a reminder of their spiritual and religious pull over the centuries.

Yet it was not a spiritual or religious calling that drew Janey to its heights on that blustery January day. Janey had climbed Hel's Tor to see for herself the place where, if gossip could be believed, unwanted babies were thrown. She paused at the top and looked down into the great natural fissures beneath her.

Her uncle's reply had finally arrived. What should have been her salvation had become a nail in her coffin. His letter was blunt and unfeeling, cursing her for bringing the ultimate shame to his family. He would not, he wrote, from this day forth recognise her and her bastard as members of his family. She must not contact him again.

Her future and that of her illegitimate baby looked bleak. They would be treated as outcasts of society, ostracised and shunned. At her wits' end, Janey had read the coded adverts in the newspaper from the baby farmers. The adverts read innocently enough: 'A widow willing to adopt a baby for a small fee', it usually said. No names, no references, nothing to tie the baby farmer directly to the real meaning behind their message. There was no guarantee what services they were really offering. After the money was paid to a third party, and the baby handed over, the mother would leave hoping her child was about to have a better life, but knowing in her heart of hearts there was a risk the baby may never be seen alive again. Despite her desperation she could not let someone else care for or, at worst, kill her baby. But could she kill it herself?

Janey faced into the wind as it whipped her skirts about her legs. She could see no bottom to the deep fissures that dropped away suddenly from the edge she stood on. She wondered how many bodies lay in their depths, how long they took to die and how much did they suffer. Perhaps if she jumped and ended her own life her death would take the pain away from her baby. No one would miss her, she thought, and she would not have to suffer her demons any more.

A fluttering in her womb, as gentle as butterfly wings, dragged her from her thoughts. Her waist had only just begun to thicken but she had been able to hide it well. Up till that moment she had purposely tried to feel no bond with the creature growing inside her. Yet the fluttering continued, refusing to quieten and be ignored any longer. *I am here*, the fluttering told her. *I am real*.

'Janey?' came a man's voice from behind her. She turned and saw Daniel standing alone against the dark grey sky, watching her.

He had seen the figure on Hel Tor sometime before and was surprised to see it still there when he returned to his fields later that morning. The length of time the person had been standing there against the billowing wind warranted a closer inspection. He realised, as he drew closer, it was a woman and that it was *her*. He had not seen Janey for some months and was shocked at how much she had changed. Her hair, usually so neat, was untidy and loose, the wind whipping up the strands and giving the appearance of angry flames dancing around her head. Her face was pale, with dark circles beneath her eyes and her cheekbones seemed more prominent as if she had lost weight. However, it was her sad expression that caught at his heart and it pained him to see her so changed. He frowned.

'You will fall,' he told her, bluntly, watching the wind buffeting her body as she stood close to the edge. She ignored him and turned to look down into the blackness of the crevices. He tried again. 'What is ailing you? You look unwell.'

'I am well,' she said. 'Leave me be.'

Concerned that she might lose her footing, Daniel came a step closer instead.

'Not until you tell me what brings you to this godforsaken place on a day like this.'

'They say people come here to end their lives. Is that so, Mr Kellow?'

'I have heard it said. What brings *you* here?'

She laughed and he could see that she was on the point of hysteria.

'I have good news for you,' she told him, theatrically. 'You were right all along. He was no gentleman. I have been used and discarded.' She bit her lip and looked away.

'What has Brockenshaw done?' Concerned, Daniel stepped forward again. 'Tell me.'

Janey stepped nearer the edge. 'Leave me be.'

Daniel's steady gaze searched her face. She was troubled and he was sure Brockenshaw was the cause. He had warned him in the dark alleyway in Bodmin to leave her be. Brockenshaw had openly boasted of his conquest of her and now he had left her. She had been *used and discarded* she had said, and he guessed Brockenshaw was the man who had done it. She stood before him looking windswept and broken-hearted, for the loss of the man she loved.

'After bedding you Brockenshaw has ended his relationship with you.' He spoke his name with the hatred he felt for the man.

Janey laughed. 'Indeed he has!' she cried out, as if addressing the barren moorland. Her eyes were wild, as wild as her hair in the gusting wind.

'Did you love him so much?' he asked, angrily.

Janey turned away, unable to look at him.

'Do you think it hurts to die?' she asked, changing the subject and looking down once more to the rocks beneath.

'No more than it does to live,' he replied, approaching her quietly.

'That, Mr Kellow, is a matter of opinion.' She stepped closer, her toes teetering on the edge. 'To live would be to prolong my torture. You warned me and I did not listen.'

'Then listen to me now. Step back or you will fall.' Daniel grew more concerned as she grew more reckless.

'Perhaps that is what I wish!' An unusually strong gust caught at her skirts; it swirled her dress and pulled her away from him, throwing her off balance. His vice-like grip caught her flailing wrist. She would have fallen if he hadn't caught her but he did not bring her to safety, instead he held her at arm's length, teetering on the edge. He pierced her with an angry glare.

'You want to die?' he asked, menacingly.

He saw raw fear in her eyes, but she did not speak. He wanted her to answer. He needed her to answer.

He shook her wrist angrily and asked her again, 'Do you want to die, Janey? Just say the word and I will let you fall.'

The wind buffeted their bodies, but he remained solid as the rock he stood upon.

'You would let me go?' she asked, in disbelief.

'Just say the word and you will find out.'

Her eyes began to glisten as they searched his face and the answer dawned on her.

'I don't want to die,' she whispered. His fingers loosened slightly, although her wrist remained locked inside his grip.

'Shout it to the wind, Janey! I cannot hear you!' he demanded.

'I don't want to die!' she screamed back at him, angrily. The wind snatched her words away but not before he had heard them. He stepped back, pulling her towards him onto more solid ground. She sank to her knees in relief. Shaking she looked up at him.

'You were going to kill me?'

A curve of a smile touched the corner of his mouth. 'No more than I could kill a kitten,' he replied, quietly.

She stood up, brushing her dress down in anger.

'I wouldn't be surprised if you drown a sack full each summer,' she accused him.

'Only if they scratch me with their claws.' He was pleased anger had replaced her melancholy mood, but he was still concerned for her. 'He is not worth your sorrow,' he added, gently.

Janey looked at him. 'Why do you care about my moods?'

'You still have my coat and my chances of having it returned are far less if you are dead.'

She found no joy in his teasing. Her sadness was so great that it still engulfed her. Suddenly he was beside her, wrapping her body in his arms and holding her close He had acted on instinct, but the movement and change in circumstances had been too sudden and took Janey by surprise. Instead of delighting in the embrace, an overwhelming panic seemed to take hold of her. A blood-curdling scream came from deep in her throat and she pushed him roughly away. He stepped back, shocked, his hands in the air in mock surrender.

'No! Don't touch me!' she screamed, before turning and running for her life.

He watched her figure growing smaller as she made her way down Hel Tor and across the moor. The wind pounding her made her journey difficult but it was evident she would rather be anywhere than by his side and in his arms. She had found his touch repulsive. She was broken-hearted for another man and no other, especially Daniel, could replace him. He felt sick with the rejection.

'One day, Janey Carhart,' he shouted after her, 'you'll want me as much as I want you now!' The gusting wind snatched his words away and lost them in the skies above the stony terrain of the moor. And he was glad of it, for showing how much her rejection had hurt him was better kept to himself.

Janey had had a breakthrough. For months she had felt nothing except numbing shame. Now she felt angry. Angry at the world for the treatment she would receive as an unmarried, pregnant woman. Angry that her only option was the workhouse. Angry that she was unable to enjoy Daniel's embrace, but, most of all, angry with James Brockenshaw for raping her. Rape was an ugly word for an ugly deed. Up to that moment she had refused to acknowledge it fully. Now she did and her hatred gave her energy for the first time since the afternoon it had happened.

She ran into her room and looked about her wildly for somewhere to spend it. In a frenzy of madness, she tore at the pages of her romantic etchings, her wildflower bouquet and her bedding, ripping, pummelling and kicking anything within reach until, finally, she fell exhausted to the floor. She stared at the rafters above her as she lay in the midst of all the destruction with the sound of her heartbeat thundering in her ears. She hated James and what he had done to her, but she was going to survive this. She let out a final roar of anger, which sent exhilaration coursing through her veins. It was time to leave for the workhouse, she decided, as her condition would soon be too difficult to conceal. She had no choice. It was a matter of when and what excuse she must use to leave without giving notice. The opportunity came just two days later.

Phillip Fitzwilliam had been with Lady Brockenshaw all morning to the exclusion of any staff. At midday the staff was assembled in the hall in order of rank. He stood before them, observing them gravely whilst contemplating his next words. The staff waited in silence for his announcement.

'As you are aware, Lady Brockenshaw has been unwell for some time,' he said, gravely. 'After much discussion she has agreed to live with me in Falmouth where I can take care of her.' He addressed Mr Tallock. 'Please arrange for her belongings to be placed in trunks. We will depart for Falmouth tomorrow morning.'

'Tomorrow, sir? So soon?'

'There must be no further delay.' He repositioned himself to the top of the line of servants. 'She will not be returning here again. My nephew will be arriving at the end of tomorrow to take over the estate, which will be sold in the not too distant future. If any of you wish to accompany my sister it may be possible to find you positions on my estate. However, I do have a butler, a housekeeper and a cook, so I'm afraid, Mr Tallock, Miss Petherbridge, Mrs Friggens, you will have to find new positions elsewhere.' He then addressed Janey. 'Naturally she desires her maid to accompany her.' Janey did not reply. 'The last year has been eventful and tragic for the family of Bosvenna Estate. I want to thank you all for your loyal support and unwavering sense of duty. Thank you for listening and good day.'

Phillip Fitzwilliam left, leaving the staff shocked, bewildered and waiting for further instruction. Mr Tallock gathered himself and delegated the packing of Lady Brockenshaw's belongings. It gave the staff purpose and they immediately dispersed to their various chores, whilst Janey slipped away to speak to her mistress. Miss Petherbridge remained, still in shock. She had always been afraid her postion would be taken from her, but the threat had come from a completely different opponent than the one she had suspected since Janey's arrival. Lord Brockenshaw was returning to wind up the estate. In a few short weeks her job would come to an end. Her world was tumbling down around her and there was nothing she could do to stop it. She had always prided herself on her ability to remain composed in times of stress, but today her dispassionate nature abandoned her as she felt the warm tears of self-pity run down her cheeks.

'Thank you for your kind offer, ma'am, but I cannot accompany you.'

Lady Brockenshaw turned her head weakly on the pillow to the sound of Janey's voice.

'Why not?'

Janey looked into her unseeing blue eyes. She did not want to cause her worry so she smiled, hoping her smile would add truth to her lies.

'My uncle wishes me to stay close to him. It will suit me very well.'

Lady Brockenshaw smiled and patted her hand, a habit she did more and more.

'If it is what you wish to do then I am happy for you.' She hesitated before adding, 'I have been so worried for you. Will you write to me? I would like to know how your life turns out.'

Janey agreed that she would, and when her employer's eyes finally closed with exhaustion, Janey slipped away to help pack her belongings.

Change and anticipation charged the air as the staff realised that soon they would be scattered far and wide by the events of the day. Lizzy and Charlotte decided to follow Lady Brockenshaw to Falmouth, whereas Mr Tallock voiced plans to retire to Fowey with his wife. Mrs Friggens had always hoped to have her own tea and cake shop and felt now was the time to attempt it. Only Miss Petherbridge did not voice her plans. Her only hope was that her brother and his wife would take her on to keep house for them, their brats and a babe on the way.

The following day Lady Brockenshaw's trunks were piled high in the hall and one by one they were hastily loaded onto waiting coaches. Janey hugged Charlie goodbye before placing him on Lady Brockenshaw's lap, who sat waiting patiently inside the lead coach. Her mistress and her brother departed shortly afterwards, followed by some of the staff, who rode in a third coach.

The house fell silent as Mr Tallock, Miss Petherbridge and Mrs Friggens retired to the servants' hall for a cup of tea and to wait for the arrival of Lord James Brockenshaw. Janey did not join them, despite an invitation from Mr Tallock. Instead she returned to her room, collected her bag and put on Daniel's coat for warmth. She noticed her uncle's scornful letter and grabbed it, as she wanted to leave nothing behind that shared her secret that she was with child. With her bag and her uncle's letter in her hand, Janey descended the main stairs of the house and stepped into the entrance hall. She thrust her chin forward in defiance, breathed in deeply and walked out of Bosvenna Manor through the grand front door, vowing never to return again.

Chapter Fourteen

The morning frost had not thawed by the afternoon so the brown winter grass of the moor crunched beneath Janey's feet. The short winter day made walking to Bodmin before nightfall impossible. Janey was hopeful that Betty, the lady from the village who she had stayed with on the night of her interview, would be kind enough to offer her a bed for one night. Tomorrow she planned to wake early, walk the ten miles to the workhouse and request admission. She followed the stone hedge that skirted Daniel's land, hoping to reduce her journey by using the short cut. She did not notice the black rolling clouds gathering in her wake and threatening to take over the sky above.

The snow fell silently behind her, insidiously gaining pace until it engulfed her lone figure. Large, fluffy flakes of lace fell quietly around her feet, beautiful yet silent, concealing its danger within an innocent façade. Janey stopped to catch her breath and tilted her head back to feel their delicate touch upon her cheeks and lashes. She watched them fall from the sky in infinite numbers, like an army of white butterflies, weightless and gentle. She smiled at her thoughts and set off again, surprised at how quickly a white blanket had formed at her feet.

Several times her foot disappeared in a hidden ditch. Such minor slips became unnerving as the light began to fade early due to the black clouds above. Janey had no choice but to continue on, as to turn back would mean being present when James Brockenshaw returned. The snowfall thickened, reducing her visibility to no more than a few yards. Her hands grew stiff with cold and her stockings and hem became wet from the snow. She continued on, despite feeling tired and increasingly more fearful.

To occupy her mind she thought of the workhouse admission procedure. Her limited knowledge had been gained from piecing together snippets of gossip and tales told to her by other servants over the years. This storytelling was now her reality and she would have to endure it at her destination.

She paused and looked around and with horror realised she had lost the stone hedge. Daniel's hedge – her lifeline – had become swallowed up in the curtain of snow. Everything around her was white, every direction looked the same. She was lost, alone and growing colder by the minute.

Janey trudged on, knowing she must seek shelter if she was to survive the night. Her hands were so cold that she could no longer feel them. She tried to move her stiff, pale fingers, her slowing mind not registering that she no longer had her bag with her. Janey looked about her, her body shaking uncontrollably with the cold. She had lost all sense of direction and time. Her throat and lungs hurt but she was forced to continue on.

Her salvation came in the form of a ruin and to her increasingly befuddled mind it looked vaguely familiar. She came upon it suddenly, without warning, but it was no less welcome. She staggered inside the stone walls of the building on legs that trembled with fear and cold. The partially fallen in roof provided some protection from the snow while its walls gave shelter from the increasing winds. In the corner lay a pile of discarded sacking; though musty smelling with age it offered a covering and meagre warmth against the freezing temperatures. Fighting to save her life and that of her baby, Janey crawled over to it on stiff hands and knees. She lifted up the layers with her useless hands and elbows, and crawled underneath them. Exhausted, she closed her eyes and fell into a deep, deep sleep.

A rhythmical thudding woke her. It was still dark despite the sun's rays threatening to break the night sky. She opened her eyes but her vision was blurred, her mind refused to work and she was unsure where she was. The thudding became louder and she could make out a dark shape of a person running towards her. The noise finally stopped as the figure slid to a halt at her side and the sacking was pulled roughly away from her body exposing her to the cold air and the growing light. She closed her eyes, unable to tolerate the harshness of reality. Daniel's coat was stripped from her and she feared she was being robbed. Her body started to shake uncontrollably. She had learnt how her life would end, a wisdom she did not wish to have.

Suddenly her arms were threaded through the sleeves of a thicker coat that still exuded warmth from the previous wearer. It wrapped around her like a comforting hug and instantly provided the warmth that the other coat did not. She tried to open her eyes but she could not. She tried to speak but only a jumbled moan escaped her lips. She felt her hands wrapped in something warm and a scarf tenderly placed around her head and as she was lifted away from the sacking, the tension in her muscles flowed away too. She put her arm around her rescuer's broad shoulders and buried her cheek into the crook of his neck. Her thoughts remained slowed, her thinking confused, but there was one thing she was sure of. She was still able to recognise the smell of sandalwood and knew whose arms carried her now.

The snow had caught everyone by surprise. Within an hour of the first flakes falling from the sky, the village of Trehale was in chaos. Sited on the side of a hill, the granite cottages hugged narrow roads that threaded their way down its sloping gradient. A combination of snow and ice soon made the road treacherous and local inhabitants knew not to venture into the village by horse in such weather. The snowfall, however, had been so quick and heavy that on this occasion horses pulling traps and wagons entering and leaving the village soon found themselves stuck halfway up the hill. The build up of traffic and noise, together with fretful horses slipping on the icy road and their drivers shouting for control of their beasts as they vied for space, brought the village women to stand at their gates and watch the mayhem unfolding before their eyes.

Daniel watched the pandemonium from the top of the hill. He shook his head in disbelief at the men's ineffectual efforts before setting off down the hill to help. On seeing Daniel's approach the men allowed him to take the lead as they knew he had a way with horses that was rarely seen in others. As expected the horses responded to Daniel's air of confidence and gentle coaxing more readily than the shouting and slapping they had been receiving up to now. One by one he led the horses to safety while the men pushed the wagons and traps from behind. Within the hour the road had been cleared.

The only signs of gratitude he received were a few curt nods. Daniel expected no more. He knew what the villagers thought of him. The snow continued to fall heavily and as Daniel trudged his way back up the hill towards home, a man fell into step beside him. It was Little Billy Bray.

'Idiots, the lot of 'em. There's always some bugger getting caught out on that road in winter. Not usually that many though.'

'It won't be the last time,' replied Daniel, pulling his collar up around his neck.

The men walked in companionable silence for some moments and although Daniel was content not to speak Little Billy was not. Little Billy liked nothing more than to gossip and there was something he wanted to talk about. He could stand it no longer.

'Some goings on up at the estate,' he stated. To his frustration Daniel kept his silence.

'Three carriages loaded up to the 'eavens! Three I tell you! Three! Seen 'em with me own eyes.' He stole a glance at Daniel to gauge his reaction but Daniel continued to stare straight ahead. 'Course it was before the snow started. Piqued my interest it did, seeing 'em 'eading out of the estate. Like rats leaving a sinking ship.'

He waited for Daniel to ask more about it and when he didn't his frustration bubbled over. 'God damn it, boy, aren't you interested to 'ear what's 'appened with your lady friend?'

The truth of it was Daniel did want to know. He wanted to know so badly it felt like an addiction. No sane man should feel the way he felt right now, listening acutely to every word the man said, yet trying to appear that he did not care. Janey had made it plain on their last meeting that she preferred someone else. Not for the first time he said the words he often said to himself.

'She means nothing to me.'

Little Billy bristled.

'Rubbish! Remember I saw you with me own eyes. I saw you lying together by the river kissing.'

Daniel stopped and turned to him.

'We made a deal. You were never to mention that to anyone or I would—'

'And I 'aven't.' Little Billy crossed himself. 'So 'elp me Lord, I 'aven't, but not 'cos of your threats. She's a nice maid. Always says 'ello and passes the time of day. She ain't stand-offish like some.'

Daniel glared at him and continued walking, quickening his step hoping to leave Little Billy behind. Little Billy quickened his step too and Daniel realised he wasn't going to get rid of him quite so easily.

Finally, he said, 'So what was going on at Bosvenna?'

The old man smiled. 'Seems like Lady Brockenshaw 'as up and left to live with 'er brother in Falmouth and took most of the staff with 'er. Only the snooty 'ousekeeper, butler and Mrs Friggens are left behind. Apparently the son is coming 'ome but they don't think the estate is going to be owned by the Brockenshaw family for much longer.'

'You seem to know a lot.'

'Well I was planning to deliver some wood and thought I would drive over and arrange it.'

Daniel raised an eyebrow at him.

'I bet you did, and found out all you could at the same time.'

'I keep my ear to the ground, there's no shame in that.'

'That is a matter of opinion.' They trudged on. Soon Daniel would reach the lane to his farm and they would part company. Daniel wanted to be alone as he had just heard that Janey had gone.

Falmouth was more than forty miles away and any chance of seeing her, whether by arrangement or accident, was now non-existent. Suddenly she was out of his life with no chance to say goodbye or part on good terms. If Little Billy had not told him he would still not know. He had shared only one kiss with her. One passionate, beautiful kiss where for one moment in time their feelings and intentions met and fitted together to make a whole. Before and after that kiss their coming together had been twisted by arguments, threats and jealousy. Yet he had always felt that their kiss symbolised what they had truly meant to each other and a promise of what could be. What a fool he had been. She had gone, without a backward glance or a farewell. Well, she could go to hell for all he cared.

'... and then the snow started and I've been worried ever since.' Little Billy's words brought him back to reality.

'What did you say?'

'The snow started and you know 'ow difficult it is to make 'ead or tail of the moors in the snow,' said the little man.

Daniel was confused. 'What are you talking about?' he asked. 'You said they left by coach.'

'Not the maid. She went to stay with 'er uncle. Cut across the moors by Curnow Downs. Saw 'er in the distance as I arrived and asked the butler about 'er.'

Daniel's steps slowed. 'She didn't go to Falmouth?'

Little Billy shook his head.

'If she was walking over Curnow, how did you know it was her? You must have good eyesight.'

Little Billy tapped his nose. 'I know it was 'er,' he said. 'She was wearing your coat. The one you gave 'er after she fell in the river. Stake my life on it.'

'But it's snowing,' Daniel said, stating the obvious.

'She probably reached the village and is staying with someone for the night. All the same, when the snow comes it changes everything and many a good man 'as got lost on the moor in weather like this.' They reached the entrance to Daniel's lane. 'Thought she might 'ave visited you when the snow started.'

Daniel glared at him. 'So you thought you would find out if I knew any more gossip of the goings on at the estate.' Little Billy for once looked ashamed. 'Well, I don't. She hasn't called in to see me and I know no more than you told me.'

They looked across to the moor now covered in a thick blanket of snow. There was not a soul in sight.

'Well, I'm sure she is fine. She 'as got to know a few people in the village now. No doubt she's tucked up nice and cosy by some fireside waiting for the morning,' said Little Billy, trying to reassure himself. 'I'd best be off.' He thrust his hands in his pockets, nodded farewell and went in the direction of his own house.

Daniel watched Little Billy disappear behind a curtain of snow before heading for home himself, with the old man's tale playing around inside his head.

He tried in vain to forget about what Little Billy had told him. After all he had no idea of the direction Janey had been heading. He wasn't entirely convinced she was planning on visiting her uncle; after all, he had rejected her as a child when she needed him most, so why would she go to him now? The light was already fading and he told himself she had probably sought shelter as soon as the snow started to fall. It would be futile to walk the moors in a vain chance of finding her, especially as there was no reason to think she was even lost. However, despite his common sense telling him to forget about her and get some sleep, he could not.

By midnight he was pacing the floor unable to settle. The snowfall, gentle at the start, had turned into a blizzard and finally blown itself out. Daniel pulled back the curtain to look out. The grey clouds were now gone leaving a clear, star speckled sky above. Not even knowing for sure if Janey was in any danger, Daniel wrestled with the idea of looking for her. A hunter's moon lit up the night with its light and it helped Daniel make up his mind. He grabbed a coat and an oil lamp and went out with the aim of bringing her home.

He had been walking for several hours before he noticed what appeared to be a bent branch sticking out of the snow. His oil lamp had long gone out but dawn was breaking and by chance he saw it in the distance, its smooth curvature catching his attention. On closer inspection it was a leather handle and, as Daniel lifted it, a woman's carpet bag, containing a meagre amount of clothing and belongings, broke free from the snow that had covered it. He had no doubt it was Janey's. Looking around he noticed slight indentations in the snow of earlier footprints. Remembering in which hand she had carried her basket when they met in the village, he realised she must be right handed. Hoping she had carried her carpet bag in her right hand the footprints suggested she had walked northwards. Although faint, he could see the tracks wavered in their direction, hinting at Janey's confusion, however the tracks also gave him hope. He knew that not far off was the tumbled down building he had found her in with Brockenshaw months ago; if she had found it she may still be alive. If she had not found shelter he feared it would be her dead body he would discover, for he knew with a certainty he had not felt before that she had passed this way and was on the moor somewhere.

Janey slowly opened her eyes to find herself sitting in a large, soft chair, with a blanket tucked snugly about her body. Before her was a comforting fire and on an iron trivet bubbled a pan of fragrant stew. She looked around at her surroundings. It was a cottage. Large slabs of slate formed a floor whilst curved wooden beams split along the grain lined the ceiling. In the far corner, lit by the light from the fire and an old oil lamp, sat an old woman darning a sock as she watched her.

For some minutes they stared at each other, neither speaking, the stabbing of the needle and the pulling of the thread the only sound in the room. The woman was old and hunched, with a weather-beaten face, a large hook nose and a scowl that showed her suspicion of the new woman in the house.

Finally Janey spoke. 'Where am I?' she asked, surprised at the weakness of her voice that was barely louder than a whisper.

'Daniel Kellow's 'ouse.' Janey's eyes widened. 'Scared are

yea?' asked the old woman, biting her thread in two with the few brown misshapen teeth she had left. 'You should be. 'E's some mazed with yea.'

She set her sewing aside, pushed herself to standing and hobbled over to the bubbling stew. She gave it a brisk stir, tapped the spoon on the pan's edge and set it aside, grumbling away to herself in what Janey supposed to be the Cornish language. Janey did not understand her, as it was rarely used now and she was too tired to care. Gradually she drifted off to sleep to the old woman's lyrical tones. For the first time in months her dreams were no longer tormented by nightmares and she fell into a fitful sleep.

Janey heard his voice first. It coaxed her from her dreams to find Daniel standing in front of her. He looked tired – and he looked angry.

'Edna says you've not eaten.'

Janey felt small next to his tall body that radiated strength. She repositioned herself in the chair to look up at him.

'I'm not hungry.' It was true; she had no appetite and felt sick at the thought.

'I don't care. You must eat.'

'I really don't feel like any—'

He pulled her to her feet.

'I don't care what you feel like. You've got to eat.' Taking her by the shoulders he roughly guided her to a chair at the table and sat her down.

'I'm not hungry, Daniel,' she protested.

He ignored her and signalled to Edna to bring over some stew. The old woman hobbled over with two laden plates and carefully placed one before him. She shoved the other toward Janey.

Janey smiled, not wanting him to discover the full extent that her life was falling apart.

'Thank you for finding me and taking care of me, but I really don't feel like eating.'

Daniel did not return her smile.

'You don't have a choice,' he said, picking up a fork and pinning her with a stare. 'Now eat.' Janey pushed the plate away. 'Eat,' Daniel repeated, barely controlling his anger.

Edna's beady eyes darted from one to the other.

'I don't feel like eating,' said Janey, her anger beginning to build. To her surprise Daniel casually dropped his fork.

'Well, if you don't eat, I won't either,' he retorted. The old woman beside them gasped.

'You've got to eat, boy. You put in a full day's work, seven days a week to keep this farm going. You can't do that on air and water alone.' She turned angrily to Janey and pointed a knurled finger at her. 'See what you've done! People depend on Daniel. 'E's a working man, 'e needs 'is food!' In her anger she reverted back to her Cornish language, spewing forth a string of words some of which sounded like insults and curses.

Daniel sat back with his arms folded, amusement glinting in his eyes as he watched Edna bombard Janey until she could stand it no more and conceded.

'All right, I will eat something.' She lifted a fork in annoyance and waved it at Daniel. 'Go on, you eat something too.'

He picked up his fork again. 'I'll eat when you do.'

They glared at one another, each holding a fork with two plates of stew steaming before them, and an old woman standing over them. Daniel took his fork and speared a cube of meat. He lifted it up between them and turned it in the light but instead of placing it in his own mouth he held it to her lips. Edna gave a toothless grin at the spectacle.

'Eat,' he ordered. She kept her mouth closed so he touched her lips with the meat, its gravy marking her lips, inviting her to lick them clean. 'Eat,' he said, more gently.

She hesitated for a second then opened her mouth and took the food. He watched, captivated, as she slid the tender mutton from the fork and ate it, finishing with a lick of her lips. It had been a long time since she had eaten a hot meal and it surprised her to find its taste made her aware of the hunger growing in her belly. Since her attack she had had no appetite and the less she ate the less she wanted. Now, tasting the meaty gravy and feeling the tenderness of the braised mutton, it awakened a desire for more. Yet Daniel had not eaten for some time and she wanted him to now join her. A silence filled the room; even Edna had become quiet. Janey lifted her fork, stabbed a piece of meat and held it out to him.

'Now you.'

He grabbed her wrist and glared at her, annoyed she had taken to imitating him, however he only saw sincerity in her eyes. He loosened his grip slightly and brought the fork she held in her hand to his mouth. Opening his lips he slid the mutton from the fork as Janey felt herself blushing as she watched his mouth move. The old woman broke into their thoughts.

'That's enough you two!' she admonished them. 'It's unseemly behaviour! Eat your own food an' be done with it or I will give yea both a clout behind the ears. Never in me life 'ave I seen a man an' woman behave in such a way,' she grumbled. 'No better than childers!'

She hobbled back to her seat, picked up her mending and returned to her sewing, her beady eyes darting between them as she sewed. Janey did as she was told and ate the rest of her stew in silence, as did Daniel. They occasionally glanced up at one another, then looked away. Janey felt a spark in the air and it wasn't coming from the fire.

The rape, and the months that followed, had left their mark

on Janey, not only by the child growing in her womb but the night terrors she had endured which exhausted her. It had become a life of contradictions. She had existed but not lived, living on her nerves yet with her emotions frozen and with her deep shame forever present in her mind. Yet for the first time since that awful afternoon, with her belly full of food and a warming fire beside her, she fell into a deep sleep.

Daniel's voice, for once tender, woke her for a second time. She listened to his voice as he spoke to Edna in the next room. It intrigued her to hear him as their conversation resembled that of an adult son taking care of his stubborn mother. She smiled as she listened, comfortable and warm by the now dying fire.

'You need a new coat, old woman,' he said, with affection.

Edna argued back. 'This coat is just fine. Don't you go bothering about me, boy.'

'But it's so old. Let me buy you a new one.'

Edna would have none of it. 'Pah! This 'ere coat will see me out, an' you too, no doubt. Stop your fussing, boy, an' take me 'ome.'

'I'm going to buy you a new one anyway.'

'Don't waste your money. I won't wear it.'

Janey could hear Daniel's soft laughter as he left the house. The old woman appeared at the door, dressed in an old worn coat and a scarf wrapped around her head.

'There's a bed made up for 'e in the room at the top of the stairs.' She flicked her eyes upwards indicating its location. 'Best sleep in a bed tonight or you'll be stiff as my knees in the morning.'

The realisation that she was going to be alone in the house with Daniel suddenly frightened Janey.

'You are leaving me?'

Edna turned to go and for a moment took pity on her.

'You've nothing to fear from Daniel. 'E's already put a lock on your door so you will feel safe.'

She was gone before Janey could argue and soon her grumbling voice, mixed with Daniel's sombre tones, grew quieter as the horse and trap carried them away. For a few moments Janey did not move. She had been in service since the age of thirteen and had never been on her own in a house. She had often felt lonely but there was always a servant somewhere within the walls. In this homely farmhouse she felt like an outsider and was alone, yet strangely not lonely. Apart from the room she sat in and the time when the old woman had shown her the water closet, Janey had not seen the rest of the house. She had spent so much of the day sleeping that she didn't even know where to fetch water for a drink. She had never felt so helpless or without a routine of chores to mark her day.

The fire still glowed but the flames were much lower now. As she watched the fire she realised she didn't even know whether to feed it or let it go out. Daniel's routine was unknown to her, as was his life here. She stretched out her stiff legs from underneath her and moved her ankles, testing their flexibility and, finding them satisfactory, she stood up. The room she had spent her time in was typical for a worker's cottage. At one end stood the granite fireplace with its clone oven for baking built into the side of the chimney, chairs positioned around it, at the other end a large table for preparing food and eating. The curtains were dull and in need of a wash to freshen them and their wooden frames were dusty. The windows were set deep in the two-foot thick granite walls, providing slated covered sills to sit upon. Despite the fading light Janey could see the garden outside. It was slowly emerging from the melting, crisp white snow, but despite the neat path which led up to the front door, the garden itself was neglected and in need of flowers and shrubs to bring it to life. Janey could see it transform in her mind, bursting with colour of flowers that she would plant if the garden were hers. She turned away and left the room to explore further. There was no point in her imagining such things, tomorrow she would leave for the workhouse.

To her surprise the second room she entered was a large kitchen, making her initial assumption that the farmhouse was like any other traditional worker's cottage quite wrong. At the far end was a black Cornish range; new and untouched, it provided a focal point in the room. Janey couldn't help running her fingers across the front, its coldness evidence that Edna preferred to use the method of trivet and cooking pot than a wood burning range. It seemed such a waste that the beautiful range was not brought to life with heat and the smells of pies and casseroles cooking in its belly, while a kettle boiled on its top. In fact, the whole kitchen looked newly built and equipped, waiting for the woman of the house to make use of it, and it seemed all the more sad that the old woman did not seem to appreciate its qualities. It had a large pantry but the shelves were bare of preserves that should have been made in the autumn to last the winter. It seemed that Edna came to make a meal and mend but the planning and running of the home fell to Daniel, who was too busy working the land.

Janey found the stairs, which led to the first and only landing. The walls of the farmhouse were bare of pictures and lacked the knick-knacks that make a house a home. She easily found the room assigned to her as it had her carpet bag placed at the foot of the bed and was the only room with a bolt. However she did not enter it but passed it by to look at the other rooms on the landing while she was alone to do so.

There was another bedroom similar in size to hers and

then, at the far end, was Daniel's. The door was ajar; she stood at the threshold with no plans to enter it but only to observe. His bed was unmade and boots lay untidily on the floor. It lacked any feminine presence, was basic and needed airing. The curtains were half drawn and a shirt had slipped onto the floor from a chair. Without thinking she entered the room and picked it up, folding it and laying it back over the chair it had fallen from. She opened the curtains and looked down on the snow covered garden beneath her and noticed for the first time a vegetable patch to the side. Neatly dug, the garden lay waiting for spring and a selection of seeds to be sown in its rich soil. It did not surprise her to learn that Daniel grew his own vegetables, most people did in the village and he was a farmer after all. She dragged her eyes away and saw the view from the bedroom window for the first time. Beyond the hedge that shielded the house from the moorland weather was the snow covered moor itself. It spread out like a white carpet for miles ahead and as the sun set in the west it cast a red fiery glow across the sky. The silhouette of a flock of birds flew across the dramatic red backdrop and Janey marvelled at the sight. The scene was beautiful and breathtaking all at the same time and Janey felt she could happily sit on the sill for the remainder of the day and watch until the sun disappeared below the horizon. She abruptly stood up from the sill she had unconsciously sat down on. She could not linger in this room, she thought, Daniel would soon be back.

She smelt the familiar smell that she had come to associate with him and turned to see his washstand and a bar of sandalwood soap in the dish. She was about to reach for it when a white figure caught her eye as it passed the doorway. It made her jump with surprise and set her heart racing as she listened to light footsteps running along the corridor and down the stairs.

Gathering her courage Janey followed to see who had been watching her but despite her best efforts the ghostly figure had disappeared and the house was empty. Her heart still beating loudly in her chest, she returned to her room and was relieved when she finally heard Daniel return and his heavy booted footsteps on the slate floor below. She sat and waited, listening to his foot tread enter each room until he finally climbed the stairs.

'I'm back,' he said, simply, as he paused at her door. He still wore his boots, which were dusted with snow that had already started to melt, forming a puddle on the floor. 'Do you like what you see?' His hair was ruffled from the wind outside and he still wore his outside coat, turned up at the collar. His eyes were black as coal and his dark brows were knitted together in a serious frown.

'The room?' she asked.

'The house,' he answered.

'It's very nice,' she replied, unsure why he should care what she thought.

He was silent for a moment, then nodded, satisfied.

'Bolt your door,' he said, abruptly. 'I know what they say about me in the village and while we are alone I don't want you to worry unnecessarily. It's not good for you, you need your rest.'

Suddenly he was gone and Janey was left alone once more. She closed the door and quietly slid the bolt across, but it wasn't Daniel that made her fingers tremble. The figure she had seen earlier had shaken her, yet Daniel had said they were alone. The figure was, she felt sure, of a young girl no older than ten or twelve. She had disappeared into thin air as silently as she had appeared, just like an apparition. The figure, which looked just like herself as a child, haunted her mind until she fell into a deep sleep.

Chapter Fifteen

Janey woke with a start. She lay for some moments not sure if the laughter she had heard was in her dreams or from the room downstairs. The house was silent, broken only by bird song from outside the window. The position of the sun told her she had slept late. She washed and dressed, pausing only briefly to observe the swollen curve of her belly in the mirror before disguising it with a shawl around her waist. It seemed, as a result of rest and good food, that her body had finally relaxed and showed her pregnant state.

She packed her belongings as she planned to leave today. She wanted to be gone before her shameful secret was out and Daniel learned of her fallen state. Through habit she finally twisted her hair in order to pin it up, a style she had used ever since entering service. She halted in the act to view herself in the mirror. Today was the first time since she was thirteen she was no longer a servant. For once in her life she could wear her hair as she wanted and wear what she wanted. Yet this independence had come at a price. She let her hair fall from her fingers to lay loose about her shoulders, got up and made her way downstairs.

The house was empty, yet evidence of its recent occupation was everywhere. A basket of freshly collected eggs lay on the table, recently washed plates and mugs lay drying on the drainer and the smell of a cooked breakfast hung in the air. She felt like an uninvited guest walking through the remnants of a now extinguished party and she wished she had woken earlier and been part of it. She had not wanted to mix with company in recent times and the feeling of wanting to seek company surprised her.

Edna arrived at the house. She took off her coat, hung

it on a hook and made her way over to the basket of eggs. Ignoring Janey, she proceeded to clean each egg with care as she mumbled to herself in Cornish. Janey watched her knurled hands work with the speed of experience, turning each egg and wiping the shell with water and soap before placing each one on a cloth to dry.

'I will be leaving today,' Janey said, gently.

Edna abandoned the eggs, cut some bread and spread it with butter and jam, and dropped it on a plate before her. 'You'd better eat something then,' she muttered, returning to her work. 'Don't want you to be taken ill before you 'ave a chance to be off.'

The old woman had made her position plain. Janey was not wanted at the farm.

Some time later Janey carried her bag down the stairs and placed it on the floor. Edna avoided her eye contact, preferring to busy herself with making bread. The woman may not want to exchange words, thought Janey, but she owed it to Daniel to thank him for his help and to tell him she was leaving.

'I am ready to take my leave,' Janey told her. 'I would like to speak to Daniel before I go.'

The woman stopped her kneading. 'Tell me what you want to say and I will tell 'im,' said Edna, craning her head up from her rounded stiff neck.

'I thank you for the offer, but I would like to say goodbye to him.'

The old woman continued to knead.

'I want to speak to Daniel,' she said again. 'Where is he?'

'He's here,' came a voice from behind her. Daniel stood in the open doorway staring at her carpet bag on the floor.

'I am leaving.'

'So I see,' he said, lifting his dark brown eyes to meet hers.

'I want to thank you for your help and hospitality,' she continued, keen for him to know she was not intending to leave without speaking to him. 'I do not wish to outstay my welcome.'

'You have somewhere to go?'

'Yes, thank you.'

'Where?'

She did not wish to lie to him but she felt she had no choice.

'I ... I ... have a position as a governess in North Cornwall. I plan to catch the train at Bodmin.'

'With who?'

'A middle class family.'

'A family with no name?'

'A family that wishes to remain discreet,' she countered. He studied her as if waiting for her to speak more but she held her silence.

'Discretion is important to you?'

'Yes, of course.'

He seemed to consider her words for some moments. She wondered if he was forming an argument that she might stay.

'I'll take you,' he said, abruptly, before leaving to hitch up the horse and trap. The two women watched him go before Edna let out a chuckle.

'Seems 'e's even more keen to get rid of you than I am,' she said, before returning to her dough.

Remnants of the heavy blizzard still lingered in places in the form of muddied white patches of crystallised snow. The wooden wheels of Daniel's cart sliced through the discoloured slush and stones in the road, which had been churned up when the main snowfall had melted. However, thankfully, Daniel took great care to drive at a steady pace, reducing the amount of jarring her body was subjected to. Neither spoke, both deep in their thoughts. Finally, Daniel pulled on the reins and brought the horse and cart to a standstill by the side of the road. He looked across the countryside to the granite built farmstead in the distance.

'Boscarn Farm,' he said, half to himself and half to her. She followed his gaze and saw his home nestled amongst the trees and sheltered from the moorland winds. To the right spread lush green pastures, on the left the barren landscape of the moor.

'You are very lucky to have such a lovely place. I'm sorry I did not stay to see more of it.' She realised as she spoke how true it was. They sat in silence for some moments before he spoke again.

'Discretion is important to you. Is that why you are leaving today?'

Fear that she had been found out pricked at her skin. 'I don't know what you mean,' she replied, quietly.

'I think you do.'

He took something out of his pocket, spread it out on his leg with purposeful movements and gave it to her. She did not need to read the letter to know what it said, as her uncle's hateful words screamed out at her in black ink.

'You had it clutched in your hand when I found you. I have not told anyone.' Janey took it. 'Is it *his*?' he asked. She nodded, unable to speak. 'I told you there was no future with him.' He stared into the distance. 'Were you making plans to get rid of it that day on Hel Tor?'

'Please, Daniel, I don't want to talk about it.'

'I knew something was wrong, but not this.'

'It is not your problem. Please take me to Bodmin.'

'To the workhouse?' he asked. She nodded and he swore. 'Do you have any idea what it's like in there?'

She shook her head. 'Not really, I have heard some things.'

'I do. I've spent time in one. It's no life for a baby. The stench of the workhouse sticks to you and taints the rest of your life.'

'I have no choice. You did all right.'

He sat silently for a moment then began to speak. 'My mother was a whore. I never knew my father. I was born in a workhouse and spent my childhood in and out of them. One day I was found eating rubbish by our landlord. My mother had run off and left me to starve. I never saw her again or wanted to. He threw me out into the street and that's where I lived amongst the tramps and prostitutes of Tudor Street. When I was ten I was caught thieving a loaf of bread. I had not eaten in three days. I was sentenced to hard labour for a year and then to a reformatory. The place was meant to make me a law-abiding citizen but life there was brutal. I survived despite them, not because of them.'

He had not taken his eyes off Boscarn Farm and Janey began to realise just how important having his own home was to him.

'One day a caretaker asked me my name. When I told him it was Kellow he made a passing remark that it was Cornish. I had a vain hope I would find family in Cornwall so the next day I ran away and came here.' Daniel dragged his eyes from the farm and looked down at the reins in his hands. 'It was a foolish dream,' he said, marking the leather with a nail. 'There was no blood kin waiting for me.' He lifted his gaze to find Janey looking at him. 'I lived on my wits and by stealing.'

Her heart went out to him. She wanted to offer sympathy, understanding – something –but words failed her while his eyes were upon her. He looked away and the moment was gone. 'One day Zachariah caught me stealing his eggs. His wife, Amy, took pity on me so they offered me work and a home. I became part of their family. They must have seen some good in me.' His dark brows furrowed. 'Not everyone does, Janey.'

A sad smile curved his lips as he watched the horizon. 'Amy told me that her own mother had a dubious past. Her mother's parents and brothers were all thieves, so it was hardly surprising. Yet she told me that she knew of no other woman who showed such courage, loyalty and love despite her being a thief's daughter. It taught Amy to believe that there was good in all people, no matter their past. I am the man I am now because Zachariah and Amy took me in and provided me with a home.'

He had not spoken so much at one time before, which made his words all the more important to hear.

'They sound like a wonderful couple,' said Janey.

The smile faded from Daniel's lips as he turned to her. 'Up to that point my life had been tainted by the start in life I had. My mother's drinking and whoring, my father not wanting to know the child he had. I paid for the sins of my parents and I kept paying. When I met Zachariah and Amy, my life began again.'

He took the letter from her hands to look at her uncle's writing. He pointed to the words *bastard*, *workhouse*, *slut*. 'It's starting again with your baby,' he said. 'Your baby's life is already tainted by its parents' deeds. Old sins cast long shadows, Janey. An illegitimate baby carries the burden of its parents' actions for life.'

The words blurred before her eyes. She knew in the society they lived that he spoke the truth.

'I have no choice,' she whispered.

'Yes, you do,' he replied and turned to look at her. 'I'll marry you. I'll give your baby my name and both of you a home. No one need ever know the child's his. No one must ever know the child is his.'

'I couldn't let you do that,' said Janey. He ignored her.

'I will provide you and the baby with a good home, but I expect the marriage to be a complete one. I have no one in the world I can call a relative. One day I want a child in my arms with my blood rushing through its veins. I want to be able to look into its eyes and see my kin. Do you understand what I say?'

She nodded but shook inwardly. Only four months before she had been brutally raped. Would she ever be able to lie with a man again and not think of that day?

'So what do you say?'

Her baby moved inside her.

'You will give us your name and bring my child up as if he was your own?'

Daniel clenched his jaw and stared off to the distance once more.

'Brockenshaw's child?' she goaded. She hated saying his name but she would rather give birth to her child in a workhouse than risk a life of brutality and cruelty by a man who calls himself father but despises the child.

'It is not the baby's fault who its father is. I will be the child's father in all ways. It will not know any difference between my own blood kin.' He turned to her with narrowed eyes. 'So what say you? Will you be my wife?'

Janey searched his eyes for some tenderness, some hint that he could love her, but in that moment there was none. Instead she saw a steely determination that what he had suggested was the right thing to do. She lifted her chin.

'I will marry you, Daniel Kellow,' she said, 'and I thank you for giving my baby a name.'

He turned the horse and cart back to the village.

'From now on it's *our* baby,' he said, snapping the reins.

'Where are we going?' she asked, holding on tightly to the seat as the wagon turned in the road, riding the bank as it did so.

'To the vicarage,' he said as the cart lurched forward. 'We have a wedding to arrange.'

Reverend William Smith had had a torturous morning. He had just conducted the funeral of Boxer Bull Edwards and it would be one that he was unlikely to forget. Boxer Bull Edwards was a brute and a bully. He was built as wide as he was tall, with fists the size of cabbages and knuckles as hard as stone. He got his nickname from his readiness to use his fists and his unpredictable temper which he meted out to anyone that crossed his path or dared catch his eye. No one called him friend and he had liked it that way; it was a life he chose and a life he forced on the woman he married.

For thirty years the villagers watched his pretty wife fade before their eyes to become a nervy, timid, skinny woman, aged beyond her years and regularly sporting a black eye or cracked rib. His domination isolated her from her family and friends and she was rarely seen except running his errands and tending to his needs in a cowering subservient manner. She rarely spoke as her brutish husband, after years of insults, convinced her she had nothing of importance to say. Reverend Smith's heart went out to her as she sat in the pew silent and in shock, terrified how she would cope without the man who had convinced her she was nothing without him. In time she would begin to bloom again but for now she was petrified at what the future might hold.

The rest of the congregation was made up of three other people. Widow Blewett sat at the back and attended every funeral in the village and even travelled to nearby villages to attend theirs 'if the pickings were scant' in Trehale. She did not need to know the departed, or even like them; it was more of a macabre hobby and started the day she attended her mother's funeral as a child. She often said she would be sitting in the back pew at her own funeral and the reverend was to make sure that her seat was not taken or she would be most upset.

The other couple sat slightly bemused that they found themselves attending a funeral at all. They had visited the reverend that morning to discuss their baby's baptism. Newly moved into the village, they were strangers, and the vicar had cajoled them into attending to make up the numbers. Fearing they might upset him, they had agreed. However, to find themselves the main mourners at a funeral of someone they didn't know took them by surprise, if not the wife of the deceased. They were too polite to say anything and acted along with the façade that Boxer Bull Edwards had meant something to them as the newly widowed Mrs Edwards thanked them for coming. As the funeral came to a close they left the church much quicker than they had entered it an hour before.

Reverend Smith took a sip of his flask before stepping out into the cemetery. To his surprise, Daniel Kellow, head down and feet crunching on the frozen patches of snow that still remained despite a part thaw, was walking determinedly towards him and in his wake walked his opposite – pretty, God-fearing, well-mannered Janey Carhart.

'Good morning, Daniel, Janey. This is a surprise.'

Daniel, in his haste, ignored the greeting. 'We want to get married, reverend.' The vicar did not hide his surprise. 'Today,' Daniel added.

'Good morning, reverend,' Janey replied, a little embarrassed at Daniel's behaviour.

The reverend gave a little chuckle as he turned to lock the old oak door of the church.

'Not today, Daniel. There's a procedure to go through.' He smiled at Janey. 'Good morning, my dear.'

Daniel would not be put off. 'What procedure?' he asked, impatiently.

'Well, the banns need to be called for three Sundays prior to the marriage date to see if anyone has reason to raise any legal impediment to the marriage. So the soonest you would be able to get married is in three weeks' time.'

'Then see to it.'

The vicar gave him a look before making his way down the church path, Daniel at his side and Janey following a step behind.

'And I need to be satisfied that you both understand the commitment you are about to make. Marriage is a sacred union before God and must be taken seriously.'

'We understand,' said Daniel, impatiently.

The vicar was not convinced. The last time he had seen Daniel he had turned his back on the girl; in fact he wasn't even aware they were courting. He told him so.

Daniel brushed his concerns aside. 'What do we need to do to convince you we want to be married?'

'I don't doubt *your* desire, Daniel,' said the vicar, but there was something beginning to trouble him. He had remembered Janey seeking him out for advice many months ago. She had told him that someone was trying to pressure her and confuse her thinking. He began to wonder if it was Daniel she had spoken of. He had just spent the last hour in the company of a woman who had become a shadow of her former self due to her overbearing husband. He did not want Janey to follow in her footsteps. He looked at Janey who stood behind Daniel's shoulder and felt a sudden desire to speak with her alone.

'Janey, take a walk with me around the church grounds,' he said. He looked at Daniel. 'Alone,' he added, pointedly.

They walked along the path in a companionable silence, while Daniel waited reluctantly by an oak tree, his hands thrust in his pockets and his collar turned up against the cold. He watched them with a worried frown.

'I have not seen you at church lately, Janey,' said the vicar.

'Lady Brockenshaw has been ill so I was required to attend to her.'

'If you marry you will be leaving your post?'

'Lady Brockenshaw left Bosvenna Manor to live with her brother a few days ago. His estate is in Falmouth.'

'And you stayed to be with Daniel?' Janey did not reply. 'How well do you know Daniel?'

'I know of his background.' She did not tell him she had only learnt of it on the ride to the church.

'I feel it is my duty to ensure you know of the rumours about him.'

'I know something of them.'

'But not all? Let me tell you so you are fully aware of the marriage you may be entering into. The rumours remain and, as his wife, you will have to live with them too.'

They stopped and turned to see Daniel watching them. In that moment she realised that he was aware of what she was about to be told. She wasn't sure if she wanted to hear yet she knew, for the sake of her baby, she must listen to what the vicar had to say.

'Daniel was eighteen when Zachariah died. He was found lying on the ground outside the house, the back of his skull was caved in and a hammer lay by his side covered in blood. Daniel said he had fallen from a ladder and indeed there was a ladder on the ground at the time. The constable was called and it seemed like a tragic accident. The rumours started when the will was read. Six months before the accident the farm had been willed to Daniel. Zachariah's wife, Amy, had already died by then, but even so it was his cousin who was expecting the farm to be left to him and not Daniel. It was also well known that Zachariah was crippled by arthritis and he could not use his hands, which were very swollen and painful at the time. Daniel's explanation started to look suspect and the rumours took wings. Only Daniel knows what happened that day and he refuses to speak about it. Some say it's because he is guilty.'

'What do you think?' she asked, not taking her eyes off Daniel, who also held hers. A sudden breeze blew through the churchyard whipping up some long dead leaves into a whirling frenzy between them.

'I know Daniel feels guilty but whether it's of murder, I don't know. Folk in the village are happy to accept his help but they don't seem to change their opinion of him. Many are jealous that a boy like him has become a man of property. Most people around here are tenant farmers and would do anything to have the opportunity to own their own ground. There is the possibility that Daniel did kill in order to own the farm and be rid of the old man. Daniel has had a rough life. His determination helped him survive. Determination can help you do a lot of things.'

'Do you think he would commit murder?'

'I think, given the right circumstances, anyone can commit murder. It is whether a man chooses to is the difference between us.'

Janey wondered for a moment whether she could. If someone was attacking her child would she kill to save their life? If James Brockenshaw had tried to rape her again while she carried a knife, would she have used it? Given the right circumstances she just might.

'Daniel keeps himself to himself but there are some who think well of him,' continued the vicar. 'Have you met Edna, the old woman that cooks for him?' Janey nodded, a half smile on her lips. 'She sees some good in him and she is not easy to please! I too like the man, although I feel he could benefit from opening his mind to God's voice and being friendlier to folk.'

'It sounds like folk aren't friendly to him,' defended

Janey. 'My father used to say that God's voice is not only heard in the church,' she added.

'I trust your father did not like attending service.'

'He preferred reading his books,' Janey replied, with a smile.

Daniel had started to pace.

'You still want to be married to Daniel, despite his background and the rumours about him?' he asked.

She nodded realising that she did. She did not want her child to grow up illegitimate with a workhouse for a home and she believed Daniel would do right by them.

'No doubt his handsome looks make up for the rest,' chuckled the vicar. The vicar was right. Daniel was a handsome man. Why had she never realised before? 'I thought so,' said the vicar as he took her arm and walked her back to him.

They watched Boscarn Farm come into view. Neither had spoken on the journey home, both coming to terms that in three weeks or more they would be man and wife. Daniel brought the trap to a halt at the top of the hill and they sat in silence for some minutes.

'Boscarn Farm,' he said, looking at the whitewashed walls of his home. 'The house and garden are yours to run how you see fit.'

'And Edna?' she asked.

He flicked the reins and they were off once more. 'Edna will always have a place at Boscarn and will be a great help when the baby arrives. She doesn't know what they say about me in the village,' he said, glancing at Janey, 'or what the vicar thinks.' It was the first time he had referred to the conversation the vicar had had with her. 'Edna cares little for the people that live in the village,' he continued, 'as they care little for her.'

'Tell me about her?' she asked, intrigued why he would hold such fondness for the cantankerous woman.

'She has a house near the Methodist chapel in the village. When her husband died she became a recluse and refused to leave her home. She spent her days cursing anyone that chatted too loudly below her window or sat on her doorstep to pass the time of day. She often threw things at passersby, even emptying her chamber pot over their heads. Some folk would stand beneath her window and taunt her, hoping to goad her into shouting and cursing. She became a freak show and the children teased her awful.

'The year before Zachariah died, she threw a turnip at me and it hit me on the head.' Janey started to laugh. 'It hurt!' said Daniel, indignantly. 'I told her she was a miserable old woman who wasted her life and was no good to anyone. It seems I was the first one to stand up to her and she quite liked that. The next morning she turned up at the farm, cooked a meal and left without saying a word. She's been coming every day, except the Sabbath, ever since. She's never left the village, or spoken to anyone else, just walks the mile to the farm and back again.'

'She doesn't like me.'

'She will be scared I won't want her to visit any more. I will speak to her. She will come around.'

'How can you be so sure?'

'She goes soft when she sees a kitten or baby chick. She will do the same when she hears you are having a baby. She will be clucking over you like a broody hen in no time at all. She never had children and I think that lays heavy in her heart. She will be glad you and your baby will be staying.'

'Somehow I can't imagine that,' said Janey as they pulled up at the farmhouse and Daniel helped her down from the trap. She felt his hand beneath her elbow and another in the small of her back.

'She has a hard shell but inside she's as soft as a feather pillow.' He halted her for a moment. 'Despite what the vicar told you, you still consider me a better option than the workhouse? He did not succeed in turning you against the idea?'

'I don't think that was his intention. He feels fatherly towards me and wanted to enlighten me.' His supportive hands left her. 'Why are you helping me, Daniel? Why are you willing to marry me and take on another man's baby?'

'I don't have a choice,' he said.

She frowned, slightly confused at his answer. 'Because of how the villagers treat you? Am I your only chance of having a family?'

He did not answer and, taking his silence as an agreement, she left him to enter the house.

Daniel took the horse by the head collar and watched her walk away. It was only when she was no longer able to hear him did he answer her question.

'Because, Janey Carhart,' he said, quietly stroking his horse's nose, 'it was the only way to make you stay.'

Chapter Sixteen

Janey listened to the banging and crashing of saucepans in the kitchen. Contrary to what Daniel had said Edna had not taken the news of their impending marriage quietly. She could not understand the Cornish language that spewed from her lips, but the tone made it clear to her that Edna was not blessing their marriage. The noise only subsided after the slamming of the back door as she left. Janey watched her through the window, striding angrily back to the village and the sanctuary of her little house. Daniel came to stand beside her to watch Edna leave.

'That went better than I expected,' he said. To her surprise, he sounded almost cheerful.

'She's furious. I've brought you nothing but trouble.'

'She's had her nose put out of joint but she will come around. Coming here each day gives her life purpose. She will sulk for a bit but I reckon she will be here tomorrow morning, like always, and act as if nothing has happened. I've told her we still want her and will need her help. When she's had a moment to remember what I said, she will make her way back here. I'll not turn my back on her.'

Edna's angry figure had now gone from their view and peace descended. For the first time that day they were alone in the house, their arms almost touching as they breathed and no bolt between them to slide across. Suddenly Janey felt vulnerable. Common sense told her that this man was helping her but panic has no rational side. Mr Tallock, the butler, flashed in her mind, his shaking and sweating evidence of his internal demons. To her horror she found herself starting to tremble and stepped away from Daniel, desperate for some distance between them.

Daniel looked at her, unable to hide his surprise at her reaction to him. She saw the hurt flash across his face before he managed to mask it with a stony stare.

'There's a rabbit pie on the table for want of a crust,' he ground out. 'I'll expect dinner at six.' He left, slamming the door behind him just as Edna had done not long before.

Janey stood in the kitchen, alone. She had hurt him by her reaction, a reaction she didn't really understand herself. She wanted the marriage to work, she wanted it to be a success, but James Brockenshaw had left his curse on her as well as a baby inside. She wanted to make it up to Daniel and the only way she could do it was to make him the best rabbit pie he had tasted. It was a pathetic attempt at an apology but at that moment it was all that she had.

Soon the range was warming the kitchen and the fragrant aroma of rabbit pie wound its way around the farmhouse. A creamy, milky bread and butter pudding had joined the pie in the oven and Janey set about cleaning and tidying the kitchen.

Time had flown by and Janey hadn't enjoyed herself so much for ages. She hummed to herself as she fed the range with more logs and moved the kettle to the side to simmer and keep warm. Suddenly instinct told her that she was being watched. Slowly turning around she saw the girl she had seen the day before. The girl emerged from her hiding place and looked at her. She appeared about twelve years old, on the verge of puberty with the awkwardness and lack of confidence of youth, but unlike Edna this girl looked like she was going to burst with excitement. This was no ghost but a living, breathing child.

'I'm Molly,' she said, coming nearer. 'I saw Granny Thom in the village. She says you and Daniel are going to be wed!'

'Is Granny Thom Edna?' asked Janey. So the ghost had a voice, she thought, looking at the girl.

Molly picked up an apple from the kitchen table and examined it. The apple had been part of last year's crop and stored over the winter, so it was always a good habit to check for deterioration or disease before eating it.

'We call her Granny Thom.'

'We?' asked Janey, still not quite believing she was talking to a young girl in Daniel's house. Her blonde hair was tied in an untidy ponytail and her dress hung loosely on her body, but she was clean, healthy and had a big smile on her face. The smile was infectious and Janey couldn't help but smile back.

'My brother David and me,' she said, taking a noisy bite. With her mouth full of apple she added, 'Is it true?'

'Yes we are, in three weeks.'

'Daniel told us to make ourselves scarce when he brought you here. He said you were too ill to put up with my chatter, but when Granny Thom said that you two were to be wed, I thought it would be all right to say hello.' She felt the heat from the range and crossed the kitchen to warm her hands and enjoy the warmth. 'Daniel put this in last year when he built this room. He said it would make Granny Thom's life easier but she won't use it.' She added in a whisper, 'I think she don't know how. She's afraid.' She waved the remaining half-eaten apple at Janey. 'Not that she would let on. She's some mazed about you and Daniel.'

'I know. I didn't mean for our marriage to make her so angry.'

Molly shrugged. 'She'll get over it. She weren't happy when me and David came to live here.'

Hiding her surprise, Janey asked, 'You live here?'

'In the cowshed. Daniel said it was best we live there.' Janey was horrified. Molly began to laugh. 'Come with me, I'll show you,' she said, grabbing Janey's hand. 'You can be our big sister, just like Daniel is our big brother.'

She pulled Janey around the corner and opened a cupboard door, pausing briefly to turn to her. 'Daniel didn't need the cowshed. He said it was too small, so he cleared it out, plastered it, laid a slate floor and even put in a chimney! Can you believe it? We have our very own fireplace. He said it was important we had our own place to sleep, our own place we could call our home. Follow me, I'll show you.'

The cupboard turned out to be an entrance to a passage, which in turn opened up into a small building. Inside were two bedrooms and a room with a table and chairs. Molly stood proudly in the middle. 'Welcome to my home.'

Janey was impressed. Molly and her brother had made the simple building into their own personal space.

'Daniel didn't tell me you both lived here,' said Janey, looking around at the cosy surroundings. According to the pictures strewn around, one of them enjoyed drawing.

'Those are mine,' said Molly, smiling, but the smile quickly faded. 'You aren't going to throw us out are you?'

'Of course not,' reassured Janey.

'Good. We have nowhere to go if you did.'

As Janey looked about the little annex, Molly explained to Janey how she and her brother had come to live at Boscarn Farm. Daniel had visited Camelford Orphanage looking for a boy to help him on the farm. He had chosen David, and on the way home he had asked David why he looked so miserable. The boy had told him he had left his younger sister in the orphanage and probably would never see her again.

'And do you know what he did?' Janey could guess but let Molly continue telling her the story which she obviously enjoyed doing. 'He turned the cart around,' she said, waving her apple core at Janey, 'in the middle of the road and went back for me. Mind you, he had to convince the orphanage but they had too many children so was probably glad to be rid of me.'

They made their way back to the kitchen. 'Daniel said to me that I must earn my keep and finish my schooling or he would send me back. So every morning I milk the cows, feed the chickens, collect the eggs, go to school and shut the chickens in at night. David helps Daniel on the farm. Look. There's David now.'

Janey almost missed seeing the boy striding up the path. He was tall and lanky, probably no more than fifteen years old and strangely familiar to her. The door opened.

'David, have you heard? Daniel's getting married … to her.' Molly pointed at Janey with the lack of manners only an excited child could get away with. Molly missed the look of shock on the boy's face as he recognised Janey, but Janey didn't.

David nodded that he had.

'Oh, I forgot to see to the hens!' exclaimed Molly, rushing to the door. She paused breathlessly in the doorway. 'Exciting, isn't it?' she said to her brother, before disappearing outside.

Janey looked at David. The boy was older than when she had last seen him, a good foot taller with a leaner face verging into manhood.

'We've met before,' she said, with certainty. 'You gave me flowers.'

The boy looked nervously out of the window. He doesn't want Daniel to know, thought Janey, and she didn't either. It was bad enough that Daniel was to bring up Brockenshaw's child. He didn't need to know that his farmhand had, albeit innocently, been complicit in James's pursuit of her. 'I won't tell Daniel, if you don't, David. It's in the past.'

The boy's shoulders sank in relief.

'The flowers were picked for you. He planned to give them to you. He just couldn't, so I did.'

'You were doing what you were told. They were lovely but I don't want to upset Daniel.'

'Nor I.'

'So we will not speak about them again.'

'No.'

'I should like to be friends.'

The boy smiled. 'Me, too.'

Molly ran into the room, her noisy chatter filling the kitchen.

'Did I miss anything?' she said, breathlessly. 'This is *so* exciting.'

Daniel sat watching the woman who would soon be his wife. As always she looked beautiful but tonight she glowed with a sense of achievement. Her pie and pudding had been a success and, he had to admit, the best he had ever tasted. It was an added bonus that she could cook. It seemed that her years in service had taught her many skills. As he watched her over the empty plates littering the table, he saw another talent he did not know she possessed. She was entertaining the children with anecdotes of her servant days with a sense of humour that had them in stitches of laughter. Molly continually interrupted her with questions, which did not surprise him, but David, the quieter of the two who rarely wasted words, was as chatty and interested as his sister. The noise and ease of conversation allowed him to sit quietly and observe this woman that seemed to be blooming before his eyes. He wondered if it was just his wishful thinking that she appeared to belong in his house. Already the kitchen had become her domain and it gave him great pleasure to discover that the range he had installed and the kitchen he had built were finally being brought to life. He remembered the words of the vicar when he had said how a woman can make a house a home by the little touches she makes and he had to agree. The house seemed to have acquired a heartbeat and it was down to her.

At some point the conversation had turned to the baby and Janey's smile left her. She glanced at him nervously as she answered the children's questions. Finally they cleared the table and disappeared leaving her alone with him. Daniel had not spoken in some time, so stood up to stand by her side at the kitchen sink.

'Do I scare you?' It was a direct question, but he saw no reason not to be.

'I'm sorry about earlier,' she replied. 'There's a lot to get used to.'

She was right. There was a lot to get used to – for both of them. The main thing for him was the baby between them.

With a single finger he touched her stomach where the buttons of her dress no longer met but were concealed by her shawl. He was careful to be gentle and non-threatening. He did not want to frighten her.

'It's getting bigger.'

She did not move away but he was still unsure how to read her. He withdrew and shoved his hand in his pocket, the touch of her body still leaving a mark on his hand.

'Amy was a large woman,' he said, gruffly. 'Her clothes are in a trunk upstairs. The old woman is good with a needle and will enjoy altering them for you to wear.' He had attempted to show her the baby would not be a problem, but he was left with more doubts than he had before. He had to leave and unravel them in his own mind.

'You seem sure she will come back.'

Daniel roughly pulled on his cap, without looking at her.

'She will come back. We are her family and she is ours.'

'Where are you going?' She sounded hurt. She had expected him to stay. He had expected to but he could not.

'Out. I won't be late.' He stepped out into the night, his collar turned up, his footsteps echoing on the stony path. He knew he was leaving her in a silent kitchen alone, but he had things to do and not much time to do them in.

Daniel had been right. Edna arrived the next morning as if nothing had happened and over the course of the morning a thaw between the two women set in. By the afternoon they were both rummaging through Amy's trunk and Janey was trying on the vast dresses that swamped her and made them both smile.

It turned out that Edna had worked as a dressmaker before her marriage and the opportunity to use her old skills ignited a light in the old woman's eyes. With a mouthful of pins, she instructed Janey to turn this way and that, as she pinned, tucked and cut to create two new dresses that would last Janey to full term. Janey was grateful for her support and her company during the day and the children's laughter and banter when they were in the house, but when they went to bed, she was often alone as Daniel chose to go out most evenings. She felt she had no right to question him further, but with the marriage fast approaching, she was beginning to wonder if she should.

'Where does he go?' she asked David, but it was Molly who answered.

'He used to visit Sally a lot. She's a friend of his.'

David kicked her under the table and Molly, in her childish innocence, could not understand what she had said wrong.

'It's true! He used to see her regular, but then he stopped. I think they must have fallen out or something but they must be friends again now.'

David tried to apologise but Janey shook her head.

'Don't worry, David.'

'Come on, you've said enough,' said David to his sister as he pulled her from the table.

'What did I say? What's wrong?'

'Out!' David shoved her out the door and into their rooms. He turned just before he shut the door. 'Sorry, Janey,' he said, quietly. 'She doesn't realise the trouble she's making.'

Janey smiled weakly as a mix of emotions churned inside her. She had come between him and his lover. How could she blame him for seeking out his old flame? Daniel had promised to give her child a name but he had not promised to be faithful to her. How could she compete with a woman who was shapely, willing and experienced, when she was growing larger by the day and unsure if she could ever respond to his desires? Despite her condition, she was very naive about pleasuring a man and after her rape, she wasn't really sure if she wanted to learn. However, soon she would be married to this man she barely knew and she wanted the marriage to work on all accounts. She didn't want the widow to come between them.

The next day Janey found Daniel in a farm building tying up a cow. She took a moment to watch him as he worked and eventually stepped inside making her presence known to him. She had not explored outside of the farmhouse since she had arrived and her appearance surprised him.

'Where's Molly?' he asked.

Janey tucked a stray hair behind her ear, suddenly self-conscious under his dark-eyed gaze.

'She has a headache so I told her to go back to bed.'

Daniel looked at the cow and stroked its head. She knew what he was thinking. It was Molly's job to tend to the cow.

'I've fed the chickens and I thought I could milk the cow for you.' He didn't look convinced. 'Really, I would like to,' she insisted.

'Have you ever milked a cow before?'

She shook her head. 'No, but I'm willing to learn.'

He thought for a moment then brought over two stools. Sitting on one he patted the other. Pleased, she came to sit beside him. Endearingly he self-consciously cleared his throat making her smile.

'You don't need to do this.'

'I want to be a good wife to you and a good farmer's wife helps her husband with the farm.'

'I don't want you to be someone who you are not.'

'Perhaps I am discovering who I am. Let me help. It would make me happy.'

With a firm gentleness he washed the cow's udder with a cloth soaked in soapy water.

'All my life I have been told what to do,' she said, watching his sweeping movements over the pink skin. 'This is different; I want to help.'

Daniel held the cow's teat in his hand. 'Hold the teat like this. To make the milk flow you need to imitate the calf's mouth sucking at his mother. Like this, can you see?'

She moved her head closer to watch his hand squeeze the teat. His fingers and thumb circled the teat and each finger in turn squeezed until the high pitched sound of the milk hit the bucket beneath. Janey, engrossed, moved closer and they bumped heads. She pulled back feeling stupid.

'Sorry,' she apologised and Daniel cleared his throat again.

'Now you have a go.'

Janey reached out and held the teat in her hand, blushing as she did so. She tried to squeeze it but nothing came out. Daniel showed her again on another and she copied but the milk refused to flow. Daniel moved closer and placed his hand over hers; his fingers were warm and naturally moulded around hers.

'Here, let me show you again,' he said, his breath brushing her cheek. He applied pressure on her fingers wrapped around the teat. The rhythm built and the milk began to flow in pulsing ribbons to the bucket below. She smiled in delight and turned to look at him, her lips almost touching his cheek. He cleared his throat again and pulled back. 'That's it, you have the hang of it now.'

'Do you enjoy farming?' she asked, trying hard to concentrate on her milking technique.

'I do, although I have plans.'

'You do?'

'Most farmers are content to be self-sufficient. I want more. I want my children to have the education I did not. I want them to have a home of their own when they are grown, so they will never know what it's like to be so poor that they have to sleep under the sky or worry where their next meal is coming from. I want things for my children that I never had and to do that I need to make money.'

Daniel took a turn at milking.

'How will you do that?' asked Janey as she rested her elbows on her knees to watch him work.

'Next year they will be bringing the railway to Trehale. It will link the village to the towns. I want to produce enough milk so I can sell to the towns.'

'But you would need a lot of cows.'

'Indeed.'

'And milk doesn't keep long so you would need to transport once, even twice a day.' Daniel stopped milking and looked at her, surprised by her interest.

'It would be hard work,' he replied, steadily.

'And take a large amount of time out of your day.'

'It would but I am willing to work hard if that is what it takes.'

Janey fell silent and Daniel continued milking, both forgetting she was meant to be learning the task.

'When I worked on the estate at Truro a dairymaid visited every Tuesday to make cheese and butter. The amounts she made were large as the family had workers living on the estate and a town house in the city. I often helped her.' Daniel stopped to look at her. It was his turn to listen. 'If you turned your milk to butter and cheese it would store longer. Deliveries could be less frequent and easier to handle as the product is smaller and more compact. Not only that, but the profit would be higher. I learnt a lot from the dairymaid. I could make the butter and cheese for you to sell.'

'We would need to buy equipment and find buyers.'

'And we would have to package it. We could call it Boscarn butter or Kellow cheese!'

'We would need more cows, but I would have to do that anyway.'

'In a couple of years Molly will finish school and she could help me make it as the business grew.'

'I could convert the Shippen, turn it into a dairy where the cheese and butter could be made. It's north facing and is the coldest building.'

They sat for a moment, their minds racing with possibilities.

He smiled at her. 'I didn't know I was marrying a businesswoman.'

'I didn't know I was marrying a businessman.' She smiled back at him, both excited at the prospect of this new venture together.

He raised an eyebrow to the bucket. 'Would you like a drink?' Janey nodded enthusiastically. 'Open your mouth,' he ordered, smiling.

Hesitantly she did, as he pointed the teat in her direction. With a rhythmical squeeze a creamy thread of milk arched through the air and pooled in her mouth. She started to laugh, gurgling and spilling some of the milk from her lips. Creamy droplets ran down her chin and along her upturned jawline, making Daniel laugh – a soft infectious laugh that caught at her heartstrings and delighted her. They sat breathless just looking at each other, feeling closer to one another than they had ever done before.

He reached out and rubbed a drop away with his thumb. She sat passively watching him, allowing him to touch her. Suddenly they were both standing; her milking stool had tipped onto its side and lay rocking by her feet. She felt his hand slip around her waist and another moved to frame her neck. Bending his head he took the drop of milk that had run down her neck into his mouth. She could hear her own heart pulsing under her skin as he travelled higher to another drop. He took that one too, into his mouth, gently licking it away. She did not stop him. Her head fell back into the cradle of his rising hand as he kissed the corner of her mouth. She could smell the sweet creamy liquid on their breaths and hear his ragged breathing which mirrored the growing urgency within him. She had come this far; it was the closest she had let any man touch her since that day. She had been enjoying it, on the verge of losing herself into the feelings that were threatening to rise in her but now his growing desire scared her.

She didn't want things to spoil. She did not want him to lose control. Brockenshaw had lost control. Had she somehow been the catalyst for his change from a gentleman to a devil? And then there was the widow. Was Daniel still seeing her? Had he lain in her arms only yesterday evening? She had to ask him and to stop the mounting desire between them before it got out of hand, and she did both by a few choice words.

'Do you kiss *her* like this?'

Daniel froze. Any closeness between them vanished as he stepped back to look at her.

'Who has been talking?'

'Molly said you visit Sally.'

'And she says I am now?'

'You go out every evening. What are we to think?'

'More of me than you do. Molly is a child, but you should know better.'

'You don't return until dark. You do not tell me where you go. What should I think?'

'I'll do better than tell you, I'll show you.' He led her across to another farmyard building but paused at the door. He turned angrily at her. 'Do you think so little of me that you would believe this? Do you trust me so little?' He raked a hand through his hair in frustration. 'Not all men are like your lover. We don't all run out at the first sign of trouble. The answer to your question is in there.' He nodded angrily to a closed door. 'But think on this ... I'll not touch you again until we are wed. It was just a kiss, but it seems even that was too much to bear.'

He strode angrily away and Janey felt like a shrew. She eased open the door and looked inside the building he had brought her to. What she saw made her heart break at what she had just accused him of. Inside the room, with its air fragrant from the aroma of freshly chiselled wood, stood a rocking crib, a large cot and a partially built high chair.

Chapter Seventeen

The wedding was fast approaching yet the bride and bridegroom rarely spoke. It was a sad way to start a marriage. Janey struggled to know what to do for the best. She wanted to marry Daniel but even to herself her behaviour towards him was confusing and unfair. She could tell him of the rape, which would explain her fear of intimacy, but she was terrified he would turn against her baby or seek revenge. If James was to be believed, he had already attacked him for merely mentioning her name. What would he do if he knew he had raped her? 'He has a temper. It will lead him to the hangman's noose, one day,' James had said and Janey could well believe it, given the right circumstances.

To her shame, when she first realised she was with child, she had prayed for a miscarriage. How could she learn to love a baby that was half Brockenshaw's and a result of rape? Yet ever since that day on Hel Tor when she had felt her baby's first feeble movements, the seeds of love had taken root and grew in her heart. The baby was just as much a victim of the rape as she was and the baby was *hers*, relying on her for its life and its survival. Its all-consuming dependence had nurtured a protective instinct within Janey that was primal in origin and filled her with wonder. The thought that Daniel might see the baby as a reminder of her rape would break her heart. It was best he thought it was conceived from an ill-judged crush than such a violent act. Yet to start her life with him based on a lie was not the best foundation to build a marriage and she struggled to know what to do.

Edna lay snoozing by the warm range as Janey mixed

a cake. The old woman had grudgingly learnt to use the 'thing', as she called it, realising its benefits far outweighed her fears. To Janey's amusement, Edna had now taken to having a catnap each afternoon, basking in its warmth. Janey didn't mind, she found it oddly comforting having her company and her naps were a sign that she was handing over the reins of running the house to her. There was a knock at the door and leaving her baking and the sleeping woman, Janey went to answer it. It was Sally.

At first no one spoke, both taken aback at seeing the other. It was obvious Sally had dressed with Daniel in mind, as despite it being early March she wore a low cut dress displaying her ample cleavage for his eyes to drink in. She was confident and alluring, with hair the colour of jet. The tight, youthful curls that framed her face were a seductive invitation for a man to coil a ringlet around his finger. She wondered how many times Daniel had done that after making love to her. This woman knew her husband-to-be more intimately than she did and that, unusually for Janey, made her want to slap her face. Instead, she gritted her teeth and gave the woman a stony stare in greeting.

'Can I help you?'

Sally tried to look beyond her. 'Is Daniel in?'

'No. What do you want?' It wasn't the answer Sally wanted to hear.

'I wasn't expecting to find you here. I heard Daniel was getting married and I wanted to talk to him.' She noticed Janey's bump. 'Seeing the state you are in it looks like you tricked him into it.'

Janey had no intention of honouring her insult with a reply and made to shut the door but Sally jammed it open with a foot.

'Daniel's always been careful. I should know. I bet the baby isn't even his.'

'Take your foot away. I want you to leave. I have nothing to say to you.'

Sally's face was bitter. She took a step nearer.

'I knew Daniel was hankering after a family. He talks to me, you see,' she added, smugly. Janey tried to push the door but again it jammed against her foot. 'Only there's not a father in the village that would be happy to have their daughter wed a man like him. That's the only reason he chose you, 'cos you probably don't have a family who cares!'

Janey saw red and with an almighty push she shoved Sally off the doorstep. *No choice* – the words rang alarm bells in her head. Hadn't Daniel said that to her when she asked him why he was marrying her? She had wondered if that was what he meant. If Sally was to be believed, she was right. However, she wasn't going to let Sally think she had hurt her with her words.

'Whether you like it or not, he's marrying me,' she ground out. 'You've missed your chance!'

Sally just scoffed. 'Do you really think a prim little thing like you can keep a man like Daniel interested for long? I know how to. Many a night he's rolled around in my bed.' She swept her hands down her body. 'It's this he prefers.'

Suddenly the heavens opened and a cascade of dirty water and vegetable peelings fell from the sky as Edna's screeching voice hurled Cornish insults from the window above. Sally was soaked to the skin, her pretty hair littered with vegetable skins.

'You evil witch!' shouted Sally to the window above. An old potato sailed through the air and hit her shoulder. Sally retreated. 'You'll never make him happy,' she warned Janey. 'You may have tricked him into marriage but you won't keep him. He'll come back to my bed and I'll be waiting!'

Janey slammed the door on Sally, but her words had

struck a nerve. All her worries about the impending marriage that had occupied her thoughts and contaminated her joy over the past three weeks were stirred anew. Sally was right, she was no match to her sexual confidence. She not only feared intimacy, but could not imagine a time when she would not. Despite what had happened, she still felt inexperienced and naïve. She wished she was more like Sally, confident in her femininity, alluring, brazen. It seemed that was the sort of woman who would keep Daniel's interest. Not someone like her who was getting larger by the day and would soon have a baby to look after – a baby that was not his. She would never satisfy Daniel or keep him. He didn't need a wife like her. She must tell him, she realised, that the wedding must be called off.

It wasn't until late afternoon that Janey had the opportunity to speak to Daniel. Molly and Edna sat at the table drinking tea and when Janey asked them where he was, they told her he was down by the river at the bottom of the meadow.

'I'm going out for a bit. I need to see him,' she called out to them as she grabbed her shawl. Before Edna had taken in her words she was gone.

'Granny Thom, does she know he's gone down to the river to bathe?' asked Molly, biting into a freshly baked biscuit.

'No,' said the old woman, pouring her hot tea into a saucer for it to cool quicker. Molly watched her as she lifted the steaming liquid to her lips and sucked it up noisily. With satisfaction she sat back in her chair. 'But she's 'avin' 'is baby so she's seen it all before.' She smiled. 'I think she will be all right.'

Molly sat and chewed her biscuit. 'Granny Thom, why do they sleep in separate rooms if she's having his baby?'

Edna had wondered the same thing. 'What folk do in

their own 'ome is up to them and none of our business,' she scolded.

Janey made her way down to the meadow. The wild flowers were delayed in their blooming due to the cold winter, which was reluctant to give way to the spring. However, today was the first warm day for a long time and despite Janey's decision to leave she knew she would miss the little farmhouse, Edna, Molly and David. They had become more of a family to her than her own and walking away from Daniel meant also walking away from them.

Her skirts brushed through the long grass as she made her way across the meadow to the wood at the bottom, where the river lay secluded under a canopy of trees. The fast flowing river bubbled and gurgled over large rounded boulders and slowed dramatically in a deep still pool. It did not cross her mind to wonder what Daniel may be doing down there as she rehearsed in her head what she would say to him.

At first she thought she was dreaming. There, standing before her in the still waters of the river, was Daniel. His back glistened with droplets whilst gentle waves splashed and teased against his hips and buttocks. Janey's eyes grew wide as she realised Daniel was naked. Unsure what to do, and in a state of panic, she retreated a step to hide behind a bush. Her mouth became dry and her breaths more rapid and shallow. Her head was telling her to leave but her feet would not move. It was only a glimpse yet the image of his body had seared into her brain like a branding iron. Perhaps it was a trick of the light. Perhaps it was not even him. There was only one thing to do, she concluded, and that was to have another look.

She hesitantly stepped forward again but the water was now still and empty. Feeling disappointed she moved from her hiding place to search him out, her eyes scanning the surface of the water. Suddenly Daniel broke through the surface. Water cascaded down his body, running along the contours of his muscles and stroking the hair on his thighs to a dark sleekness. Janey's mouth fell open.

She had seen a naked man only once before in her life. It was an illustration of a statue called The Flood, which depicted a beautiful, muscular, godlike man rescuing a victim from deep water by carrying the unconscious figure over his shoulder. Heroic and strong, Janey had been mesmerised by the illustration until her mother, red-faced with embarrassment by the indecent image, had torn the book from her hands. How odd, Janey thought, that the next time she would see a man naked was as if the illustration had come to life. She licked her lips but did not move. He was washing, she realised as she watched him rake his hands through his hair.

The light caught the movements of his muscles as his body moved. She felt no fear or repulsion at the sight of him, only primal, melting desire deep inside her. He was, without doubt, beautiful to look at. Wet, sleek and clean, his body ignited a surprising desire in her to touch him and be touched by him as she was sure that only he could fill the aching emptiness inside her. The realisation that she felt such lustful feelings towards the man that would soon be her husband meant there was hope for their marriage. She watched, open mouthed, as he strode out of the river to his pile of clothes, confident, unashamed and athletic in his movements. He was unhurried and relaxed as he neared the bank and, to her horror, she realised he was looking at her. She had been caught.

He reached for his trousers.

'You will have to marry me now,' he joked as he pulled them on. He did not seem to mind at all that she had been watching. Janey, on the other hand, was mortified. Belatedly she shielded her eyes.

'I did not know you were bathing.'

'I had hoped you sought me out knowing I was.'

'I'm sorry to disappoint you.' She peeped over her hand. His chest remained bare and he made no further attempt to dress. She let her hand drop.

'Sally visited, she was looking for you.'

'Why?'

'To speak to you. She thinks we are not matched well. She says you are only marrying me because no other man will let his daughter marry you. She thinks I tricked you into marriage.'

'She is wrong.'

'Which is what I told her ...' Daniel raised an eyebrow in surprise. '... and so did Edna ... in her way,' Janey added, a little uncomfortably.

'I can imagine.'

Janey began to pace up and down, wringing her hands as she walked.

'What is ailing you?' Daniel asked. 'It's best to speak plainly.'

Janey took a deep breath and faced him. 'She did bring up certain issues which perhaps we should discuss.'

'Go on.'

She started to pace again. 'From my current situation you must think I am experienced in the bedroom.' Daniel did not respond so she carried on. 'But the truth of the matter is I am not. It was only once. I only tell you this in case you expect me to be a certain type of woman with experience. I am not.'

'I do not judge you as I do not expect you to judge me. All I ask is that you are faithful when we are wed. I will not be the decoy while you two carry on meeting.'

'That would never happen.'

'Yet you loved him.'

'At one time I thought I did. It was a mistake.'

'One I warned you about.'

'And one I will forever regret. But I do not want our marriage to be blighted by your recriminations.'

It was the first time in a while she had retaliated back. She was beginning to resemble the Janey she once was, the one that threw stones at him by the river, the one that had kissed him first.

'And I will not have you accusing me of seeing other women.'

'I will not, if you do not.' He had taken a step nearer. She halted in her pacing and faced him.

'Which leaves the baby,' said Janey. 'Do you promise me that my baby will not be treated differently from your own?'

A muscle worked in his jaw. 'I said I would not.'

'My baby has become precious to me. I need your reassurance.'

'Or you will call off the wedding and go into the workhouse?'

'I will if I have to.'

He came towards her, stopping just less than an arm's length away. 'Have I given you a reason not to trust me?'

She shook her head. 'No.'

'I said I would treat your baby as if it was mine,' he said, taking her hand in his, 'but I did not promise to love it.' He placed her hand on his chest above his heart. 'Love comes from here,' he said, and reaching out with his other hand he brazenly placed it on her breast. She gasped but did not slap it away. 'And here.'

Janey did not move or drop her gaze from his.

'But love cannot grow unless there is a willingness to nurture it,' she told him.

'On that we disagree,' he said, removing his hand and dropping hers. 'Love can still grow despite the best attempts to crush it.'

Daniel observed the graceful swing of her hips as she returned to the house. For once she had not flinched at his touch. She had asked for patience and he was willing to give her that. She had also asked for reassurance and that too he had given but it would not change how he felt. He watched her walk away, her hair blowing in the breeze and Brockenshaw's brat in her belly.

Janey looked at herself in the mirror. It was not how she had dreamed her wedding would be. With Edna's help and alterations she wore the smartest of Amy's old dresses for her wedding. It was deep blue which highlighted her dark chestnut hair and green eyes. She had dressed her hair up in a style more befitting a lady of the upper class than a soon to be farmer's wife, but it was her wedding day and she wanted it to be as special as she could make it.

After going missing for much of the morning, dear, excited Molly ran into her room with the largest bouquet of wild flowers she had ever seen.

'They're lovely, Molly, I love wild flowers.'

Molly grinned. 'I know. I thought you could carry them to hide your bump and put some in your hair.'

'Where is Daniel?' Janey hadn't seen him all morning.

'I've just seen him leave with Edna. He wanted to get to the church early.'

They spent the little time they had left threading flowers into their hair before David arrived with the trap to take them to the church.

Janey felt nervous and a sense of foreboding as the trap

drew up to the little church. To her surprise the graveyard was filled with people from the village waiting for her arrival. They stood in groups around the graves, silently watching her as she was helped down from the trap by David. She knew why they were there. They had come to see who had been fool enough to marry a man with a murderous reputation. The villagers thought they got their answer when they saw her – a woman fool enough to fall pregnant by him.

Janey took a deep breath and tilted her chin in defiance as she threaded her arm through David's, while Molly followed on behind. She recognised some of the villagers, but not all. Little Billy was the only one to smile at her and she smiled back, grateful to see a friendly face.

The cool air of the church hit her inflamed cheeks with a suddenness that surprised her. It took a moment for her eyes to adjust to the dark gloom inside. As she proceeded to walk up the aisle, she noticed the pews to her right that should be filled with Daniel's friends and relatives were empty except for Edna and Matt. Her own pews on the left were no better. Her uncle had not replied to her invitation. It was foolish of her to have sent it. One lone young woman sat on her side of the church. The woman turned and smiled at her and Janey was grateful to see her. It was Mary, home on leave from her nurse training.

Finally she saw Daniel standing squarely at the front, taller than the rest and the only one not to look at her. As she approached him she willed him to turn and smile and reassure her that what she was doing was right, but he did not. As she came to stand beside him, their arms brushed. The touch caused him to look down at her and his glare immediately softened as he took in the wild flowers in her hair.

'You came,' he said, softly.

'So did you,' she replied.

'Are you sure you want this?' he asked, frowning. She nodded, not feeling at all sure she did. The softness left Daniel's face and he turned to the vicar. 'Let's begin,' he said. 'The villagers are waiting for a wedding, let's not disappoint them,' and with that they were married.

Matt had insisted the bride and groom returned to his home for some food and drink. The tension of the wedding melted away briefly as Matt and Mary, along with their parents and numerous siblings, turned the gathering into an impromptu party.

Mary carried a small plate of food aloft as she weaved her way through her younger brothers and sisters towards Janey. She offered it to her, smiling.

'It's not much but Mam insists you have something to eat. After all ...' She dropped her gaze to Janey's thickened waist. '... you are eating for two now.'

Janey took the plate, although in reality she felt too anxious to eat. The wedding service had passed without a hitch, but she still had the wedding night ahead.

'Now I know why you didn't write,' said Mary, selecting one of the two buns from Janey's plate. She used it to indicate Janey's bump. 'You had other things on your mind. You are a dark horse, Janey Kellow. I didn't think you would ... you know ... with Daniel ... before the wedding night.'

Janey looked away. She didn't want to lie to Mary. Her gaze searched for her husband in the crowded room. She found him with Matt, his head bowed as he listened intently to what his friend was saying. He looked so handsome in his wedding clothes. How she wished the baby had been his.

'Nor did I,' replied Janey, evasively. She turned back to Mary, who was tucking into her bun, intent on changing the subject. 'Thank you for coming. It's so good to see you. You look so well.' It was true. Mary looked radiant, a far cry from the servant she used to know.

'I am happy,' replied Mary. 'The matron is ferocious, but I am kept busy. The infirmary has a new west wing and an operating room which means—'

Two of Mary's younger sisters ran between, interrupting them by their excitement and laughter. Mary shrugged and laughed too as she watched them run out of the room. 'They are excited. Sisters!' she exclaimed. 'Who would have them?' She realised her error immediately and was horrified. 'Oh, Janey! I am sorry! My tongue always gets me into trouble.'

Janey waved her apology away. Mary meant no harm. 'Are you enjoying the training?' she asked, keen to change the subject yet again.

'We are the first trainee nurses at the hospital to be trained following the principles of the Nightingale Home and Training School in London,' replied Mary, proudly. 'I can't imagine doing anything else now.'

'Not even marriage?'

Mary hesitated briefly, then added resolutely, 'No, not even marriage.'

Her friend was holding back, Janey could tell. 'Mary?' she coaxed.

Mary relented and dropped her half-eaten bun on Janey's plate. 'Well, there is one doctor who is very handsome, but he is arrogant and, as you know, I am not good at holding my tongue. He is not used to a trainee nurse being so outspoken. It's no surprise that we do not get on. If Matron knew of our spats, I am sure I would be dismissed. But he riles me so and I cannot help myself.'

'Daniel and I did not used to get on well,' ventured Janey, with a teasing smile.

'That's different,' replied Mary. 'There was something

between you … a spark that I never had with him. I hated to see it as Daniel only had eyes for you. And this …' She placed her palm gently on Janey's belly. '… is the living proof of his love for you.' She let her hand fall away. 'Daniel must be overjoyed to have a child of his own. You will have made him very happy by giving him one so soon. I am pleased for you both. Truly I am.'

Janey looked over at Daniel again. He was the one who was talking now. She suspected he was telling Matt about their ideas for the farm. Despite their plans, she had the gnawing feeling that she had already let him down.

'I am not sure that he liked me from the very beginning, Mary,' said Janey, quietly. 'However, it doesn't matter now. I do not intend to dwell on the past, as it can sap one's strength. It is the future that counts and our future is together.' *Whatever that future might be.*

The wedding celebration kept the bride and bridegroom apart, not by design but by sheer numbers of bodies in the tiny house. Several times Janey looked across the room to Daniel, and he to her, but the noise and chatter of the family they had been persuaded to join continued to act like a human barrier to any intimate words or touch. Yet time was passing quickly and each minute spent meant that the wedding night drew closer.

The evening ride to Boscarn Farm was no better as the trap also carried an excitable Molly and a tired David. It was only when they finally retired to their rooms were Daniel and Janey finally alone as husband and wife.

Janey sat nervously on the bed in her nightdress as she waited for Daniel to come to bed. Someone had already placed her clothes and bag in his bedroom making it clear to her that her place was now with him. She wondered whether to get in the bed, or stand beside it to wait for his arrival as she listened to him walking around downstairs turning down the lamps and drawing the curtains. She stood up and took a quick look at herself in the mirror. A nervous woman standing in someone else's bedroom looked back at her. The door opened and Daniel came in.

'Are you tired?' he asked, taking off his shirt. Janey wondered if it was a loaded question.

'A little,' she replied, feeling self-conscious. His gaze followed the length of her nighty and returned to her face.

'You've taken the flowers from your hair,' he said, taking her hands and gently pulling her toward him. He brushed a stray lock of hair away from her face.

'They were beginning to wilt.' They had not discussed the wedding night and she was unsure what he expected.

He slowly untied the neck of her nightdress and eased her gown to the side to expose her shoulder. She felt him stroke her skin with the back of a finger.

'I won't hurt you,' he whispered as he watched the candlelight flicker on her smooth skin. She forced her breathing to remain steady.

'I know,' she said, quietly.

With a lift of one finger he eased the gown completely off one shoulder and it fell limply around the top of her arm, exposing half of her breast to his eyes. Her breath caught in her throat.

'Your breasts,' he said, softly, as his hand glided down to expose her breast fully, feeling its heaviness and softness in his hand, 'have changed since the day I pulled you into the river.'

Janey suddenly felt self-conscious of her breasts, which had grown larger as her pregnancy had progressed. She attempted to cover her breast with the nightgown.

'There's no shame in how a woman's body changes,' he added. 'It is nature, it's natural.'

'I feel fat.'

Daniel smiled at her confession and tilted her face up to his. His deep brown eyes looked into her soul, whilst stripping her naked before him. She felt her nipples grow painfully taut, aching for his touch again. Instinctively she arched toward him, but he did not notice as his gaze had already dropped to her mouth. He ran a thumb along her bottom lip, feeling its softness and fullness. As if he could wait no longer he bent his head to hers and briefly touched her lip with the tip of his tongue. Her mouth opened in invitation. Needing no further coaxing, he kissed her again, tasting her, wanting her, sharing the same breath with her – and Janey was lost. She no longer felt self-conscious of her pregnancy. She felt desired, she felt sexual and she wanted him like she had wanted no other man. In a building urgency he cupped her face, kissing her jawline and her neck. As she floated away from reality on a sea of sensation she felt him ease both shoulders of her gown down to her waist and pull her into his embrace.

In a ragged whisper, he asked, 'Do you want me?'

'Yes.'

'Show me.'

Tentatively she reached up and threaded her fingers around his neck to kiss his breath away. Any memories of that *awful day* did not cross her mind as there was no comparison to how she felt now. She wanted him to touch her, to love her, to be inside her.

He slid his hand down her back to cup her buttock beneath her white cotton nightgown. He pulled her body to him so she could feel his desire. She gasped.

'Do you want me as much as I want you now?' His tone had changed; his breathing was unsteady but his voice had an edge.

'Yes,' she whispered, wanting more of him. Suddenly he

held her at arm's length and looked at her. She faltered in her confidence as she saw a struggle in his eyes. It was as if he was battling some demon inside him.

'Daniel? What is the matter? What's wrong?' she asked bewildered, bereft that he had drawn away.

'I've wanted you for so long but you only had eyes for him. I've wanted you to want me, but you saw me as a "heathen", as if I was beneath you.'

She shook her head. 'Never!' she cried. 'If I gave you that impression, then I am sorry. You were so different to anyone I'd met before.'

'Right now I should want to make you suffer, as I have suffered these past two years,' he said, searching her face. He sighed as if in defeat. 'But I can't,' he said, finally. 'I want you more than ever.' He kissed her hard with a passion of a man possessed and claiming her as his. He caressed her with the right only her husband had and she was lost in his embrace once again. His hand swept down her body, taking in the curve of her breast and her belly. Both had forgotten the baby inside her, both too absorbed in discovering each other's bodies. As if demanding their attention the baby chose that moment to kick violently to the outside world and right into the palm of Daniel's hand.

Their lovemaking came to an abrupt halt and Daniel looked down as if in shock. The baby kicked twice in quick succession and Daniel felt it clearly in his palm once more. He withdrew his hand, balling it into a fist to take away the sensation of its touch.

'You won't hurt it.' Janey smiled, taking his hand to feel the baby again. She hoped this would be the chance for him to feel more bonded with the baby he was to call his own, but his hand recoiled from hers.

'Did you know Edna had eight children?' he said, staring at her belly.

'No, I didn't.'

'She lost each one before her seventh month.' He eased the straps of her nightgown onto her shoulders again so she was no longer exposed to his eyes. She felt like an unwanted gift being handed back. 'I have spent the last eight years being blamed for someone's death. I will not have you blame me should you miscarry.'

He pulled the covers of the bed back and told her to get in, and she did, in a state of shock at how things had suddenly changed. 'We will wait until after the birth. I have waited long enough, I can wait a few more weeks.' He lay down beside her, his hands cradled behind his head, staring up at the ceiling whilst Janey lay beside him. There was less than two inches between them but it might as well have been a chasm. She knew she should feel grateful that he was protecting her baby's health but as she lay beside him, just on the brink of experiencing something wondrous with the man that was her husband, all she could feel was a sense of utter rejection. It seemed even on their wedding night James Brockenshaw was still coming between them.

Chapter Eighteen

On the surface their marriage appeared to flourish as Janey settled into the life of a farmer's wife. Edna taught her how to gut the poultry that Daniel reared for their table, whilst Janey returned the favour by sharing cooking secrets from the cooks she had worked under as a kitchen maid. Together, they prepared the spare bedroom for the baby and whilst Janey baked, Edna would sit by the range, warming her toes and knitting for the new arrival as if it was to be her own.

Under Janey's instruction, David dug up patches of the front garden so Janey could plant shrubs and flowers that would add, she insisted, colour and interest. Daniel found the idea amusing that she would want to waste her time growing plants that had no use, but she knew, come the summer, he would take as much pleasure in seeing the garden transformed as she would. She also commandeered a small patch of Daniel's vegetable garden at the side of the house to nurture back to health the herbs that Amy had grown.

Daniel didn't know where she got the energy from as the inside of the house began to transform before his eyes. The furniture now shone with beeswax polish, the windows gleamed in the sunlight and the air always smelt fresh as she had a habit of throwing the windows open each morning. She also got into the routine of beating the carpets weekly and cleaning the slate floor each morning. Even David joked that they needn't bother with plates as they could just eat off the floor. Daniel felt a sense of peace that at the end of his working day, he came home to a clean, well-organised home with good cooking waiting for him, a warm fire in the grate and laughter and chatter to make him smile.

The changes, however, did not stop there. After

encouragement from Janey, Daniel set about transforming one of the outbuildings to a dairy for butter and cheesemaking. After searching the sale pages and visiting several markets he eventually found all the equipment they needed. There were two specific days that made Daniel feel that his dream of expanding the business was finally going to become a reality. The first was arriving home with the cheese presses. Janey, Molly and Edna watched as he and David unloaded them from the cart and installed them in the dairy. As the men stood back to rest from the exertion, the women, led by Janey, broke into a spontaneous applause. Daniel smiled, pleased that there were others as excited as he was about the new business venture.

The second time happened when he and David brought a small herd of new cattle home from the market. Only Janey was at home but he saw her look out of the window then quickly disappear again as they made their way down the lane. She came out into the garden and watched them go by with a big smile on her face.

'They're beautiful. What are they?' she called to him.

'They are South Devon cattle. They are docile, hardy and live for a long time, which means they will not need replacing as quickly as some breeds. They also mature quickly so I can breed from them sooner.' Daniel patted the curly, light red coat of the nearest cow to him. Janey's smile was infectious and he couldn't help but return it with one of his own. 'They also produce creamy milk. Just right for cheesemaking. It will put our cheese and butter one step ahead of the others.'

Janey leaned over the granite hedge at the bottom of their garden to watch the gentle giants walk past. He felt a surge of pride and pleasure at his achievements and that Janey was there to witness them. He would have liked to have run over to her, picked her up and swung her around in appreciation of her support, but he did not. He had a small herd of cows to control, he told himself, so instead he just nodded at her in acknowledgement and passed her by.

'I really think you are the best to sell it. They won't buy from me.'

'Nonsense,' said Janey, pinning her hat on her head, 'but if that's how you really feel, I will.' She looked at Daniel's shirt and instantly recognised it as the one he wore at the dance. The pocket had been expertly mended by Edna, but the button was still missing. 'Wait, I'll be back.'

She disappeared for some minutes before returning with a sewing basket and something in her hand. She ordered him to sit. 'I should have mended this shirt ages ago,' she said, threading a needle and kneeling before him.

'Don't kneel down.' He patted his leg. 'Sit here.' She looked around embarrassed but Edna and David were nowhere to be seen. Not wanting to offend she sat down primly on his lap. Daniel watched her at work. 'That's lucky. It matches the others exactly,' he said.

'That's because it's the one that is missing,' replied Janey.

Daniel frowned. 'Where did you find it?'

'When I tore it, it came away in my hand.'

His eyes narrowed. 'And you kept it all this time?' His scrutiny of her actions took her by surprise and she blushed. She finished the sewing, cut the thread with her scissors and stood up.

'I hate to throw things away.' She busied herself packing her sewing box away. 'Besides, I thought I might return it one day.'

Her answer did not satisfy Daniel, but it did give him hope. 'I would have thought returning a button to me would be the last thing on your mind when you fled Bosvenna estate, Janey,' he said, in a gentle tone.

Janey straightened and hugged the sewing box to her chest. She dared not look at him, preferring to take an interest in the polished wood in her hands.

'You were never far from my mind, Daniel. I did not want to leave it behind.' She turned and gave him a shy smile. 'Now, we must hurry. The shop owner is expecting us and we must create a good impression by being on time.'

Arthur Jones greeted Janey with a smile and looked warily at Daniel as he entered his shop behind her. Ignoring the mixed greeting, Janey put out her hand and, a little surprised, Arthur Jones took it.

'Thank you for seeing us, Mr Jones. I am Janey Kellow. I believe you know my husband, Daniel.'

Daniel, not used to mixing with the villagers, followed his wife's lead and shook the shopkeeper's hand.

'We have arranged this meeting as we have something you may be interested in selling in your shop.'

Janey took out her samples of butter and cheese for the shopkeeper to try. The samples were not from their first batch. It took several attempts and tasting sessions, involving everyone at Boscarn Farm, before they were happy with it. To ensure they made the best quality product, Janey and Molly had attended a dairy course in the nearby town of Camelford. They could not persuade Edna to join them.

'I 'ave not travelled further than two miles outside this 'ere village an' don't intend to start now!' she had told them, and nothing Janey or Molly could say would change her mind. However, their own successful participation had resulted in them both gaining a dairy certificate, which Janey proudly showed the man standing before her.

'These cheese samples are from our mild cheese range and this is our butter,' said Janey, laying out her samples. 'They are both made from South Devon cattle which produce rich creamy milk. We will be able to produce medium and mature cheeses over time. It's the age of the cheese that determines the maturity, as I'm sure you know.'

The shopkeeper nodded and selected a sample of butter, moving it about his mouth to taste the full flavour. He then reached for a cube of cheese and took a bite. He took his time as he savoured it on his tongue. Daniel and Janey held their breath.

'They are very good,' said the shopkeeper, reaching for another. 'It melts in the mouth.'

Janey smiled and released the breath she had been holding.

'So you will be happy to sell our cheese and butter in your shop?'

'Now I didn't say that. Mrs Tholly makes my cheese and Hawkens makes the butter. The locals are used to their products,' he said, glancing sheepishly at Daniel.

Janey couldn't believe what she was hearing, or rather what he wasn't saying. The shopkeeper did not want to do business with Daniel Kellow, despite the cheese and butter being a far superior product to the ones he sold at present. From the look on Daniel's face he was thinking the same.

'Mr Jones, our cheese and butter taste better than any I have tasted for a very long time. I'm sure the villagers would prefer to buy ours.'

'That is your opinion.' Arthur Jones showed them the door. As far as he was concerned the meeting was over.

Daniel stepped forward. 'Mr Jones, I understand you are wary of doing business with me, sir. If I was in your shoes I would feel the same.'

The shopkeeper eyed him suspiciously.

'I know I have a lot to prove, but I feel that the product we are producing is far superior to anything available in this area at the moment. We plan to sell to St Mabe, Port Wella, Bodmin and Wadebridge in the coming months, however we wanted the local village shop to be the first to have an option to buy and to offer you privileges the other shops will not have.'

'Privileges you say? Such as?' Daniel had secured Arthur's attention.

'Such as a short notice order delivery privilege and a ten per cent discount. As our first buyer you are important to us.'

Janey felt pride for her husband surge through her. He was talking to the shopkeeper as if he had been doing negotiations for years. However, Arthur still remained doubtful.

'You still seem unsure,' Daniel said. 'I am willing to provide the first block of cheese free and you will have one hundred per cent profit from the sales. When it is a success, which I have no doubt it will be, will you do business with us?'

'A free block of cheese and a ten per cent discount on all future orders?'

'Yes, Mr Jones. I give you my word our products will remain pure, with no bulking additives and our deliveries will be reliable. As our first customer you will always be special to us.'

Arthur thought for a moment, as he selected another sample of cheese and popped it in his mouth.

'Of course, Mr Kellow, you know as well as I do it will sell before the week is out.'

'I have no doubt it will, Mr Jones.'

The shopkeeper nodded in resignation. 'I believe we have a deal,' he said, offering his hand. The deal was confirmed with a firm handshake.

As a young woman Janey always thought she would

fall in love in a romantic setting, perhaps watching the red sky of a perfect sunset or dancing to the sound of a waltz. She never envisaged that it would be in a crowded little shop with the smell of cheese filling her nostrils. She watched Daniel's lips move as he spoke to the shopkeeper but she no longer heard his words. It seemed every day she was discovering a new side to Daniel Kellow. Daniel, the serious, stubborn and aloof man who had dipped in and out of her life over the past two years, had today conducted himself in a polite, self-assured manner. His behaviour had been akin to a gentleman. She wondered how long she had been in love with him. Mary had seen a spark between them from the very beginning. Perhaps she had been in love with him all along. The truth of the matter was she simply didn't know. She did know, however, with a certainty that she would stake her own life on, that in the dimly lit shop, surrounded by sacks of flour and holding cheese samples in her hand, she had realised that she loved her husband – and it felt glorious.

Edna turned the handle of the mangle as Janey carefully threaded the wet clothes through the wooden rollers. There was something rewarding about seeing the water squeezed out of the washing and drip into the bucket below. Janey was approaching her eighth month. She was beginning to tire and Daniel had insisted on taking on extra help in the dairy as orders were beginning to build. The first batch of cheeses was nearly mature and ready for delivery but the shops who were willing to sell them had also expressed an interest in their butter samples.

The first Kellow butter was delivered to the outlets last week with a resounding success and the cheese and butter making was becoming a full-time job. So when Daniel arrived with two of Matt's younger sisters, Janey couldn't help feeling a little relieved. While they did most of the work, she and Edna supervised, tested for quality and prepared the orders. Daniel and David then made the deliveries. It was a small business but one that was fast growing a good reputation for reliability and quality. Daniel soon realised that, if it continued to grow at the same rate, they would need more land to accommodate a bigger herd.

Edna and Janey chatted about the success of the business as they worked, resting now and then to take a drink from the water they had drawn from the well, before returning to the laundry pile. Edna had begun to look upon Janey as the daughter she never had and told her just that. Perhaps it was this closeness that led Janey to confide in her about what was recently troubling her.

'I worry about giving birth. What if something goes wrong?'

'Things do go wrong, there's no doubt about that,' replied Edna matter-of-factly. 'I carried all my babies for the first four months but after that date they would start to slip away from me. None lived past seven months. But you 'ave good child bearing 'ips an' your time is nearly 'ere. We 'ave Bertha in the village, she delivers all the babies around 'ere an' then there's the doctor nearby who lives in the big 'ouse at the bottom of the 'ill. There's 'elp at 'and.'

'Did you have Bertha?'

'In time, but I 'ad Agnes first. She was the midwife back when I 'ad my first. She was the wise woman of the village, tended all the deliveries an' laid out all the dead. If she 'ad been born a 'undred years earlier she would be called a witch. ''Er 'ouse is full of concoctions for this an' that, an' she's not averse to casting the odd spell or two. 'Owever, give 'er 'er due, she was a good midwife. If I'd taken 'er advice my babies may 'ave survived and I might 'ave 'ad a brood of my own.'

Janey sat down and Edna followed suit.

'What was her advice?'

'After my first miscarriage she told me to kill a bird and wrap it in cloth soaked in the blood from the afterbirth. She told me to 'ide it in the 'ouse. She said by offering the life of a small animal it would prevent further miscarriages in the 'ouse where it was buried. She said that all future babies born there would be 'ealthy and survive.'

'But you didn't do it.'

The old woman shrugged. 'At the time it sounded like a lot of mumbo jumbo. We 'ad a big row an' we never spoke again. I didn't know I would 'ave seven more babies to bury but by then I was too proud and grief-stricken to make up with 'er. She still lives in the village but she 'asn't delivered a baby for twenty years now. She got fed up with people knocking on 'er door at any time of the day and night. Bertha will be around. She will look after you. You need not worry on that score.'

The baby kicked inside her. 'It's kicking again, Edna.'

The old lady chuckled and reached over to feel the bump. 'You've got a strong baby in there. I don't think you need to worry about the birth. This little one is fighting fit.'

'Daniel won't feel the baby's movements,' Janey blurted out. She could hardly blame him but it concerned her none the less.

'Men are funny sometimes. 'E will come around. When 'e sees the little one staring up at 'im 'e will be all over the baby. You just wait and see.'

Janey smiled weakly at Edna. 'I hope so. I hope so very much.' She stroked her belly but couldn't help feeling a sense of foreboding about the month ahead.

Daniel felt the smack to his face before he was awake. Its suddenness wrenched him from his dreams and into reality with lightning speed. He sat up, rubbing his jaw, and looked down at his wife as she slept beside him. She was having another nightmare. She whimpered between bouts of fighting, flailing her arms as if it was for her very survival. The first time he had seen her like this he was at a loss what to do. He had tried to hold her tight to provide comfort but it only made things worse. In the end he had woken her but it took a long time for her to settle and he feared he had made things worse. In the morning he had asked her what she had been dreaming about but she had been evasive and did not want to talk about it. She had asked if she had spoken and appeared relieved when he said he could make no sense of her mumbling.

In the first few weeks of their marriage she had suffered these nightmares at least twice a week. They were occurring less frequently now but after the first he had resolved not to tell her. She had not wanted to share with him the contents of her dreams and if she remembered them she did not tell him. He no longer woke her. He had learnt that stroking her hair and whispering her name seemed to soothe her and chase the nightmare away.

He turned and propped himself up on his elbow and did just that, troubled to see the beaded perspiration upon her forehead as he spoke softly into the night. He had his own ideas of the cause as he had seen her fight like this before. It had been when she had fought hard to be released from the arms that held her. He remembered how she looked in minute detail; he remembered the weather, the time and the place as clearly as if it had been yesterday. He could even remember her anguished cry. He closed his eyes shut, hating knowing who she was fighting in her dreams because when he had seen her fight like this before it had been on Hel Tor and the arms about her were his.

*

Janey leant against the gate of the meadow and took a deep breath. The air, as always, was fresh and clean and she inhaled it deep within her lungs, savouring it before letting it out once more. The sun shone down on the wild flowers that carpeted the little meadow and Janey watched in delight as butterflies fluttered haphazardly from flower to flower. She had felt restless all morning so when Daniel had told her that he would have to move the herd to eat the meadow grass soon she had taken the opportunity to go for a walk and drink in the sight of the flowers before they were eaten. Their destruction was part of farming life, and next year they would grow back stronger from the richly fertilised soil. David arrived and leaned on the gate beside her.

'I'm looking for Daniel, do you know where he is?' he asked.

Janey shook her head. 'He may have gone to the top field. He did say there was a tree up there that needed cutting back. I'm not certain though. Why?'

David picked up a blade of grass and started to chew it.

'There's no problem,' he said. 'I just wondered if he wanted me to clean out the water troughs. What are you going to do this afternoon?'

'I'm feeling a bit restless, I may take a walk into the village later.' They stood quietly admiring the flowers. 'They're beautiful. Wild flowers are my favourite,' Janey said with a sigh, and was surprised when David said he knew. Molly had said the same thing when she gave her her wedding bouquet. Janey was intrigued. 'How do you know?' she asked.

David tried to swat a fly that had started to annoy him. 'Daniel said.'

'He did? When?'

David returned to his chewing. 'Oh ages ago. Two year or more.'

Janey turned to him. How would Daniel know that they were her favourite flowers? She only remembered telling James Brockenshaw when she returned from walking Charlie. He had struck up a conversation with her in the courtyard behind Bosvenna Manor, and only a few days later he had given her a bouquet of wild flowers or at least David did on his behalf. As Janey recalled the events a growing sense of pain grew in her chest as she realised that Daniel had been present at the time.

'Tell me about the day you gave me the flowers, David. How did it come about?'

'I suppose that now you are wed, there is no reason not to tell you,' said David as he leaned against the gate. 'Daniel had got himself all dressed up in his best clothes. Well, you know how Molly is; she kept asking where he was going. He eventually said he was going to ask a girl to walk out with him and he paid Molly a farthing to pick a bunch of flowers from the meadow as they were the girl's favourite flower.' Janey hid her surprise as she quietly listened. 'He asked me to go with him,' continued David, 'to look after the horse while he walked up the drive of Bosvenna Manor.'

'Why didn't he give them to me?' asked Janey, not quite believing what she was hearing.

'When we got to the gates he changed his mind ... not like Daniel at all. He said that he was on a fool's errand, that you were too good for him. I said Molly would be really upset if he didn't give you the flowers so he told me to run down the drive and give them to you but not to say they were from him. So I did what he asked.' David lifted his cap and scratched his head before sliding it back on. 'After I gave them to you we rode home. He never mentioned your name again until the day he brought you home.'

'I saw you speaking to James Brockenshaw when you left,' said Janey, quietly.

'That awful man nearly rode into me. He asked me what I was about and I said I was running an errand. He then told me to get off the estate and be sharp about it or he'd have me whipped for trespassing.'

'They were beautiful flowers,' Janey said, lamely, but her mind was on Daniel.

'They were just ordinary flowers but you seemed to like them at the time. I'll go and look for Daniel in the top field. He might need a hand with the tree.'

Janey watched David leave, but her thoughts were elsewhere. Daniel had wanted to walk out with her? Yet every time they had met they had argued. He hated James Brockenshaw and took every opportunity to warn her off him. Yet the more she thought of those meetings with Daniel she realised that the stubborn man, who was always giving her his words of wisdom, was really a man that was jealous of her interest in James. How could she be so blind? He had been in and out of her life, often helping her, often annoyed with her – but always wanting her. Janey needed to speak to him but it would have to wait until this evening when Molly and David were in their annex and Edna had gone home. It was a conversation she did not want interrupted by anyone.

Still feeling restless she decided she would take a walk into the village and visit the haberdashery. A sudden desire to make a new dress that would show off her figure once the baby was born had taken hold of her. She wanted to look desirable for her husband and if she ordered some material now, the dress might be ready by the time the baby arrived, with Edna's help.

Janey entered the farmhouse by the back door and reached for her shawl and reticule. It was Daniel's voice she heard first, followed by Edna's soothing tones. She was about to call out to them to let them know where she was going and that David was looking for him, when she heard her name mentioned. She paused, hesitating whether to listen or leave.

'I try but I just can't,' said Daniel. Edna replied but Janey could not make out the words. She waited for Daniel's reply. 'I see her belly getting bigger, I know she wants me to take an interest in it, but I can't. I feel nothing for the baby. I don't know if I ever will. It's like a thing growing between us.' She could hear the anguish in his voice. 'She wants me to love it but at the moment I can't. I hate myself for feeling this way but I don't know how to change things.'

Her initial joy at realising he wanted her faded. He may want her but he did not want her baby and her baby was part of her. Janey half stumbled, turned and fled.

She walked fast and furiously to the village turning over the conversation in her head. By the time she reached the village some sanity had taken hold once more. Could she blame Daniel for having doubts about the baby? Did he not have the right to express his concerns to Edna and seek her advice? She must remain calm and not judge Daniel too harshly. She had had far longer to get used to the idea of the pregnancy and parenthood than he had. She wanted the marriage to work. She loved Daniel. Maybe, with time and understanding, love for her child would grow. Daniel had said once before that love could grow despite the best attempts to crush it. She didn't know if she was evading the problem or being philosophical about it; either way she would visit the haberdashery as she had planned. The visit would take her mind off her problems and her pregnancy, which was becoming more uncomfortable as the days went on.

David saw Daniel walking towards him through the farmyard.

'There you are. I've been looking for you. Janey didn't know where you were either.'

'I've been talking to the old woman,' said Daniel, not stopping to speak further.

'Did Janey find you?'

Daniel became wary and slowed his step. 'No, why?' he asked.

David scratched his head. 'She said she was going to the village so I assumed she would let Edna know.'

'When did she come to the house?' he asked, concerned that his conversation with Edna had been overheard. When David answered he knew, without a doubt, it had. 'I'd better go to the village to give her a lift home,' he said, marching off to prepare the horse and trap. 'She shouldn't be walking so far in her condition.'

Janey had a successful visit to the shop and was making her way home across the village green. Two large oak trees grew in its centre, forming a canopy of leaves providing cooling shade on the hot sunny day. Janey's mind was still filled with Daniel as she stepped amongst its leafy shadows. She did not notice the man waiting for her to approach until he stepped out into her path.

'Well, if it isn't my little vixen, come out of her den to bathe in the sunshine,' James teased.

Janey felt the earth tilt beneath her feet as she looked up to see the man in front of her. Drink had aged James, mottling his skin and reddening his eyes, and despite his well-tailored suit and matching top hat, he looked slightly dishevelled. She wondered if he had been drinking today; if not she had no doubt he would be in his cups by the evening. He raked her body with his gaze and took in that she was with child.

Janey moved to the side to walk past him but he blocked her way.

'That's very impolite of you, Janey. It is customary to reply to a greeting.'

Janey often wondered how she would feel if she ever saw him again. Would it be fear or humiliation? Now she knew. It was anger, and she was grateful for it.

Through gritted teeth she hissed. 'I see no one I wish to greet. Get out of my way.'

'You seem upset.'

'You amaze me with your arrogance,' she retorted. 'I have no wish to speak to you. I hate and despise you and will do so until my dying day.'

Daniel brought the trap to a halt and searched the street for Janey. He could not see her so turned his attention to the green. At first he overlooked the couple standing alone under the shade of the twin oak trees but something in the way the woman stood caught his attention. His gut twisted in anguish as he realised it was Janey and that she was talking to Brockenshaw. They stood close together, oblivious of the people around them, and they only had eyes for one another.

'What is the matter with you? Can we not be civil?'

'Do you really not know?' Janey was incredulous. 'You raped me.'

Brockenshaw examined the end of his cane. 'Rape is a serious allegation.'

'You raped me,' she repeated, clearly. 'Call it what you like to evade responsibility but I know what you did and so do you.'

'You enjoyed my attentions. In the grotto your eyes were like a puppy … begging.'

'You took advantage of your station and position. Do not try to pass the responsibility of your attack onto me.

There is only one person who has that and that is you. Now get out of my way.'

'Janey,' he said, reaching out to touch her cheek, 'let us be friends. I have taken a room in the inn down the road. Come back with me and let us talk about it.'

Daniel saw Brockenshaw caress his wife's cheek and could stomach no more. With a flick of the reins he turned the trap around and headed for home.

'Take your hand off me,' ground out Janey. 'You make my skin crawl.'

James's hand fell away.

'I am Mrs Kellow now. You have no hold over me. The sight of you makes me feel sick!'

Janey turned around and set off for home, turning only briefly to reassure herself that he was not following. With some relief, she saw him entering the village inn.

There had been something cathartic to have faced him after all this time and tell him how much she hated him. His avoidance of any responsibility to the act dumbfounded her, yet, on reflection, what did she expect? She had been blind to his conceitedness, his false charm and his spoilt ways. She had been a fool. Yet she knew she had also been naive, a dreamer and he had seen her weakness and taken advantage of it.

She paused to catch her breath. She rubbed the base of her bump to ease the cramp like ache that had come back again. She had experienced the pain, which was not unlike her monthly curse, when she started her journey. Thankfully it had passed off but now it had returned. It was not unduly painful, but it was uncomfortable nonetheless and she waited for it to pass before she started her walk again.

A few yards down the road she was forced to stop again

as the discomfort had returned. Perhaps the baby was in a strange position and pressing on her somewhere? She heard the horse and trap before she saw them and it was with some relief when she saw it was her husband coming to collect her. She smiled at him and waved, but her smile faded a little as he approached and she saw how angry he looked. Daniel expertly turned the trap and horse in the road and waited for her to climb up.

'I'm so glad you have come. I was beginning to regret walking into the village. Did David tell you where I was?' Daniel did not answer. Janey grabbed her seat for support as the trap lurched off. 'I have some news. I hear from the vicar that the bank is finally selling the Bosvenna Estate. I thought perhaps we could rent the two fields that border our top fields from the new landlord. You said we would need more land. Of course it would be better to buy but we can't afford it at the moment. I could write to Lady Brockenshaw and ask her to let us know who the new landlord would be. I've been meaning to write to her and tell her I'm now married. We had a close relationship when I worked for her and I'm sure she would be interested.'

'Why did you go to the village?'

Janey frowned at his angry tone. 'For this and that,' she said, evasively. She wanted the dress to be a surprise. 'What is the matter?'

'You tell me,' he replied.

They arrived at the farm in silence, Janey perplexed by his angry mood.

Daniel jumped down and grabbed the horse's bridle. 'David. David!' The boy came running out of the house. 'Unhitch the horse and put the trap away.'

The boy took the bridle and gave Janey a questioning look. Janey shrugged, she was as confused as he. Carefully she got down from the trap to follow Daniel into the house.

'Daniel, what is the matter? Why are you so angry?' Daniel had taken the stairs two at a time and stood looking down at her from the top.

'Why did you go to the village?' he asked again.

'I had errands to run, nothing of importance. I know I should not have walked there,' she said, unconsciously rubbing her pain away again, 'but I'm home now. I won't do it again.' She had almost reached him before he turned and strode off to their bedroom.

Angrily he changed his shirt for another one, pulling at the buttons and throwing the one he had worn across the room. Janey watched him, bewildered.

'You are lying.'

Janey shook her head. 'No, I'm not,' she replied, quietly.

He finished buttoning his shirt and stood in front of her with a tortured look on his face. He leaned toward her until she felt his breath on her cheek. 'I saw you!' he whispered.

The blood drained from Janey's face. He had seen her talking with James. Daniel pushed past her and descended the steps two at a time. Janey followed, almost tripping on the hem of her dress in her haste.

'It's not what it looked like, Daniel. It was not planned.'

'Don't lie to me, Janey.' His hatred for the man was palpable. 'You swore to me you would not make a fool of me. You promised me you would not meet with him behind my back. How often have you arranged your lover's trysts? Or did it never stop?'

'You can't believe I have any feelings for him, Daniel? It is you I love, not him.' It was not the time to confess her love for him. Even to her own ears it sounded false, a lie to be told to get out of trouble.

Daniel paced around the kitchen like a caged animal. His anger at her perceived betrayal had no outlet and he wanted to tear the house apart.

'I saw you. I saw him touching you.'

'You saw me telling him how much I hate and despise him.'

Daniel scoffed in disbelief. 'You have always loved him. You made no secret of it. I was nothing to you ... just someone to mop up his mistakes. One day you are kissing me, the next you are in his arms. Marriage has changed nothing.'

Edna came into the kitchen and watched in horror at the argument unfolding in front of her. Guarding the door to keep David away she felt powerless to help.

Janey's eyes blurred with tears. 'I don't love him. It was nothing more than a young girl's crush. It is you I want, it always has been, I just didn't realise it.' She grabbed his arm to keep him still. 'Please believe me!'

He shook her off and resumed his pacing. He had seen them together, his eyes did not lie.

'How often have you met? How often have you made love?'

'Today was the only time we've met since we married. It was not arranged, I did not want to see him. He just appeared!'

'Did you make love?'

'No! I was only in his company for a few minutes.'

'You expect me to believe that?'

'I told you before we were married it has only ever been the one time.'

'Once? Why should I believe you?'

'It is the truth!'

'Where?' He wanted the details; it was as if he had a sore he could not help but pick.

'Please, Daniel, don't torture yourself.'

'Where?' he asked again.

'In my room ... in the servants' quarters.'

'Do you still love him?'

'No, I hate him.'

'Why would a young girl's crush turn to hate when you have a baby in your belly to bind you together?'

Janey turned away but he grabbed her by the shoulders and forced her to face him.

'See, you cannot look at me. You still love him!'

'No!'

'Then tell me why? Convince me!' he shouted, giving her a little shake. 'Convince me!'

'Because he raped me!' she screamed.

No one in the room moved. Now she would know if he believed her. Now she would know if he thought she had brought it on herself. Just a look from him, just a hesitation in his voice or manner and she would know.

'I'll kill him!' he roared, heading for the door.

'Don't!' Janey cried. 'Stop him, Edna.' Edna had already blocked the door.

'Now don't go doing anything 'asty, boy,' she said. 'You'll get yourself in all sorts of trouble if you go an' do something stupid.'

'Get out of my way, old woman! He's going to pay for what he's done!'

Janey clutched Daniel's arm. 'It's not him that will pay; it will be you on the end of a hangman's rope. It will be me because you will be lost to me.' He tried to shake her off. 'It will be Molly, David and Edna.'

Daniel turned away from her and moved the old woman to one side.

'He can't be allowed to get away with it. I'll take the chance. I've got to make him pay.' He lifted the latch.

Janey reached for a butcher's knife. 'If you harm him,' she said, calmly, 'as God is my witness, I will kill myself.' Daniel turned to look at his wife holding the butcher's knife to her own throat. 'I swear on my life, Daniel, if you harm Brockenshaw, I will slit my throat right here and now.'

'I can take the knife from you.'

'But you won't be able to watch me forever. I swear I will kill myself. I will not live my life waiting for them to arrest you for murder. I will not live my life with memories of seeing you swing from a rope …' Her eyes brimmed with tears. '… and I will not live my life without you.'

Daniel turned to look at the door latch and lifted in his hand.

'Please, Daniel, swear to me you won't harm him,' she begged.

He rested his forehead on the door, a man defeated. As much as he hated the man and what he had done, Janey knew he loved her, and his life at the farm, more.

'I swear,' Daniel promised, hating the words he spoke. He turned to look at her. Janey tried to smile to reassure him, but under his gaze she could no longer hide the pain. Her hand began to shake as she slowly lowered the knife to her side and let it fall.

'Well, I'm glad that crisis is over,' she said bravely, 'as I think another one is about to begin.' Daniel looked down. Fluid was silently seeping from beneath her hem, its finger-like rivulets surrounding the blade at her feet. Her waters had broken. Brockenshaw's baby was on the way.

Chapter Nineteen

The accusations of betrayal were forgotten as Daniel and Edna helped Janey to bed. Edna took charge and shooed him out of the room, claiming that this was 'woman's work' and ordering him to get Bertha from the village.

Daniel sent David off to fetch her, and sat in the kitchen to wait for news. As generations of expectant fathers before him, he was unable to settle and paced the room as he listened to the groans of pain above. Molly arrived home from school, and in a whirlwind of excitement on hearing the news, ran upstairs to help. Daniel remained downstairs to wait. Finally David returned – alone.

'Bertha's at a birthing down by Willford Crossing,' he told them, still breathless from the ride. 'Her sister says she will be finished there soon and she will send her up here.'

'Well, I 'ope she won't be long,' Edna said, cheerfully, as she fetched a towel that hung in front of the range warming. 'I've never delivered a baby before.'

'How is she?' asked Daniel, concerned. Time was passing and he hated to hear Janey so distressed.

'She's strong, it shouldn't be long now. I just 'ope Bertha will arrive soon.' Edna disappeared upstairs again before Daniel could question her further.

Several hours passed. Edna came to the bedroom door to call down to Daniel and David for the fourth time.

'Is she 'ere yet?'

'No.' Daniel came to the bottom of the stairs to talk to her. 'I'll ride over to see where she has got to.' As he turned to go Edna spoke again.

'Daniel,' she called. 'If you 'ave to drag 'er from the other labour, do so.' The worried look on Edna's face sent Daniel running to his horse.

Daniel banged on Bertha's door with the side of his fist, causing it to rattle on its hinges. A middle-aged woman answered with a look of horror on her face.

'Oh no,' cried Bertha's sister. 'I forgot to tell her!' Daniel felt his heart drop in his chest.

'Is she here?' he asked, hopefully. 'I'll take her back on my horse. My wife needs her.' The woman shook her head.

'I'm so sorry,' the woman looked genuinely stricken. 'She's not here. She's gone to Mevagissey to visit our brother. She won't be back tonight ... or tomorrow. Ride on to Doctor Barker. I know doctors usually leave the birthing to the women but he will be better than no one.'

Daniel thanked her for her advice and leapt back into the saddle. He was angry with the woman but she looked genuinely mortified that she had forgotten the message and taking his frustration out on her would help no one. Digging his heels into his horse's flanks, he galloped recklessly down the road to the big house at the bottom of the hill. It seemed like an age before anyone answered the door. Between pacing back and forth, Daniel rang and knocked several times. Eventually a maid opened the large neatly painted door.

'Doctor Barker is attending a function in Truro and will be staying overnight. Doctor Billingsworth is meant to be taking his calls. He lives in St Tude but I'm afraid he will be of no help to you. Someone else sought him out this afternoon and found him drunk in the Pig and Whistle. He was fit for nothing then and he still had a brandy in his hand.'

Daniel swore, returned to his horse and pulled himself back into the saddle. The sooner he let Edna know the bad news the better.

When Daniel arrived home he knew something was wrong. Molly came downstairs looking close to tears. Gone was her earlier excitement and she couldn't bring herself to speak for fear of crying. She went to fetch Edna, who came down to speak to Daniel.

'Is Bertha 'ere?' she asked, immediately.

'No. She's left for Mevagissey, Doctor Barker is in Truro and the doctor in St Tude is drunk. I don't know who else to fetch. How is she?'

Janey's moans were quieter and he hoped it was a good sign. It was not.

'It's not going well. There's something wrong. The speed and strength of 'er pains are strong but the baby just won't come. She's getting weaker, Daniel. I don't think she can last much longer.'

Daniel stared blankly at her unable to absorb what she had just said. Edna turned her attention to David who was looking at her with glistening eyes.

'Fetch Agnes, she lives at Myrtle Cottage. It's the rundown 'ouse with the ivy growing over the top windows and an overgrown garden. Tell her Edna needs 'er 'elp. Tell 'er Edna's sorry for what she 'as said in the past. Tell 'er anything, just get 'er 'ere.'

David ran out of the house and galloped off on Daniel's horse. Daniel finally found his voice.

'What's going on, Edna? She's going to be all right, isn't she?'

'No, Daniel, I don't think she is. I think she's dying. You'd better come in and spend some time with 'er. It may be the last chance you get.'

Daniel opened the door. The room smelt of stale sweat, immediately infiltrating his nostrils like a sickly poison. A frightened Molly was holding Janey's hand, but on seeing

Daniel made an immediate retreat to allow him access to her.

'We'll be outside the door if you need us, Daniel,' whispered Edna and she quietly pulled the door closed behind him.

Daniel looked down at his wife. She looked pale and weak as she lay sprawled on the dishevelled bed. She wore her white cotton nightgown, which was stained pale pink in places. Her hair was wet from effort and her legs shook with pain. She opened her eyes and reached out her hand to him, whispering his name with dried, cracked lips. He had never seen her so close to death, for that was what she was. Yet the eyes that looked up at him were her eyes; much duller, etched with pain, but they were her eyes all the same. It was her soul looking back at him, proving her spirit was still on this earth. He reached for her and cradled her in his arms.

He tried to soothe her as he did when he chased away her nightmares in the depths of the night, but this nightmare would not end. Her limp body shook as another contraction reared its ugly head, building and building like a violent torturer enjoying inflicting pain to its victim. In agony she buried her face in his chest, clinging to his arms for support, yet even in this she felt weak. As the pain passed, she lay like a limp doll in his arms.

'This is my fault,' Daniel said, stroking away the wet hair from her face, 'I shouldn't have argued with you.'

She shook her head weakly. 'Hush now,' she soothed. 'The labour had started long before our row. I just … didn't realise.' It was an effort for her to speak and he knew it, yet even now she was soothing and reassuring him. 'They don't think I know,' she whispered, weakly, 'but I do. I'm dying, Daniel. I know I am.' He told her she was wrong but she would have none of it. 'I don't have the time for untruths.'

She touched his cheek and to his horror her hand felt cold. 'I want you to know, I do love you, Daniel Kellow. Always have. I just didn't realise it.'

'You seem to not realise a lot,' Daniel said, trying to lighten things. She smiled weakly at his remark.

'I heard you speaking to Edna about the baby.'

'I know. I'm sorry.'

She shook her head weakly again to quieten his words. 'Don't be, Daniel, I understand.' Her lids fluttered shut for a moment and she tried to gain some strength. 'It must be hard for you to bring up another man's baby as your own. Please, Daniel, promise me you will not ...' she faltered; the effort of speaking was getting too much.

'Hush, Janey, rest. You need your strength,' soothed Daniel, tears stinging his eyes. Janey ignored him.

'... will not make my baby suffer for the way it was conceived or who its father is. Please promise me.'

'I promise. The baby will never know that I am not its real father in deed or word.'

Janey sighed and relaxed in his arms for a few seconds, savouring his promise until another contraction racked her body. The contraction was more violent than the last but Janey's reaction was weaker. She was dying in his arms and he felt useless to help her.

After it had passed her eyes remained shut as she weakly smiled to herself.

'You have always helped me when I was in trouble ... on the night of the dance ... by the river ... in the ruin ... even on Hel Tor when I was thinking of killing myself.'

'I can't help you now, Janey. Only you can do that. Don't give up. Don't give up on us.'

'I don't have the strength.' Her voice was so quiet he could hardly hear her. 'I'm so ... tired.'

He held her tightly. 'Don't leave me,' he pleaded.

'I have no choice.' She was slipping away from him like water through his fingers.

'Haunt me if you must, just don't leave me.' He was becoming angry in his distress. 'Walk in my dreams, be by my side in the day, just don't leave me alone on this earth without you!'

'I'm too tired, Daniel. Just speak to me. Let me hear your voice.'

As the life flowed out of Janey's body, Daniel rocked her in his arms. She was too exhausted to fight for life and he knew it.

'From the first day I saw you,' he said, gently, 'I wanted you as my wife. You were standing on the moor, surrounded by lambs bleating for their mothers, with your arms outstretched to the sky. The sun was shining on your face and you were sighing in pleasure.' Daniel smiled at the memory. 'You didn't know I was watching, but I was. You were so happy and I knew from that moment I wanted to spend my life making you feel that way again.'

He stroked another wet strand away from her clammy forehead. She was smiling but her eyes remained closed and he was unsure if she could still hear him. 'You wore a blue dress and a bonnet with matching blue ribbons. You had one single strand of hair that had come loose and it bobbed and bounced against your neck as you walked. You were the most beautiful woman I had ever seen and I was lost for words. By the time I had found my tongue you were gone. I thought I would never see you again. I even wondered if I'd dreamt you up.' He kissed her limp hand and held it to his cheek. 'If you had a brood of children hanging on your skirts, I would still have married you. I was so afraid you would not turn up to the church that day. Then suddenly there you were, looking as beautiful as ever with flowers in your hair.'

The smile from Janey's face had gone and she lay quietly in his arms. She looked dead; if it wasn't for her shallow breathing he would have thought she was. The door opened and Edna entered with an old woman. Agnes, the wise woman from the dilapidated cottage in the village had arrived.

She was older than Edna and twice as ugly, with a hooked nose and a whiskery chin. Her expression was grave when she saw Janey. She did not waste time on polite greetings and immediately rolled up her sleeves.

She looked at Daniel. '*You* can get out of the 'ouse. I don't want men around while I work.'

Edna nodded to the door encouraging Daniel to do as Agnes had instructed. Daniel briefly hesitated – it may be the last time he saw Janey alive – yet if he did not let this strange creature do her job, she would be dead before the night was through. He gave his wife a heartfelt kiss on her forehead, carefully laid her head back on the pillow and left the room.

Daniel could not bear to leave entirely. He sat at the kitchen table waiting, unsure if his legs could support his weight any more. His whole body seemed to be shaking as he listened to the floorboards creak above his head. Molly came downstairs with a small pouch in her hand and he watched her pouring something from it into a cup; on this she poured hot water from the kettle. She no longer looked like a twelve-year-old. The events of the evening had aged her ten years. Daniel asked what she was doing.

'The woman says it's yarrow herb and it treats fever and bleeding.' She put down the kettle and turned to Daniel. 'I'm scared, Daniel. She says the baby's in the wrong position and it's not turned right. She's up there prodding and pushing Janey's belly … she's being really rough. She's mumbling words I don't understand, bit like Granny Thom does, but it sounds like spells and chanting. Granny Thom is just watching and doing nothing to stop her.'

Daniel buried his head in his hands. He knew she wanted him to reassure her that Janey would be all right but he didn't have the confidence in Agnes to give it. Molly disappeared upstairs with the brew and almost immediately Edna came down. Daniel looked up hopefully but the expression on the old woman's face told him things were no better.

'How is she?' he asked but Edna ignored him. She was looking for a knife. Daniel came to her side. 'What are you doing?'

Edna found the knife she wanted and made her way back to the stairs.

Daniel blocked her way. 'Edna, for God's sake, what's going on up there?'

'Death's going to visit this 'ouse tonight, Daniel. We will be lucky if one of them lives. Now get out of the way, boy.'

Daniel did not move. 'Don't let it be Janey who dies.'

'Neither will survive if you don't move, let me pass.'

'Let me go for the doctor in St Tude. Better a drunk doctor than that crone up there, casting her spells and mixing her potions!' Edna lifted a knife to him.

'Move out the way, boy. I love Janey dearly but they are both going to die if I don't give this to Agnes. Now move or I'll use it on you.' The old woman pushed past him and Daniel, helpless, watched her climbing the stairs. 'If I'd done what she said years ago I might 'ave 'ad a brood of my own an' you must do the same. She wants you an' David out of the 'ouse. Don't come back until sunrise. Don't risk not doing as she says or there'll be two deaths in this 'ouse for sure an' not just one,' called back Edna.

'Why should we trust her, Edna?' Daniel called after her.

Edna paused at the top of the stairs and turned to look at him, the knife glinting in her hand. ''Cos she's my sister, boy, an' she knows what she's doing,' she said, quietly, before disappearing into the bedroom.

At first Daniel could not move but then a powerful energy welled up inside him and he had to get out of the confines of the house. He fled to the stables where he collided with David, knocking the boy to the floor and winding himself. Through gasps of breath he warned the boy not to enter the house before sunrise. If they needed him they would send Molly to fetch him.

'Where are you going?' asked David, looking up at him.

Daniel could not remember mounting his horse; nothing seemed real in this unfolding nightmare. 'I don't know. I just need to get away, but I'll be back. I'll be back to see the wreckage left of my life.' He dug in his heels and the horse, bareback and bridle-less, leapt off into the night with Daniel holding its mane.

The horse and rider thundered along the moonlit road, leaving clouds of dust in their wake. At first Daniel had no plan in his head but as the events of the day tormented his mind his destination became clear to him. He turned the horse northwards and headed for Bosvenna Manor.

The estate was now under the bank's control and awaiting sale. Although the house would be empty, Daniel wanted to ensure he had the freedom to explore it unseen, so upon arriving at the entrance to the drive he took a route through the side gardens. Once the manor came into view he slowed to a trot, jumping to the ground when he finally stopped. Leaving his horse by a tree to graze, he ran across the remaining woodland gardens, his figure disappearing intermittently among the shadows of the trees and shrubs. Eventually he reached the dairy window, opened it and climbed in.

The coolness of the dairy hit his face as his feet landed on the floor. He hadn't been in this room for ten years or more, yet nothing had changed. He did not stay to reminisce over teenage adventures. He was on a mission and was soon on his way. He strode through the corridor and into the main kitchens as if the house was his. The rooms were eerily quiet except for his boots echoing on the slate floor. His path was lit by moonlight that poured through the windows along his route and with ease he found the servants' stairs and ascended them two at a time.

He wanted to see the place where his wife had been raped. It was utter madness, of course, but it befitted his crazed mind. He wanted to share the pain she had endured and to do that was to see it, envisage it and feel it, as she had done. He reached the first floor and then the second in quick succession. He had no interest to explore the rest of the house. This was no leisurely sightseeing tour, he was not there for pleasure. He was there to experience hell.

On the third-floor corridor that led off from the servants' stairs a flickering glow caught Daniel's eye. He stopped. It was the glow from an open fire reflecting on the wall. He was not alone and he knew, without a doubt, who the other person might be.

James Brockenshaw sat slumped in the chair looking at the dancing flames in the fire. He had run out of brandy and sat sulking over his misfortune and too lazy to move. He knew he shouldn't be here but the landlord of the inn where he had been staying had evicted him for non-payment of his rooms. Tomorrow he would go to Wadebridge and stay with some friends until the sale of the estate was complete; after that he did not know where he would go. His friends were becoming less tolerant of his visits. They had started to lecture him on his drinking and his gambling, the very same friends who only a few years ago encouraged him in such antics. Even his mother had refused to see him, calling him a drunk and a disappointment. Disappointment was the same word his father had used to describe him. Even that servant girl had looked at him with pure hatred. What was her name again, his befuddled mind tried to recall, Janey Carhart now Kellow. Kellow. His mind worked slowly in the haze of brandy fumes. Kellow, he knew that name. Suddenly it was as if the man himself had come out of his head, reached down and grabbed him by the collar. Hauling him to his feet, his face no more than a breath away. Daniel spat in his face.

'You bastard!' Daniel roared, shaking James by the collar.

'Get your stinking hands off me!' James demanded, struggling to free himself from the vice-like grip.

'I should kill you for what you did,' Daniel ground out.

'What are you talking about? Get off me.'

James's breath stunk of spirit but Daniel did not care. He pulled him up towards his face so their noses almost touched.

'You raped my wife and I'm going to make you pay!'

Daniel began dragging him from the room like a heavy sack of flour. James fought to free himself, pulling and clutching at Daniel until both men fell heavily at the base of the servants' stairs. Daniel quickly regained his balance and proceeded to climb the steps with James in tow.

'Where are you taking me?' cried James.

'You are going to show me the room where you raped my wife.' Daniel was possessed, consumed with a steely determination to succeed in his quest.

'I didn't rape her,' cried James.

Daniel pulled his face close to his. 'Are you calling my wife a liar?'

James's eyes widened. 'It was a mistake, nothing more.'

Daniel slammed him against the wall. 'A mistake, you say? Are you calling my wife a *mistake*?'

James tried to break free but failed. Once again Daniel

was off, climbing the steps and heaving a stumbling man behind him. Panting, they both arrived in the dark servants' quarters. Daniel pushed James ahead of him.

'Which room was it? This one?' He slammed James against a door. 'Or this one?' Again James's body hit a closed door. Daniel suddenly recalled from which window he had seen Janey's candle light on the evening of the dance. 'I know which one it was.' He dragged James with him to the closed door at the far end of the corridor. 'It's this one, isn't it?' He forced James to face it, by holding his arm painfully high behind his back, but he didn't wait for an answer. He opened the door and pushed James inside, who fell sprawling to the floor.

Daniel had expected to see an empty room, perhaps a bed and a chest of drawers but nothing more. He had not expected to see Janey's uniform hanging neatly on a coat hanger on the wardrobe door or the white lace cap on her bed as if waiting for her to pick it up and place it on her head. A delicately embroidered picture hung from the wall, sewn, no doubt, by her hand. Daniel blinked. He had not expected to see the room as if she had just left it for a moment and would soon return. His gaze fell on a pair of wooden patten shoes placed neatly by the wall. The same ones he had concealed in his coat in order to trick her into taking a ride on his horse.

He should be near her, not here in this house wallowing in the pain of self-pity. She needed him and he was not with her. She may even be dead. How could she be dead and he not be by her side? Daniel did not see James's fist fly through the air but he did feel the pain as it found its target. His head snapped back but he remained standing, although dazed.

James fled the room. Coming to his senses, Daniel followed in hot pursuit, along the corridor, down the stairs and onto the third level of the manor. He chased him through several dimly lit rooms, empty but for the odd piece of furniture covered in white sheets. Although James had the advantage of knowing his route, Daniel was the faster and more agile. Dodging tables and jumping over stools, Daniel soon gained on the drunken man who tripped and stumbled his way through the house that had once been his home.

James opened a door that led out onto the balcony of the grand staircase. The ornately carved stairs wound their way down to the ground floor and into the front hall. James looked behind him and was shocked to see Daniel so near. He stumbled backwards against the banister and disappeared from view. Daniel slid to a halt, his breathing coming hard and fast. He waited for the thud of James's body to hit the tiled floor below, but no sound came. Slowly he stepped forward and looked over the broken banister to the ground floor.

Hanging by his fingertips, James swung precariously from the ledge. His face crumpled in terror as Daniel smiled down at him. Daniel slowly lifted his foot and placed his heel on his fingers.

'I should crush your fingers to a bloody pulp and watch you fall to your death,' he said, in a chillingly relaxed tone as he felt no empathy for the man hanging below him. 'No one would mourn you. You are a disgrace to your family name. I am the wealthier of the two of us as I have Janey. Whereas you ...'

He left the sentence unfinished; they both knew he was highlighting the mess James had made of his life. He lightly pressed his heel on his fingers and James, fearful that his life was about to end, whimpered as he felt the warmth of his own urine seep through his britches.

'I would die a happy man knowing I rid the world of

you,' Daniel mused. He looked up and noticed the sky beginning to lighten. Agnes had told him to stay away until sunrise. It was time he returned home. 'Dawn is breaking and I have somewhere else I'd rather be, and as much as I want to kill you, I promised my wife I would not end my life on a hangman's rope because of you.'

With one movement Daniel reached down, grabbed James's hand and pulled him to safety, but he had not forgiven him. With all his might he kicked Brockenshaw in the stomach where he lay, expending a small part of his hatred for the man. Unable to look at him further he spun on his heel and walked away to find out if it was his wife or this man's baby that had survived the night.

'I'll make you pay for this, Kellow!' James shouted after him.

His threat meant nothing to Daniel. 'I have a house full of witnesses who will vouch I am at home on this night, and what would you say?' shouted back Daniel. 'That I came after you because you raped my wife? That I saved you from a fall? You have no case to charge me. You are a fool, Brockenshaw. A drunken fool, with no home, no money, no family and no future!'

Daniel did not look back again at James, who remained curled on the floor. He wanted to see Janey and discover what was left of his life.

Chapter Twenty

Edna scampered from room to room to reassure herself that the farmhouse was empty. Satisfied that it was, she returned to the main downstairs room and used all her strength to move the sideboard away from the wall. She disappeared but returned within seconds with a crowbar in her hand and proceeded to loosen one of the smaller slates and ease it to the side. Reaching into her apron pocket, she took out a small spade and dug a hole in the rich dark soil that had not seen daylight since the house was built. Following a furtive glance over her shoulder, she reached into her apron pocket again and brought out a small parcel, which she carefully placed in the hole. She sat back on her heels to rest.

She had followed her sister's advice to the letter. The sacrifice and burial of the bird, wrapped in the bloodstained cloth of the childbirth bed, would be the only way to prevent any further miscarriages or deaths due to pregnancy within the house it was hidden. This house is cursed, Agnes had told her, and only this spell would break it. Edna believed her sister was right. Amy and Zachariah's marriage had been childless. To fill the void they had taken in a thieving boy called Daniel. Edna did not want Daniel to suffer another labour like Janey's. She covered the bird with the soil, replaced the slate slab and finally the sideboard over the top. Edna felt a great weight lift from her shoulders now that the spell was complete and she knew, with a certainty that surprised her, that any future pregnancies and births in the house would be happy and healthy ones.

Daniel heard the baby's cry from the other side of the farmyard. He had been working and had no wish to confront the perpetrator, however, the wailing continued to grow, so, with long purposeful strides, he eventually crossed the yard and entered the farmhouse by the back door.

The house appeared empty but for the cradle by the range and its occupant. Seven days ago, while his wife lay dying in his arms, he had promised her that he would look after her baby. For seven days he had avoided the baby girl who had eventually been dragged from her body. It had been Janey's choice to call her daughter Grace and the baby, born three weeks premature, could wake the dead with her cry.

'Edna!' he called out, irritably, 'the baby's squalling!'

It was unlike Edna to not be cooing over the baby. He glanced in the front room and up the stairs but there was no sign of the old woman. He looked warily back at the cradle. The persistent crying was beginning to grate on his nerves but it wasn't himself he was concerned about. He edged towards the cradle and looked in.

The baby, mouth open wide and eyes closed shut, screamed for attention. Her thin arms and balled fists punched the air with frustration. She had kicked off her blankets showing spindly legs with overlarge feet. Her face, flushed red in anger, hinted at the obstinacy in her that had helped her to survive. She stopped her crying and tried to catch her breath, gulping and hiccupping. Daniel, frightened she was having difficulty breathing, called for Edna again. Edna did not come. He need not have worried; the scrawny thing began to cry again, demanding attention and refusing to give up.

By now Daniel was looking directly down on the strange miniature human that seemed oblivious of his presence. Since her birth he had avoided her, unable to look at the baby that had caused so much pain. Her screams changed as she began to tire and her bottom lip trembled between each cry. One finger unfurled from each fist and Daniel thought she looked as if she was conducting an orchestra. Without realising it the thought made him smile. He found himself engrossed in the jerky movements of the little person in the cot. Particulary when she accidently poked herself in the eye. She began to cry louder again, until her thumb found her mouth and she clamped down upon it to suck.

How powerful her suck is, thought Daniel. As if listening to his thoughts the baby raised her eyebrows causing him to smile again. How strange to see such a tiny mite have all the same movements as an adult. He wondered if she was dreaming. Do babies dream? Was she dreaming she was having her dinner or was it all instinct to survive and nothing more?

He reached down and touched her other hand with his finger. The skin, almost transparent, felt as soft as a petal. His finger was grabbed by her little hand and she held on to it tightly, with a strength that surprised him. He noticed her cheeks were covered with a soft downy hair. He had heard Edna tell Molly that the hair would fall away over the next few weeks. Now, for the first time, Daniel had taken the time to see what they were talking about.

With a struggle he prised his finger away from her grasp but immediately felt the urge to reach down and pick her up, as he had become inquisitive to the cuckoo in his nest. Carefully he held her against his chest, supporting her head just as Edna had taught Molly. The baby immediately snuggled into him, her warm head cradled under his jaw. He was glad he had taken the time to shave that morning as he felt her delicate head against his skin. She was warm and had the sweet smell of milk and sleep about her. The little hair she had felt like wisps of frayed silk against his lips as he ran his mouth against the top of her head.

Carefully, he walked to the kitchen window to look for Edna, but instead his reflection in the glass stared back at him. It was a strange sight to see. Daniel Kellow carrying a baby in his arms. She had fallen asleep against him, her little lips now quiet and at peace. Her trust in him was total and unquestioned. She did not fear him, she did not judge him, she did not question him.

He had wanted a family and Grace had come into his life. He had not asked for her or wanted her but she had come all the same. She also had no choice in the matter. Thrown together as father and daughter, he realised they had more in common than not. She moved slightly in his arms and he soothed her with his words. She soon settled at the sound of his voice and he felt his heart swell in his chest for her.

'Hello, Grace,' he whispered into her hair, enjoying her little body snuggled up against his chest. 'Do you know who I am? I'm your father and you are my little girl.'

Edna selected a second slice of Hevva cake and smiled to herself. She knew Daniel would forgive her for not answering the baby's cry but it was something that had to be done. She had watched with growing concern how Daniel had avoided the little mite and she could not let it go on any longer. If Janey knew what was happening she would have been distraught.

Edna didn't blame Daniel. Grace's birth had been traumatic for all involved and people have their own ways of dealing with such things. Then, of course, there was the discovery of how she was conceived. Edna would not tell anyone who the real father was. After all, there were many children in the village brought up by men who were not their fathers. As she often thought, any boy can make a child – it takes a man to make a father, and Daniel would make a good father. He just needed a nudge in the right direction.

So when Grace had started to cry and she saw Daniel

working in the yard, Edna had made herself scarce. She had taken a chair into the pantry, shut the door and sat down to wait for Daniel to investigate the cause of the crying. She wasn't in the habit of hiding from her duties, but it was a means to an end. She sat chewing on the sweet, flat cake feeling rather smug that her plan had worked. Grace had not been the only one to hear her father's words; so did the old woman sitting not ten feet away behind the pantry door.

Daniel looked across the field of waving, golden yellow corn. Daniel liked this time of year, as he was able to see the benefits of his hard labour growing strong in his fields. The sunset cast blood red shadows across the evening sky and he wished Janey was here to share the view with him. If it wasn't for her encouragement he would not have started the dairy business this summer. Its success still surprised him. Never feeling accepted by the villagers before, his reliability, excellent produce and reasonable prices were gaining the respect of the shopkeepers and villagers. Today, for the first time, a couple had raised their hand in greeting to him. He knew that the change in their opinion of him was down to Janey. Oh how he wished she were here now so he could hold her as they watched the sunset together.

He heard a woman's voice call his name from the gateway. He turned to see Janey carefully shutting the gate behind her and making her way over to him. She was smiling at him as the gentle breeze lifted strands of her hair away from her face. She wore a new blue dress he had not seen before, which showed off the curve of her bust and waist in a most enticing manner. Not for the first time, his body stirred as he drank in the vision of her.

But the figure walking towards him was no apparition. It had been two months since that terrible day when she lay dying in his arms and he still couldn't believe Grace and her mother had both survived it. He did not know what Agnes did in that bedroom, what spells the wise woman had cast or what strange concoctions she had brewed. He just knew that when he arrived home from Bosvenna Manor he had found his wife still living and a baby girl in Edna's arms.

Janey had remained very ill for the next two weeks and each morning he had woken wondering if she had survived the night. Edna and Molly cared for the baby and at feed times placed her on Janey's breast for nourishment. After a slow start Grace began to gain weight and it was around this time Janey also improved.

She had nearly reached him and the smile had not left her lips. The healthy glow had returned to her cheeks and to his eye, her womanly post-baby figure looked beautiful and alluring. She stepped into his arms and for a moment they held one another in companionable silence before she twisted to look at the sunset. Daniel rested his chin on her head as he held her to him, enjoying the feel of her bottom against him.

'Beautiful, isn't it?' She sighed, looking at the sun going down.

'Mmmm,' Daniel agreed, enjoying her warmth against him. 'Where's Grace?' he asked.

'Edna's having a last cuddle before she goes home. She's spending tomorrow with Agnes, and of course she never visits on a Sunday, so she won't be back until Monday. I'm glad Agnes and Edna are spending time together. They want to make up for the years that have passed.'

'Yes, thirty years,' agreed Daniel.

Janey watched as a wave of wind flowed over the crop.

'It looks almost ready to harvest.'

'Another couple of weeks and then it will be. I just hope it stays dry so we can get it in safely.' They stood quietly watching the sun, enjoying the peace and quiet.

'I wrote to Lady Brockenshaw today,' said Janey. 'We had become quite close before she left for Falmouth and I have always felt guilty not keeping in touch. Doctor Barker visited this afternoon and he mentioned he was paying a social call on her this evening. I asked him if he would pass on a letter to her. I hope you don't mind.'

'I don't mind,' Daniel said, rubbing his cheek against her soft hair. 'What did you say?'

'I said I was happily married, that I had a beautiful daughter and that we had started a business making cheese and butter. I said we would be limited to how much we could produce as we did not have the acreage for a larger herd. I stopped short of asking her if she knew who the new owner of the Bosvenna Estate was. Doctor Barker says she is unwell and I didn't want to trouble her.'

'Our neighbour, Tommy Hawk, wants to give up farming but he doesn't want to leave his house. It would suit us both if we could rent his fields from his landlord. It would allow Tommy to stay at the farmhouse and it would give us more land for our cattle. It was not only Lady Brockenshaw's son that could not handle money. Her husband has also been short of funds in the past and had to sell some of the farms belonging to the estate. Tommy's farm was one of the farms he sold. He has never met his new landlord as his rent is collected through a third party. We could ask Tommy who this third party is and track down his landlord that way.'

'I would rather do that than trouble Lady Brockenshaw. From what Doctor Barker said, she is not long for this world. He felt he could say that as he is not her doctor but visiting her as a friend. She has a doctor in Falmouth attending her now.'

Janey rested her head back on his shoulder. 'Doctor Barker saw Miss Petherbridge yesterday. She now lives with her brother at Killywith.'

'That squalid looking house north of St Mabe?'

Janey nodded. 'She is helping keep house for his wife and their brood of children. It sounds like his wife has a fine old tongue on her and makes a fine match for Miss Petherbridge. She takes great delight in ordering her about. Miss Petherbridge was emptying the slop bucket when he came to call. By all accounts she had a face on her like she'd just eaten a lemon.'

She felt Daniel chuckle silently behind her, which made her smile too. They lapsed into silence once more. Eventually Daniel spoke.

'Why did Doctor Barker call here? Are you unwell? Is Grace all right?'

'We are both well. In fact, I asked him to call to confirm that I am fully recovered, which he did after examining me.' She turned in his arms and threaded her fingers through his. She was looking up at him with a provocative glint in her eye and she was smiling. She kissed her finger and placed it on his lips to pass the kiss on. 'This means that you have a promise to keep.' She was flirting with him and Daniel broke into a smile as she tugged on his hand to lead him back to the farmhouse.

'I do?' he teased, pretending to have forgotten what he had said.

'You said that you would not touch me again until I was fully recovered from the birth. Well, I am and I have waited long enough. Edna is waiting to go home, David is out and Molly has gone to her room. Grace will be fast asleep so we have the house to ourselves when you have returned from taking Edna home. So come on, Daniel Kellow, we have both waited long enough.'

Despite her provocative flirting earlier, Janey suddenly felt nervous. As Daniel had left to take Edna home he had whispered in her ear to remain dressed as he wanted to be the one to undress her. The soft caress of his voice against her skin had ignited a sense of anticipation within her and she struggled to know what to do to occupy her time as she waited for his return. Despite the energy building inside her she had nothing to do but wait. She spent her time alternating between pacing their bedroom and brushing her hair to a shining curtain of softness. Finally she heard the wheels of Daniel's cart arrive home. From behind the curtains, she watched him strip to the waist at the garden pump and wash himself in the cold water. She bit her lip in excitement as she heard him take the stairs two at a time. The bedroom door opened and he was standing there, his hair wet and sleek, and softness in his eyes as he looked at her. In two strides he was cupping her face like a precious chalice and kissing her lips.

'I've wanted this for so long,' he murmured as he savoured the moment against her cheek. 'I won't hurt you. Just tell me if you want me to stop.'

Janey shook her head and reached up to wrap her arms around his neck.

'I won't want you to stop. Not now, not ever,' she reassured him, as she wanted this as much as he.

Slowly he unbuttoned the bodice of her dress and eased it down over her hips, letting it fall like a cloud around her feet. He embraced his wife and lifted her away from the folds of material to stand near the bed. As each undergarment was undone and eased from her body, it was replaced with his kisses and caresses. Janey was taken away from the reality of the day; only the two of them mattered now. She followed his lead, touching him, kissing him and tasting his cold, freshly washed skin that warmed as their passions grew.

He sat down on the bed and pulled her between his thighs to kiss her hips and her belly, whilst his hands cupped her buttocks through her drawers. With one gentle pull of the cord at her waist her drawers lay loose on her hips. He eased them over her curves with trembling hands.

Janey looked down at his head and threaded her fingers though his hair, enjoying the power that her body had to affect him so. This feeling of power made her bold as Daniel desired her and feeling desired was a potent aphrodisiac.

It did not surprise her to learn that Daniel was a skillful lover. It did not surprise her that his pleasure came from seeing hers. The more she relaxed, the more he took her to another world where her senses were heightened and she felt no shame. She wanted him as much as he wanted her and as their bodies explored and became entwined in erotic embraces, the thrilling sensations within her own grew and grew. It built to a crescendo, finally climaxing with exquisite pleasure that made her shake and tremble with desire.

In the aftermath Janey could do nothing but lay exhausted, feeling the pulsing pleasure flow away from her like the falling embers from an exploding firework. She lay dishevelled on the bed, shaking as her nerves continued to ignite at the briefest touch, but Daniel had not finished yet. Daniel moved to lie above her and nestled his body between her legs. She felt his desire against her throbbing softness. It was his turn now and when he asked if she was ready all she could do was nod and faintly smile. She felt him gently enter her and fill her as they became one. He lay above her, kissing her and she returned his kisses with a contentment born from feeling complete. Then the rhythmical dance of their lovemaking began and Janey was lost yet again as they both hit the sky with their climax and consummated their marriage for the first time.

The first rays of dawn peeked through the chink in the curtains casting dancing rays of light upon the sleeping couple. Daniel and Janey slept peacefully in their bed, deep in their dreams. A dawn chorus from the birds outside did not wake them, or the horses' hooves and metal-rimmed wheels of the wagon that rolled into the farmyard. It was not Grace stirring slightly in her cot when disturbed by the sound of men's boots approaching the house. What tore them from their dreams, with a sudden brutal force that set their hearts racing, was the thundering knocking on their front door.

Suddenly the house was in confusion as Daniel quickly dressed and Janey went to comfort a distressed baby. A call on a house so early in the morning was never good news but with a questioning look at one another it was clear neither Janey nor Daniel knew what it could be. Daniel left her, descending the stairs in haste before opening the door downstairs. Janey listened. She didn't recognise the other men's voices and could not make out what was being said. She quickly dressed, and carrying Grace in her arms, went down the stairs to see who the visitors were.

Daniel stood between two tall constables, his hands shackled with cuffs and a chain. His face was grave as he looked at her.

'Daniel? What is happening?' she asked.

The heavier built constable replied.

'Mrs Kellow?' he asked. She nodded numbly. 'We are arresting your husband for murder.'

Janey's eyes darted to Daniel.

'Whose murder?' she asked. He had sworn to her he would not kill James Brockenshaw. Had he broken his promise to her while she lay giving birth? Daniel saw her silent question and shook his head.

'We are arresting him for the murder of Zachariah Trebilcock.'

'But he died years ago. Why now?' asked Janey as they began to leave, roughly pushing Daniel ahead of them.

'The charge has been made and we have a duty to act. He will face the magistrate on Monday morning at the Guild Hall in Bodmin.'

Janey ran after them desperate to know more. 'Where are you taking him?' she shouted.

'There was a drunken brawl in St Tude last night,' said the thinner of the two constables. 'Our lock-up is now full with the culprits. Considering the seriousness of the charge we have been granted permission to take him directly to Bodmin gaol.' He opened the prison van door and motioned for Daniel to climb in. Daniel hesitated, before doing so.

'Daniel!' screamed Janey, running to the door.

'Take care of Grace,' he told her. His voice was hoarse and sounded unfamiliar to her. She wanted his reassurance that all would be well but he would not look at her.

The door of the prison van shut with a bang and the wheels started turning. Suddenly she was left alone, except for the babe in her arms, watching the prison van disappearing down the bumpy lane with her husband handcuffed inside.

David and Molly ran out to join her, a plethora of questions spilling from their lips, but Janey did not hear them. Daniel knew he was at risk of losing everything he held dear, yet he would not look at her as he left. She had seen him swallow to clear the choking in his throat and she had seen his stricken face. It was not a sign of guilt that he could not meet her gaze. It was in order to avoid falling apart.

Janey was distraught. She wished she was braver but she wasn't. For the next hour she was inconsolable, sobbing until her lungs ached and she had no more tears to fall. Molly was no better and David sought solitude by tending to the animals and crying alone. The man that had come to mean so much to them had been taken from them and they felt powerless to help.

An hour later, Janey's distress had turned to a growing anger and anger has an energy all of its own. It gave her the strength to dry her tears and it sharpened her brain to make plans. After ensuring the necessary chores were done to keep the farm running, she prepared to leave by dressing in her smartest clothes and her best boots. Daniel had helped her on many occasions and now it was her turn to help him. She knew nothing of the judicial system, what to expect or how she could help, so there was only one thing she could do. After harnessing the horse she climbed up into the trap, Grace strapped to her body by a makeshift sling.

'Where are you going?' asked David, anxiously holding onto the horse's head.

'I'm going to Bodmin to find out what I can do to help Daniel,' she said as she positioned the reins in her hands. 'Look after the farm for me and direct Matt's sisters to which milk needs turning to butter and cheese. I want this farm in good order for Daniel when he comes home on Monday.'

She gave the reins a shake and the horse moved forward into a trot in the direction of Bodmin town. It was only when she had disappeared from sight that David realised she had never driven the trap alone before.

Bodmin was built on a slope. To the north, lurking in the shadows at the bottom of the hill, stood its imposing grey gaol behind a high stone wall. Access to the internal small courtyard was gained by a single arched entrance. As Janey walked through it, a hundred or more evenly spaced windows, of equal size, looked down on her and witnessed her approach. Behind those windows, thought Janey, were four hundred or more convicts awaiting trial or serving their sentence, and one of those was Daniel. She shivered and moved on to the reception office to speak to the warden on duty.

She could tell by his expression that he was not expecting a visitor or one as smartly dressed as she was. He eased himself to a more upright stance as Janey approached.

'Good day, sir,' she greeted him, in what she hoped sounded like a businesslike manner. 'My husband was arrested in the early hours of this morning and brought here to await the magistrates on Monday. There has been a dreadful mistake. He should not be here.'

The warden laughed. 'I suspect given the opportunity, ma'am, most of the prisoners here would claim they are innocent.'

'In this case it's true.'

'Then you have nothing to fear when he appears before the magistrate,' came the reply.

Janey observed the warden behind the desk and the futility of her visit became apparent. She hadn't really expected to walk out of the grounds with Daniel on her arm but she was here and she must make the most of it.

'Sir, I will speak plainly. I'm not accustomed to the system or what to expect, I don't even know what happens on Monday. I would be grateful if you could share your knowledge.'

The warden visibly puffed out his chest at her flattery.

'On Monday the magistrate will hear the charge at the Guild Hall. Witnesses for and against the prisoner will be heard and the magistrate decides if there is a case to answer. If he feels there is not enough evidence then your husband will be set free. If he feels there is a case to answer then he will sentence him to go on trial at the Assizes in a few months' time. He will be brought here again to await trial by jury.'

'So I must find witnesses for his defence?'

'Indeed, ma'am, if there are any.'

Janey thought for a moment. If she could not find any

she would try to find someone who would vouch for his character.

'May I see him, sir?'

The warden shook his head. 'That is out of the question,' he said. 'Criminals must have served at least three months of their sentence before visitation is granted and then only twice a year.'

'But my husband has not been convicted,' she countered.

'I am only a warden. In special circumstances visits can be granted by the governor but this is hardly a special circumstance.'

'It is to me.'

'I'm sorry, ma'am.'

Janey was at a loss what to do and as she considered her next steps her gaze wandered from the warden's face to the wall behind. She looked at the photograph displayed in a fine gold frame that hung on the wall. It did not register initially as her mind was on Daniel, but the more she looked the more the figures came into focus and she recognised the people in it. Staring back at her was the late Lord Brockenshaw and Lady Brockenshaw and a man she did not recognise. The warden saw her surprise.

'Did you know Lord Brockenshaw?' he asked.

'Indeed I did. He died last year from scarlet fever and I nursed him in his final days. Lady Brockenshaw and I became quite close. I consider her a friend.' She omitted that they were her employers; better he thought she was on their social level, as it might prove beneficial to her needs.

'Lord Brockenshaw was a magistrate for several years. He also helped fund the female wing years ago.'

'Who is the third person?' Janey asked.

'It is the present governor, Mr Porter.'

'May I see Mr Porter? I would dearly like to speak with my husband.'

The warden, once adamant that visits were out of the question, was now uncertain. Janey opened her reticule and pulled out the reference Lady Brockenshaw had given her some months before. Smiling she offered the letter to the warden to read.

'Sir, I have here a reference as to my character from Lady Brockenshaw herself. I believe Mr Porter would accept that these circumstances are exceptional and special. Do you not agree?'

Moments later, after being introduced to the governor and enduring idle chit-chat for politeness' sake, Janey was being escorted into the bowels of the prison itself by a warden. As they made their way up the stone staircase that spiralled from floor to floor, Janey could glimpse the wings of the prison that spread out on each level. She had expected the sound of prisoners crying or shouting from their cells but inside the stone walls there was an eerie silence, except for the sound of wheels turning in the distance.

'What's that noise?' she asked, nervously.

'Prisoners on the treadmills,' replied her escort. He gave no further explanation. Janey followed him up another flight of stairs.

'I don't hear anyone talking. Why is everyone so quiet?' she asked in a whisper. It was unnerving to be in a building with up to four hundred people and not hear anyone at all.

'It's the *silence system*. Prison is not meant to be a pleasant place. Maintaining silence means criminal habits cannot be passed on. Prisoners are not allowed to speak to one another; if they do they are punished and their food rations reduced.'

'Prisoners are not allowed to speak for the whole of their sentence?' asked Janey, incredulously.

The warden nodded.

'But that could send a man mad,' exclaimed Janey.

'It often does,' agreed the warden, stepping into a wing on the third floor. 'Here we are, ma'am, prisoner three hundred and thirty-two is on this wing.'

The wing was long, with a wide central corridor. On either side were rows of single cells, no more than seven feet by twelve feet in size with one small window. The windows were situated so high and recessed so deep in the thick stone walls that no prisoner could see out and only a small amount of light filtered through their bars. The light from the windows, however, was the only light to enter the dark, foreboding wing unless a warden walked the floor, whereupon the light from their oil lamps cast eerie demon like shadows across the damp walls made of brick.

Janey tried to appear confident, matching her steps with the strides of the warden as they entered the wing but inside she was frightened. The sound of their footfalls echoing within the prison wing brought faces to the cell doors. She could not make out their features, as the barred windows in the doors were so small, but their eyes looked desperate as they drank in the vision of a woman amongst them carrying a baby.

The warden cast her a glance. 'They cannot hurt you. Ignore them.'

Janey tried but she found it difficult, especially when she saw that some of the prisoners were no older than David. She held Grace a little tighter to protect her from the horrors around her.

The warden stopped by a cell and motioned to Janey that they had arrived. With some apprehension she looked through the door window that was no bigger than her outspread hand. At first she could see nothing. Gradually her eyes grew accustomed to the darkness and she could make out a figure of a man sitting on a wooden board that substituted for a bed, his elbows resting on his knees and his head bowed.

'Three hundred and thirty-two, you have a visitor,' directed the warden. The man lifted his head to look up. Within seconds Daniel's face appeared at the window.

'You shouldn't be here, woman, this is no place for you.' His words were not unkindly said. Janey's legs shook as she heard the familiar voice of her husband. Seeing what she cradled in her arms, he added, 'And Grace too. She will catch a chill.'

'Grace is fine. She's taking warmth from my body. I had to come. I had to see you.'

'The farm? The orders?'

'Don't worry about them, Matt's sisters are helping and Matt will come tomorrow. We must worry about you and help you get out.'

He shook his head in despair. 'If I am to go to trial and am sentenced you must sell the farm and forget about me.'

'Never! You are innocent. It's one of the reasons I am here, to tell you I don't believe what they say about you.'

Daniel rested his forehead against the bars. 'That means a lot to me but I know what the villagers say about me,' he said, sadly.

'Was anyone there that can be a witness for you?'

He shook his head. 'No. Edna arrived moments later and Doctor Barker a while after that but Zachariah was dead by then.' He threaded a finger through the bar and Janey kissed it. 'Oh, Janey, don't cry. It will be the undoing of me.'

'I'm sorry, I promised myself I would be strong for you but I hate to see you here.'

He stroked a tear from her cheek and brought it to his lips to taste a part of her.

'If they should hang me, at least I will die with the memory of having you as my wife these past few months.'

Janey clung to the bars. 'Hush now,' she said, softly, 'don't talk of hanging. You will walk free again and we will fulfil our dreams together as we have planned.'

'I love you, Janey Kellow.' He rubbed his cheek along the softness of her fingers as he spoke. 'From the first day I saw you on the moor I have loved you. Of all the bad things I have done in my life the one good thing was taking you as my wife.'

'I will find someone who will speak for you before the magistrates.'

'There is no one.'

'There must be. I will find someone.'

'God only knows who will speak for me.' He took a deep breath, as if summoning courage. 'I want you to go now.' Janey shook her head. 'Go. I cannot bear to look upon you any more. Go. Go!' Daniel tore himself away from the cell door and stepped back into the shadow. He stood with his back to her, unable to watch her leave.

The warden took her arm. 'It's time to leave, ma'am, before the prisoners become unsettled.'

'I love you, Daniel,' Janey whispered. She saw his shoulders brace before she turned and was escorted away.

As she stepped out of the prison entrance and back into the daylight, the bright sunshine hurt her eyes, forcing her to squint. A faint breeze passed over her face, reminding her that her cheeks were still wet from her tears. Using her sleeve, she roughly wiped her face dry. Tears would not help Daniel, she thought. Only determination would free him and she had plenty of that for the both of them.

Chapter Twenty-One

Janey had not slept well but she had too much to do to worry about her lack of sleep. Matt arrived at the farm to help out and Janey gave him a list of orders that would need to be delivered first thing Monday morning when she was at the magistrates' court. As she pinned her best hat on her head and gathered up her shawl she directed Matt, David and Molly to what needed to be done.

'Where are you going?' asked Matt, surprised at how in control she appeared to be.

'I'm looking for character witnesses for Daniel's defence. I thought of you, but as you are best friends I am concerned the magistrates will not give your evidence much weight.'

'So who are you going to ask?'

They both knew Daniel had not gone out of his way to seek friends from the village. Unknowingly, Daniel had given her an idea where to find such character witnesses and she was on her way to secure them. Satisfied Grace was fast asleep and in Molly's care, she wrapped her shawl about her.

'I'm off to church to speak to God's flock,' she answered, decisively. 'I'm sure there will be a few willing to give up their time once I have had a word with them.'

Reverend Smith stood up before his congregation and opened the Bible. It was not the sermon he had planned to give this morning but Janey Kellow's unexpected visit had made him change his plans. He had always had a soft spot for the young woman but she had gained his respect this morning as she relayed the events of the previous day to him. She had been the only person he knew who did not judge Daniel based on the rumours about him and he respected her for that. Even he, in his premarital discussion with her, had brought up the gossip about him, yet, as she very wisely stated, there was not a shred of evidence to support the accusation that Zachariah had been murdered. Janey Kellow, with immense diplomacy, had held up a magnifying glass on his own behaviour. By not eradicating the rumours years ago he had been complicit in them. After all, as his father had instilled in him, an act of omission is no form of defence.

He looked at the faces in front of him, and with his voice echoing within the church stone walls, he began to read from James, chapter three, verses one to ten.

'Taming of tongues ...' he roared, looking down on his congregation, and began to read with a passion he had not felt in many years. He had a message for his flock that was long overdue. A message that condemned idle gossip and warned of the dangers and hurt it could inflict.

He thumped the Bible, making them jump. 'The tongue is like fire,' he continued as perspiration formed on his forehead. 'The tongue must be tamed, or it will become unruly, evil and as deadly as any poison!' Reverend Smith took off his glasses and looked at the faces below him. Not one could meet his gaze. 'We have all been guilty of partaking in idle gossip. Often it is harmless. Often it is to spread good news.' He rested his glasses carefully on the Bible before him. 'But there are times it has been started with malice in mind and sometimes what started as an untruth becomes truth along the way. The tongue is a deadly weapon, it can hurt as surely as any knife. It can destroy a reputation as surely as any deed. To wound, to destroy our fellow man in such a way is a sin. Yet all of us here have been guilty to one in our parish and we must right the sin we have revelled in for the past few years.'

The congregation turned as Janey stood up and made her way to the front of the congregation. In the past she would not have had the courage to address so many people but the woman that stood before them now was not the one that arrived at the Bosvenna Estate two years before.

'Some of you may know me. I was Lady Brockenshaw's maid. I am now married to Daniel Kellow. He has been wrongly arrested for the murder of Zachariah Trebilcock. Zachariah was not murdered. He fell from a ladder and it was a terrible accident, but it was not murder. Tomorrow my husband is being brought before the magistrates' court in Bodmin who will assess if he is to go to trial. I am looking for people who are willing to testify to Daniel's good character.' Someone coughed uneasily in the congregation. 'Daniel is a good man,' Janey persisted. 'I know his start in life was difficult, but he is a fine man and does not deserve such treatment.'

It was not going well; the people sitting in the pews were looking everywhere but at her. Janey spied the shopkeeper. 'Mr Jones, Daniel has been true to his word regarding reliability and quality of your cheese and butter orders.' Arthur Jones nodded in agreement. She turned to the vicar. 'Reverend Smith, Daniel mended your wall, without being asked or requiring payment.'

'Indeed he did, when half the congregation had walked by without so much as an offer,' he replied, looking accusingly at his flock.

'Mr Wills, I understand Daniel saw your lame horse last winter and offered his advice.'

The old man nodded. 'Indeed he did. The horse has been well ever since.'

'And didn't Daniel help a number of villagers by leading their horses to safety when the road was covered in ice at the beginning of the year?' A few more nodded in reluctant agreement. 'Daniel is a good man. Is there anyone here who will stand up for him?'

No one answered or volunteered. She could understand their reluctance; it would be a day away from their work, it would mean travelling the twelve miles to Bodmin and it would mean entering the alien world of the judicial system. Janey realised she would have to use another tactic.

She turned to the vicar and, in a voice that carried across the pews, she played her last card. 'Thank you, Reverend Smith. I had hoped for help, however the Methodist service is about to begin so I will seek help from the preacher and his congregation down the road. I understand they are quite vocal in standing up for what they believe in and they have a good strong sense of what is right and wrong. I thank you for allowing me to speak. Good day.'

As Janey left the church she could hear the murmur grow behind her. If there was one thing that could rile up a congregation it was competition from another church or chapel. Janey stepped out into the sunshine and headed for the Methodist chapel down the hill.

For a second night Janey did not sleep well but the drive that gave her energy to prove Daniel's innocence had not left her. She rose at six o'clock and, together with David and Molly, fed the animals and milked the cows. Churns of milk were already waiting when Matt arrived with his sisters an hour later. To Janey's surprise Mary was with them, offering her services on her day off. After a joyful reunion, Mary insisted that Molly and David accompanied Janey to the court as she could take over their chores. Janey agreed, grateful for the company.

As Janey finished wrapping Grace in a shawl in preparation for taking her daughter with her, the door opened and in walked Edna. Janey looked at her in horror as she realised Edna was not dressed for the court appearance. In fact, she didn't even seem to notice the amount of people standing around her as she made her way across to the sink and began to wash the eggs, a chore she did every morning – except on Sundays.

'Edna!' Janey cried. 'Why aren't you dressed? We are about to leave for Bodmin and you aren't ready.'

Due to her arthritic neck Edna looked about her with some difficulty. For the first time she noticed that the room was crowded and Janey, David and Molly were dressed in their Sunday best.

'What's going on 'ere then? Ain't anyone got a 'ome to go to?'

'Edna, didn't you get my note? I knocked on your door yesterday but received no answer, so I pushed a letter through your door.'

Edna returned to washing the eggs. 'You should know better than that maid,' she said. 'I don't answer my door to people and I don't read anything but for the Bible on a Sabbath.'

'It's Daniel, he has been arrested for the murder of Zachariah. He's up before the magistrate this morning. You are to be a witness for his defence!'

The old woman dropped an egg and it smashed in the kitchen sink. Its golden yolk ruptured and slid from sight down the plughole.

'Who would think a thing like that? Daniel wouldn't kill Zachariah, 'e thought of 'im like a father.'

'It's been village gossip for years that he did. Didn't you know?'

The old woman turned pale. 'Don't you know me at all, maid? I don't talk to no one. I 'ad no idea. 'E never mentioned it to me.'

'He didn't want to worry you, Granny Thom.' Hearing

Molly's frightened voice beside her Janey put an arm around her.

Edna dried her hands on her apron. 'Well, it ain't what I look like that matters but what comes out of my mouth. If I'm going to be forced to leave this village I'd rather go for a good cause an' save Daniel's neck than for any other reason. The eggs can wait. Come on you lot or we'll be late.'

After the initial euphoria of Edna agreeing to be a witness, by the time they reached Bodmin town Janey had begun to question whether it had been a wise decision to ask her. Matt had driven them to Brock station to catch the train to Bodmin. When the train arrived, with its billowing steam and noisy engine, Edna had run for cover and had to be reassured it was safe to board. During the journey Edna succeeded in insulting four fellow travellers, a ticket collector and a luggage handler. Janey felt a sense of relief when the train finally pulled into the centre of the town and they could get out to walk the quarter of a mile to the Guild Hall.

As they approached, a man at the door told them the Justices of the Peace would be sitting at the Shire Hall County Court in the main square due to unforeseen circumstances. When questioned why the magistrates' court was now being held in the main County Court building the doorman told them that one of the cases had caused much interest and a crowd had started to gather outside. As the Guild Hall was sited on the main road through the town there was a very real danger the road would become blocked. They were, therefore, using the Shire Hall County Court, which was more suitably sited and could cater for the larger numbers.

Frustrated and anxious, Janey, Grace, David, Molly and Edna headed for the County Court building, which was not far away. As they approached, they could see a large crowd had gathered in the square outside and was threatening to spill into the road.

'Who do you think they have come to see?' asked David, concerned.

'I don't know,' replied Janey. 'I hope there won't be a riot.'

Two constables guarded the main entrance. On informing them who they were, they were granted permission to enter. Just as Janey was guided through the heavy doors she managed to take one last look at the crowd outside. She recognised two heads in the midst of the bodies and gasped.

'What is it?' asked Molly. 'Who did you see?'

'It's all right, Molly, everything is fine,' Janey reassured her as she ushered her on ahead. She glanced over her shoulder to look back at the crowd before they disappeared out of sight. She had not been mistaken. In the midst of the crowd were Reverend Smith and Preacher Jago, each fronting their own congregations and arguing for all they were worth. Oh Lord, thought Janey, what have I done?

Daniel had been transported to the Shire Hall County Court some hours earlier and was locked up in the holding cells below ground level. The holding area was dark and damp, with a row of cells lining one wall. Each cell held a man and was just big enough for him to stand or sit down in. Besides the cramped conditions, the air was polluted with the odour of sweat and the offensive stench of an earth pit latrine. The windowless room echoed with the clanking of handcuffs and leg shackles as the prisoners voiced their fears and frustrations of what was to come. Only Daniel remained quiet, waiting his turn.

'It seems the magistrates want you up before them first, Kellow,' said the warden. 'They hope that the crowd outside will disperse if they deal with the murderer first.'

Daniel was led up a flight of enclosed, narrow, stone steps that took prisoners from the holding area directly to the courtroom. It was a cheerless and dark route. At the top was an open door. Daniel paused, took a deep breath, and entered the courtroom beyond. Suddenly everything was bright and ornate. Crowds of people sat around watching him as he was shown to his seat and a hush descended on the room.

He had not slept for two days and not been able to wash. He felt dirty and his wrists hurt from the shackles around them. He looked around him at the unfamiliar faces. They were already sizing him up and forming their opinions about him. He braced himself for what was to come, and then he saw *her* and took strength in her presence.

Janey turned Grace around so Daniel could see her face. Although he looked tired, she saw him half smile at her and she returned it with a trembling smile of her own to give him courage. As if to reassure her, or perhaps remind her of another time, he winked, just as he had done two years before when he caught her staring at him through the kitchen window at Bosvenna Manor. Her smile grew wider at the memory.

Three Justices of the Peace sat at the bench. The longest serving of the three, and therefore the main speaker, was William Menhennit, a wealthy property owner who made his fortune through his mines. He ordered for silence and for everyone to be seated. Outside the crowd had begun to sing hymns but unfortunately the two congregations had chosen different ones. Rather than sounding in harmony the singing grated on the ears, causing Mr Menhennit some concern. He beckoned a clerk over.

'What's that noise outside?' he asked.

'It's the crowd, your worship, they are here to support the defendant and want their voices heard.'

'Their singing voices are not fit for a pig to hear. I hope they sing better on a Sabbath for it sounds like hell is outside at the moment.' He addressed the people in the room. 'May I remind all who are present that this is not a trial of the defendant. We are here today to assess the evidence. If I, and my colleagues, feel there is no case to be answered then the defendant will be discharged. If, however, we feel that there is enough evidence that the defendant may have caused an indictable offence we will commit him to be tried before a judge and jury at the Assizes. While awaiting his trial the defendant will be held in Bodmin gaol.' He looked around the courtroom. 'Defendant, please stand.' Daniel did as he was told and stood tall and proud, dwarfing the constables at his side. 'You have been brought before us charged with the murder of Zachariah Trebilcock. How do you plead?'

'Not guilty, your worship,' replied Daniel, clearly. His voice was strong and steady and Janey couldn't help but feel a surge of pride for the courage he was showing.

'Sit down, Mr Kellow.' He turned to the constable. 'Bring forth the witnesses for the prosecution.'

The office clerk called in the first witness and Molly and David had to grab Janey's arms to stop her from standing up in rage. Entering the courtroom was a smartly dressed man, carrying a top hat and gold tipped walking cane. His black boots shone as he walked confidently into the courtroom and took his place before the magistrates.

The man looked across at Daniel and smiled. Placing his hand on a Bible, he took an oath to speak the truth when giving his evidence and then braced himself for questioning.

'I am Lord James Brockenshaw of Bosvenna Estate,' he said, clearly. 'Zachariah Trebilcock owned the farm that neighbours my estate. Usually in cases of an offence the victim prosecutes. In this case the victim is dead.' A murmur of agreement went through the audience. 'I feel it is my duty to bring the case to court and see that justice is done. I have therefore brought the case before you.'

William Menhennit looked over his glasses at him.

'What evidence do you have that the accused committed murder?' asked one of the other magistrates who had, until now, remained silent.

'Since Zachariah Trebilcock's death there have been widely spread rumours that Mr Kellow killed the farmer by hitting him on the head with a hammer and with such ferocity that the back of his head was greatly distorted. He was seen fleeing the scene with his clothes covered in blood and he was heard admitting to the crime. The farmer, who had supposedly died by climbing a ladder, suffered badly from arthritis and was in no state to climb anything, which suggests that the tale is a false one.'

'Did you witness any of this? Were you present?'

'I was not, your worship, but I have witnesses who were.'

'Then I think it is best we heard from them. Rumour is not evidence enough for indictment. Let us hear the next witness for the prosecution.'

Janey could tell James was a little put out. He had expected that his word, as a gentleman, would hold greater weight, but it seemed that the magistrates wanted something more solid than hearsay. Janey gnawed her bottom lip. Why would someone say that Daniel had confessed to the murder? Why would they say he was fleeing the scene? She looked nervously across to Daniel, who did not meet her eyes.

The second witness entered, took the oath and was asked to confirm his name and the events of that day as he recalled it.

'My name is Simon Rosevear. I was a gardener for Doctor Barker. On the day Mr Trebilcock died I was trimming Doctor Barker's hedges. At about eleven o'clock in the morning I heard a commotion so I put down my shears and looked over the gap in the hedge. I saw Daniel Kellow jumping down from his horse and running to Doctor Barker's front door. He had blood on his arms and shirt front and he was banging on the door with both fists, like this.' The thin little man held up his fists and pretended to bang on an invisible door. 'The door opened and the doctor came to the door. I heard him say, "Come quickly, Zachariah is dying and it's my fault".'

There was an audible gasp from the people around her and Janey felt sick. Even to her ears it sounded like an admission to murder. The magistrates asked a few questions to verify his position in relation to the door and then it was the turn of the next witness. Without realising it, Janey had taken hold of David and Molly's hands. Together they sat stony-faced, hardly daring to breathe. She recognised the next witness; it was Doctor Barker and he looked uncomfortable as he stood before the magistrates. It was his turn to take the oath.

'My name is Richard Barker and I have been the doctor of Trehale Parish for more than twenty years. I knew Zachariah Trebilcock well, as I did his late wife, Amy, and Daniel Kellow. When I was asked to be a witness it was not made clear to me that I would be a witness for the prosecution. I will tell you what I saw but I want it noted that I consider my witness testimonial as neutral.'

'We have taken note,' said William Menhennit.

'At about eleven o'clock there was a banging on my door. My maid answered it and called for me. Daniel Kellow was at the door and visibly distressed. He was covered in blood. He told me Zachariah was dying and he felt he was to blame. I fetched my bag and followed him to Boscarn Farm. On the way he told me Zachariah had fallen from the ladder and he thought he may already be dead. On arriving at the farm I found Zachariah. He was lying on his back and he had been covered with a rug. Edna Thom was praying over him. There was a pool of blood about his head that had congealed. This told me that he had died very soon after the accident. If he had died some time later the bleeding would have continued and there would have been non-congealed blood present. I examined the farmer and the back of his head had multiple fractures. I know this as the back part of his skull was moveable beneath my fingers.'

Daniel dropped his head and Janey could see the muscles in his jaw move. Her heart went out to him having to relive the awful day in such detail.

'I pronounced him dead shortly after my arrival,' added the doctor.

'Please describe the scene to us, Doctor Barker.'

The doctor gathered his thoughts for a moment. 'I had no reason to doubt what Daniel had said. There was a ladder lying on its side, Zachariah was near the ladder and by his head was a hammer. The hammer was covered in blood but only because it lay in the pool of blood by his head.'

'In your medical opinion was Zachariah fit enough to climb a ladder?' asked a magistrate.

'In the last year of his life he suffered badly from rheumatism. It was a sudden onset that was ferocious. There were days he could hardly lift a knife and fork. In my opinion he would have had great difficulty climbing a ladder.'

The reporters present scribbled in their notepads, each envisaging the headlines they would use in the broadsheets the following day.

'However, anyone who knew Zachariah knew him to be a stubborn mule at the best of times. If you ask me *should* Zachariah have climbed the ladder ... I would have said no. If you ask me *could* Zachariah have climbed the ladder … I would have said no. If, however, you ask me *would* Zachariah have tried to climb the ladder … I would say, without a doubt. If he had wanted to try, no one on this Earth would have been able to stop him.' He looked over at Daniel. 'And that includes the accused, Daniel Kellow.'

'Yet he confessed,' replied the third magistrate.

'In my opinion he expressed his guilt at not preventing the accident. I did not think at the time, or at any time since, that he expressed his guilt of murdering him.'

Janey relaxed a little in her seat and Molly gave her a quick hug. Things were beginning to go their way.

After confirmation that all the witnesses for the prosecution had been heard it was Daniel's turn to stand before the Justices of the Peace. Janey watched Daniel take his place.

'Everything is happening so quickly.' Janey looked to the door. Where were Daniel's witnesses? she asked herself.

David tugged her arm. 'Is that a good sign?' he asked, quietly.

'I don't know,' Janey whispered back to him.

She looked at Daniel who now stood proudly before them, his feet planted squarely with his shoulders. As his hands were cuffed he had to place them both on the Bible when he took the oath.

'My name is Daniel Kellow.' His voice was steady; only the clearing of his throat showed his inner nerves. 'I am no angel. I was brought up in the slums, workhouses and reformatories of Bristol. While still a child, I ran away to Cornwall to search for my family. As luck would have it, I met Zachariah and Amy Trebilcock soon after I arrived in the county. Rather than take me to a workhouse, they took me in. Zachariah was a good man who became someone I admired, my father and my friend. True, he was a stubborn man, but he was a wise one. He taught me a trade, he gave me a home and he made me part of their family.'

Daniel swallowed again, his cracked lips evidence that he had not drunk anything for some time. 'For three days before the accident it rained. The roof of the farmhouse had started to leak due to two slipped slates. They needed to be pegged back into position, however the ground was so wet and the rain so heavy that I refused to mend the roof until it was dry. I knew that if I fell there would be no one to do the work on the farm, so we placed a bucket under the drips.'

He looked across at Janey who encouraged him to go on with a nod of her head.

'On the day that he died it was dry and I got the ladder out and the hammer I needed to tap the loose slates back into position. I got no further. Each time I went to mend the roof something would happen to take me away. It was a busy time of year; the cow calved and then the pig got loose. It was one thing after another. Zachariah was getting frustrated, he could see I was busy and he was never a man to sit still at the best of times. I told him not to climb the ladder. I told him that if I didn't get around to mending the roof that day it would not hurt to have a bucket catching the drips for a few more days. After shutting in the pigs I returned to the farmhouse. I saw him on the ladder. I saw him slip on the runner. I saw the ladder topple sideways. I heard the thud ...'

For a moment Daniel could not speak. He bowed his head and took some deep breaths before lifting his chin and continuing.

'I ran to him and I held him in my arms. There was blood everywhere.' He looked at his hands as if he was seeing it all again. 'His eyes were open and he turned his head to look at me. He smiled, can you believe that?' Daniel asked the magistrates. 'As he lay dying he actually smiled at me. As I held him I saw the life go out of his eyes. They stayed open but I knew he was gone. Edna came running out. She told me to fetch the doctor and so I did. I don't remember getting on the horse or riding to the doctor. I remember him answering the door but I don't remember what I said. It felt like I was in a nightmare. I don't even remember riding back with the doctor. I do remember seeing Edna praying over Zachariah's body and a rug over him. I just stood there and the doctor took over. He arranged the funeral director, or perhaps it was Edna ... I don't recall. I was in shock. I think I've blanked it out. I was eighteen years old at the time.'

The courtroom was deathly quiet; even the haphazard singing outside had stopped for a moment. The magistrates whispered to one another and were about to speak when the singing began again. However, this time both congregations had joined forces and sang the same hymn. Their steady and tuneful voices rose through the air and into the courtroom like angels' voices from heaven.

William Menhennit sat quietly listening for a moment. Finally, appearing to ignore the singing outside, he raised his voice so he could be heard and said, 'Thank you, Mr Kellow, you may sit down. Next witness, please.'

Janey turned to see Reverend Smith enter the courtroom and stand before the bench. As instructed he too took the oath.

'I am the vicar of Trehale, Reverend Smith. I also speak on behalf of Preacher Jago from the same parish. He is outside directing the singing.'

'It was brought to our attention that they required some directing,' interjected one of the magistrates. A ripple of laughter flowed through the courtroom.

'Sometimes people are stronger when they stand together than when they are apart, which is why the congregation of both the church and chapel are here to support the defendant.'

Daniel's surprise showed on his face.

'Some of the villagers have been guilty of feeding on the unfounded gossip of Daniel Kellow over the years. It was harmlessly meant but the villagers now realise it is no longer harmless and that a man's life depends upon it. They have come here today to offer their support to a man that came to live in their midst. As a young boy he was an unruly lad, but that does not make him a killer. Zachariah was a good man and he thought a lot of the lad. Zachariah was a man you could trust, yet we were guilty of not trusting him in his opinion of Mr Kellow. We realise that is our sin and we must ask God for forgiveness.' Reverend Smith addressed the public. 'Mr Kellow has been modest, he has quietly gone about his work and he has often offered his help, without obligation, to the villagers that have, until now, spurned him. It takes a good man to turn his cheek time after time as he has done.' He turned to Daniel. 'I would like to say to you, Daniel, on behalf of my congregation and that of Preacher Jago's, that we apologise for the bad words spoken about you over the years. We hope you can forgive us.'

Janey saw Daniel swallow again and give a slight nod.

'Strong words indeed,' said the magistrate, 'but we deal in fact in this room. Are there any more witnesses?'

'Edna Thom,' replied the office clerk.

'Send her in, time is getting on and we have twenty more prisoners to deal with before the day is at an end.'

Edna shuffled into the court looking more like a witch than a principal witness. She stood up and took her oath as did all those before her.

'State your name,' said the clerk.

'You know it! Why ask me to say it?'

'Just say your name and give your evidence. Tell us what happened on the day in question,' replied the clerk through gritted teeth. Janey realised he had probably already had some trouble from Edna outside the courtroom.

'I'm Edna Thom. I cooked for Daniel an' Zachariah at the time of 'is death. Zachariah an' Daniel were outside and preparing to mend the roof. I was in the spare bedroom and saw the ladder placed against the wall. I had found a trunk of clothing that I discovered later belonged to Zachariah's late wife, Amy. I did not know that at the time. I took a dress out an' was 'olding it up against me. I then saw Zachariah climbing the ladder. 'E was struggling and tucked in his shirtfront was an 'ammer. I watched him climb 'igher an' as 'e passed by the window 'e looked in and saw me. 'E was not expecting to see me staring back at 'im. It made 'im jump but 'e kept 'is footing.' Edna turned to the public watching her. She saw Janey and told the rest of the story to her. ''Owever, the jump must 'ave unsteadied the ladder, Janey, as when 'e started to climb again the ladder started to move, slowly at first then it gathered speed. Suddenly 'e 'it the ground. I looked through the glass an' saw 'im lying there, eyes open and bleeding. Daniel reached 'im an' started to 'old him. I ran down the stairs an' told 'im to fetch the doctor. 'E was no more than a boy back then. 'E couldn't quite believe what 'ad 'appened. I knew Zachariah was probably dead but I wanted to get Daniel away so 'e didn't 'ave to see 'is body. As soon as 'e was gone I covered it over an' started to pray.'

'Are you telling us that you witnessed the incident and it was an accident?'

Edna turned her attention back to the magistrates. 'I am. Daniel did not kill 'im an' if I'd known all these years 'is reputation was suffering because of idle gossip I would 'ave told my story long before now!'

The three men at the bench brought their heads together and whispered for some moments before William Menhennit spoke again.

'Daniel Kellow,' he said, 'we have listened to the

evidence for the prosecution and the defence and we are in no doubt you have suffered a great injustice for the past eight years. There is no evidence whatsoever that a crime has been committed.' He addressed the reporters. 'Let it be related in print that the Magistrates' court believe that Zachariah's death was an accident and Daniel Kellow is not guilty of murder as no murder occurred. The defendant is discharged ... and will someone please tell the singers outside that he is free and that they can go home. I've had enough hymns for today!'

The court was in uproar as everyone started to talk at once. Reporters rushed out to their respective newspapers as Daniel was led out through another door. Janey, with Grace in her arms, David and Molly made their way through the bodies blocking their way to spill out into the hall outside. Edna, reverting to her Cornish tongue to shout her insults, roughly pushed her way through to reach them. Janey hugged her, as did the others.

'Thank you, Edna. Thank you,' cried Janey, holding her tight; then she saw Daniel coming towards her and she was suddenly in his arms.

'It's over,' he whispered into her hair. 'The nightmare is over.' He held her close and their bodies moulded together as they took comfort in one another's embrace in the crowded hall.

James was outraged. As the witnesses, reporters and general onlookers left the courtroom and witnesses and families for the remaining cases filed in, he confronted the senior magistrate.

'You have made a laughing stock of me, Menhennit! What happened to solidarity between gentlemen?'

The magistrate set his papers aside and slowly stood up. James's father had been his friend and they had worked together as magistrates for several years. It was a shame, thought the magistrate, that his son was not cut from the same cloth. James had once owed him money and he had to endure the embarrassment of asking his father for the debt to be paid. He straightened. Despite his age, he was taller than the younger man and the balance of power was in his favour.

'I see no gentleman,' he said, quietly, 'and as for making a laughing stock out of you ... you managed that all on your own. You are in my court and I take offence how you have addressed me. I am to be addressed as your worship or sir. Do I make myself clear? Now I have more pressing issues to attend to.' He spoke to the constable at the door. 'Escort this man off the court premises. If he refuses to leave arrest him for riotous behaviour. It will be a great pleasure to commit him to fourteen days' hard labour in gaol.'

Chapter Twenty-Two

Daniel sat by the crackling fire and watched the amber flames dance and twist. It had been a busy two months since the trial. Not long after his return it was time to harvest the corn. As soon as it was cut, a steam engine and wooden threshing machine had arrived and chugged away in the fields for two days until the straw had been harvested and the corn separated. On the last evening of the cutting he performed the 'Crying of the Neck' ceremony and the workers, his family and friends celebrated the end of the harvest with pasties and ale.

Taking advantage of the public's gruesome interest in crime and punishment, the broadsheets reported the magistrates' findings and ran the story for several days. It did, however, proclaim his innocence, the news of which soon spread through the village like wildfire. Over the years Daniel had got used to people avoiding him in Trehale; now he had to get used to his sudden popularity. People greeted him as if he was an old friend, asked for advice on their animals and orders for his cheese and butter doubled overnight – and then there was Grace's baptism. In contrast to their wedding, the church had been packed. Women cooed over the delightful baby girl and the men shook Daniel's hand. Daniel could not remember feeling as proud as he did that day and Janey had been delighted to see Mary return to be part of the celebrations as godmother. Grace smiled throughout the day and enchanted everyone. His heart swelled with pride. It did not cross his mind that she did not have his blood in her veins. Grace was his daughter and he was proud to be her father.

*

'Come, sit on my lap,' he said to Janey as she came into the room. He gently tugged on her hand to encourage her but instead of sitting primly on his lap, she lifted her skirts and a leg and straddled him. 'Has anyone told you that you are a flirt, Mrs Kellow?' he said, smiling, enjoying the feeling of her close to him.

'I only flirt with you, Mr Kellow,' she replied, threading her fingers behind his neck and giving him a kiss. 'Molly and David have gone to the harvest dance tonight and we are alone, but for Grace.'

'Ah, another dance.' He smiled. 'I seem to recall you called me a *heathen* at a dance once.'

'I may have, but of course my definition of *heathen* is quite different to what you may think it means,' she teased.

'You must educate me,' he replied, sliding his hands up each of her thighs and feeling the cotton of her drawers beneath her skirts.

'Perhaps I should show you,' she murmured, kissing him again.

A loud knock on their door brought their kissing to an abrupt halt. The last time someone knocked on their door their world had collapsed around them. After hesitating for some moments Janey answered it.

Phillip Fitzwilliam stood on the doorstep and took off his top hat in greeting.

'Good evening, Mrs Kellow. May I come in?' The tall man entered their cosy little farmhouse and introduced himself to Daniel with a shake of his hand. 'I am Phillip Fitzwilliam. Your wife was my sister's maid, although I understand that perhaps *companion* would be a better term to use.'

He lifted his coat-tails and sat down on the chair offered to him. Indicating for them to sit with a flap of his hand, Daniel and Janey also took a seat. His unexpected call had momentarily struck them dumb until Daniel found his tongue.

'To what do we owe this unexpected visit?' he asked.

Mr Fitzwilliam looked about him and placed his top hat on the floor by his chair. He crossed his legs.

'I am here to inform you both that Lady Brockenshaw passed away three weeks ago. She had been ill for some time and never really recovered from the stress caused by her son bankrupting the estate. In the end I think her death was a release to her as well as those that loved her and hated to see her suffer.'

Daniel took Janey's hand to comfort her. She did not speak but he intuitively knew that the news had distressed her.

'Her funeral was a private affair, just as she wanted. She is buried in the Fitzwilliam family plot in Falmouth.'

'I should like to visit her grave,' Janey said, quietly.

Daniel squeezed her hand. 'We could travel by train whenever you want.'

They sat for a moment in silence with their thoughts, and then Fitzwilliam spoke again.

'Giving you this news is not the only reason I am here. I think I should start at the beginning as I think a full explanation is in order.'

'May I offer you some refreshment first?' asked Janey.

'There is no need. My visit will be a brief one.' He sat back and made himself more comfortable. 'The late Lord Brockenshaw, my sister's husband, was a good man but he was not a businessman. He was rather too generous with his money and he invested unwisely in several business ventures. He tried to protect my sister from his financial worries. It is a common mistake that when one is blind, people think they can communicate without the person knowing. He was wrong. My sister was a clever woman and she picked up ... from a tone of voice, a pause in speech, an evasive reply to a question ... that there were problems.'

He settled back further into his chair. 'Ten years ago I inherited a substantial sum from our aunt. She left it to me, but her intention was that both my sister and I had an equal share. She knew, as a married woman, my sister's fortune would automatically pass to her husband and she did not want that to happen. She wanted the money kept safe for my sister's use. She was proved right. Lord Brockenshaw was incapable of holding on to his money and over the years was forced to sell several farms that were part of the estate. As each farm was sold, I, under my sister's instruction, bought them on her behalf. Her husband never knew he was in fact selling the land to his wife and he died never learning the truth. Unfortunately James is even worse with money than his father. Where his father was over generous and with a poor business mind, his son gambles, drinks and is reckless.' Seeing Janey's expression, he added, 'Forgive me if I sound harsh on the Brockenshaw family, Mrs Kellow, but our side of the family was never happy with the match and it seems we were proved right.'

'I'm not sure, sir, why you are telling me all this,' interrupted Janey. 'How does this affect me?'

'All will become clear, Mrs Kellow.' He gave her a reassuring smile before continuing. 'It is common knowledge that James squandered the estate's fortune within months of inheriting it. He foolishly took out a loan and bought shares in gold. Last September, the market collapsed and he, as well as many others, lost everything overnight.'

Janey squeezed Daniel's hand. The collapse of the market was around the time she had been raped.

'When my sister became a widow she could own property and her inheritance in her own name for the first time in her life. Naturally, I immediately transferred the land and rental payments that it had incurred to her. She planned to leave it to James in her will. However their relationship deteriorated drastically when he lost the remains of the estate. The bank has now sold the Bosvenna Estate to a member of parliament who resides in Kent.' He brushed a speck from his trousers with a casual sweep of his hand. 'What he plans to do with it I do not know.

'Shortly after receiving your letter and reading in the broadsheets about James's slanderous accusations and the stress you endured as a family at Bodmin Magistrates, my sister insisted on seeing her solicitor. The result of which is that she changed her will. She told me she wanted to "right a wrong" before she died and this was the only way open to her.'

He withdrew a sheet of paper from his pocket and handed it to Janey.

'This is my sister's will. You will see that she has left you the sum of four thousand pounds and three farms totalling one hundred and fifty acres. One of the farms borders your land and the other two are further east towards St Tude. You can do with them as you wish. You may decide to keep them and collect the rent or sell. The decision is yours.'

He reached into another pocket and brought out another letter. 'My sister dictated this letter to her solicitor. I do not know the content, I do not wish to know, but she instructed that it should be handed personally to you. As I am the executor of her will I am carrying out her wishes.'

'Her son will not like it,' said Daniel.

Mr Fitzwilliam stood up. 'You need not concern yourself regarding James. He does not know his mother had money or property and as he is no longer a beneficiary, he does not have access to read her will. I will provide him a small allowance. He is not destitute if he uses it wisely. I believe he is staying with friends in Somerset at the moment, however I suspect he will outstay his welcome very soon and move on elsewhere. I have no interest in the man. He may be my nephew but apart from my obligation to my sister's memory, I want no part of him.'

He retrieved his hat. 'All in all, you are a very rich family. I do not know why she chose to bestow such gifts on her maid that she has known for only a few years but she said she had her reasons. As I said, my sister was a very clever woman so I trust her judgment.'

He shook Daniel's hand and then Janey's. 'I will arrange a meeting with my sister's solicitor so the deeds and money can be transferred to you. I have taken lodgings for the night in Bodmin and will return to Falmouth tomorrow. It has been a long day.'

'Sir,' blurted Janey, who was a little in shock at what he had told them, 'before you leave, may I ask how Charlie is?'

Mr Fitzwilliam smiled. 'He is in the carriage, if you care to find out for yourself. He pines for his mistress and, I suspect, his moorland walks with you.'

'I miss him too.'

'Then accept him as a gift. I like my hounds; Charlie is too much of a lapdog for me.'

Daniel and Janey saw him to his carriage and, after a boisterous greeting from Charlie, returned to their kitchen with the dog circling their feet.

'This house is getting more crowded by the minute,' said Daniel as he tried to avoid stepping on the dog. He glanced up, smiling, to find Janey reading Lady Brockenshaw's letter. She looked up.

'What does she say?' he asked.

Janey held the letter in shaking fingers, tears threatening to spill.

'She knows about Grace. She has not said so in so many words, but the implication is there,' she said.

Daniel came over and held her in his arms.

'We must leave it in the past, Janey,' he said, gently. 'We have a bright future together ... with Grace. We must not allow Brockenshaw to taint our lives any more. Lady

Brockenshaw has given you this fortune to make amends. It is time to move on.'

She rested her head against his chest.

'He does not even acknowledge what he did was wrong. It did not even cross his mind that Grace is the result of what he did to me.'

'Let us be thankful for that, as she is our daughter now. She will grow up to be a well-educated, financially secure woman.' They stood in silence for some moments until Daniel spoke again. He jerked his head towards the dog. 'Charlie has made himself at home,' he observed as the dog lay down to sleep in front of the fire.

'As we all have. You have brought us all here, Daniel. Molly, David, Edna, and I have found a family with you.'

Daniel kissed the top of her head and allowed his lips to linger there.

'Our family will be even bigger by next year,' added Janey.

'Bigger?' he whispered.

'Grace will have a brother or sister to love her and be loved by her.'

Daniel's hold tightened around his wife, but the emotion deep inside him was too great and he was forced to bury his face into the crook of her neck to savour the news. She stroked his hair, smiling.

'The future looks bright, Daniel. We will walk toward it ... together.'

'Together,' he managed to reply, 'as a family.'

The huntsman blew his horn and the chase was on. James, dressed in his scarlet colours, kicked his horse into a gallop and followed the pack of baying hounds. The misty weather and the wet boggy ground made the ride challenging but it all added to the excitement of the hunt where man and hound pitched their skill against the fox.

James revelled in the adrenaline pumping through his body. His mount and his riding colours were borrowed and the money in his pocket was fast dwindling away. He needed this excitement to make him feel alive when he was not in a drunken stupor.

The hounds snaked over a stone stile. In order to avoid the slippery mud the riders took a firmer route around the bottom of the field. James, however, preferred to remain close to the hounds and with a vicious dig of his heels, he forced his horse to jump it. They landed awkwardly on the other side but stayed upright. He pulled his horse around and set off again into the mist. The baying of the hounds faded into the distance and he could no longer see his fellow riders. Realising he had become isolated from the hunt, he angrily turned his horse again and dug his heels into its flanks. It leapt forward into the unknown, white foam spilling from its mouth.

James did not know if he or his horse was the first to see the red-coated vixen that ran across their path. The solitary hunter stopped and stood her ground, whilst her accusing amber eyes stared back at him. Spooked, his horse reared upwards with flailing hooves. James became unbalanced and found himself falling. He landed with a thud onto the soft ground. Splattered in mud, James looked up to find the vixen still watching him. It was the last thing he saw before his horse fell with its full weight on top of his body, crushing the life out of him.

The vixen casually turned away and went to ground at the base of the hedge. Reaching her cubs, she curled her body around them and settled down to sleep. The sound of the hunt receded into the distance as they lost her scent and moved away. Peace resumed. The huntsman who had threatened her would not disturb her again – she had survived and the chase was at an end.

Thank You

Thank you for reading *The Captain's Daughter*. I feel honoured that you chose to read it when there are so many other books available to you. I hope you enjoyed following Daniel and Janey's journey as they discover the true meaning of love and form a family of their own.

I started writing *The Captain's Daughter* in 2010. At the time I lived on the edge of Bodmin Moor and the rugged landscape was one of the many locations that inspired the novel. It took two years to write and many more before it was taken on by a traditional publisher. Every time I walked on the moor, I felt that Daniel and Janey were waiting for me, eager to learn that I had finally published their story so it could be shared with others.

I was the caretaker of Daniel and Janey's story for many years. Now it is in the hands of its readers as positive feedback and word of mouth recommendations will help determine its success or failure – and ultimately its longevity. With this in mind, if you enjoyed *The Captain's Daughter*, I would be so grateful if you could take a moment to write a review on the retail site where you purchased this book, Choc Lit's website, or Goodreads (if you are a member). A review can be as short as one sentence or longer if you are so inclined. Your opinion and recommendations really do matter.

Thank you again for taking the time to read it. I do hope you enjoyed the story, because I enjoyed writing it and Daniel and Janey have waited long enough for their story of love and survival to be told.

Love,

Victoria Cornwall x

P.S. Daniel Kellow was adopted by Zachariah and Amy. Amy once told Daniel about her mother, who she greatly admired. You can read her mother's story for yourself, in *The Thief's Daughter*.

About the Author

Victoria Cornwall grew up on a dairy farm in Cornwall. She can trace her Cornish roots as far back as the 18th century and it is this background and heritage which is the inspiration for her Cornish based novels.

Victoria is married and has two grown up children. She likes to read and write historical fiction with a strong background story, but at its heart is the unmistakable emotion, even pain, of loving someone.

Following a fulfilling twenty-five year career as a nurse, a change in profession finally allowed her the time to write. She is a member of the Romantic Novelists' Association.

For more information on Victoria:

www.twitter.com/VickieCornwall
www.victoriacornwall.com
www.facebook.com/victoriacornwall.author

More Choc Lit

From Victoria Cornwall

The Thief's Daughter

Cornish Tales series

Hide from the thief-taker, for if he finds you, he will take you away …

Eighteenth-century Cornwall is crippled by debt and poverty, while the gibbet casts a shadow of fear over the land. Yet, when night falls, free traders swarm onto the beaches and smuggling prospers.

Terrified by a thief-taker's warning as a child, Jenna has resolved to be good. When her brother, Silas, asks for her help to pay his creditors, Jenna feels unable to refuse and finds herself entering the dangerous world of the smuggling trade.

Jack Penhale hunts down the smuggling gangs in revenge for his father's death. Drawn to Jenna at a hiring fayre, they discover their lives are entangled. But as Jenna struggles to decide where her allegiances lie, the worlds of justice and crime collide, leading to danger and heartache for all concerned …

Available in paperback from all good bookshops and online stores. Visit www.choc-lit.com for details.

The Daughter of River Valley

Cornish Tales series

Cornwall, 1861

Beth Jago appears to have the idyllic life, she has a trade to earn a living and a cottage of her own in Cornwall's beautiful River Valley. Yet appearances can be deceptive ...

Beth has a secret. Since inheriting her isolated cottage she's been receiving threats, so when she finds a man in her home she acts on her instincts. One frying pan to the head and she has robbed the handsome stranger of his memory and almost killed him.

Fearful he may die, she reluctantly nurses the intruder back to health. Yet can she trust the man with no name who has entered her life, or is he as dangerous as his nightmares suggest? As they learn to trust one another, the outside threats worsen. Are they linked to the man with no past? Or is the real danger still outside waiting ... and watching them both?

Currently available as an eBook on all platforms. Visit www.choc-lit.com for details.

Introducing Choc Lit

We're an independent publisher creating
a delicious selection of fiction.
Where heroes are like chocolate – irresistible!
Quality stories with a romance at the heart.

See our selection here:
www.choc-lit.com

We'd love to hear how you enjoyed *The Captain's Daughter*.
Please visit **www.choc-lit.com** and give your feedback
or leave a review where you purchased this novel.

Choc Lit novels are selected by genuine readers like yourself.
We only publish stories our Choc Lit Tasting Panel want to
see in print. Our reviews and awards speak for themselves.

Could you be a Star Selector and join our Tasting Panel?
Would you like to play a role in choosing which novels we
decide to publish? Do you enjoy reading women's fiction?
Then you could be perfect for our Choc Lit Tasting Panel.

Visit here for more details…
www.choc-lit.com/join-the-choc-lit-tasting-panel

Keep in touch:
Sign up for our monthly newsletter Choc Lit Spread for
all the latest news and offers: www.spread.choc-lit.com.
Follow us on Twitter: @ChocLituk and Facebook: Choc Lit.

Where heroes are like chocolate – irresistible!